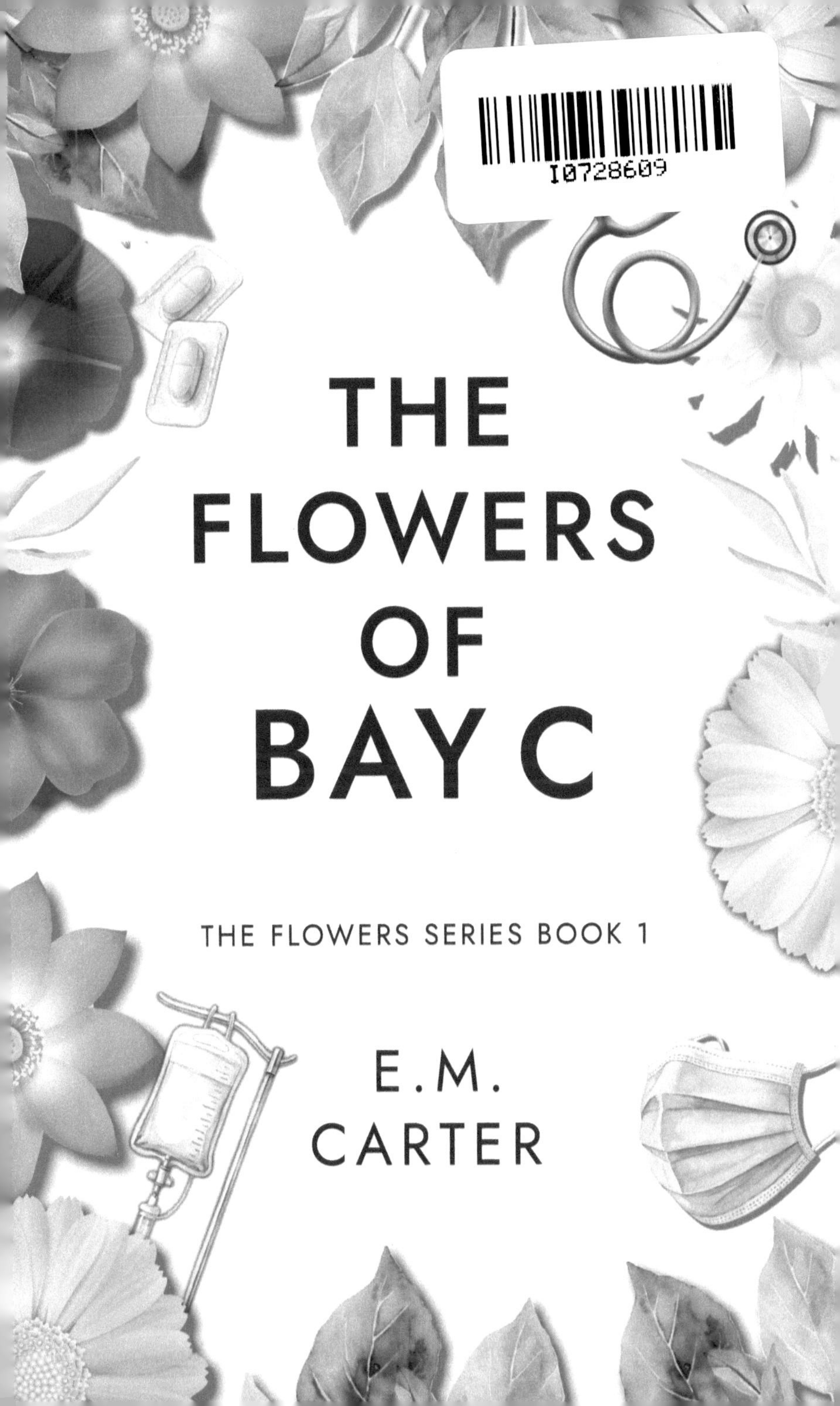

THE FLOWERS OF BAY C

THE FLOWERS SERIES BOOK 1

E.M. CARTER

Copyright © E.M. Carter 2025

The right of E.M. Carter to be identified as the author of this work has been asserted by her in accordance with the Copyright, Designs and Patents Act 1988.

All rights reserved.

No part of this publication may be reproduced or transmitted in any form or by any means, electronic or mechanical, including photocopy, recording, or any information storage and retrieval system, without permission in writing from the publisher.
All characters and events in this book are fictitious, and any resemblance to real persons, living or dead, is purely coincidental.

No AI was used in the writing or design of this book.

Published by Resolute Books
www.resolutebooks.co.uk

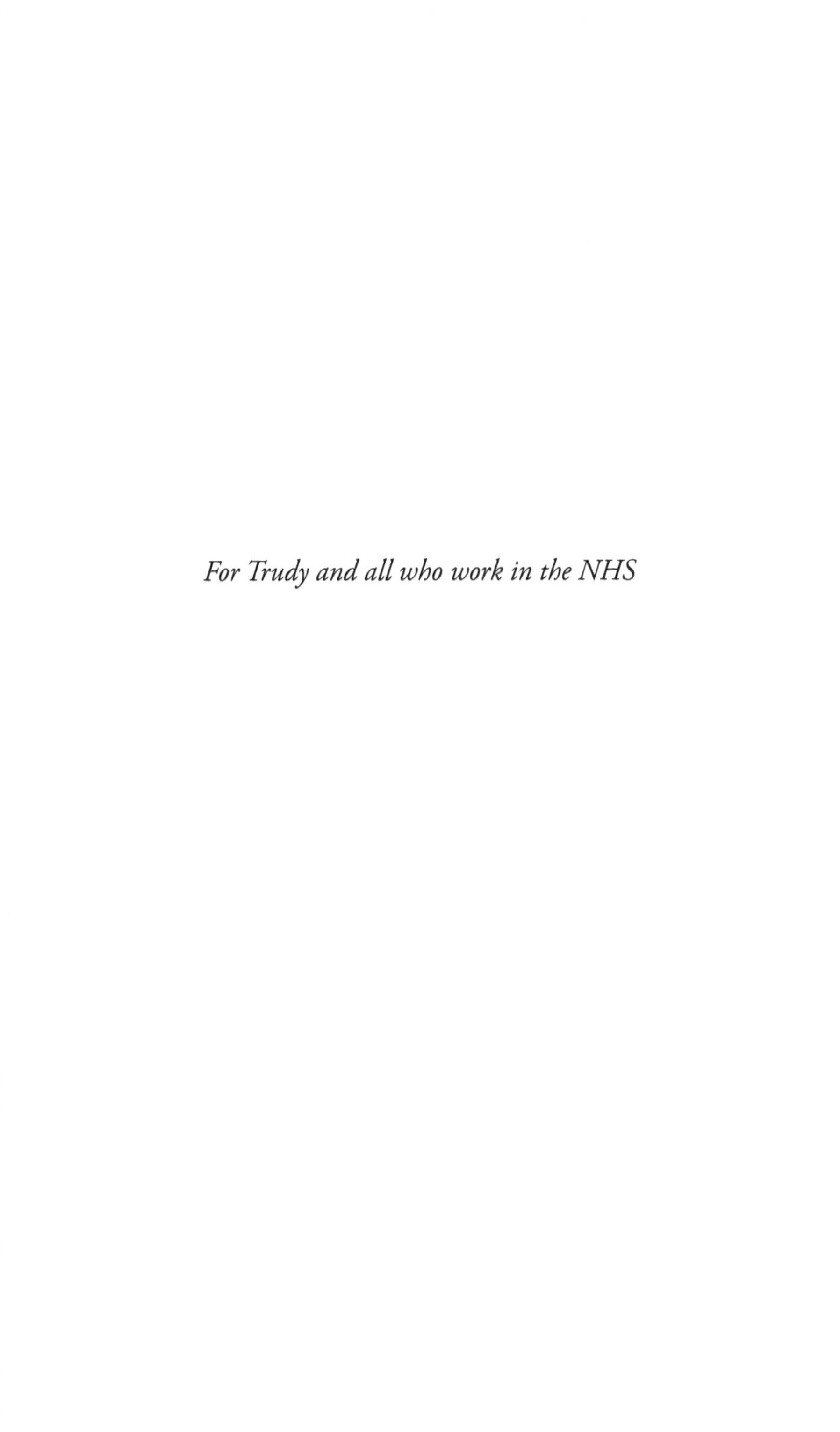

For Trudy and all who work in the NHS

From: Diane Harris <dharris@radh.nhs.uk>

Subject: Urgent

To: Joy Nyoni <sisterjoy@radh.nhs.uk>

Joy,

What on earth is all this I hear of missing patients, illegal alcohol, newspaper reporters and animals running rampant on my ward? We're the NHS, not a veterinary surgery! Why were processes not followed? Heads will roll for this, and I assure you that one of them won't be mine. I expect a full explanation in my inbox by 9am tomorrow.

Diane

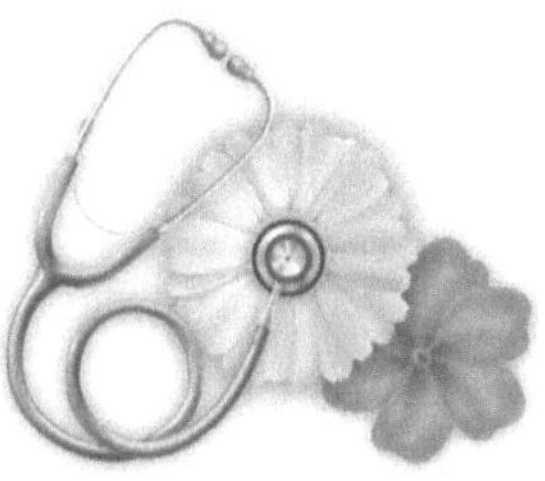

Chapter 1

I CAN TELL the man by my bed is judging me. Probably because I'm wearing a scraggy nightshirt emblazoned with the pink-sequinned words *Sorry Not Sorry*. Then again, perhaps I just think everyone is judging me these days.

I always mean to pack a bag for these occasions – silk pyjamas, a fluffy dressing gown, like I'm actually staying in a lavish hotel. But I don't own any silk pyjamas, my dressing gown died in the noughties, and I'm in hospital. Again.

'I'm sorry,' I say to the nurse, who maybe isn't judging me at all. Maybe he's thinking about something else entirely, like when he's going to get off this endless shift. And I don't even know why I'm apologising.

'You're not sorry,' he says, pointing to my nightshirt and grinning.

I try to smile at him, but my lips are too cracked. 'Sorry,' I say again.

He shakes his head, winking at me as he walks away.

I didn't think I'd end up in here tonight. It was a normal day, really, Jake in school and me at home, a little more tired than usual. It was only after lunch when it smashed into me suddenly, the infection, whipped me off my feet and slammed me to the ground. 'Again?' Jake said when he got home, tossing his bag into the corner and opening the fridge. 'Hospital?'

Hospital.

Jake grunted, checked me over and moaned at the lack of anything in the fridge. Then he called the ambulance. Then he held my hand while we waited. Then he asked if we had any biscuits.

We didn't.

The air is too thick in this ward. Cloying waves of disinfectant and over-boiled cabbage. All around me it presses in, spattered walls and faded concertinaed curtains, with its discordant symphony of buzzers beeping, phones ringing, machines singing.

'You. You, girl.'

I pull my brain out of its fog and cast a glance around the ward. What girl? What You?

'Yes, you, girl, I said.'

Turns out it's me, even though I left the girl in me behind over twenty years ago. She's still there somewhere, though, desperate to be something more than I've made her.

The elderly woman in the bed next to me is pointing at me, her bony finger quivering. What does she want? What does she think I can do for her from here?

A healthcare assistant shushes her. 'Come on, Edna lovely. Settle down. Leave the nice lady alone.'

'Go away,' she says to the healthcare assistant, her voice so reedy the words are almost swallowed by her breath. 'I only want her.' She tries to sit herself up; her face is grey round the edges, her eyes ringed with shadows. She sags back down, sinking into her pillow. 'I only want her. Eighteen, she is. We had a nice cake.'

The healthcare assistant sighs, flicking her glance upwards. 'She's a patient, Edna my darling. She's poorly. She can't talk to you now.'

She doesn't say, *and there's no way she's eighteen*, but I'm sure she's thinking it. She shoots a weary grin over at me, rolling her eyes. I can't smile back and can't do anything much else, either. I'm hemmed in by an oxygen mask, a drip, and agony like knives needling my skin.

I couldn't say anything even if I were eighteen.

I'm forty-five and I want to go to sleep. I want to sink into wide-open night spaces where I am allowed to live in colour.

SOMEONE IS TOUCHING my arm.

I open my eyes and the light batters my pupils. Was I asleep? Jake's face is in my mind, his eyes that shimmered when he left me here earlier. Has he had a good dinner? Maybe he'll be cooking for my parents, perhaps his famous enchiladas; I catch the scent for seconds and want to wrap myself up in it.

'Nurse.' Edna is weeping, and no one takes any notice.

'Miss Fielding?'

A heavy weight presses down on my eyelids, and I try to fight against it, to focus on the person speaking to me, the soft, uncertain touch on my arm. A man in scrubs with a stethoscope around his neck hovers next to my bed, clipboard in one hand, iPad in another, clearing his throat. He looks about sixteen. 'I just need to talk to you for a few moments, if that's okay?' His voice is kind but he flutters with tension, his gaze flicking around the busy ward as if there are far more important things to do. 'I'm Doctor Wood, I'm a medical junior doctor.'

'Oh.' I slump a little bit inside. Junior doctors: sweet and young and serious and a little bit naïve.

'On a scale of one to ten, with ten being the highest, what would you say your level of pain was?'

The question crashes into my foggy mind. What is my level of pain? My eight might be someone else's four, my five might be someone else's ten. How do you quantify pain? I think back to when I was in labour with Jake. I would have given that a sure ten. But this is a ten too, just a different kind of ten. This is a ten without joy at the end of it, without the hope of it being over soon, without my body knowing what to do with it. This is a sharper ten, a ten that might crush me into tiny little pieces.

My pain is lots of colours, but they are all harsh ones. A purple so deep it is the depths of blackness, a bruise of despair. A red so bright it slices me open. A green so bitter it clinches me into spiky embraces I do not want.

Fifteen and a half, I think.

'Eight,' I say.

He writes it down. 'Okay, so I have your x-ray here.' He shows me the tablet, tracing his fingers over the image of my messed-up lungs. 'You have a pneumococcal infection here, you see. Both lungs. I'm afraid we'll have to keep you in a while. We'll get you started on some IV antibiotics.'

I try to find words. I could reel off the drugs and the dosages, the times they should be administered, but fog wraps up the words and smashes them away. I squeeze my eyes closed.

He clears his throat and I force my eyes open, force myself to focus on his face, all floppy hair and black-framed glasses, a blur of youth and newly minted authority, a fight between arrogance and uncertainty.

'We'll start you on one gram amoxicillin.'

I shake my head. 'No.'

He grips his clipboard tight, his shoulders rising and falling, as if he is weary of patients who tell him that they can do this better than he can, as if he knows that he needs to learn bedside manner but it's sometimes just too hard.

I swallow and my throat is choked with razor blades. 'Not that.'

He frowns at me and then glances at my notes and starts flicking back through the pages and murmuring words to himself. I know he's going to tell me what I'll have now, as if it's his idea. It'll be tobramycin that makes you tired and sad, once a day for fourteen days. And then ceftazidime that tastes like rotten onions in the back of your throat as it sears through your veins, three times a day.

'Right.'

I close my eyes as he collects up his notes and his ruffled dignity and shuffles away to another poor weary patient who probably won't argue with him about medication.

'We're just taking you to Ward Nine, Mrs Fielding,' someone says. A porter in blue scrubs with a hipster beard and a rainbow lanyard. It's Miss, I want to say to him. Not married. Not anymore. But I don't want to think about that, because it might make me sink and I have to hold on.

Edna squawks as he wheels me away. 'Where's the eighteen-year-old going? Where are you taking her? I need her.'

She's leaking bewilderment as the porter wheels my bed away, tears creeping down hollowed-out cheeks. I turn my gaze away, longing to be more for her.

The temperature drops as we push through the acute medical unit doors and into the long hallway. This is the Victorian wing of the hospital – an infinite corridor, harsh strip lights surging above. I can't breathe. I see Jake's trainers kicked off by the front door at home and wish I hadn't wasted so much time nagging him to clear them away.

We stop at a set of lifts and wait. The hipster porter hums a tune I vaguely recognise, tapping his feet. Somewhere in the bowels of the building a clanking, grating sound starts up, as if the lift has woken from a hundred-year slumber. It arrives with a sulky hiss that sounds like Jake's grumbles when I make him do homework. Doors opening, the automated voice chants, the doors crawling open with a suck of air. Doors closing. Lift going down.

'Here we go,' the porter says, pausing at double doors and buzzing the intercom. He shifts from foot to foot and rubs his hands together as we wait.

A nurse looks up as we enter. Ward Manager, it says on her badge. Official dark-blue tunic and trousers. Weary piercing eyes. I know her.

'Where for Mrs Fielding?'

She glances at the electronic board behind the nurse's station, then points down the hall. 'C Bay. Be there in a moment.' She looks more closely at me, and I see the usual recognition sweeping through her eyes. 'Oh, it's you again, turning up like a bad penny!'

That's me. Bad Penny. Waste of space Penny. Drain on the NHS Penny.

She flushes. 'Oh! I didn't mean… I forgot.'

The porter turns and grins at me, working gum fiercely around his mouth. 'You look tired. You get any sleep up there?'

I shake my head.

He makes a wry face. 'Ward'll be quieter, love.'

The ward isn't quieter. A machine that sounds like a jet engine in trouble squeals from Bed 4, a cacophony of beeping wails out around the bay, and all the lights are on. 'Has no one put these lights off?' No one answers him so he deposits my bed in the middle on the left side, and strolls out, waving. 'Hope you feel better soon.'

He doesn't turn the lights off on his way.

I don't want to be here. I want to be home in my bed with Jake safe in the next room. Will I see my boy again?

'You woke me up.'

I peer through the half-closed curtains to my left where a blonde woman in a *Frozen* nightshirt is propped up in her bed, her stare a thousand daggers.

She shrugs at me and then shifts her body around, shoves her feet into huge fluffy bunny slippers on the floor by her bed. Grabs a ratty pink dressing gown from the plastic chair next to her bed. 'Going for a fag.' She staggers out of the bay, trailing an oxygen cylinder.

The world presses in and angry clouds shudder through half-waking dreams. There's noise in the dreams, but it's blurry at the edges. I don't know where I am.

Something is biting my arm in two.

'Miss Fielding. Penny. Sorry, flower, I'm just taking your blood pressure. Relax, now.'

I blink and glance at the clock on the wall above the door. Four o'clock. Did I sleep? The main lights are still on. A healthcare assistant in a light green dress looms into my vision. 'Oh dear,' she says, releasing the cuff. She grabs my finger and places it in a pulse oximeter. 'Eighty-eight.' Her brow knits as she flips through my chart.

I try to form a word. 'M…'

She lifts my wrist, placing a gloved finger on my pulse point. 'You what, flower?'

My tongue is stuck to the roof of my mouth. 'Morphine… please.'

Marcus would've scorned me for that. Drugs are weakness, he'd say.

'Sorry, petal, you'll have to wait for the nurse. She'll be round later with your IVs. Try and get some sleep. Just turn your head, lovely, just got to do your temperature. Oh. Thirty-nine point eight. Right, well, try and rest.'

Frozen woman is back in the bed next to mine, mouth open wide, pneumatic snores spilling out and reverberating through the bay. She looks lost there, like I feel, falling into a void. I am tumbling over myself, and somewhere down there I know it is quiet and I want more of it.

Weak sunlight straggles through the windows, and I remember I left the washing outside. Jake won't notice; he has a great knack for ignoring those things. It'll flap around out there for the next two weeks, lonely and cold and waiting.

'Shh, now, flower.' It's the healthcare assistant from before. I know her, I think, from more stays in here. I recognise her spiky red hair and wide-open smile. 'Just doing your obs again. Try to sleep.'

A nurse comes up behind her, drip-bag in hand. 'S'cuse me, Nicki. She needs hydrating.'

'Just give me a sec.'

She shows the oximeter to the nurse, who raises her eyebrows.

The nurse hooks the bag up to my drip-stand and connects it to my cannula. 'There you go, Penny. That'll help.'

I wonder what will happen if I allow myself to sink deep into the enticing murk, to drown. It is black as night and maybe it will hide me away forever. No one will miss me, not very much. Jake's old enough to cope by himself more now, and that scares me.

Then, suddenly, I feel it: his hand in mine when he was small. He knew I'd always keep him safe, even when my body let me down.

Whatever's dragging me down can't win, because he has to be okay.

He still needs me, so I'm not allowed to go.

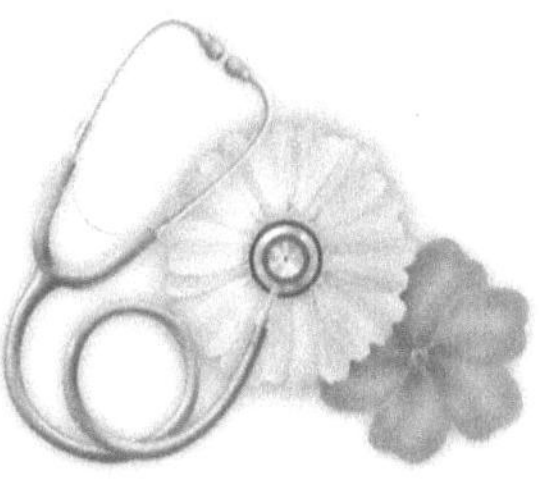

Chapter 2

YOU ARE SO inspirational, Penny, they say to me. So brave. They don't know how they'd cope if they were me. You're strong, people say to me, and then I have to pretend to be strong, and that makes me weaker still.

We laugh about it on the Facebook group. We call ourselves The Braves and admit to one another we don't really feel brave at all. We have a thread for those in the Five Star Hotel. Whose turn is it this time, we wonder, to be pampered all day and all night, to sample the extensive menu. Some of us visit the hotel more regularly than others. Some push right to the front of the queue and get to indulge in its comfort far too much. Like me. Grabby, that's what I am, taking up more than my fair share.

We have a thread for those who don't make it out, as well.

It doesn't feel like a hotel this morning. The ward sister is on her medication round and Nicki is in the ward with the breakfast trolley; what-can-I-do-you-for-today-flower? Must be on a double shift. I like her, with her big warm smile she casts around so freely. She's the kind of nurse patients always hope for: tender and funny all wrapped up together. She grins at me. 'Back again, then, Penny?' I nod, because I haven't got any words in me this morning. 'You look pale, flower. Can I do you some porridge? Bit of sugar?'

I shake my head.

'Toast?'

No.

'You sure? Anything? What about some yoghurt? Need to keep your strength up.'

I shake my head.

'Okay, lovely. Just shout if you want something later, won't you?'

My oxygen mask bites into my face and I move it away for blessed seconds until the air is sucked out of the room. The ward sister looms up out of the choking haze. 'Got to keep that on, Penny. You know that.'

I know her. Sister Harris. She's been here for years. Abrupt but kind.

'Come on, love. Put it back.'

'Can I have a nasal cannula?'

She sighs, shaking her head at me as if she is a teacher scolding a difficult child. 'You're on the high flow, dear. You know that. Don't want CPAP, do you?'

I know that. And no, I don't want the positive air pressure machine. I know it's essential to fill my lungs, but it makes me feel like my face is trapped in a wind tunnel.

I roll onto my side to reach for the bed remote to sit myself up a bit. The healthcare assistants will be round in a minute to get the beds made before the doctors come on their ward rounds, but I'm not sure I can make it out of bed. I hope Jake's up, getting ready for school, not skiving off like he did last time I was in. I close my eyes, sink back down against the thin pillow.

'You just get in yesterday?'

Open them again. It's the girl in the bed to the left of me, the one with the *Frozen* nightshirt in the night. The one I woke up.

I nod. 'Was in the acute unit.'

She grimaces. 'Like a nightclub in there, just as noisy. Not as fun, though.'

'Mmm.'

'What you in for?' Her accent is heavy west country, her skin shockingly pale. Her blue eyes are almost translucent, stark with her tale of sickness. 'I been in a week already.'

I try to form the word. 'Pneumonia.'

'What?'

Daggers are stabbing me. Piercing my side.

She shakes her head. 'Don't worry, my lovely. You're in no state, are you? Get to sleep. I'm Jodie, by the way.' She sticks her hand out, as if to shake mine, then pulls it back and does a little wave. 'I'll leave you alone now.'

Looks like she's forgiven me for the early wake-up call.

I glance over into the far corner where an elderly lady lies still, a huge mask the size of a dinner plate pressed to her face, screwed on at the sides. The Mask, the staff call it, and patients always dread it; much worse than a mere oxygen mask. She is like a bundle of sticks, so diminutive the pillows almost swallow her whole, her eyes skittering wildly below the mask. *Rescue me*, they are shouting. *Get me out of this thing.*

Jodie catches me looking. 'That's our Barbara. Been in longer than me. Not so good today, but she has better times.'

The one other occupant of the ward is in the bed in the far-right corner. A middle-aged woman with a purple scarf draped over her head. Jodie follows my gaze. 'That's Amina, I think she's called. Don't say much, though. Only came in yesterday.'

The lines on Amina's face cut deep with exhaustion. She's picking at a bowl of porridge, an oxygen mask lying by her side. She sees me staring and smiles gently.

I close my eyes and drift back into the fog.

THE DOCTOR COMES in trailing his entourage of registrars and students. He's my favourite consultant, Doctor Chowdhury, who sees me in clinic and tells me to go easy on myself but remember to do more exercise, and I always nod and smile, like I'm going to turn over a new leaf first thing in the morning and start couch to 5K, like I will suddenly snap out of all this and feel able to take on the world.

'Penny Fielding! In here again?' He spreads his hands and smiles at me. 'We see far too much of you. No offence.'

I pick at the loose skin around my fingernails and wish I wasn't wearing this nightshirt. Karen bought it for me for Christmas once. Let's get you out of all that black, she said. Bit of sparkle, that's what you need. It was the only one I could find when the ambulance came for me.

Some place inside me I want sparkles, but I don't want to sparkle at anyone else in case they see me.

He's serious, all of a sudden, scanning the x-ray and blood results. 'Hmm. Have you done us a sample yet?'

'Sent one in, few days ago.'

'Okay. We'll need another now you're in, too.'

He picks up my hand, scrutinises my fingernails with his brow furrowed, his face all shifting in great vivid worry-lines like Van Gogh's self-portrait. 'More signs of clubbing than before.'

I look at my nails, at the white blotches, the unnatural curve, the tale told of long-term lung disease.

'Your infection markers are up, high white blood cell count. You'll be in for fourteen days, at least.'

I slump even more than I was slumped already.

'I'm a bit concerned about your x-ray here. It's showing too much fluid. Here, see, you have fairly severe pleural effusions. We could do a chest drain, but we could try a pleural tap first – a procedure where we insert a needle into your pleural cavity to see if we can drain enough out for you.'

Not that, again. Last time they tried that one they decided it was a good idea to make me a practice dummy for a junior doctor who couldn't get the needle – the biggest, thickest, longest needle ever – into the right place, and I yowled like a cat in the night.

'You'll do it?' I implore him with my eyes, which are most definitely the furthest from enticing as eyes can get right now; reddened, veiny and raw.

'Someone will be round.'

Oh good.

I sleep in snatches, between nebulisers and pills and IV drips, Jodie's strident voice loud into her mobile, shouted conversations between staff, the screeching of machines, the constant shrilling of the phone out by the nurse's station. The cycle of meds, observations, drinks and food passes me by in my daze. The tap gets done and the phlebotomist takes five vials of blood. I refuse the bed change and refuse a wash, refuse another cup of tea (the first still sits, untouched and tepid, on my table) and the toast Nicki keeps offering me. Just leave me alone. Just give me more morphine and leave me floating in my ocean of far away.

It's only Jake who wakes me from my stupor, loafing into the ward with his earbuds in and his phone stuck out in front of him. He scans the beds, settles his gaze on me and then grunts, raising his chin at me slightly, and if I'm making generous assumptions this might be interpreted as something like, 'Hey, Mum, I miss you and hope you're feeling better.'

'Did you walk here?'

'Bike.'

Jake is not easy to have a conversation with at the best of times. He is my darling boy, but he is fifteen and doesn't yet know how to use multisyllabic words, or entire sentences. And his ability to use any words at all varies with his mood, which in itself varies as much as the English weather.

He removes his earbuds, at least, and slouches onto the bed. Nicki will give him a ticking off for that if she sees him. He sweeps his long fringe from his eyes and glances around the bay at the other patients. Barbara is fast asleep in the corner, pinned under her mask, and Jodie is not here. Amina is surrounded by four great tall lads who are all talking at once in soft but animated voices, and a smaller older man sitting on the blue plastic chair by her side, holding her hand. He looks about ten years older than her. They are ignoring the boys and staring at one another as if they have been starved.

'You okay?' Jake says at last, having summoned up a great amount of energy to bring these arduous words forth from great depths.

I nod. Then shake my head, because it's no use lying to Jake. It's only ever been me and him, and so he knows if I am okay or not.

He narrows his eyes at me. 'You're not.' I stare up at him, at the darkness slicing into his smooth forehead. He still has a baby face in so many ways, round at the edges and yet just sharpening that tiny little bit as adolescence morphs him out of childhood and into the stinking, grumpy unknown.

'No,' I say. 'But I… I'll be all right.'

My fingers are crossed under my blanket.

He gazes at me. Looks at my oxygen mask, my chest rising and falling too quickly, my face that I know will be pasty and flushed all at the same time, my hair all mussed up and unbrushed. I hate it when my hair is messy but don't have the energy to do anything about it. And I don't want to put that on Jake.

'You be in here two weeks again?'

I nod.

'I hate being at Nan's. She fusses too much.'

'I know.'

I hated growing up with her, too, and I hate having to rely on her for Jake when I'm in hospital.

He shrugs and rams his earbuds in again, lost too soon in the world of his phone. The conversation, such as it was, has run dry. I stare at his thumbs working so frantically away, wishing he was small again, the little lad whose smile lit a room and who never stopped talking.

But that little lad was heartbroken every time I had to go into hospital. My father would wrap him in his arms and drag him kicking and screaming out of the ward. Maybe he's still kicking and screaming inside, but just doesn't know how to show it anymore, in his great scary brave new adolescent world. I want to kick and scream, too, to pummel my fists into someone's chest.

Jodie shambles back through the bay, dragging an oxygen cylinder on wheels with one hand and a drip stand with the other, her tatty fleece dressing gown gaping open to reveal a T-shirt with the words 'OK Millennial' printed in great big black letters. She holds her curves like a proud goddess, sticking out her chest, her copious belly hanging out over her pink leopard-skin print pyjama bottoms.

'Cool T-shirt,' Jake says, and she stops and stares at him.

'You her son then?'

Jake makes a noise that might mean yes in some strange alien language but sounds more like 'duh' in ours.

'I'm Jodie.'

'Jake.'

'What you playing?'

Jake cocks a sardonic eyebrow at her.

'Go on, let's see.'

He shrugs and shows her his phone.

She narrows her eyes, leaning in and scratching her head. 'That's a rubbish score.'

Jake's mouth twitches. 'Actually, I'm in the top one hundred.'

'Get you!' Jodie sheds her dressing gown and sinks onto her bed. 'I'll show you what I'm on.'

Jake shifts closer to her bed, and I feel like he's interacted more meaningfully with a stranger nearer his age in thirty seconds than he has with me in twenty minutes. I close my eyes and lie back. I'm done with this day.

I don't hear Jake leave.

It's LATE EVENING and I'm waiting for the last IV round when I hear the raspy voice. 'Have you seen my mouse?'

I open my eyes. Try to focus. What? Is someone saying something to me? Jodie is here but she's quiet, on her phone with headphones in. Amina snores gently across the ward.

'You! Have you seen my mouse?'

It's Barbara, mask-less, speaking in urgent tones, eyes flicking around the ward, her white hair wild. Is she talking to me?

'You there. Girl. Come over here.'

She means Jodie, or maybe she wants one of the nurses.

But she's beckoning to me. She's sitting bolt upright with her mouth hanging open, like a baby bird waiting for dinner, her limbs like twigs, shipwrecked on a great island of cotton wool whiteness.

I drag myself up to a semi-sitting position and look at her, raising my shoulders.

'Yes. You. Come over here, please, darling.'

I don't have the strength to leave my bed, let alone make it across the ward. I try to say something, but my voice is stuck in my throat. I think about Edna from the night before and think about how I seem to be regularly letting down elderly women at the moment. Sorry, I'm sorry, I can't help you. I am just failing you, like all the other times. Like I fail my son and fail myself. I look down as a flash of pain blazes through my finger and notice I am picking at my skin again, and it is red raw.

Barbara's voice quavers as she calls to me, 'You have to help. Help me!'

Jodie yanks out her earbuds and clambers off her bed. She goes to Barbara and pats her hand. 'It's okay, Barbara my love. She's just a patient like you. She's really poorly. Leave her be.'

'But my mouse,' Barbara says.

'Don't worry about your mouse. We'll find it.'

'She's by the sea. I have to go to the sea. Why does no one ever help me? I ask everyone and no one ever wants to help. I say to them, I say please help me. Please do this one thing. But no one cares. No one left to care.'

Jodie tenderly takes hold of Barbara's hand and whispers something to her. Barbara stares at the ceiling, mumbling something incomprehensible. Jodie turns to me, shakes her head and makes a spinning motion with her finger. 'Bit dippy, bless her. Thinks she's lost a mouse.'

'Oh,' I say.

I dream of hundreds of mice scurrying round the ward, calling to me in sad, quivering voices, in my tiny, restless snatches of sleep.

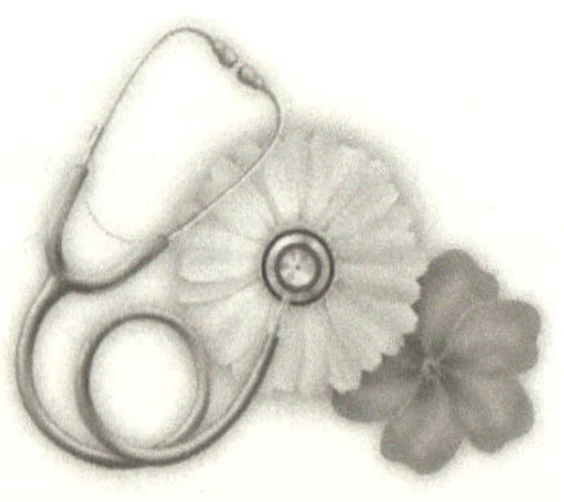

Chapter 3

MY COLOURS HAVE all been washed away and I want to swirl with them into a universe of nothingness. In dreams I wear purple tights and short flowery dresses that flow loose and make me skip through blue skies with rainbow clouds. In dreams I don't hide my colours but in life I wear black leggings and grey jumpers and they help me to not take up space. Once I bought some purple tights and Marcus told me I was ridiculous and then I threw them away. Now my colours have faded, and I can't grab hold of the edges of them anymore; there is a black hole underneath me and it looks like all the clothes I wear, and it is dragging me down, and I don't want to resist anymore.

But then Jake's face is there, and he is holding all the colours with him, and I have to fight for them.

IN THE MIDDLE of the night I'm wide awake. A young Filipino healthcare assistant called Ernesto has been taking my observations every hour because my sats are too low and they are worried about me, he says. He is short and wiry, the vital signs trolley towering over him as he trails it around the ward, wheels squeaking like a disgruntled seagull on every turn. He has a smile like sunshine in the rain.

A new patient is arriving, the same porter who brought me to the ward pushing her bed into the bay and winking at Ernesto, who grins back at him and grabs the front of the bed. They pull her in next to me, and I stare at her. She's not much older than me but looks a bit scary; all nose piercings and purple hair and tattoos crawling over her arms and neck. Her eyes are dark pools of exhaustion, like everyone else's in here, including most of the staff.

Jodie is up on her feet in seconds with her cigarettes tucked in the pocket of her dressing-gown, her oxygen cylinder trailing behind. 'Hey,' she says to the new woman. 'Nice tats.'

'Thanks,' the woman says, her voice worn.

'I'm Jodie,' Jodie says, and I wonder what it is about this Jodie, that she needs to announce herself so quickly, that she wants everyone to know who she is. She's unlike most patients I meet in here, people who just want to sleep the days away until release. She's loud and crass and I don't want to know her. I want her to go away and leave me alone. I want everyone to leave me alone.

'Kat,' the tattooed woman says, and turns her back to us, coiling herself up into a tiny ball. I can read the pain on her, see it in the stiffness of her body, in the set of her shoulders. Her hospital gown is open at the back, the tie loosened, and through the opening a large tattoo of what looks like a phoenix is visible.

Jodie whistles. 'Woah. Must've hurt.'

Kat doesn't respond.

A shock wave of agony snakes through my body, intensifying in waves with every breath. I call out to Ernesto, a thin reed of a call, but he doesn't hear.

I pinch the skin on my arm and button my lips together. Stop bothering them, Penny. Stop making their lives more difficult, those nurses who work tirelessly, battling through twelve-hour-shifts with little break, hardly off their feet. I want to be a nurse, to have a body that will stay on its feet for twelve hours. I want to be a Tesco checkout girl or an Amazon packer, a teaching assistant or a lorry driver. I want to be anything at all.

I will squeeze my eyes tight and lie as still as I possibly can because that helps just a little bit. Maybe if I lie still enough I will disappear altogether, stop taking up this bed and let it go to someone more worthy.

DOCTOR CHOWDHURY IS standing at the foot of my bed, clutching an iPad, with stooped shoulders and his most pitying gaze levelled at me. I know that look; it's the one that shouts out this-is-not-good-Penny, but his tones are calm and measured as he relays the damage. 'It's the big three again, like last time, I'm afraid. The Unholy Trinity.'

I am empty. I am numb. He does not tell me what I do not already know.

'Pseudomonas, some heavy growth there. Aspergillus. Mycobacterium abscessus, again. Thought we'd seen that one off last time.' He smiles gently, as if he is making a little joke.

'Oh.' *I'm sorry,* I want to say. *I am sorry for being such a fertile breeding ground.*

'You know why we call these the Unholy Trinity, don't you?'

I shrug.

'Bacteria, fungi and mycobacteria, all three conspire to do more damage to your lungs.'

'I know.' I do know. They are my friends. I have made them a nice, warm home to hang out in over the years, and they are reluctant to leave. Just when we think one has been successfully evicted, it pops up again, laughing in my face. Marcus would say I don't try hard enough to kick them out the door.

'We'll do our best with these IVs. They're the big boys. We should review your anti-fungals, too.' He taps his pen against his mouth and gazes at me. I don't want him to gaze at me. He has more important patients to see. Patients who are dying.

'You are brave,' he says unexpectedly, and I dig my nails into my palms. He doesn't know how I get under my duvet and pinch myself at night, to try to make myself cry, because the tears are there in my throat and they push at me until I think I will burst into pieces. He doesn't know I scream at the sky and at God or whoever is up there. He doesn't know that I am really a coward.

'Your infection markers are very high, still, and we are not happy with your oxygen saturations or your temperature. We'll repeat the x-ray later to see if we need to put in a chest drain after all.'

Not a chest drain. Please not a chest drain.

'Is your cannula okay?'

I hold out my hand. They put it in the wrong place; it'll be blown within hours. Dried blood crusts around the site and it stings deep.

'I'll ask the nurse to do you a new one,' he says.

At lunch time, a catering supervisor I don't recognise slams a tray down on my table. 'Dinner,' she says, walking away.

'Wait.' My voice is a weak croak. 'Sorry. I'm vegetarian. Sorry.'

She gawks at me as if I am an alien from another planet. 'It's fish,' she says, slowly, as if I am hard of thinking.

'Sorry. It does say, up there.' I point to the board on the wall behind my bed. VEGGIE scrawled in great black shouty letters. It could as easily say PICKY or DIFFICULT. That's what Marcus thought about my food habits, anyway.

She stares at the word as if it is written in a foreign language. 'But it's fish.'

I sigh. 'Fish is not vegetarian.'

She rolls her eyes. 'All the other vegetarians eat fish. No one else ever complains.'

I have been veggie for much of my life. I think I know what constitutes vegetarian. But I don't. I say, 'I'm sorry.'

She shrugs and walks away, and I'm left filled with self-rancour and nausea at the offending fish on the plate I will not touch.

'I'll have it,' Jodie says, up from her bed and hanging over my table. 'I'm hungry and this dinner is far too small. I'll eat anything, me. Well, apart from hospital food.' She laughs, her whole belly shaking like a jelly.

Amina says, 'Can I have the food?' On her table is a tray with pork chops and overcooked, mushy broccoli. 'I must not eat this pig.'

Jodie raises her eyebrows at me.

'You have a problem with this?' Amina says.

Jodie shakes her head. 'Nah. Just… I think you should get to make your own choices, that's all.'

Amina says nothing. Jodie shrugs, takes the fish to Amina and the plate of pork back to her own bed.

I wasn't hungry anyway. The nausea still churns through my stomach like a washing-machine on its spin cycle.

Barbara doesn't have the mask on today. Nicki is sitting with her, spoon-feeding her yoghurt and chatting away. 'You're doing well today, lovely, aren't you? We'll have you home in no time! The doctor's pleased with you, isn't he?'

Barbara dribbles yoghurt down her chin. Nicki scoops it up, spooning it back in. 'Come on, flower, you need to get your strength back, don't you?'

Barbara pushes the spoon away. 'Did you see the mouse?'

'No, Barbara, I told you, no mice in here.'

'There's rats.' Barbara's voice is a low growl of anger.

'No rats, either.' Nicki casts a sideways glance back at Jodie.

'I have to go to the sea to find her.'

'Find who, petal?'

'Do you not listen, woman? My MOUSE.'

Nicki scoops more yoghurt into Barbara's wide gape of a mouth, and Barbara splutters.

'Come on, get this down you. Stop worrying yourself about rodents, my lovely.'

Barbara is quiet and obedient for the remainder of the yoghurt.

When Nicki has left the bay, Barbara sits bolt upright and points over at me with a wizened, crooked finger, as if she is accusing me of something. Jodie follows her gesture and sits forward. 'What you doing, Babs?'

'You'll take me there, won't you?' Barbara says, her watery eyes still on me, finger quivering.

I don't know what to say.

'You have to take me. You have to.' Her voice is rising in volume.

Jodie throws off her blanket and goes to Barbara. She takes her hand. 'It's okay, chicken. It's okay.'

'You take me,' Barbara shouts in Jodie's face, droplets of yoghurt spraying over her hair. 'You get me to the sea. You will, won't you?'

'Shh,' Jodie says. 'We will. I promise we will.'

Barbara grips Jodie's hand tightly between hers. Even from here I can see the translucency of her skin, mottled and veiny and stretched so taut I wonder if it might rip to shreds any moment and the bones all spill out. She leans in closer to Jodie and says something in a raspy croak. I think it might be something like, 'It's the only thing I've got left in the world now.'

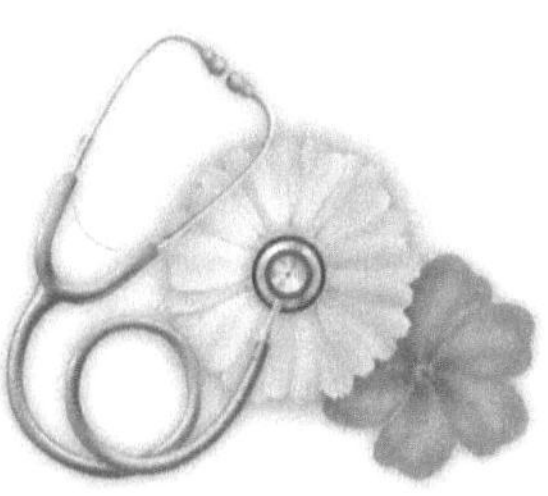

Chapter 4

EARLY EVENING JAKE is visiting me again. 'Grandad dropped me off,' he says around mouthfuls of Twix. He sees my eyes on it. 'Want some? I was hungry. Nan makes rubbish food.'

This is true.

'No thanks.'

'Still can't breathe too well?'

I shake my head. Wish I could ask for a drink. Some squash, maybe, something cold, something that's not hospital tea or tepid water. But the words get stuck in my iron-clenched gullet.

Jake shrugs his shoulders and turns his attention back to his phone.

Jodie sits on the edge of her bed, watching us. 'Oy,' she says, kicking out at Jake, 'you should talk to your mum more. She's well poorly.'

Jake grunts. 'Whatever.'

Jodie gets up, kicks him again, and he laughs. How does she get away with that? If I did that he'd cry child abuse. 'Yeah, yeah,' he says, instead, and turns back to me, laying the phone down on my bed. 'Sorry you're feeling so crap.'

I try to smile.

'You look like Helena Bonham-Carter,' he says randomly.

'What?'

'All mussed-up hair and pale as a ghost, and this weird kind of not-smile.'

True, I suppose. But I wouldn't actually mind looking like Helena Bonham-Carter, so I'll take it.

There's a commotion at the doors. A bed being delivered, another patient, a full house in Bay C. Two of the healthcare assistants move the empty bed out of the way in the space opposite me. A logjam is forming at the door of the bay; Nicki hovering with a commode for Barbara, several of Amina's family just arrived in for visiting. The porter pushing the new patient's bed rolls his eyes. 'Give us some space?' A different porter to my rainbow hipster one. Amina's sons move back, apologising, all polite and sweet and toweringly tall.

Kat, the new patient from the night before, is fast asleep with her back turned to us, as if she is trying to shut out the world.

This new patient is probably mid-sixties, a close-cropped bob of greying hair fighting a battle with garish yellow dye, pursed up mouth, and frown lines slashing her face into ragged slices. A nasal cannula sits lopsidedly in her nostrils.

'I don't want to go here,' she says to the porter and the nurse wheeling her bed into place. The effort of speaking sends her into a convulsion of hacking coughs and I wince. Do I sound like that?

The porter and the nurse ignore her and chat among themselves. How are her wedding plans, he is asking. Good, she says. Except her fiancé hasn't sorted the caterer and promised her he would. Men, hey! Yeah, useless creatures, the porter says.

'Excuse me,' the new woman says. 'I know your conversation is… *cough* – vital – *cough*, but I actually said I don't want to go here.'

Her accent is a jarring mix of try-hard King's English and earthy west country twang.

The nurse just smiles. 'Right, Violet, let's get you sorted and checked in then, shall we? Be back in a min to do you.'

Violet's pasty face turns shades of red vivid against the slight blue tinge of her lips, her several chins wobbling along with her outrage. 'I want my own room.'

Jake clears his throat. 'Boomer.'

Most people over forty are boomers to Jake.

His lips twist in a sly little grin. 'Bet her middle name's Karen.'

Jodie splutters in the corner.

I sigh. I cannot find the energy to berate him about his careless use of the name Karen as a misogynistic slur for a certain type of middle-aged woman. I've done the spiel once too often – how do you think it makes all the lovely people feel who happen to be called Karen? What about Aunt Karen? Case in point, he always says, and smirks louder at me.

He stares at me now with one eyebrow raised, as if to question my poor parenting in its lack of challenge to his unwarranted attack on the personality of someone he does not know. I close my eyes.

The nurse blithely ignores Violet's plaintive and increasingly loud demands, shoving the bed brake down with her foot and bustling out of the ward, bantering with the porter. Her husband-to-be apparently forgot to ring the vicar like he promised he would. Men!

Nicki delivers Barbara's commode, pulls the curtains round her space and grabs the observations trolley from the corner by Jodie's bed. She strolls over to the new patient, winking at Jodie. 'Hello there, Mrs Oddens. Violet, right? Is it Vi? Just going to get your sats done, flower.'

Violet's narrow mouth puckers itself even further in. 'It's *Oh*-dens. And no, you may not call me Vi. Violet is my name. And I'm not a flower, thank you.'

Jake mouths *Ohhhdens* at me and I try not to grin.

Nicki laughs. Nicki always seems to laugh easily, a flower herself, open to sunshine and dragging it into the ward for the rest of us.

'Don't you dare make fun of me,' Violet says. Nicki winks back at Jodie who is on the edge of her bed, drinking it all in with her direct blue gaze.

'I want my own room,' Violet says.

'This is the NHS, not the Hilton,' Nicki says, and I smile to myself.

Violet narrows her pale eyes, grabs Nicki's arm and gives a non-too-subtle sideways nod towards Amina. 'I don't want to be next to *her.*'

Everything about Violet is a scream of brashness, from her faded and smudged blue eyeshadow through to her loud floral polyester nightie and bright pink fluffy slippers. Jodie catches my eye and I lower my gaze, but not before seeing the mischievous grin playing around her lips. This one is going to be interesting, I think. She's like a real-life Hyacinth Bucket, all bluster and faux-posh accent, and now adding bigotry to the mix.

'Boomer,' Jake says again. His voice is as smirky as a voice could be if it was a smirk. He leans over towards Jodie. 'Plus she has Lego hair.'

Jodie cackles.

Amina says nothing but her face tells the truth of a long litany of similar comments poured over her through years. I want to go to her, to say we're not all like that, but my energy is drained like water wrung from a cloth.

One of her sons stands up, stretching himself taller than before, if that were possible, his head almost touching the curtain rail. He stares hard at Violet. 'What's your problem with my mother?'

Violet does not seem troubled by his words or by the presence of the other three equally large young men. She pouts like a child and then huffs, 'She's one of them Islams.'

Nicki has the blood pressure cuff wrapped around Violet's arm, and I'm sure she yanks it off harder than she should. 'Stop it.' She's the formidable primary teacher to Violet's stroppy five-year-old, scolding her for her petulant silliness. 'That's the end of that kind of talk in my ward.'

Surprisingly, Violet simmers down and says nothing more, just casts a disdainful glance over at Amina, and then, for some reason, turns and nods at me, curving her mouth in a kind of tortured smile. Jake laughs out loud. 'You've made a friend, Mum.'

I hope not.

Amina's sons gather around their mother's bed and speak quietly to her. One of them grabs the curtain and yanks it along its rail, screening out Violet.

'My boyfriend's coming in today,' Jodie announces, scuffing her bunny-slippered feet on the floor beneath her bed.

I don't know what kind of response she wants, so I say, 'That's nice.'

'You'll love him. He's wicked, really cool.'

Jake snickers. 'No one says 'wicked' anymore.'

Jodie shrugs. 'No one says 'Boomer' anymore.'

'Boomer,' Jake says.

A shaven-headed man as broad as he is tall with a tattoo of a snake crawling around one arm and an arrowed heart with 'Jodie 4 eva' inked on the other bicep struts into the bay wearing a grubby vest top and low-slung Adidas joggers. Jodie stands up, smoothing out her long blonde hair. 'Everyone, this is Kane. My boyfriend.'

When she says 'everyone', she really means me and Jake. Barbara is snoring in her corner, without visitors once again,

Amina is concealed behind her curtain, Kat is sleeping and Violet is lying back against her pillows, her face a picture of disapproval as she stares at Jodie's boyfriend. He is oblivious, not because he's drinking in Jodie with love in his eyes but because he is staring at his phone.

'Hi, Kane,' I say.

'S'up,' he says, or at least I think he does. It's more of a murmured grunt, much like Jake's preferred manner of communication. He slumps onto the chair by Jodie's bed, splaying his legs out wide, and continues to scroll through his phone.

'You on that game again?' Jodie says.

Nothing.

Jodie sinks back onto her bed, her face fallen in on itself, as if all the hope she was storing up for his visit has been extinguished and she's facing reality again. She pulls at his arm but he bats her away. 'Just got to finish this level.'

'Oh. Okay.'

Jodie is different with him. It's as though with the rest of us she's a rose in bloom, all opened out to the sun, but with him her petals wilt. The way she acts is a little familiar, a little uncomfortable. But I don't want to think about that. I'm probably reading too much into it, anyway. Maybe Kane is just finishing a game off, and then he will sweep Jodie up in his heavily muscled arms and hold her tight and tell her he loves her and she is beautiful.

Violet is faffing round with her overhead TV system. I thought those things were obsolete, with their old-fashioned phone handsets, the coiled wire that snags your hair with its vicious grip. With the pointless little keyboard that was too tiny for the tiniest fingers and never quite succeeded in calling up the internet. When Jake was born I tried to announce his birth online using one of those things because my phone was out of charge, but it flickered and froze until I slammed the wretched thing back in its cradle, my frustration mixing up with post-birth shock, leaving me a curled-up heap on my bed, staring at this tiny new life in his plastic crib beside me and wondering how on earth I was ever going to do this thing on my own if I couldn't even work this stupid machine.

Violet is grappling with it now, stabbing at the keyboard, brows knitted together in vexation. 'You. Young man,' she shouts, gesturing to Jake with the phone, 'can you make this work?'

'Please,' Jake mutters under his breath, but dutifully stands, lumbering over the bay to Violet and studying the unit, a sneer creeping over his features. 'What even is this thing?'

'I want to watch *Eastenders.*'

'You'll be lucky.' Jake takes the phone off her and hangs it up, then fiddles with the buttons on the TV. 'This thing came out of the ark. Don't you have an iPad?'

'Don't like those new-fangled things. They don't have buttons to press.'

Jake raises an eyebrow and fiddles round some more. 'You need to get a payment card for this, or use a credit card to pay for it. Damn! They're ripping you off.'

Violet is unruffled. 'Just get it working.'

'Okay Karen.'

'I don't know what that means. My name is Violet.'

'Nothing. Look, can you get your family or whatever to do the payment for you? Or do you have a card?'

'But my husband won't be in until tomorrow, and *Eastenders* is on in ten minutes.'

Jake shrugs. 'Sorry.'

'Youngsters today have no staying power,' Violet mutters, and shoves the unit away from her at Jake, who stumbles back.

'Woah. Okay then. Good luck.' Jake comes back over to me, slouches down onto the chair by my bed.

I muster up my strength and the edges of an outrage that isn't as large in me as usual. 'The Karen thing is tedious and offensive.'

Jake laughs. That worked well, then.

Jodie leans over to Jake, ignoring Kane who is immersed in his phone, all morose and silent. She tilts her head over at Violet, her eyes wide and dancing with mirth. 'She's gonna be a right one.'

'She is that,' Jake says.

'I need a fag.'

'I'll come with,' Kane says, leaping out of the chair and hightailing it out of the bay, leaving Jodie in his wake, struggling with all her paraphernalia.

'I do, too,' Violet says, unexpectedly. 'You got one I can have?'

Jodie stares at her. 'You look like you should stay here.' Violet's lips are bluer than before, her face pale as the moon.

Violet shakes her head, as if Jodie is being ridiculous. 'I know what I can and can't do. I'm high up in the National Trust, you know.'

Jodie and Jake gaze at one another with snarky grins dancing on their lips.

Violet turns her body away from us. 'Nurse!' she shouts at Nicki, who is hovering over by Kat's bed. 'Take me outside in one of those chairs. I need a cigarette.'

Nicki takes a long breath in and puffs out her cheeks. 'Righto, Mrs *Oh*-dens. If I could just finish what I'm doing—'

'I'll take her,' Jake says, dragging himself to his feet. I stare at him, taking in the sheer wonder of him, his gawky teenageness, endless arms and legs all sharp awkward angles, dark hair swept low over his eyes in messy disarray. 'Not to talk to her or anything. Just 'cause they've got enough to do round here without her demanding her rights all the time.'

'I'll look after him,' Jodie says, hovering in the doorway and winking at me. 'C'mon, Mrs National Trust, let's find you that chair.'

Jake says, 'We should put a thistle on it.'

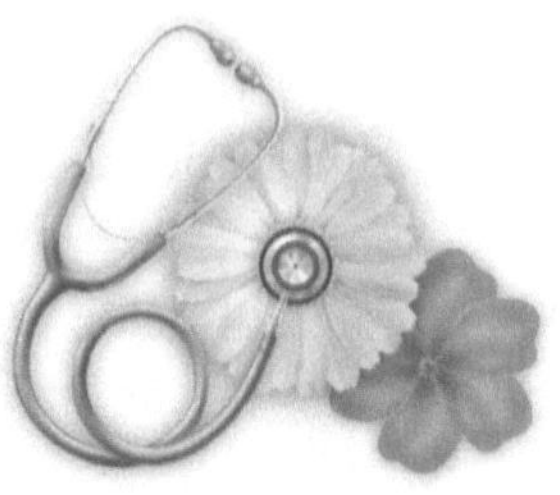

Chapter 5

I AM NICE Penny.

I am Penny who says yes to everything, because I cannot be a person who lets others down.

Like when I said yes to joining the Parent Teacher Association and got mercilessly sucked into the life of a mum that does school things. I baked a thousand cakes, took meticulous minutes of long and pointless meetings, and organised discos for overexcited children who got high on all the sweets I got cheap from Costco and then traumatised the dazed-looking DJ with their squealing and squalling. I was swiftly promoted to vice chair, but never chair, because Lucinda Williams would never dream of relinquishing her power. Then I got myself voted onto the governing body and sat through endless meetings where I said yes to a lot of things I did not understand. I said yes to going on courses about safeguarding and British Values and then had to give presentations at the full governing body meetings to scary people who sat and judged my poor communication skills. But I was reliable, for a time, so I got asked and asked again, until I started being unreliable. I sent my apologies to meetings and school trips I'd been earmarked for as an extra adult to herd reluctant Year Fives around the Botanic Gardens or eager Year Ones around the Farm Park. I berated myself then; why did I ever sign up? Why did I ever think this would be different, that I would cope, that I would suddenly magically be well enough? I resigned and watched as a look of relief crossed the headteacher's face and disapproval blazed in Lucinda Williams' eyes.

I am nice Penny who wants to please, and I am disappointing Penny who always lets you down.

I can be nice Penny in hospital, though, without the pressure of performance. I'm the helpful patient, that kind and polite one who doesn't shout at them or spit in their faces. I don't tell them that their laziness is a complete disgrace, like Violet did to a healthcare assistant in the night. I can be different. I can make their job easier. And then, maybe, they won't notice me too much.

This morning I spot Dr Chowdhury making for my cubicle flanked by a group of what can only be medical students. Incredibly young, fresh faces set with keen enthusiasm woven with edges of fear, clinging their iPads close to their chests and almost drooling in the wake of this renowned consultant who is deigning to allow them in his presence.

They squeeze together at the bottom of my bed and smile hopefully at me. Dr Chowdhury clears his throat and sweeps his hand towards them. 'Good morning, Penny. These are some of my trainee doctors. Would you mind if they had a chat with you and examine you?'

I can hardly say no, can I, not with them hanging on his words like excited puppies, squished into my cubicle. Not when I don't know how to say no, even when I just want to sleep. Barbara called all night for the nurse, crying about the rats and the mouse, and Violet was angry. 'Will someone please shut that woman up?' Kat wept in her bed and asked for morphine that didn't come. My own pain was worse through the early hours, the burden of it pressing me into the bed like a brutal version of sleep paralysis.

I nod at Dr Chowdhury, and he yanks the curtains round their rails, shutting us off from the ward, enclosing us in a blue cave. Too small.

He turns to the students. 'I'd like you to ask Miss Fielding some questions. Diagnose her. Tell me what is wrong with her.'

What is wrong with me. If only they could actually diagnose all of the wrongs-with-me.

Dr Chowdhury smiles at me. 'Penny. If you wouldn't mind, please don't reveal your condition. Just try to answer their questions and see if they can get it.'

I nod again, sit myself up more, wish I'd got myself dressed and washed and respectable. Wish I'd brushed my hair, brushed my teeth, brushed the ravages of the night off me. They must be thinking about how awful I look. Their eyes tell the tale of their judgment or maybe their incomprehension of me, out of their privilege of health and youth and beauty. Can't this woman make a bit of an effort?

'Are you in pain?' A boy who looks about fourteen years old stares at me, blue eyes bright and intense, an echo of ginger fuzz shading his chin and top lip.

I don't wish to dignify that with an answer so I just nod. I'm like that dog in the advert. Nod, nod, nod. I'll nod myself right over and fall flat on my face.

A girl with a hijab and dark, intelligent eyes opens her iPad and opens her mouth. Takes a deep breath. Closes it. Opens it again. 'So, what brought you into hospital?'

An ambulance, I so want to say, feeling a smile playing at my mouth. But I will be good. I will scatter enough clues and yet not too many. This is a familiar scenario, an oft repeated tableau, hey guys, here's an intelligent and articulate and fairly young person with a rare disease. Perfect for those trainees to cut their teeth on. Go on, ask her, she'll say yes, she's compliant, she's nice.

'I had chest pain and more sputum than usual. And just general aches in my body, temperature, low sats.'

They gaze at me as if I'm an attraction at the zoo. I can just imagine the cogs turning in their heads. She knows the lingo, they're thinking. She's not new to this. She's probably a chronic case.

Hijab girl says, 'And what colour is your sputum?' The others stand there like fishes out of water, like they have no voices of their own.

'Dark green. Some brown. Streaks of blood.'

They tap furiously at their tablets, as if taking down highly important notes in a lecture.

'And would you say you were breathless?' the boy with the fuzz says.

Well look at me now, I want to say. Look at my oxygen tube and the colour of my skin. Nice and blue. What do you think?

'Yes,' I say.

They shift uncomfortably, taking tiny glances at one another as if to encourage someone to pick up the baton. A tiny girl with huge glasses and vivid red lipstick swallows and steps forward slightly, eyes on Dr Chowdhury. 'Is she asthmatic?'

Dr Chowdhury stands with arms crossed and expression inscrutable. 'Don't direct your questions at me. Penny is a person.'

The girl shakes her head as colour floods her cheeks. 'Sorry. Sorry, Dr Chowdhury. Um… Pen… Miss Fielding, do you suffer from asthma?'

'No,' I say. She nods fiercely then steps back into the shadows as if her work is done.

The girl with the hijab takes up the challenge. She's the confident one here, the one who's going to go far. 'What medication are you on?' she says, her finger hovering over her iPad.

I take a breath and it stabs me hard. 'Do you want the whole list?' She nods. 'It might take a while.'

'That's okay.' She smiles at me.

I begin to count on my fingers. 'Well… carbocisteine.'

A young man who hasn't said anything yet says, 'Could you spell that, please?'

I sigh.

At the end of my list most of them don't look any the wiser. Fuzz-boy's face is crinkled in a deep frown and glasses girl stands with her finger on her mouth, staring into space. Spelling boy looks like he wishes he was taking no space up at all, like he is an awkward add on. Only hijab girl is clued in.

'Do you have cystic fibrosis?'

Dr Chowdhury smiles. 'Continue,' he says. 'Close. Ask her about her history.'

She blushes. 'Of course. Sorry. Uh… Miss Fielding, can you tell me about how you were as a child? Have you been ill for a while?'

'Since I was a child. About five or six.' I stop to take a breath and they're there, hanging on, as if my words will rescue them. 'I caught whooping cough, and well, since then really things got worse.'

Things got worse. It sounds so understated, so run-of-the-mill, not like something that has blighted my life since in ever-increasing ways.

'Is it chronic bronchitis?' the clued-in girl says.

None of them have got it. None of them ever get it.

The consultant fills them in on what's really wrong with me, the rare disease very few have heard of, then lays into them in his gentle yet deadly style. They should have introduced themselves to me, he says. Should have greeted me, asked me how I was feeling, treated me like a human being. They are meek and hangdog, staring at the floor, cheeks flamed with their humiliation. Dr Chowdhury laughs at their confusion. 'You'll learn,' he says, and I know they will, with him as their mentor.

Dr Chowdhury tells me the chest drain isn't necessary after all, and relief washes over me. But I might need another manual drain tomorrow, depending on the fluid levels.

That's fine, as long as he doesn't ask one of his students to do it.

IN AFTERNOON VISITING, Jake is here again and so are Amina's sons, and her husband, too. I look at him and wonder how two such tiny people produced four such great big hulks of sons. One of them pulls the curtain, shutting off Violet, who tightens her mouth so much her lips might crack and shatter into tiny dried-out pieces. Jodie greets Jake like he is a long-lost friend, and Jake makes fun of her slippers. 'Did you kill some poor bunnies for those?'

'Funny.'

'Is that useless boyfriend coming in?' Jake says, and I stare daggers at him.

Jodie seems unruffled, as she does by most things. 'He should be. And I'll tell him you said that. He'll have a right laugh about that.'

I bet he won't.

Jake is morose today with me, flicking at crumbs on my bed and huffing and sighing.

'What's up with you?'

'Nothing.'

'Don't lie, Jake. What is it?'

He rolls his eyes. 'Nothing. Just leave it.'

But I can't leave it. You can never leave it, see, when you're a mother and your child is in pain. You press and you push and sometimes you take it too far.

A MUFFLED BANG. It's coming from Jake's bedroom. And a sob. I drag myself upstairs, stomach churning. What's wrong? He's seemed withdrawn, lately, even more grumpy than usual, communicating in an ever-shortening series of grunts.

I push his door open. He is sitting on his bed, head in his hands, iPad sprawled on the floor with its cover half off and a crack creeping across the screen.

'Did you… did you throw that?'

He shrugs.

I pick it up, noticing it's still open to an Instagram post. He grabs it off me, slams it onto the bed face first. 'Leave it, Mum.'

'What is it?'

'Nothing.' His nothing is so packed with somethings it is glaringly obvious it is not nothing at all.

'Jake? Tell me, love. I want to help.'

He glowers up at me, eyes narrowed. '*You* can't do a thing.' His voice so drips with resentment that I flinch.

'Jake, please, what is it? Is it someone at school?'

'You could say that.'

I grab his iPad. I know in this moment that I shouldn't do that, that fifteen-year-olds need their privacy, but I do it anyway. I grab it and I find the Instagram post and see the picture and the comments. It's one of those meme things Jake is always showing me, but this time it is a picture of Jake's head badly photoshopped onto the body of a skinny, frail old man and the word 'FAIL' in big shouty letters stamped across the image. And then the comments, etching themselves into my brain so sharply I know they will never peel away.

> **2010alex**: so that happened
> **charlotte2011**: what happened?
> **gamer_boyunseen**: so you know that thorpe park trip? We lost it cos JF skipped school again and so yr 10 got it instead
> **charlotte2011**: how is that fair???
> **2010alex**: that's how it works. U have to get like 99% attendance to win the trip, sirs been yabbering on about it all yr
> **gamer_boyunseen**: yeah and if it weren't for him we'd be going. We should do something
> **taylorrules**: why didn't he come into school? Was he ill? Cos that seems a bit mean tbh
> **gamer_boyunseen**: nah it was his stupid mum again shes always sick shes like one of them hypochondriac people, u know. Hes always skipping school cos of her and so we keep missing out on the class attendance things like we did last yr too remember?
> **taylorrules**: yeah but it's not really his fault
> **2010alex:** how's it not his fault, he's 15 not 5
> **gamer_boyunseen**: we should sort him out

The tears push at my eyes but freeze there as they always do. Jake sits on his bed, picking at his fingernails and ignoring my gaze. His mouth quivers just a tiny bit and I want to go, to take him in my arms and tell him that I love him, to tell him it will all be okay.

'I'm so sorry,' I say.

'Not your fault.'

But it is my fault, isn't it? It's my fault that Jake sometimes misses school because I'm so sick I need him to keep me safe or I can't take him if the bus doesn't come. It's not my fault the school has a ridiculous system that penalises students who are absent for any reason at all, but it is my fault that I can't always manage to get Jake there, like a good parent should.

I bend down and take his hand, but he slaps me away and turns his back on me. I know that I shouldn't have pushed, that I shouldn't have looked on his iPad. I know it is something he just has to deal with. Just another layer of guilt for me to take away and feed into the recurring script scrolling through my mind. Useless mum. Useless me.

I GAZE AT him now, remembering how he was with me and gritting my teeth. Don't push, Penny. Not this time. Don't press him so hard he runs away.

'Well,' I say. 'You know where I am if you need me.'

He looks up at me, eyebrows raised. 'Yeah. Yeah, thanks, Mum.'

Jodie is watching us, staring without apology.

'What d'you want?' he says, rolling his eyes at her.

'Nothing,' she says, in an eerily precise parody of his own *nothing* from a moment ago, a kind of exaggerated adolescent grunt. His mouth curls up at the corners.

I look over to Barbara's corner. 'Does she never get visitors?' I ask Jodie.

'Not while I've been in, and that's over a week now.'

'That's so sad.'

'Yeah.'

'I wonder where her family is.'

Jodie shrugs. 'Dunno.'

Violet is propped up in bed, listening in to every word. She's dressed in pink satin pyjamas and a hideous monstrosity of a dressing gown, all loud purple and red flowers clamouring for space on padded staticky polyester. It's a shapeless beast, reaching the floor, straight up and down with a zip all the way down the front. 'It's like a seventies toilet tent,' Jodie said earlier when she first donned it. 'She should take it to Glastonbury.' Violet didn't hear her but I giggled and it hurt.

'My husband will be here any minute,' Violet says in a voice so dripping with pomposity it sounds like it wishes to audition for the role of a BBC presenter circa 1950 but doesn't quite make the grade. 'He's bringing me some proper coffee.'

'Good to hear,' Jake says, and I nudge him. He rolls his eyes at me.

'And a proper walker, at that.'

'Walker?' Jodie says.

'These ones in the hospital are hopeless. Squeaky. And dirty.'

'Oh—'

'And I want to get to the toilet myself, thank you very much, not have some filthy cardboard pot in a chair brought over to me like I'm some helpless old woman. When I have my own walker, I can do that. It has a little seat, you see.'

Jodie nods, eyes wide and guileless. 'I see.'

Jake's mouth curls in great snarky coils.

A man walks into the bay. He can't be Violet's husband. Far too young and un-Violet like. He stops in the entrance, searching the beds, settling on Kat's. Relief and something more upturns his mouth in a great big grin, white teeth gleaming in the straightest smile I've ever seen. I watch Violet watching him. The lines and etchings on her face veer up and down in great animation, a mix of disapproval and incomprehension. The man is holding a packet of chocolate hobnobs and a big purple Bible. He's wearing a dog collar tucked into a neat blue clerical shirt. Violet's eyes have almost disappeared into the folds of skin crinkled up on her face and waves of disdain emanate from her as he bends and kisses Kat full on the mouth. It's not only that Kat is married to a vicar, though. I can read Violet's thinking, almost plain as day written across her face. It's that Kat, with her purple hair, her tattoos and her piercings, is married to a tall Black vicar in ripped skinny jeans.

Jodie is agog, too. 'He's a bit of all right, isn't he? I'd go to church if he was vicaring it or whatever.'

Kat just beams. It's the first time I've seen her sitting up, engaged, smiling. I'm glad. I was worried for her in the night, when her soft, choked sobs carried over to my bed in waves. There's colour in her face now, whether through feeling a little better or seeing her husband, who blatantly adores her. 'Hobnobs and my Bible,' she says. 'My hero.'

That's when Violet's husband walks in. I know he's Violet's husband, just in the way that anyone knows anything. He looks a lot like her, in his facial features at least, despite an arresting bristly moustache. Maybe it's his expression, one of slight antipathy and distaste, as if he has taken a bite of the world around him and found it wanting, ready to spit it out in disgust. He stares around the ward, taking us all in, Jodie and Jake staring right back at him. 'Why does he have a toilet brush on his face?' Jake whispers, and Jodie laughs out loud.

He's much smaller than her, though, thin and wiry, sinewy where Violet is softened by age and plumpness. He ignores us and walks over to her, each step measured and careful, grimaces at the plastic chair by her bed, and perches on the very edge. 'Hello, dear.'

'Hello, dear.'

'Hello, dear,' Jake says, and Jodie laughs again. I'm going to have to watch these two. Maybe it's like having another child, like trying to deal with siblings who wind one another up. I never got a chance to find out what that would be like, at least for myself.

My own sister is much older than me and far distant, even as a child, always achieving more and better and being the one my parents liked to wax lyrical about in their Christmas Round Robins. *Karen has passed her Grade 8 violin this year, as well as coaching primary age children in gymnastics, getting her gold Duke of Edinburgh award and scoring A*s in all her A Levels. Penny has only been in hospital twice this year.* That kind of thing.

Watching Violet and her husband is mesmerising. They seem to mirror one another in all their words and actions, like an ultimate version of his 'n hers. I bet they have matching orange cagoules and walking boots.

Her face is all scrunched into a slicing glare. 'Where is my coffee? And my walker?'

He opens his eyes wide; a rabbit in the headlights. 'Oh. Oh. I… I forgot.'

Violet folds her arms and flattens out her lips.

He lays his hand on her knee. 'I'll bring them tomorrow. I promise.'

She raises her chin and then slowly turns her face away.

'Forgive me,' he says.

'You'll bring in some Garibaldi, then, too? From Waitrose, not Asda?'

He nods, his moustache all animated in the fervent rhythm of it.

Jake clears his throat. 'Fly biscuits.'

'Are you well, dear?' Violet's husband says.

'Could be better. That woman screamed all night.' She points at Barbara, who is oblivious, slumped low in her chair with her head thrown back and mouth open in a slight snore. She looks tiny, lost like a small child in a huge beanbag.

Mr Oddens' mouth is an oh of outrage. 'They should give you your own room, out of this awful place.' He lowers his voice.

'With people like *that.*' He's looking at Barbara still, but I know who he's really talking about. Thankfully Amina is screened behind the curtain pulled between them, deep in happy conversation with her family.

'I know. I said that to them when they brought me in here. But they took no notice.'

'That's disgusting.'

Jodie sniggers and mouths something at Jake.

Kane walks in with his phone in his hand, nods to Jake and me, glances at Kat and her husband and then does a double take, another furtive glance. 'See we've got the reverend in here.'

'Yeah, and he's hot.' Jodie simpers up at him, searching his face, waiting for him to laugh.

He flops on the chair and picks up her hand. Rubs it gently. 'Say again?'

Somehow, he manages to load soft words with a ton of menace.

Jodie stops. Gulps. 'Um… I mean, he's hot, it's hot in here, isn't it?'

It's always unbearably hot on the wards. But Kane is not taken in, and his response takes me hurtling back into a time I don't want to revisit.

He doesn't say anything. He just sits, with his hand flat over Jodie's hand, staring into her eyes.

I shiver.

KANE DOESN'T STAY long today, but his presence casts a shadow over the ward, like an arctic wind creeping in and cooling the atmosphere. Jodie is quiet for a while after he leaves, silent even when Kat's and Violet's husbands leave. Jake is still here, playing

Tetris on his phone, flouting visiting hours. 'I don't want to go back to Nan's, Mum.'

I don't ask him why they haven't come to visit me.

'So,' Violet says to Kat. 'You're a vicar's wife, then?' Her tone is loaded with incredulity and derision all at the same time.

Kat shakes her head. 'Actually, *I'm* a vicar. And so is my husband. He's called Nate.'

Violet's mind is blown. You can see it in the whites of her fingertips clasping the neck of her polyester dressing gown tightly around her. '*You're* a vicar?'

'Yup.'

Violet sniffs. 'Well. That's new.'

Kat catches me listening in and winks. I avert my gaze, thinking about the faith I had as a child that faded over years of pain, something echoing in the far reaches of me.

Jodie peels herself off her bed and collects up her smoking equipment. She eyes Violet then turns to Jake. 'Wonder if her husband has the Dressing Gown of Doom as well as her.'

Jake giggles. 'Probably.'

Jodie turns to Kat as she leaves the bay. 'Didn't know you was a Bible bashing type. Don't get that myself, but each to their own.'

Kat just smiles a weary smile and leans her head back on her pillow, closing her eyes.

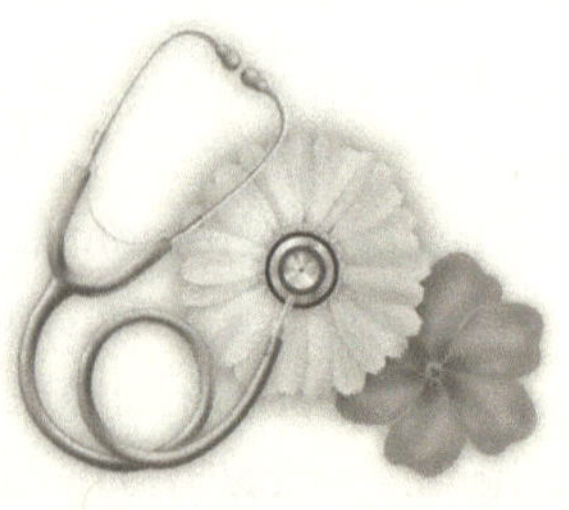

Chapter 6

'YOU CAN START getting out of bed a bit, now, Penny,' Dr Chowdhury says to me the next morning. 'Your oxygen's up and your infection markers slightly down. Some encouraging progress for you.'

I smile and then wince. I might look better clinically, but the pain in me hasn't read the memo yet. Getting out of bed and walking across the ward, even to the bathroom, seems an impossible dream, something from a faraway land I once lived in, a time when nurses didn't have to come with their bedpans and commodes, summoned by my red call button, when I need a wee.

'The physio will be over later to help you with some clearance,' he says. 'And maybe a little walk, yes?'

I nod, but inside I shake my head.

The physiotherapist is an impossibly young, implausibly energetic boy named Dan. He's full of cheer and motivational soundbites, all delivered in a soft Welsh lilt. I like him, but he's exhausting and punishing on my frail body. This morning he is more joyous than ever, bouncing into the bay and loping over to my bed. 'Good to see some colour in your face! How's that breathing?'

I shrug.

'Not so good still?'

'No.'

'We'll do some clearance, if you're okay with that, then?'

I nod.

I'm not really okay with it. He always claps my back until I feel bruised and battered, loosening the resistant mucus on my chest. He's the most brutal of all the respiratory physios in here, but he gets the best results, so I have to be okay with it because it will help me get better.

'Good. Let's get started, then. On your right side first? That's your worst, isn't it? Lower right lobe?'

'Mmm.'

'Okay then.' He helps me over onto my side, a slow process of grunting and groaning agony. He grabs the bed remote and flattens it down, then pulls the curtains round so we're enclosed together. I close my eyes. 'Just do some active breathing cycle first to get started, then I'll do some percussion.'

I breathe slowly. Shallow breaths. In-out-in-out-in-out. Deeper breaths, six of them, slow and steady, as far in as I can get, which isn't far, even with the oxygen.

'Good, good,' Dan says, though it's not really good. It's a bit pathetic, really. 'Same again, try and breathe more deeply on the second bit.'

Not going to happen.

I go through the cycle again and then he starts his percussion and vibration. It sounds like fun, when I think about it like that, like there's a full brass band in here with me, blasting away the rubbish.

Not fun.

'Okay?' he says.

'Kind of.'

'It's working well. I can hear it loosening. Can I keep going?'

'Yes.' I want to say no, but he's just doing his job. Just grit your teeth and bear it, Penny.

When he finishes I am sore and exhausted. I lie there, unable to move, as he adjusts the bed and then makes some notes on my chart. 'I'll send that sample off to the lab. The doctor mentioned going for a little walk. How do you feel about that? Just to the ward entrance, perhaps?'

'I... I—'

'You not ready? It might help with recovery. Bit of exercise, get those legs working?' His eyes are twinkling. 'You might be able to get those sexy stockings off.'

I look down at my unattractive off-white hospital support stockings and feel my lips curving upwards.

'Ah, see there, I saw a grin! We'll have you up and about, you'll see.'

He writes more onto his chart. 'What is it you do, again?'

My heart sinks. Not that, again. The how-do-you-justify-your-existence question. I lie in bed and claim benefits, that's what I do, and that's hard enough, navigating the hell that is disability benefit applications and appeals.

I wish I could be like you, Dan, and bring meaning to people's lives.

❦

IT'S A FREEZING January day and I am sitting in my car, shivering and wondering what on earth I am going to do. I am at the centre for my work capability assessment for my Employment and Support Allowance claim but there are no disabled parking bays. There are no parking bays at all. It's on a main road and the driver behind me is revving his engine and flashing his lights.

By the time I've found a space and dragged myself up the road to the centre I am in pieces. Inside the centre it is no better; it's on the first floor, I'm told, and no, sorry, there's no lift, there are the stairs dear, you can manage those can't you? I wonder why an assessment centre for ESA doesn't have a lift, but I say nothing, like usual.

The assessor tells me she is a healthcare professional but doesn't tell me which kind. She watches as I stumble through the door, but makes no move to help, just waves to a chair and sits reading something on her computer screen, perhaps my claim form. Her brow furrows, her mouth moving as she scrolls down the page.

'My mum had bronchitis,' she says, looking up at me. 'Was nasty at the time, but didn't do any lasting damage. She's a hard worker, she is, never takes a day off for anything.' She raises her eyebrows at me as if this random anecdote will somehow propel me out of my sickness, out of her way and straight back into work.

'Not bronchitis,' I mutter, enunciating the name of my disease slowly.

Her left eyebrow is cocked so high I think it might set there forever, a bushy question mark stamped on her face. 'Oh. Never heard of that one, I must say.' She says it in a voice that belies a great scepticism about whether this thing actually exists or if I am just making it up.

It sets the tone for the whole thing, with me trying to explain how it affects my life and her face set in a kind of incredulous disdain. But I look fine, she says, I'm dressed and clean. I don't tell her about the tunnel of blackness I'm heading into, or the scent of sickness that weaves through my nostrils and wraps my body in its evil potion.

'Can you cook for yourself?' she asks, fingers poised in the air over her keyboard.

'Well, yes, but only sometimes. I mean, I can cook, like I mean I know how to and all of that, I am bringing up a child on my own, after all. But some days… a lot of days really, I can't actually cook at all.'

'How do you mean?'

'Well, I mean I feel so ill that I can't get out of bed, or off the sofa, and even lifting a pan is painful.'

'Oh.' She purses her lips and I know I am messing this up. I know that I am not explaining it as well as I need to be, I know here and now this woman thinks I am some kind of lazy skiver who just slouches on my sofa all day.

'But you can lift a pan – physically?'

'Well, yes, but it doesn't mean I can actually do the cooking with it. I get so breathless, I have a lot of pain, it makes me bend double, it makes my head hurt… I often have infections. Here.' I pull out my repeat prescription to show her my long and complicated list of medication, but know she must have already seen that. It's on my form and it's on the letters of support from my GP, my consultant, my physiotherapist, my respiratory team. But I wonder if she's really seen it. If she has really understood it.

'Hmm.' She waves it away. 'And do you do your own shopping?'

I know that if I say I do she will say that I am well enough to work because I can get round a supermarket. 'I do it online. I can't carry shopping or walk for long.'

'And how did you get here today?'

'I drove.'

'Oh! So, you walked a bit of a way, then?' She looks up at me, the bushy question mark bristling with suspicion.

What am I doing here? Why don't they believe me? I think back to all the advice I've been given: tell the assessor how your condition affects you, including on your worst days. Tell them what you are not able to do, because they are set on finding out what you can do to get you into work.

I can read the assessor's thoughts on her face and later on I know I will see them writ large in the decision maker's letter. Sorry to inform you…

And then the mandatory reconsideration. And then the tribunal, where the panel look on horrified at the poor decision-making and award me my support group Employment and Support Allowance.

Rinse and repeat.

'I DON'T HAVE a job,' I say to Dan now, staring at the soulless blue curtain behind his head. I am too exhausted to spin justifications this morning.

'Oh,' he says.

Oh. That's about right. Oh. A woman of my age, a woman who should be earning her living, a single mum too – why not play into all the stereotypes while I'm at it?

'Loads of jobs you could do, intelligent woman like you.'

Loads of bosses who wouldn't want a weak, unreliable flake like me.

'What did you used to do?'

Used to do? Used to want to do a million things, to travel, to write, to run, but mostly to paint and draw, to craft worlds apart from my own, to lose myself in great wide skies and jewelled depths. I'm good at it, I know that. I almost managed it, for such a short time, in a job I was too sick to keep. My tutor at art college said that I was talented, that if I was prepared to put in the hard graft I could go far. You just have to believe in yourself, she said, because only you can make the decision to succeed in life, and you've been given a gift. It's all about attitude, you see, if your attitude is right then you'll nail it, but if you give in to weakness then life will pass you by. I lapped up her words, crossing my fingers behind my back, knowing she was right, I could do this if I really tried. That word, echoing back through so many years of school reports; *try*. Just try harder, Penny.

I worked at an advertising agency after college, all fresh and new and full of resolve, ready to take on a world that hadn't been so kind to me so far and so surely owed me something now. Maybe I would, in the end, be a children's book illustrator, as I had once hoped, back when I was small and my paintings made people gasp. Perhaps now my parents might be proud of me, at last.

It was during my first sickness absence review meeting, just six months after joining the company, that reality crashed the party. We expect your attendance to improve from now on, the HR lady told me. I took my union rep to the next meeting, but I'd just not worked there long enough, HR lady said. Sorry, Penny. Dismissed, I was alone and adrift in the world, my shattered dreams lying in shards at my feet.

That's when Marcus saved me. Exercise, my doctors said, that's what will help you with all this, just try it. So I did. I tried, and joined a gym where, it turned out, a man named Marcus worked, a man who wanted to collude in the bettering of me.

'I've been ill all my life,' I say to Dan.

He nods and smiles at me as if he gets it.

But he doesn't, really. 'You should pursue your dreams,' he says gently, his voice all empathy. 'You can do anything you want to.'

No I can't.

'He's well fit,' Jodie says as Dan strolls out of the bay, leaving me lying there failing to catch my breath. She hunches on the edge of the chair by my bed. 'Wouldn't mind him doing a bit of pummelling on me.'

My laugh comes out like a strange gurgle.

She doesn't seem to notice. 'I had that woman do mine. You know, the one who looks about six.'

They all look about six.

'She's good though. So how you feeling?'

'Better,' I say. 'You?'

She shrugs. 'Just waiting to get sent home. Doctor said it might not be too long. Been in nearly two weeks now.'

I sit myself up a bit, gather myself together. 'What were you in for?'

A line carves into the smoothness of her forehead. 'Just the usual.'

'Usual?'

'Like you, I guess. Chronic lungs. COPD and all that.'

She's young to have Chronic Obstructive Pulmonary Disease. 'Oh. Yeah.'

'I know, I'm only young. Well, thirty, anyway. Been chesty most my life, though.'

'Me too.'

We sit quietly, allowing the unspoken understanding to pass between us, the magic of solidarity.

'That must've been really hard.' It's Kat, propped up in her bed, leaning over at us, a little less pale than yesterday. 'Suffering like that, even as a kid.'

Jodie doesn't seem to care that Kat was listening in. She's up on her feet again, wandering over to sit on the chair between Kat and me. She's like a pinball machine; back and forth, back and forth. 'What about you? What you in for?'

'Pneumonia,' Kat says. 'Never had it before, it was a complete shock. Can't imagine living with that kind of thing.'

I look at my bitten-down fingernails and say nothing. It's strange, hearing the kindness in her voice. Not something I'm much used to.

Jodie says, 'But you're getting better now?'

'Bit. Doctor says I'll be in another week or so.'

'Me too,' I say.

Jodie looks over to Amina, as if inviting her to take her turn in this great revelation of our diagnoses and terms of stay. 'What about you? Amina?'

Amina is silent, her face deep in a book.

'What's with her?'

'She's probably just feeling ill,' Kat says, and Jodie shrugs.

Amina lays the book down. 'I don't have such good English.'

'It sounds good to me,' Kat says.

'I do not really always understand. Sorry.'

Kat smiles at her. 'You don't have to be sorry. We were just wondering how you are doing.'

Amina stares at Kat, and then at me and Jodie, eyes widened, hands curling and uncurling in her lap. 'I… thank you. I am doing well. But the doctor, he says I will be in here more days. I want to go home to my family.' And just like that, where the light was in her eyes the tears begin to gather, shimmering and then spilling out. She brushes them away. 'Sorry. I have felt so ill.'

Violet tuts loudly. 'Well, don't we all want to go home? None of us are exactly loving this.'

Nobody replies, but I watch as a shade of anger crosses Kat's eyes.

'Where's that boy of yours?' Violet says to me. 'I need him to take me down to the shop and outside for a little cigarette.'

I find myself smirking exactly how that boy of mine does, at the sheer entitlement of her. Jodie catches my eye, and I wheeze out a cackle, and then I hold my ribs, grimacing.

'He's hardly going to be here at this time of day, Vi,' Jodie says. 'He's not your personal porter, you know.'

Violet fixes her with a look that might kill a lesser person.

Amina grunts as she rotates her body round and stumbles out of her bed, her face grey with the effort. She's wrapped in a blue silk dressing gown, a loose floral turquoise scarf covering her hair. She shuffles towards the toilet in her jewelled flip-flops. A nurse I vaguely recognise comes into the ward, pushing the white medication cart ahead of her and smiling at Amina on the way, telling her to take it easy. She looks kind, grinning widely around at us all, dark eyes full of sparkle. 'Hello, ladies! I'm Sister Joy. I've got your nice lunchtime tablets.'

'There is that man in our toilet now, again.' Amina is back, eyes troubled, spreading her hands wide.

Jodie blows out her cheeks. 'Not again.'

I hadn't noticed, but I haven't made it as far as the toilet yet.

Sister Joy looks up from the chart she is studying. 'Again? That man is so naughty. He has his own toilet.' Her soft Caribbean lilt becomes more pronounced in her rising tones of disapproval. 'I will sort him out, this man in your toilet.'

This man in our toilet lurches out, flinging the door wide with a loud creak. He is wobbly on his feet, sparse white hair all askew, sprouting in odd places over his mostly bald head, blue striped pyjamas loose around his lanky frame. 'Harold,' Sister Joy says, rolling the r for seconds loaded with censure, 'come on. You have your own men's toilet. You cannot take the ladies' one. Poor Amina, she is waiting.'

Amina looks down at her feet, blushing.

'I don't like the men's toilet,' Harold says.

Sister Joy lays her chart down and marches over to him, a finger held forth in admonition. 'Don't be naughty. You use your own. Why do you not use your own?'

'It is too dirty and the men pee on the seat,' Harold says sulkily, like a teenager being asked to tidy up his room.

'Well, you pee on our seat,' Jodie says.

Harold shakes his head. 'I do not.'

'Yes you do. Amina, look now, has he peed on the seat?'

But Amina is back on her bed, clutching her book, face hidden away.

'I don't. And I will keep going to this toilet. It's my right to go to this toilet. I have paid my taxes all my life.' He waves his arms around in great outrage.

Jodie snickers and tilts her head over at him, catching my eye.

He's poking out through his pyjama bottoms, wizened and shrivelled.

Sister Joy sighs.

Violet says, 'Put yourself away, man.'

AFTER LUNCH I am drifting off into woozy sleep. Barbara is snoring in the corner. Jodie is not tired, though, it seems, and plonks herself down by Amina's bed, much to Violet's glaring annoyance. 'So, what country you from?' she says without guile, and I cringe a little bit.

Amina seems okay with it, but I wonder if deep down she's just resigned to it. 'I'm now from here, from this town, but I was living in Pakistan until I was eighteen years old.'

Jodie settles in, waiting for more, and I watch, curiosity cutting through a daze of weariness.

'It was so beautiful, my country, it was always so filled with colour and big wide skies. Here the skies are too often grey.'

Violet tightens her lips.

'Why'd you come to England?' Jodie says.

Amina is quiet for a moment, smoothing down her blanket.

'I was brought here to marry my husband, Bilal.'

Jodie is all outrage. 'What, you don't mean like one of them arranged marriages, do you? Like I mean like when you don't even know him and you have to get married to him, 'cause your parents force you?'

Amina just nods.

Jodie is raging with wounded self-righteousness. 'Well, why don't you leave him now? Now, like, you're older and all that, and you know you don't have to be tied to some dude as his slave no more?'

Amina just smiles, and Jodie gets more riled.

'I mean, it's not as if you'd be penniless now, you'd get help from the state, right? Like most of us do. You could go live on your own and be happy. You could get rid of that headdress and all that.'

A shadow of a frown crosses Amina's brow. 'We made a life together, Bilal and me.'

Jodie is incensed. 'But—'

Amina holds her palm up. 'No. You don't know everything, you know. It does not have to be like you think. And I like my hijab. I choose it myself.'

I sit up slightly, studying Amina's face: earnest and, somehow, contented.

Violet mutters something to herself. I think it's something about headscarves and the Conservative Party going all soft, but I can't be sure.

Jodie rolls her eyes as she clambers to her feet. 'Well, you stay in your controlling marriage then. Whatever.'

For someone usually so laid back and tolerant, she seems incredibly flustered. Is it that her worldview is being challenged, or is it that she thinks Amina really is an oppressed woman? Because she doesn't look like one to me. But what do I know? I didn't tell anyone about Marcus.

Jodie shakes her head as she makes her way to the bay entrance. She casts a glance back over her shoulder, at no one in particular. 'Women shouldn't have to be with men who control them.'

Has she looked at Kane lately?

Amina says, 'Bilal has never controlled me in my life.'

I MUST HAVE dozed off, because when I'm next aware Jodie is back on her bed, flipping through a magazine, and Jake is here, on his phone. Violet is shouting about something, her tones caustic and whinging through the general clutter of noise on the ward. 'Those nurses just sit and twiddle their thumbs all day. It's not like they have anything better to do.'

Her husband is there, too, nodding along at every word and exuding disgust like a haughty cat facing up to an overexcited puppy.

'I've been asking for it for hours,' Violet says. I've no idea what 'it' is, but guess that it's something she feels should be rightfully hers right this minute.

'It's a disgrace,' Mr Violet says.

Jake rolls his eyes at Jodie, but she is oblivious, her attention taken up by her magazine. 'Lot of moaners going on about smokers in this article. I have the right to smoke if I want to.'

Violet picks up on that one. 'All those anti-smoking types out there, wanting to take our rights away.'

'It's a disgrace,' Mr Violet says.

Jodie nods fiercely. 'Yeah, and they think we shouldn't smoke in like pub gardens and that now. It's all we've got left after they took our inside smoking away.'

Jake clears his throat. 'Ahem millennial ahem.'

Jodie scrunches her nose at him, but a tiny smile quivers at the corners of her mouth.

'Shall we go for one now, then?' she says to Violet, who nods and instructs her husband in bossy tones to stop lolling around and go and get her a wheelchair. Jodie and Violet are in the habit of going for their smoke together. They huddle under my window in the Peace Garden because the smoking shelter is too far to walk and there's a nice bench to sit on. The smoke drifts up and curls through my nose and my lungs and the pain batters my chest. Can I close the window, I ask the nurse. That one doesn't close, she says. Can they not be told not to smoke there, I say. No one takes any notice of us, she says. So I shut up and say nothing at all to Jodie and Violet who are, after all, sick as well, and as deserving as anyone else of some pleasure in life.

'You should say something to them,' Kat says. 'They'll move somewhere else.'

But I can't and I won't. I am Penny who wants to please.

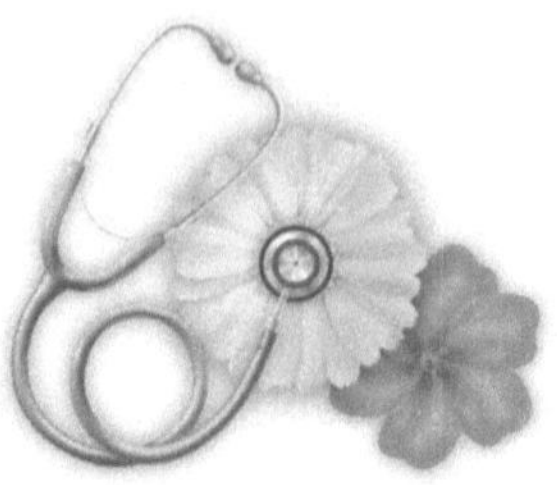

Chapter 7

I'M EIGHT YEARS old and my mummy is cross with me, I know that because at breakfast her eyebrows were angry, like when I make a mess or tell a lie. Her eyebrows never do that with Karen because she is always good.

I feel very poorly today and it's hot in my room. The window is open but it doesn't stop the sun burning through to me in my bed. I want to be outside with my friend Haki, playing hide and seek behind the houses where the trees are close together and it's sometimes a bit scary. Karen says I am babyish for playing hide and seek but I like it.

My mummy and daddy are in the kitchen and I can hear every word they are saying. They don't think I can, they think the wall is enough to stop the words coming through but it isn't. My mummy is whispering at my daddy but it is more of a shouty whisper. She is talking about me, I know that because she just said my name. She just said that Penny is too expensive and my daddy said that it will be fine and we will get through it. I don't know what he means, but his voice makes me feel better.

I sit up and put my ear closer to the wall. I try not to cough even though a cough is trying to come out of me. My chest is hurting and I want to cry a little bit but I stop the tears because Karen teases me when I cry and says that I am a silly little baby.

'We're going to have to go back to England,' my mummy says. I have never been to England but I know it's colder and greyer than here because Mummy says that she would never want to go back because of the weather and the gloomy sky. I was born here, like my sister, and I don't want to go away from it. My tummy feels cold.

'She'll probably grow out of it,' my daddy says.

I am growing every day, my daddy measures me sometimes and my mummy sighs and humphs and says that I grow out of all my clothes too quickly, that I am like a weed. I wish I was like a flower instead but I have to be a weed. Perhaps that is what Daddy means now, that if I grow out of something we won't have to go to England. But I don't know why he says that.

'The bills are getting too high,' Mummy says.

'I know, but—'

'You tell me where we'll get the money, then, if you're so very insistent on staying here. You tell me how we'll get treatment for her? We haven't got the NHS here, in case you hadn't noticed.'

My daddy sighs really loudly.

Mummy lowers her voice, but not much. 'If only you'd not come home so drunk that time.'

Daddy laughs out loud. 'You didn't seem to mind, at the time.'

'Well, I minded nine months later, didn't I? And now... our dream life, Martin! It's going down the drain in front of me. And it's all because of *her*.'

Sometimes when my mummy talks about me she says *her* in a way that makes me feel smaller and like I want to curl up and disappear. I wonder what she means now, what she said about Daddy being drunk. Sometimes they both have a lot of wine and they giggle a lot and dance out on the veranda, but I don't understand what that has to do with me.

'We've no choice,' Mummy says, and I am sad because her voice is sad.

'Look, we should wait. I still think it could get better. That… she could get better, and we could stay here.'

'We have no money, Martin. And she's not getting better. She has an incurable disease. Stop living in denial. We have to go home, so that we can get doctors for her. Unless you want to leave her to get worse? Is that it?'

'Of course not. Of course not, Chrissie. Who do you think I am? I want her to get better.'

'Well, that's that then.'

There's a sudden silence and then the sound of a door slamming. My sister has come into the kitchen, I know it's her because she always slams doors. She is a teenager and teenagers always slam doors, Daddy says, they are always noisy.

'What's what then?' Karen says. 'What are you two plotting in here?'

'Shh,' Daddy says. 'Keep your voice down, Karen. We're just talking about Penny's health.'

'Oh.' Karen sounds disappointed, as if my health is a very boring thing to talk about. Which it is, really.

There's the sound of a chair scraping on the linoleum. 'Karen,' my mummy whispers, and I can hear her voice even clearer now because she is closer to the wall, just on the other side of me. 'We might have to go back. To the UK.'

'Really?' My sister sounds eager. Happy, even, maybe. 'Why?'

'Because of your sister's health issues.'

Karen laughs, and it's that laugh she always uses when I get poorly, it's a laugh that says she thinks I am being silly and making it all up and pretending I am hurting. It's like the laugh that

Mummy does when Daddy says he has tidied up the kitchen or made the tea.

'Because of money, really, love,' Daddy says. His voice is all soft, like it always is for Karen.

'Can we go soon?' Karen says.

'You… *want* to go?'

'There's nothing to do round here. And in England they have discos. And I can get records and tapes easier. And make-up. And, oh, just everything. Can we go soon?' Karen's voice is all high, like a buzzy bee all excited as it flies round in the air.

My mummy tells her that yes, we can go soon, and that if she is a good girl they will buy her a new tape at the airport. Karen says can she have a new Walkman please because hers is old, and Daddy says yes of course she can because she is being so good and understanding and patient and they are so proud of her.

I don't think I will get a new Walkman, because it is my fault that we have to go to England and be able to take me to the doctor to get my medicine. And because I am not a good girl like Karen. I am a naughty girl who keeps on disobeying my parents and also keeps on being poorly which makes life hard work for them.

But I so wish I could have a new Walkman and a new tape to go with it.

❧

SOMEBODY IS STABBING my arm. Stop it, I want to say, stop it. My mind is shouting but my mouth is pinned closed. Then a wetness, a burning, and I cry out.

'Shush.'

It's not a kind shush. It's a hassled shush, a shush loaded with frustration. I open my eyes and blink at the nurse ramming a syringe into my port. 'It'll take one more,' she mutters.

The pee-stinking liquid is leaking all over my skin and soaking my sheet. Blistering through my vein, collapsing it down until it explodes into a bruise, strewing my forearm with purple blossom. I cry out.

She tuts. 'Just another minute.'

No. I have to say no. To tell her to stop. It's my body.

I've got nothing. She keeps pushing and I bite down on my lip. She disconnects the syringe and slams it into the cardboard tray, huffs some more. 'The day staff'll have to sort it,' she says, storming off. No sorry, no ouch that looks bad, no kind words. I whip the cannula out myself, ripping off the plaster and grimacing. It was half out already, the stinging medication congealing in with the fresh blood running from the wound.

I close my eyes and wish I could collapse into nothing, just like my vein. Wish my bruise would blossom so large it would swallow me up, suck me into purple depths.

Something is touching my arm. Pulling me back from clenching blackness. A light touch, a feather of gentleness and warmth. 'Penny? Penny? Wake up, lovely. Good morning, darling. My name is Patience. I'm your nurse today.' Patience speaks in a gentle, musical lilt and in my semi-comatose daze I'm lulled back to the wide open skies of my early childhood, running free through our village in rural Kenya, where my parents had met as engineers on a water project, and stayed on when Karen came along. An idyllic childhood, my mother always said, that's what they wanted for her, that's why they stayed. Several years later, I arrived unexpectedly. I ran in and out of low roofed homes where warm women who called themselves aunties fed me with fresh mangos and avocados, and sat under the great cedar tree in the centre of the village watching the world go by. My father took me on safari once. I don't remember many of the animals, but do remember an elephant with her newborn, her trunk wrapped around him, her face a picture of protection and patience. What I remember most is nights under the sweeping African skies with multitudes of stars like diamonds studding the velvet canvas, the beauty and grandeur of it taking my breath away. I still have dreams where I am lying out flat, gazing at the sweep of the heavens, the colours of sunset painting the skies in glorious hues. I want to fall into the colours and stay there forever. In my dreams the majesty of it all invades my pain and eases it, and I wake up yearning for more.

When we returned to the UK I was lost in a world that was alien to me, that still is alien in a million ways. My mother became sad and depressed, like the grey skies of England, and my father made bitter comments about how my disease ruined their lives. My sister was happy, though, in a world she could escape our parents' expectations and go and have some fun. She rebelled, sneaking off with unsuitable boys and smoking weed, and that, apparently, was my fault too. It would never have happened if we'd stayed in Kenya, if I hadn't been ill, if I hadn't been born.

'Penny, wake up,' Patience says again, touching my shoulder softly. I open my eyes and focus on her. She's small and round, dressed in a light blue tunic and flat black hush puppies. 'I'll be round with your medication in a while. I understand you need a new cannula? Your other one is hurting, yes?'

I show her my battered arm and the discarded cannula detritus on my tray.

'Oh dear. That looks nasty. I'll ask the specialist nurse to come and do one for you on your other arm, okay darling?' She looks closer at me, her eyes filmy pools of empathy. 'Are you okay?'

I hadn't realised it, but now I feel it. My cheeks are wet. And I never cry.

'Are you in pain?'

'Yes,' I say.

I DIDN'T ONLY make them come back from Kenya. I tied them to a life of doctors and hospitals and disappointments. I failed to strive for a brilliant career like Karen the golden child, the high-achieving solicitor who worked hard for everything she got and so deserves it. If only I could have put more work in, my mother said. If only I'd shown some spark about me, some motivation, some passion for something useful, like Karen who excelled at everything, who was captain of the netball team, who brought home the trophies that took pride of place on our mantelpiece.

Thinking of my sister, I drag myself to a sitting position and dig my phone out of the drawer in the cupboard by my bed. I haven't picked it up since I was admitted; I couldn't take the brightness of the screen or of everyone's lives going on as usual outside. There's not much charge, but enough to see I have a pile of messages on WhatsApp and Messenger. Karen's name is at the top of them, several messages, let me know how you are, would love to visit but yada yada, Jake keeps us filled in, love you sis, you'll be out of there before you know it. I tap out a short response. Thanks, Karen. I'm getting better. Miss you xxx

She messages back immediately. Miss you too. Xxx

And it's true. I do miss her. Since I left the toxic environment of home we grew closer. There's still a wall between us, though, neither of us ever quite strong enough to scramble over the top. She's not the one I run to when things are tough. She breezes through life with a can-do attitude and doesn't understand why I don't. But I wish she would come and visit me, despite her high-powered job and her million-pound home in central London with the full time nanny for her two equally high-attaining daughters. My parents adore them; they are everything they want in grandchildren, and Jake, like me, knows he somehow doesn't quite make the grade.

I scroll through all the messages, feeling increasingly guilty about my lack of response. Heard you were in hospital! You ok hun? When you getting out? Can I visit? Hope you're feeling better xxxx

I don't have the energy to reply to them all. My head thuds harder, a woodpecker attacking me with its long sharp beak. I go to my Facebook page and update my status: Thank you so much to everyone who has sent me messages. Sorry I'm being rubbish at replying.

Always sorry.

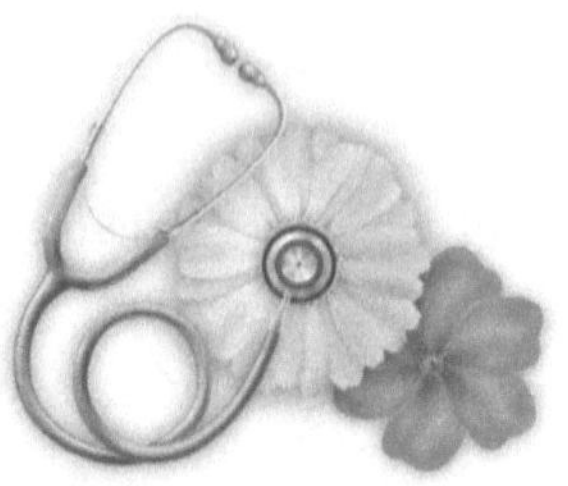

Chapter 8

'L ET'S GET YOU out of bed today, flower,' Nicki says to me after the ward rounds. 'The doctor says you're doing better, and you're off the oxygen, aren't you, so let's get you to the bathroom.'

'Okay.'

'Don't look so mournful! It's a good thing.' She flings back my blanket and takes my arm. 'Here you go, just lean on me.'

I place my stockinged feet on the floor and drag myself off the bed. I weigh a thousand tons, my feet are made of concrete, my lungs of bricks, weighing down in my chest until I'm afraid they will shatter my ribcage and fall out of me.

Nicki steadies me. 'Okay, now, take it slowly. I'm going to just get you a walker to make it easier for you.'

When she returns with the walking frame I'm flopped back on the bed, my breathing thick and laboured. Jodie sits on the edge of her bed, cheering me on. 'You're gonna do this! Just breathe slowly.'

Nicki helps me up and I lean on the walker. 'Deep breaths now,' she says. 'No rush.'

Each step seems like a mile, the toilet door a hundred miles, stretching out into a whitewashed, bleach-stinking expanse in front of me. Impossible.

'One step at a time.'

When I make it there Nicki gives a great big whoop and high fives me. 'You did it!' Jodie echoes her whoop from the corner.

I did it. I walked to the toilet. I laugh at the tininess of the achievement, thinking about my parents' Christmas letter: *Karen became a QC. Penny walked to the toilet.*

Inside it smells faintly of cigarette smoke, and I wonder if Violet was having a crafty one during the night, avoiding the rain. I try to avoid the mirror, but it drags my eyes, and I reel back at the sight of myself. Greasy, ratty hair lying in lank strands on my shoulders. My cheeks are white and hollowed out, my eyes haunted and darkened with pain. My collarbones stand out more than they did, sawing through sallow skin. 'Looking good, girl,' I say to the mocking mirror, which snorts back at me. I wonder if I will ever have the energy for a shower again.

'Let me brush your hair,' Nicki says when I'm back in my bed, shaking with the effort of it all. She brushes gently, in long soft strokes, then deftly gathers it into a bobble on my neck. It's still lank and dark with sweat and filth, but I feel better, like I might be human again, sometime soon.

'Harold was smoking in that toilet earlier,' Amina says to Nicki as she goes to leave the bay.

Nicki blows her cheeks out. 'That man thinks the world owes him everything.'

'He should use his own toilet.' It's a real issue for Amina, I can see, that her dignity might be compromised by a man. 'He might walk in on us. That lock doesn't work very well.'

'I'll have a little word with him,' Nicki says. 'I'll tell him what's what, don't you worry.' She strolls out of the bay, humming a little tune.

Jodie perches on my chair with her phone in her hand. 'You okay?'

'Yeah. Bit worn out.'

'You did good.'

I shrug. 'One day at a time.'

Jodie scrolls through her phone, then stops, her face creasing up, dark shadows flickering in her eyes.

'What's wrong?' I ask.

'Just this.' She shows me her phone. 'On my Facebook. Some loser started a petition about disabled parking spaces.'

I take the phone and read through the post. It's not fair on normal people, the post claims, all those spaces, too many of them. I look up at Jodie. 'Normal people?'

'Right? And about two thousand people have signed it, too.'

'I bet whoever started it parks in them anyway,' I say.

'His type are always so entitled.'

'Like Harold,' Violet pipes up. Jodie's mouth twists with something like amusement. Violet, setting entitled people to rights? I can't help smiling, too.

Kat leans forward in her chair. 'People shouldn't judge. Not all disabilities are visible.'

❦

IT'LL BE A great girls' night, Jen says to me. It'll be good for you.

I get myself ready, psyching myself up for a rare night out. I'll only have to sit down for a couple of hours, after all, watching a play won't be too taxing, surely? It's *Calendar Girls*, Jen says. You know, like the film, and that was funny, right? I nod along. Yeah. Great idea. I'm strong enough for this.

By the time I arrive at the venue, the exhaustion is setting in. I drag myself too slowly through the narrow corridor, other people jostling me to get to their seats on time. The foyer rings with raging whispers, bouncing back at me and hitting me square in the gut.

The theatre is all faded opulence; heavy red brocade velvet curtains and gold swirls dancing on the walls, seating in steep tiered layers, and we're up on the balcony at the top, up in the heavens with the angels, Jen says, up two long and windy flights of stairs. I have nothing left when I get to my seat, and I sink down, head in hands. Jen brings me a glass of wine and tells me to relax. Jen and Pen, Jenny and Penny, partners in crime, let's have a good laugh tonight. We deserve it.

By the interval I need the loo and regret the wine. When I stand up my bones are molten liquid, draining down my legs and through my feet until I stagger and grip hold of the back of the seat. 'You need some help?' Jen asks, but I shake my head. It's only going to the loo, for heaven's sake.

I stumble down the two sets of stairs, heading for the ladies', but stop short at the straggly queue snaking up the hallway towards me, gaggles of giggling women, stumbling in their stilettos and shrieking with mirth.

I can't stand there. I can't. My legs won't hold me up.

The disabled access toilet is back down the corridor to my left. No one's in there, so I lurch in and lock the door behind me before sinking onto the toilet seat. Deep breaths. Get a hold of yourself, Penny. Breathe in. Breathe out. In. Out.

Why did I think I could do this?

I close my eyes and rest my aching head on the grab rail next to me. Dig in my bag for more painkillers, swallow them down.

A knock on the door.

I need to sort myself out. Get out of here. Someone else needs it.

Every movement is like forcing myself through a vat of setting fudge, undoing my jeans too difficult for clumsy, aching fingers. I push myself through, sweat forming in beads on my brow.

I manage to turn the lock after several failed attempts. A woman is sitting there in her wheelchair staring at me, her friend standing next to her with arms folded and an expression full of antipathy. 'You're in the disabled toilet.'

I don't know what to say. I should stand up for myself, say I am disabled, too, that I need it, too. But I don't. I push the door wider and try to move out of their way.

The friend is not ready to move on. 'This is a *disabled* loo.'

'I know. I… I'm chronically ill.'

She laughs, but the smile goes nowhere near her eyes. 'Yeah. As I said, this is a disabled loo, and a disabled person needs it. You don't look disabled.'

'I couldn't stand in the line.'

'You couldn't stand? What about Jane here?' She thrusts her chin in the air, her glare hard on me. A small crowd is forming around us, others joining in with their *yeahs* and their *wows*.

Jane puts one hand in the air, palm out. 'It's okay, Chloe, I didn't mind waiting, looks like she needed it too. It's fine.'

Chloe hunkers down next to Jane. 'But that's not the point, is it. All your life you've had to put up with all this crap for being in a wheelchair. All the time. And you shouldn't have to. Not on a night out. It's not fair.'

She's right. It's not fair. None of it is fair.

'Sorry,' I say, and skulk away, face turned to the floor, hisses of rancour chasing me through the hall. I leave the theatre, text Jen that I'm ill again.

'Oh Pen, you could've seen it through,' she texts back. 'Now I have to watch it on my own.'

'Sorry.'

Sorry. Sorrysorrysorry.

JEN COMES IN for visiting today. 'I saw your post on Facebook. Didn't want to visit before in case… you know, in case you weren't up to it.'

'Thanks,' I say. Inside I'm thinking, she should know me better, by now.

We met in antenatal classes. She was a single mum too, and Jake and Alice were inseparable as youngsters. She was kind to me, stepping in when I could barely move, taking Jake to nursery or one of his clubs. It's no problem, Pen, I'm here for you and always will be. Then she met Simon and began to retreat, laying ever frostier barriers between us, dropping hints about being taken for granted. I love her, but there's always a catch with her now, it's never as wonderful as it was in those early days when we put the little ones to bed and sat up all night putting the world to rights with a couple of bottles of wine.

I miss that Jen.

Jake straggles in, clad in a black beanie and fingerless gloves but no coat. 'Where's your coat?' I say. 'It looks freezing out there.'

The soft rain of the morning turned into frozen shards of sleet, clattering against the windows insistently through the afternoon.

Jake shrugs, grabbing one of the black bucket chairs and slinging it down by my bed. 'I don't like wearing a coat. You know that, Mum. Hey, Jen.'

'Hi, Jake. How are you?'

'Okay.'

Jodie leans over, her long blonde hair hanging in two messy plaits. 'Jake,' she says, stretching out the name. 'What's up?'

'Not much,' Jake says, turning away from Jen and me and dragging his chair closer to Jodie. 'You?'

Jodie leans further towards him and whispers something, and they both splutter into loud laughter. Jen narrows her eyes, all affronted, as if to ask why Jake would be much more interested in a patient he'd known for all of five minutes rather than his godmother.

Kat's husband Nate wanders into the ward. He's holding a large red cloth Aldi bag, and sets it on Kat's bed. I catch a glimpse of something brown and furry as he starts to draw it out. Has he smuggled a puppy in?

Kat stares up at him. 'What have you…?' She stops as he pulls out the item and holds it up to her.

'Tada!'

'Why did you bring that?' Kat is grimacing, but then a wan ghost of a smile skips around her mouth.

Jodie shouts, 'What you got there, Mr Vicar?'

She calls him Mr Hot Vicar when he's not there, and Kat always laughs and says yeah, he is.

Nate whirls around and proudly holds up a large fluffy brown thing. It's a Chewbacca onesie, complete with ears on its hood.

'Cool,' Jake says.

'I thought you'd be chilly,' Nate says to Kat, turning back to her and laying Chewbacca on the bed. 'You having pneumonia and everything.'

Kat laughs, a raw, tired chuckle. Then she pulls him close and snuggles into his neck. Jodie whistles.

'Have you felt the temperature in here?' Kat says.

Nate shrugs. 'Just wanted to make you feel better.'

'I know.' She kisses him. 'You're adorable. But please take Chewie home with you. He'd boil me alive in this place.'

Okay, he says, but when he eventually goes Chewbacca is still strewn across the bed, Kat cuddling him close to her and waving to her husband. I love you, he says, I love you too, she says, and I wish I knew a love that would bring me a Chewbacca onesie in hospital.

'You've got a gem there,' Jodie says to Kat.

'What's that even supposed to be?' says Violet, gesturing at Chewie with her eyebrows knit together. 'Is it one of those fur rugs?'

Jodie and Jake snort in unison.

Barbara is awake in her corner, her eyes fixed intently on the onesie, and I am sad for her, with no one to visit her, no one to see how she is. I reproach myself for being jealous of Kat. I have a son who loves me in his own gruff way, I have friends and family who aren't always ideal but are still there for me. Barbara has no one.

'It's the rat,' she says, pointing with a withered finger. Her chest crackles so loudly I wonder if her ribs might splatter into tiny pieces. 'It's going to get the mouse.'

'Big rat,' Jake whispers, and I shush him.

Barbara's voice is higher, quavery. 'Get the rat out of here!'

Kat walks over to her, slow, stumbling, wobbly steps, clutching the onesie. 'See, Barbara, it's just some daft pyjamas my husband brought in. I'm never going to wear this in here, am I? Silly sod.'

Violet's mouth is agape and I can read the thoughts on her face. The vicar said sod!

Barbara reaches out her hand and touches the onesie tentatively. 'The rat's not here?'

'No, darling, the rat's not here.' Kat sits down on Barbara's chair, laying Chewie on her lap. Barbara keeps her hand on the material, stroking up and down.

'Will *you* take me to the seaside?' she says.

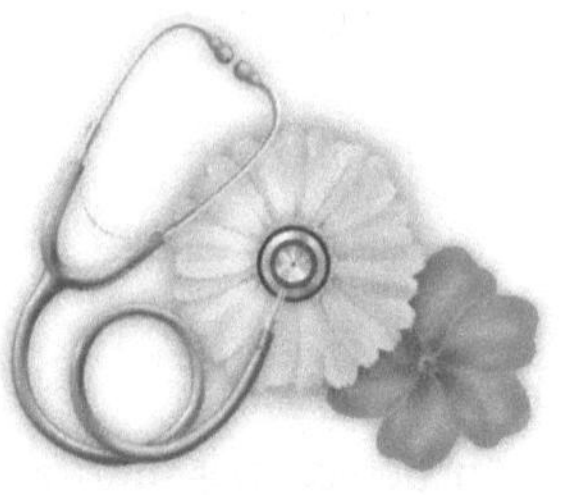

Chapter 9

Dr Chowdhury is pleased with me the next morning. 'You've been up, I hear?'

'Well, as far as the bathroom.'

'Good, good.' He strokes his chin. 'Everything is mainly heading the right way, although your temperature is still a little high.'

'Oh.'

'You should keep going on little walks. It will help your circulation and strengthen you a bit.'

I know I should, but my body heaves a great sigh at the thought of it.

'I'll ask the physiotherapist to come by again today,' he says. 'Get you clearing a bit more again. And a bit of moving, today, perhaps to the garden?'

The Peace Garden seems a million miles and another lifetime away, but in reality it's only round the corner. And if Jodie and Violet can manage it, then I can, too.

'Okay,' I say.

Dan breezes in later with his usual purpose and vigour. 'Penny, *cariad*,' he says, playing up his Welsh accent. 'I'm told we're going to get you out into the sunshine today?'

I look out of the window at the grey November morning. 'Hmm.'

'We'll do your drainage afterward, so as not to wear you out too much.'

As Dan leads me through the doors to the garden, the damp air hits me square in the chest and I bend over in a convulsion of coughing. Dan holds onto my arm and steadies me. 'No need for the histrionics, my lovely.'

I roll my eyes at him and get my breathing back to a stable place. 'Can I sit on the bench?'

Dan helps me over and supports me as I sit. It's seen better days, this bench, all flaky green paint and exposed shards of wood. But it's a place of wonder for me, after days enclosed in the warm heaviness of the bay. I turn my face up to the watery sunshine and close my eyes.

The garden is mostly bare in the winter months, a few hardy blooms clinging to life, the winter jasmine and cyclamen a welcome surge of colour through the grey. In the spring and summer it blazes with vibrancy and soothes all those who sit in it, but even now it is what it says it is; a place of tranquillity and escape from the ravages of hospital life.

'Good?' Dan says.

'Mmm.'

It's good for a few minutes, and then it's cold, and then it hurts, but I did it. I made it. Penny made it to the garden sounds better than Penny went to the toilet, doesn't it Mother?

I'm woken later by the clatter of the tea trolley. 'Tea?' the plastic apron-clad healthcare assistant says to me. It's not Nicki today, it's a tired looking middle-aged woman with short brown hair and glasses held together with sellotape. She looks like she needs a holiday.

'Yes please.'

A tiny elderly woman with a mouth full of teeth like chipped piano keys spread in the widest grin I've ever seen walks into the bay. She's going round all the beds asking patients if they want to come to chapel on Sunday. Their team will come and fetch them in hospital wheelchairs, she says. We all say no, thank you, apart from Kat who says she'd like that, and would they like her to lead the service?

The smiley lady chuckles, patting Kat's hand. 'Away with you. You are a one, you are. You're here to get better, not take services!'

'I might just liven them up for you. Wake up all those sleeping patients who snore through the sermon.'

Smiley Lady laughs harder, a great guffaw that matches her larger-than-life beam. 'What are you like, Rev Kat?'

As she leaves the ward, Jodie is on her feet, cigarettes in hand. She stops at Kat's bed. 'Why are you a vicar?'

Kat suddenly looks weary, like the weight of everything comes crashing down on her all at once. She leans back, her head sinking into the pillows, closing her eyes. Jodie shrugs and starts to walk off.

'Because I can't not be,' Kat whispers.

Jodie doesn't hear her.

Violet says, 'I'm coming. Wait for me.' She shuffles out of the bay behind Jodie, leaning on her walking frame. 'Brian brought it in for me,' she says, seeing me watching. 'Much better than those awful hospital ones. Filthy things.' Her walker has a seat with a basket underneath it and looks like something I could do with but prefer to shun under denial along with mobility scooters and walking sticks. You don't need one of those things, Marcus said to me, you just need to strengthen your body.

It's quiet in the bay, with Kat sleeping, Amina watching something on her tablet and Barbara on her chair, staring into space. I pick up my book, neglected since Jake brought it in for me, the words swimming through my weary brain. Maybe today I can get some reading in. I settle back on the bed, sipping my tea and finding my place. It's not a challenging book. Pappy chick-lit, Jake calls it. Jilted quirky thirty-something called Emma with tumbling red curls who loves knitting and triathlons leaves the city and starts a bakery by the sea where she meets a mysterious, rich young man who wants to sample her baps. He sweeps her off her feet and helps her save the bakery from the hands of the nasty man who wants to knock it down and build new houses over the site. And they all live happily ever after.

'Hey! You, girl,' Barbara shouts across the ward to me. I look around the bay, hoping for rescue. But no one is around.

'Come over here, darling,' Barbara says.

I breathe out slowly. I've spent days ignoring her plaintive calls to me, but now I have some strength I should show her I'm not heartless. I drag my weary body across the ward, ignoring the rush of blood to my head, and hover near her chair, which is loaded with clothes and medical detritus. She pats her bed.

I shouldn't sit. Infection control, the ward sister always says, stern little lines slashed over her face. Patients must not sit on other patients' beds or chairs. The word *Covid* lingers in the air but never gets said. No one wants to hear it. We all heard enough of it when it raged through the world. I shudder, thinking about the months of shielding, trying not to go too near Jake, not to hug him.

Most of the staff turn a blind eye when we sit on one another's chairs, but Sister Harris shoos us off, squawking like a riled-up mother hen. And beds are a complete no-no. She's here today, Sister Harris, on the warpath, eagle eyes scouting for any of her staff slacking off or making mistakes. I have to sit now, though. My legs are water and I will splash to the floor in a few seconds. I squat on the end of Barbara's bed, anxiously scanning the station outside the bay like a schoolkid in trouble trying to evade a teacher.

Barbara grabs my hand and I can't wrench mine away. Can't hurt her feelings. I've heard the doctors discussing her, the nurses in the night in hushed tones as they replace the mask she's pushed away once again, the whispers of the short time she has left. So I squeeze her hand softly. It feels like thin tissue paper wrapped around a bunch of those flimsy matches that always break when you try to strike them.

'I want to go to the sea,' she says, piercing into me with her watery gaze. 'Just one more time.'

'I know you do, Barbara.'

Her IV drip machine squeals at me through the uneasy silence. Occlusion in the line. I press her call button and drag myself up off her bed. 'The nurse will come and sort it out,' I say to her.

'The sea,' she says.

I try to smile at her but can feel my mouth distorting, my face sagging into some kind of leer. 'It would be nice, wouldn't it.'

'I lost my mouse.'

I make a soothing noise.

She grips my arm. 'I lost my mouse, and I want you to take me to the seaside.'

I squirm and back away a little. I don't know what to say. I wish Jodie was here. Jodie is good at this stuff, she would joke and chat with Barbara and defuse the moment. Nicki would too, she would warm the place up with her chatter and her quips and her Lovelies and her Flowers. But I have little to say. 'I wish I could help you.' I watch as her face falls.

'Well, you can. You can get me to the seaside, can't you? You can drive?' Her rheumy blue gaze is insistent, weary, haunting.

'I… yes, but… maybe you can go when you are better?' Inside I'm thinking, she's not getting better, and she never has visitors, doesn't have family, she's never going to go to the seaside again. 'Sorry,' I murmur.

'Tell us about the sea, my lovely.' Jodie is back, slinking into the ward unseen. I breathe out slowly. 'Tell us where you'd like to go.'

Barbara beams a wide grin. 'I want to go to Sand Bay,' she says. 'Where the sand stretches for miles. I want to sit on the beach. I want to eat ice-cream and watch the surf lap at the sand. I want to feel it on my feet.'

'Sounds like heaven,' Jodie says. 'We should go tomorrow.'

Barbara laughs, a great wheezy rasp followed by a frenzy of hacking. She sparkles up at Jodie. 'You're a wicked one.'

'Bit on the chilly side for ice-cream, though.'

'So, what's up here, then?' It's the stressy healthcare assistant, reaching over to silence Barbara's buzzer and checking her IV line. 'I'll just get the nurse to sort this out for you.'

The machine screeches at us. *Beep beep beep I am blocked sort me out.* It accuses me for my impotence, my inability to help an old lady with what is evidently the most important thing in the world to her.

'Back to bed, ladies. You shouldn't be over here, you know that. Sister Harris'll be in here and won't be happy.'

Barbara grabs Jodie's hand as she turns away. 'But you do mean it, don't you? You promise?'

Jodie stops, mouth opening then closing, flicking her eyes to me and then back to Barbara.

'Yes,' she says.

'You should not make promises you cannot keep.' Amina is standing in the middle of the ward in her long silk dressing-gown, frowning. I'm taken aback by the anger written across her face. 'It is not fair on her.'

Jodie shrugs. 'Who says I can't keep it?'

Amina's eyes darken as she grabs Jodie's arm, beckoning her away from Barbara. 'Don't be such a fool. You cannot take her to the sea.'

Barbara is oblivious, drinking cold tea from a sippy cup with no handles, her hands shaking as she tries to keep purchase on it.

'Well, what if I can?'

Amina's eyebrows knit together more tightly. 'You think you know best about everything.'

'Woah!' Jodie steps back. 'What gives you the right to say that?'

'You think you know all about my marriage, all about my family. You think I am not strong, that I am, what do you say, jailed in by my husband because we did not fall in love like in one of your movies.'

'Okay—'

'You are all, look after number one, be your true self whatever it does to others, you are the most important person in your life. But I don't see it like that so much. You say to me I cannot be happy in this marriage that was arranged for me, I say who are you to tell me what happiness is and that I do not have it? I have been married to Bilal for nearly thirty years now and I love him more all the time. He is the gentlest man I know. The best man I know.'

'Woah!' Jodie says again. 'Where did that all come from?' She grins over at me and Kat, and I wonder at her ability to bounce things off. 'Anyway, actually, I was thinking about others. I was thinking about making Barbara feel happy.'

'But if her happiness is then shattered because you do not mean what you say, then it will be no happiness at all.'

Jodie says nothing, opening and closing her mouth like a goldfish.

'You said it to make yourself feel good, not to help Barbara, not in the end.'

'I—'

'Do not try to justify it.'

I sit on my bed, amazed at Amina. It's like a light has been switched on, a candle lit where there was darkness, where there was a quiet woman hiding away in her bed there is now a formidable woman of strength.

'I just wanted to help,' Jodie says.

'You wanted to feel like you were helping, no?'

'Well, yeah, I guess, but also actually I did want to make her feel better.'

'But you understand you have to mean what you say?'

'I kind of do – mean it, I mean.'

Vivid lines cleave through Amina's forehead. 'But how can you?'

'I'll think about it, okay?'

'It's better that you just be kind to her without making promises.'

Jodie doesn't reply.

'You see,' Amina says, hands on hips and face flushed, 'sometimes you must think about what and how you say things to people.'

'Well said,' Kat says.

Violet trundles back into the ward behind her walker, the Dressing Gown of Doom soaking wet, her hair straggly and wild, bumping into Amina as she turns back to her bed. Violet staggers back, arms wide in alarm, as if she is afraid Amina will do something bad to her. Amina ignores her, sagging onto her bed and closing her eyes as if all the effort she put into standing up for herself has drained out of her, like water churning down a plughole.

'Rude,' Violet says.

No one replies.

'Harold's been in the toilet again,' she says.

Chapter 10

A HUGE RAT stares at me with slitted evil eyes, creeping up the bed towards me with its tail slashing to and fro, to and fro. I'm coming to get you, I'm coming to bite you, I'm coming to—

'Shut up, you cantankerous old hag.'

A hissed whisper, from Barbara's corner, behind tightly drawn curtains. A smothered giggle. 'Never stops yakking on about mice and rats.'

'Crazy old coot.'

I try to sit up. Try to grab the moment and make it make sense, but I am pinned to my bed and the words keep coming.

'What a mess, shit everywhere.'

'It's disgusting. Look at these sheets. Some of us round here have to clean up after people like you.'

A tiny, wavery sound, like a cat in pain. Followed by more harsh laughter, then, 'Shhh, Julie. You're making too much noise.'

Crying, now, that's what I can hear. Raspy sobs. Scratchy words. 'My mouse. My mouse. Please.'

I am frozen.

'Your mouse, your mouse, oh please, oh please,' in a mocking whisper and a barely snuffed out cackle.

I have to call a nurse. Have to tell them what is happening. What they are saying to Barbara. But my body will not listen to my mind. My limbs are bricks. I can't let this happen to her. Can't let—

A scramble. A flurry of light and curtains and shock. 'Who the hell do you think you are?'

Jodie.

'How would you feel if I called you a cantankerous old hag? Not so good, right? I'm reporting you, and you're totally getting binned for this.'

They go quiet then, but I can still hear the watery waves of Barbara's bewildered grief. I squeeze my eyes shut and wait for the night to swallow me up.

'Penny.' A soft whisper. 'Wake up, love. I'm just here for a little bit of blood from you.'

The phlebotomist ties a tourniquet round my arm, squeezing tight until it goes numb. 'Sharp scratch.'

I like it when the phlebotomists do my bloods. Their sharp scratches are a whole lot less sharp than other healthcare professionals' sharp scratches, especially doctors. Especially junior doctors. Their sharp scratches are so sharp it's like being bitten into by a raging tiger. But the nice phlebotomist's sharp scratch barely registers as anything beyond a tiny sting.

She takes several vials of blood this morning, all with different labels quickly and competently attached, neat and tidy and well-practised. 'There we go. All done.'

'Thank you.'

She goes to Violet next, shakes her shoulder gently. 'Mrs Oddens? Violet?'

Violet splutters and coughs. 'What do you want now?'

'Just here for some bloods, love.'

'They took some yesterday! Don't you dare stick that thing in me!'

'Doctor asked for some more.'

'If you lot could do your job better this wouldn't happen. They took about a pint of the stuff yesterday. What business do you have stabbing me again? This is disgraceful.'

The phlebotomist doesn't even flinch. 'Doctor needs more today.'

Violet catches me watching and narrows her eyes at me. 'Well, try not to stab me too hard. The one yesterday, it was disgusting, she wasn't at all careful, I can tell you that much.'

The phlebotomist presses her lips together, with one slightly raised eyebrow, wrapping her tourniquet and readying her needle. She doesn't mention that she was, in fact, the one who took Violet's bloods yesterday. I wonder about her, about how many times she goes unseen by patients, trekking round the wards with her trolley, hated for her needles.

'Sharp scratch.'

Violet screeches like a derailed train. 'Ouch! That ruddy hurt!'

The phlebotomist doesn't reply, just as she didn't yesterday when Violet went on a long rant about how much she hates needles, how she'd refused the Covid vaccine because she hates them so much but mostly because they put microchips in them to control us, and she'd had Covid anyway so what was the point?

'You lot with your tiresome needles, all the time, disturbing my sleep. It shouldn't be allowed. Can't you come back at a reasonable hour?'

I close my eyes, grinning to myself. I know what Jake would be saying if he were here now.

SNATCHES OF CONVERSATION float through my window from outside. It's Jodie and Violet, out for their early morning smoke. I smile wryly at their blossoming unlikely friendship, two women diametrically opposed in background and character, bonded together by tobacco and disease.

'She's a bit up herself, isn't she, that Sister Harris,' Violet is saying.

'What, you mean like the rod up her backside?' Jodie says. Violet rasps out a snort, and then a laugh, and then she's cackling away and Jodie's joining in and they sound like the three witches from *Macbeth* without the third, yet more than making up for her absence.

'And that one too,' Violet says, her voice lower now. 'Up herself, a bit, I mean.'

She's talking about me. I can picture her now, pointing up at the window surreptitiously. I try not to laugh out loud at the irony of Violet calling someone up herself.

Jodie is quiet for a few seconds. Then, 'Nah, she's all right, that one. Just a bit buttoned up sometimes.'

Buttoned up? I guess that's true, really.

'But you know, she raised that kid alone, with that bronchithingy she's got too, and that useless dude what just naffed off and left her.' I wonder how she knows all of that, and then remember Jake, their whispered conversations, their trips to the garden, all the time they've spent together in the past few days while I have been lying in drug-hazed agony. Has Jake been opening up to someone, for the first time in his life? 'He's a good kid too, that Jake. Bit of an annoying bugger sometimes, thinks the world revolves round him. He told me I was a millennial snowflake yesterday, like he was inventing a clever new term, said I was wittering on about the food here or something, that I should check my privilege and think about refugees. I told him he should stop generalising about entire generations, and he got this grump on him and said he was being ironic, that Alphas never use the word snowflake 'cause that's for Boomers and Xers who think that anyone who doesn't have a stiff upper lip is a let down to the nation. He's all right, and so is she.'

There's a moment of silence, and I can almost smell the waves of Violet's bafflement, curling up through the window with her smoke.

Then, 'I think I'm one of them baby boomers.'

Jodie laughs. 'Yeah, you are. You definitely are.'

I feel a little bit of something warm in my belly at the way Jodie talks about Jake and me. It's like the soft edges of a possibility, that maybe, after all, I could be proud of myself, and those edges make me feel a little less insignificant than before.

And then I remember what happened in the night, and I look over at Barbara, and I hate myself anew.

Marcus didn't believe in self-pride. At least, he didn't believe I had anything to be proud of, only him who worked hard from dawn to dusk to keep a roof over our heads. And I knew he was right.

'I'VE BEEN WATCHING you,' Marcus says to me. 'I can't help but notice you're struggling a little.'

I swipe my arm over my sweat-soaked forehead, too aware of how I must look. I've been watching him, too. Watching how he works his clients until they drop, all those impossibly beautiful women hanging on his every word, women who exude confidence like rays of sunshine, strutting around the gym with their perfect toned bodies in their branded lycra and ignoring me entirely.

He crouches down next to where I am sitting on the leg-curl bench. His dark eyebrows knit together, and I follow his gaze as his eyes flick over the pitiful single ten pound weight I'm using, my legs straining at their limit. Heat blossoms in my cheeks.

'You're cute when you blush.'

I dab at my face with my towel, as if I can hide the increasing redness, aware of the intensity of his gaze, piercing into me.

'Seems to me you need a targeted training programme,' he says.

I shake my head. 'Oh, no, I can't afford a personal trainer or anything like that. My doctor prescribed me a six-week membership, to help me get stronger, but—'

'Who said anything about payment?'

His eyes are oceans of empathy, and I want to drown in them.

'Little bit of work would sort you out. You could be quite pretty, you know, if you put the effort in. Good bones. And I can help you.' He smiles at me then and I am lost.

Quite pretty. I'm certain he doesn't mean those words in the way Keira Knightley means them in *Love Actually*, all fresh-faced with youth and health and stunning beauty. He means that maybe if I work out harder my skin might sag less, I'd be less sallow, perhaps.

He reaches out and chucks me on my chin, then tucks a strand of hair behind my ear. 'Mind me asking what's wrong?'

Honesty. Come on, Penny, it's the only way. 'It's my breathing.'

'I know something that can help a whole load with that. Come over here.'

He leads me to a cross trainer, the machine I avoid, mocking me every time I walk into the gym with its unreachable heights. I shake my head. 'I don't think… I mean, I've been working on the bike. I'm doing okay, actually.'

I feel proud of myself, I want to say. I'm persevering and it's paying off.

He waves his hand over at the bikes, dismissing them with a twist of the lips. 'Nah. This'll build you up more. Look.' He climbs on and starts it up, and in seconds he's a blur of movement, arms and legs whirring in a rhythmic dance, all energy and bulging muscles.

'Now you.'

'I can't—'

'That's no attitude to take, is it? I know you can do it. I have faith in you.' He's not even broken a sweat. He stares at me, his brow all crunched.

I don't understand why he has faith in me. He doesn't know me.

'I can only do that because I've worked so hard at it.' He spreads his hands, gesturing at his body, all toned and fit and glowing with health, and grins. 'You could, too. And I want to help.'

But why would someone like him want to help someone like me?

'You're a little slow,' he says, as I brave the cross trainer, forcing my legs to co-operate and my chest to stop crushing so hard.

I nod furiously. 'I know. I know. I'm sorry.'

He lays his hand on my arm and I shiver. 'It's okay. I have some ideas. Shall we go for a coffee? Get something down on paper? A plan?'

And that's how it started.

I was caught up in his optimism and charm, in his certainty that he was the answer to my troubles. He was like a breath of fresh air after living in the shadow of my successful sister – he was going to reshape me, mould me into a new and better version of myself, a version my parents would, at last, be proud of. How did I get so lucky?

THERE'S A TRAFFIC jam at the entrance to the bay after breakfast. The little man from the Hospital Friends is pushing his trolley laden with newspapers, magazines and chocolate into the ward while Nicki is pushing a commode laden with something else out of it, and Sister Harris is trying to get through with the meds cart. Ernesto hovers behind her with the obs trolley.

'Anyone for papers today?' the Friends man calls.

'Got any beer?' Jodie says, and the man giggles and waggles his finger at her.

None of us want anything. I'd quite like a newspaper but he only has the *Mail* and the *Sun*, no *Guardians*, so I don't bother. He looks deflated, so I buy a Mars bar and he bounces over to me like a grateful puppy.

Sister Harris is sharp today, any soft edges filed away by stress or exhaustion or just life. She is impatient with the Friends man, pushing through and sighing heavily, telling Ernesto to get a move on because the observations are late. She's coming round with the morning drugs and heparin injections. 'Little pinch of stomach please?' she says to me and I lift my pyjama top up. 'Ooh, you're all the colours of the rainbow here, aren't you.'

I look down at my stomach, a map of blotches of varying colours, the daily blood thinning injection taking its obvious toll. She pinches some loose stomach flesh and plunges the thin needle in. 'Sharp scratch.' The drug is a fiery dart. This one really is a sharp scratch. 'There you go. All done. Ernesto! Get those obs done!'

The staff are a bit scared of Sister Harris. I haven't seen any of the other nurses here only addressed by their title and surname, but Sister Harris looks like she'd bite your head off if you called her Diane, even though it's printed on her name tag. I can tell they're in awe. They're like a class of eight-year-olds, all tedious righteousness, scampering around and falling over one another in their eagerness to be the one to get some rare praise from their teacher today. Ernesto almost bows to her as he rushes towards Kat with the obs trolley. With Sister Harris the praise rarely comes, but they're still hungry for it; I see it in Ernesto's eyes, right now.

The doctors are scared of her, too, and defer to her like a soppy golden retriever backing away from next door's imperious Persian cat as she wanders through their rounds, her voice a sharp cut through the waffle and the apologies. She is fiercely protective of her patients, stopping by our beds when she has no time to, asking if all is well and if there is anything we want to talk about with her. Most of us nod and say we are fine, but Jodie likes to embroil her in long conversations about the food and that grumpy nurse on the night shift who cannulated her wrong and exploded her vein and then told her off for not staying still. Today is different, though. Jodie beckons her over, speaking in more lowered tones than usual, hands flying everywhere, her face a jagged crevice of outrage. She keeps pointing to Barbara and I strain towards her bed, catching snatches here and there.

'I'm not making that up.' She looks towards me. 'Hey, Penny, I'm not making that up, am I? I don't do that. I don't lie. You heard them, yeah? Those care workers in the night.'

I nod. 'Well, yes.' I look down at my hands and pick at the loose, red-raw skin. Why didn't I mention it to Sister Harris? Why did I leave it to Jodie, content to pretend it never happened?

'They were literally being that rough with her, telling her to shut up, 'cause she was crying and going on about her mouse. And they was laughing at her too. Telling her she'd made such a mess when she shat herself. I had to say something so I was over there giving them a piece of my mind.'

'I think they assumed we were all asleep,' I say.

Sister Harris sits down heavily on Jodie's chair. 'Do you know who it was?'

Jodie nods. 'It was that grumpy one, you know, the one who chews gum all the time and shouts like a banshee. Think she's called Julie. And the other one, I don't know, think she was agency 'cause she had a different colour uniform.'

'Hmm.'

'I was shocked, to be honest. To be fair, most of you lot are always kind and go out of your way. That's why I was so upset about it and had to tell you, Sister.'

'Thanks for letting me know.' Sister Harris' face is set in a firm grimace, barbed with ominous purpose, and I'm slightly afraid for the staff in question. Not sorry for them, though.

I've seen it before, with patients with dementia or just confused in their illness, like Barbara. I've seen them dehumanised and laughed at and wondered how it will feel when I get to that age and it's me they are mocking.

In my head I know I was mocking her, too, because I didn't try harder to stop it.

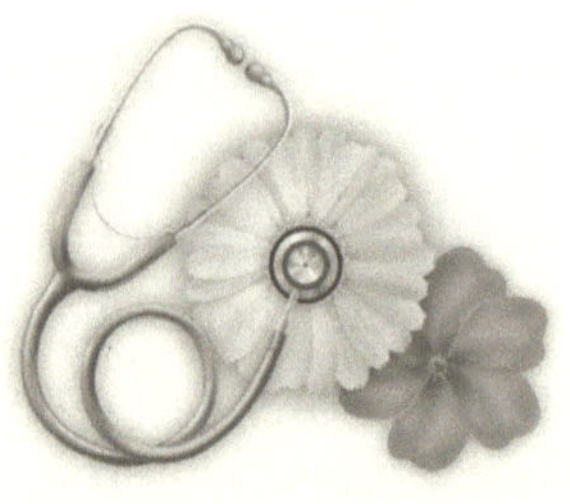

Chapter 11

MAGAZINES MAKE ME weary these days. Karen used to pass her copies of Cosmo and Red on to me, and I would curl up on my sofa with a cup of tea, all eager to escape into their shiny, scented pages, to gape in awe at the prices of the fashion I would never dare to wear. They were a window on another world, a life that I craved but seemed scary at the same time. When Jake was born I traded them in for Mother & Baby and Take a Break, scouring the pages for tips on how to breastfeed, how to be a better mum, how to get stains out of carpets, how to be happy. The pages were full of busy mums juggling their work and play and their children's activities with ease; vitality shining from their perfectly made-up faces, bursting with health and wellbeing, living their best lives. As the years went on, I stopped buying them, only flicking through in the waiting room or when I was in hospital and someone brought me one for a treat.

Only it's not a treat, not really, not anymore. It's a reminder of my frailty and my lack. It's the same with Instagram, which I installed in the hope it would transform my life into something that looked a little more perfect than it was, that if I could capture the good bits in little filtered squares that gave off the pretence that I had it all sorted, maybe I would be a little more sorted, after all.

I didn't take pictures of my hospital bed or my thousands of daily pills, because honesty was too brutal for me, and before long I ran out of things to take pictures of. So I deleted the app and deleted my best life all in one go.

Jodie buys new magazines every day and Kane brings more in for her, *Heat* and *Hello* and *OK*. She flips through them, crowing over the outfits and perfect homes, reading out the quizzes; what sort of Disney princess are you? Who were you in another life? Kat scorns them and says they are shallow and only propagate envy. Violet likes to read them and complain about the terrible manners and lifestyles of the celebrities, she would never do things like that, how common. Amina doesn't touch them.

Jodie tries to pass them on to me. 'You'll love this one. It's got Ed Sheeran in it.'

I smile politely and thank her. Today it's a scraggy copy of *Woman's Own*. There's an article about building yourself up when you're feeling tired and low. I turn the pages slowly, scrutinising the page numbers, until I find it. A picture of a perfect woman with bouncy auburn hair holding a plate of avocado salad and smiling with her perfect teeth. She doesn't look very tired or low. 'Ten pick-me-ups for down days,' goes the headline, and I read through, sighing. Eat more fruit. Do more exercise. Try meditation. Try mindfulness. Sleep better. Read more books. Put your phone down. Make things. See friends. Hug people.

That easy.

It's like when Marcus used to tell me that his brand of exercise would cure me. He went slowly with me, his voice full of kindness, taking it an exercise at a time, patiently standing with me while I lifted weights and shook with the effort of it, guiding me as I dragged myself painfully slowly through the hills programme on the bike. My muscles became more defined, my stomach flatter, my legs stronger, and I stood up straight, holding myself differently. He'd fallen in love with me, he told me one glorious day, he thought about me all the time. If I could just keep on following his programme, I'd be cured for good.

It's like all those miracle cures. All those multi-level marketing schemes promising the world. People telling me that if I buy their products I will get better immediately, so what am I waiting for? If I don't reply, or say no thank you, I see those cold edges of disappointment creeping over their faces, so better to obediently swallow down the smoothies and aloe vera drinks, and get sick anyway.

People in this ward are not like that. How strange it is that it's when I'm in hospital I feel most understood, most at home.

'Let's have a ward feast,' Jodie says. 'I'm bored of the food in this place.'

'A ward feast?' Kat says, sitting on Jodie's chair and watching out for Sister Harris or any of the other staff who might tell her off. 'You mean like order in? I'm down for that.'

Jake is here, and Kane is here too, slouching on Jodie's bed, pushing her over to make space for himself. Sister Harris wouldn't like that at all. 'You don't need more food,' Kane says, munching through a family size bag of crisps. 'You should take the opportunity to lose a bit of weight.'

Jake glares at him but he takes no notice.

Jodie flushes. 'I meant… well, I meant for Penny, and Amina and everyone really. I mean, Penny is veggie and they give her fish and such, and they don't always even give Amina something if there's nothing halal or whatever.'

Kane sneers. 'She should take what she's given.'

Violet nods vehemently, flicking a disdainful gaze over at Amina.

'I think it's a lovely idea,' Kat says. 'Should we get Dominos? Maybe Kane could go and pick it up for us, if they don't deliver to hospitals?'

Kane grunts.

'Please,' Jodie says. 'You'd do that for me, wouldn't you?' She pushes herself up against him, pouting up at him and batting her eyelashes. He pulls her in tightly, squeezing that little bit too hard. She coughs and gasps and he doesn't let go.

'Anything for you.'

I squirm inside, exchanging a glance with Kat. Marcus held me tight, too, squeezing in hard as he told me that he loved me so much that he needed me to be better for him, that I just wasn't quite pretty enough, or fit enough, or funny enough.

'Can I have some?' Jake says.

When Kane comes back with the pizza, we descend on him like a pack of hungry labradors. Even Amina is up, face all animated, digging out her purse and pressing too many notes on him with copious thank yous. He doesn't give her any change.

Jodie is grinning widely. Her wonderful boyfriend, doing this for all her new friends, going out of his way for us like that. She's a beacon of light, all sparkly eyes and glowing cheeks, delighted that Kane is, after all, what she needs him to be.

'You can have one slice,' Kane says to her, 'and I'll have the rest. Take it home for my dinner.'

Her face falls.

'But…'

'Tosser,' Jake hisses under his breath, and Kat nods, her face tight with anger.

Jodie says nothing more. She eats her slice slowly, bravely, blinking back tears, her mouth quivering with tiny I'm-okay-really smiles. 'This is delicious. Thanks, babe.'

'You shouldn't have any more dinner tonight,' Kane says. 'Remember what we said?'

Jake explodes through a mouthful of veggie supreme. 'What right have you got to tell her what she can eat?'

Kane lumbers off the bed, squares up to Jake, all tattooed muscle and shaven aggression. 'Pardon?'

Jake shrugs. 'You heard me.'

It's not like Kane can start a fight with a fifteen-year-old boy in a hospital ward, after all.

Jodie's shoulders are tight with tension. 'It's okay, Jake. He's right. I was on a diet, and… and he's just trying to help me.'

'But you're ill,' Jake says, his brow creasing up in baffled sadness. 'You need to get strong. And have a treat too, being stuck in here all day.' He sweeps his arm in a large arc around him.

'It's okay,' she says softly.

All I can think about is Marcus, and how he convinced me that he was only doing these things for my good, too, and how I believed him for so long. How I was his project, his trophy to show off when he succeeded in reforming me.

Except he didn't, really.

'Kane will do anything for me,' Jodie says, taking hold of Kane's hand and leaning forward to kiss him.

'Anything,' he says.

'THANK YOU,' VIOLET says later to Jodie, 'for the pizza I mean. It was a welcome change from the pigswill they call food around here.'

I'm amazed at Violet actually saying thank you to something. Maybe that's Jodie's effect on her, of the cumulation of hours they must have spent together with their cigarettes, out in the cold together. Violet saying thank you is like a light being switched on somewhere in a place full of too much gloom. Jodie grins at her. Kane has left, and she is back to her effervescent self without his shadow hanging over her and pressing her down. 'No worries,' she says.

'My grandson likes that pizza stuff. Oh, I mean my granddaughter, I suppose. He's one of those transvestites now.'

Jake buries his head in his hands. 'You mean transgender.'

'Well, I don't know,' Violet says, her mouth a tight line of uncomprehending disapproval. 'I never know what these kids are doing nowadays. Never know if I have to call him a boy or a girl.'

'Probably kindest to call her what she asks,' Kat says.

Jodie stares. 'Bit woke for a vicar, aren't you?'

'No one says woke anymore,' Jake says.

Jodie screws up her nose at him. 'Careful, or I'll yeet this Coke at you.'

'Yeet,' he scoffs.

I wonder what it is about Jodie. She has made my son smile more than he has in months.

'Where does she live?' Kat says to Violet. 'Your granddaughter, I mean.'

Violet sniffs. 'Oh. Well, they're all over in London, see. Moved away from here as soon as he could, my son, got married to some bimbo he met in a bar. Doesn't deign to visit his mother very much, even when she's in hospital.'

'Sorry to hear that,' Kat says. 'That must be hard.'

Violet nods, and I'm surprised to see tears begin to form in the corners of her eyes, then track a slow crawl down her cheeks. Kat goes over, takes her hand. 'It's okay to cry.'

Barbara is rigid in her chair, listening avidly. 'I cried, when Bill died.'

Violet gazes at her. 'Was that your husband?'

Barbara nods. 'Sixty years.'

'That's amazing,' Kat says. 'When did he pass away?'

'Five years ago.' Barbara stares into space. 'That awful corona thing.'

Kat keeps silence for a long moment.

Then, 'Do you have children?'

Barbara hesitates, the lines around her eyes animated, crawling outwards like ivy creeping up a house in time-lapse motion. 'No.'

'Sorry,' Kat says, 'I didn't mean to be intrusive.'

Barbara says nothing. Just stares out of the window opposite her, beyond Jodie's bed, her faded blue eyes reflecting the grey day.

Poor Barbara. She's lost the only person she had in the world. I watch each day just in case an errant son or sheepish niece turns up with illegal flowers and apologetic murmurings, but no one ever does. She just lies in her corner bed, wasting away. She doesn't eat and she doesn't sleep. She stares at the ceiling and whispers about the rat on the floor.

'Hey,' she calls over to me, snapping out of her staring silence, 'The rat is on your bed! The rat is on your bed now. Get it off. Get it off! Nurse!'

'Does she think I'm a rat?' Jake murmurs.

I shake my head. 'Shh. No, she has a thing about rats and mice. Leave her be.'

'Nurse!'

Nicki walks in with a pile of sheets under one arm. 'You calling me, flower?'

'It's the rat. There. On her bed.'

Nicki glances over at us and then pats Barbara's hand with great tenderness. 'There's no rat, lovely. Try not to worry. Just a great big lad who shouldn't be there because visiting is over.'

Jake takes the hint and throws his hands up, dragging himself off the chair. 'I was going anyway.'

'I saw it,' Barbara says, her voice a quavering moan.

Nicki puts the pile of sheets on the bed and kneels down by her chair. She takes both her hands and looks into her eyes. 'It's okay, Barbara. The rat's gone, see? You're safe, flower. Now, I've brought these sheets to sort your bed out while you're out of it, seeing as what we couldn't get you up for love nor money this morning. So let's get your bed all nice and then me and Claire will get you washed and changed and settled back for a nice little nap. Is that okay?'

Barbara pushes out her bottom lip.

'Now now, Barbara, you're my good girl, aren't you? You going to let me help you?'

'But the rat…'

'The rat isn't here, flower. Just you and me.'

Nicki gets up, holding her back and flinching as if she is in pain, then winks at us as she drags the curtains round Barbara and shuts her off from the scary, rat-filled world outside.

Jodie balances on the edge of my bed, ready to launch herself off when Sister arrives. She looks at me and beckons me closer. Whispers something.

'What?' I say, shrinking back from her tobacco heavy fumes.

'I said we could take Barbara to the seaside.'

'What?' I say again.

'You heard me. We could take Barbara, you know, she said it was her last wish or something, right? We could make it come true.'

I stare at her incredulously. 'I don't think…'

I look over at Violet and Kat, Kat holding Violet's hand, listening to her talk and weep about her family.

Jodie shakes her head and leans in closer. 'Listen. I've been thinking. They like us all going for our little walks, getting some fresh air, the doctor is always telling us we should do that, isn't he? See, Kane has this minibus thing, and the sea's not far away, right?'

'Um—'

'I don't mean like tomorrow or anything. I mean when we're all feeling a bit better. Maybe in a few days.'

'I—'

'Look, I've thought it all through. We could take her in a wheelchair and everything. Only need to have a little sit on the beach, like a few minutes. We'd only be gone about an hour all in if you think about it, if that. They wouldn't even miss us.'

'But we can't do that. Barbara's not always all there, is she? She's too frail. And we probably won't all be here in a few days – people go home, they move us around, you know that.'

Jodie pouts. 'Don't be such a Debbie Downer. We've been in this long together, haven't we? Nearly a week? They'll not move us now until we go home, and none of us are ready for that yet, are we? You're not going home yet, are you?'

I shake my head. 'No, I mean, I have another week or so.'

'Right? And my doctor says to me this morning, you're not ready for home yet, Jodie, however much you try and convince me you are. My blood levels or something. Though I feel fine.'

'Yes but… we just can't. We'd get in trouble.'

'Why would they know, though?'

'We don't have the strength. I don't think I can drive, on all these meds.'

'Kane will help us. I already asked him. He'll do anything for me. There's this beach, see, just a small one.'

I swallow. 'I… why don't we wait, maybe one or two of us come back when we're better and out of here, take her then? Just as visitors? I could drive.'

Jodie taps her finger against her mouth and gazes at me, her blue eyes more intense than usual. 'Haven't you heard the nurses?'

she whispers, her eyes darting from right to left. 'They keep saying she's near the end, don't they?' Her shoulders slump. 'We have to help her before she goes. To do this one thing for her. It's only a little thing, and it's not like we're prisoners here, is it? What if we could give her her dying wish? Don't you want to do that?'

I stare at her then laugh.

'What's so funny?'

'Well, uh…'

'You think we couldn't do that? Kane's a builder, right? He's super strong. He can help us. And Kat, she's up for it I reckon. And Violet, well, she's up herself and all, but she reckons she'd be up for it. I asked her earlier when we was smoking, she was like, don't be stupid, girl, but then I explained it all and she was like, well maybe, but only if she can just sit in the van 'cause she don't like sand or seawater. Says to me she's feeling a whole load better. Amina, I don't know if she'd want to come, but no harm asking, yeah? Unless she'd sneak to Harris.'

I can't think of what to say. She must be doing this for a bit of fun, a fairy tale we can all collude in the telling of to pass the time, a dream of better things.

'Well, I suppose,' I find myself saying.

Part of me wishes it was a real plan, that we could really do it, that we could really let Barbara feel the salty air on her face and the sand between her toes. I lean back into my pillows and close my eyes, conjuring up the blue sky and the gentle waves.

We could pretend, I suppose.

I'M NOT SURE Violet really is feeling better, even though she told Jodie she is. In evening visiting she looks pale, clinging on to Brian's hand as if she's drowning and he is her lifebelt. Her frown is more twisted than usual, screwing up her face and pinching her eyebrows together in one straggly line as she glowers over at Amina's family. Amina's husband Bilal and three of her four sons are there with her, quiet and gentle as always as they lean in towards her with tender words, faces etched with concern.

'Shouldn't be allowed,' Violet mutters in Brian's direction, while keeping her eyes narrowed at Amina's sons. 'Think they can get away with anything. Says three visitors on that sign, clear as day, but these people think they can do as they please.'

'It's disgusting,' Brian says.

'Gadding about, disturbing everyone's peace.'

'It's a disgrace.'

'See this is why I needed my own room. They don't care about getting us better, really, not when they let hundreds of people come in with no thought for the ill people in here.'

Violet coughs and then explodes into a frenzy of coughing, leaving her gasping for breath and blue around the edges. She bends over, her shoulders heaving, and Brian strokes her back. 'It's okay, dear. Calm down. Shh.'

But Violet is riled. She points to Amina with a wavering index finger, her lips quivering with outrage. 'That's what happens when she has all those people over. That's what it makes me do, Brian! It's intolerable!'

'Intolerable,' Brian says.

'And they all talk in that foreign Indian language and all. No respect.'

Amina and her family are talking quietly, as they always do, but they can't help but hear her accusations. I wonder what it is like to be so accused when you have done nothing wrong, and suspect Amina knows only too well. Her glance shifts towards Violet for a second, and then over to me, and I lift my eyebrows at her and smile gently, rolling my eyes in Violet's direction. Urdu, Amina said to Kat when she asked about her mother tongue. She and Bilal whisper together in Urdu, but the boys prefer to speak English, even though they are all bilingual. One of them, their eldest, he can speak five languages, he has a flair for them, she told us with pride shining from her eyes.

'They give me no peace,' Violet says, her voice a pitiful rasp now, choked up with tears and the edges of her coughing fit.

'Disgraceful,' Brian says, and I think to myself that I have never seen anything less disgraceful than Amina's caring, gentle family.

'Nurse!' Violet cries out, as Ernesto comes into the ward with the obs trolley. 'Nurse!'

Ernesto sighs dramatically and wanders over to Violet, swaying his hips as Jodie gives a low whistle. 'What is it, Violet?'

'Give me some painkillers.'

Ernesto casts a sardonic glance back at Jodie. 'I'll ask the nurse to come and see you, Violet. Are you in pain?'

'Of course I'm in pain, you silly little man. Why did you think I was asking for painkillers? I'm in pain because people keep giving me a headache.'

'I'll ask the nurse. But it could be a while, they're just on changeover.' Ernesto whirls round with the trolley and slaloms it over to Jodie. 'Time for a blood pressure check, young lady.'

'No one cares in this place,' Violet says loudly. 'They all think they have better things to do with their time than get some pills for a lady in pain.'

'Well, I think they do an amazing job,' Kat says. She's sitting up on her bed with Nate balanced on the edge, both leaning forward, listening in raptly to the exchange.

'Huh,' Violet says.

Brian says, 'They're a disgrace.'

There's a clamour at the door as several women come into the ward shedding wet coats and grabbing chairs. 'Kat!' one of them says. 'Good to see you out of bed!'

Kat has visitors all the time, different people every day, old and young, men and women. Her congregation, I suppose. They come armed with biscuits and grapes and chocolate and a whole lot of love, and I envy her community. The four women grab themselves chairs and draw them up to Kat's bed, eager with news and chatter and life. One of them takes out a soft knitted shawl, all the shades of purple, and presents it to Kat with a kiss on the cheek. 'We made this for you in the knitting group,' the woman says, flushing slightly. 'It's for you to feel our love. And our prayers.'

Kat has tears in her eyes. 'I don't know what to say. Thank you.' She drapes the shawl around her shoulders, still managing to look edgy and eye-catching, as she always does, even in checked pyjamas. The tears spill down her cheeks and one of the women passes her a tissue.

'We love you,' the woman says.

I want to cry, too, but don't know how to.

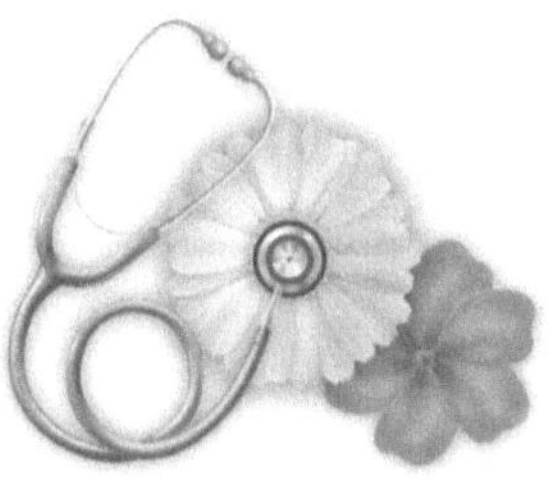

Chapter 12

'M iss Fielding?'

Someone is tugging at my arm, gently but insistently. 'Miss Fielding, I just need to take you for a bronchoscopy.'

Oh no. Not that. Dr Chowdhury mentioned it yesterday, or was it the day before? The days bleed together in here, hours go by without you realising, then drag by until you want to grab them and concertina them all together so they go quicker.

I don't like bronchoscopies. We'll sedate you, they always say, but the sedation is never enough to mask the cold scope shoved down my throat, choking me, the suction through parts that sting with the pain of it. It'll help us see what's going on down there, he says, and clear you out a bit more in the process, get rid of that deep seated stuff that refuses to budge with even the most violent percussion Dan has to offer. That's great, I say, as if I can't wait, as if it's a trip to the cinema.

As the porter wheels me out of the ward, I notice Violet lying still in her bed, an oxygen mask pressed over her face, which is devoid of its usual blotches of high colour.

'She is very poorly,' Amina says. 'She was very sick in the night and could not breathe.'

I must have slept through it all.

Amina looks worried, her brows pinched as she watches Violet's chest rising and falling too quickly. 'She seemed so much better, yesterday. She was – how you say it – sprightly? She was saying she could go home soon.'

'She has COPD,' Kat puts in, and I immediately feel guilty that I don't even know that, that I'd never bothered to ask. 'She had Covid really badly too, last year, she nearly died and it made her COPD worse.'

'Oh no,' I say, staring at her, lying there in her polyester nightie, a blue waffle blanket tucked in around her, eyelids quivering, arms still at her sides, all exposed and pale and floppy.

'We need to go.' The porter pushes my chair out of the bay into the cool breeze of the corridor, and I brace myself for what is ahead.

❧

My throat aches.

I'm taking a sip of some insipid hospital tea when Dan strolls in with a chart in one hand, pushing a walker with another. 'Right, Penny! Hope you're feeling energetic. We're going to get you walking up the stairs today.'

I swallow and my throat is too small and I gag. 'Just had… bronchoscopy.'

'Ah, nice. You must be feeling nice and clear.'

'Nice and sleepy.' The sedation still hits me in waves. It seems stronger than usual because I barely remember it, only the feeling of the cool scope hitting my throat, the feeling someone was trying to drown me, the desperate need to cough, to get it out of me, but then nothing. I woke up back here in my bed tasting something metallic. There's blood on my lips.

'Ah no, *cariad*. It's hours since you had it. Let's get you up.'

'You sound like thingy,' I say blurrily.

'Thingy?'

'From *Gavin and Stacey*.'

He laughs. 'You ready?'

No.

I teeter behind the walker, gripping on for dear life, fighting through the fog. 'Good girl!' Dan says, as if I'm a schoolgirl who's just got all her spellings right. I glance at Violet again on my way out, but she's barely moved from her prone position, and her face seems whiter still. I've not been very kind to her. What if…?

The stairs stretch out before me, all concrete and frigid with cold, like the outside has nudged its way into the building and been made to feel too welcome. 'Brrr,' Dan says, hugging his arms round himself, 'bit chilly in here, isn't it?'

The stairwell is always cold, in summer and in winter, but just now the temperature feels too much, it feels like alien terrain impossible for me to traverse. The cold hits me in a stab of agony and I stumble.

'Okay?'

I swallow and nod, clinging to the walker.

'Righto. So, leave this here at the bottom and just hold on to the rail. Anytime you need to stop, then just tell me, we won't go further than you can. Okay?'

'Okay.'

He keeps hold of my arm as I pick up my foot and place it on the bottom step, grabbing hold of the cool metal rail. My leg shakes as I lift my other foot. One at a time. One foot on the step, drag other foot to the same step, rest a moment, next step. I can do this.

'You're doing well,' Dan says, and I wonder where he gets his chipper patience from, that he can hang round cold stairwells with wobbly middle-aged women all day and never get frustrated.

It's around the tenth step where the world starts to spin and my stomach churns as though I'm on *Oblivion* and going over the big drop. Not that I've had energy for Alton Towers for years.

'Woah there.' Dan grips hold of me as I sway, blood rushing to my head and pounding at my eyes.

'I feel… faint…'

The world is black.

I'm collapsed on the stairs, Dan beside me, my head in my hands. 'That's it. Keep your head bent low. Give it a few seconds. Okay there?'

I breathe out. 'Sorry.'

'Don't be a daft bint. You have nothing to apologise for. I should probably have realised you still have sedative in your system.'

I breathe in. Breathe out. In. Out.

'Better?'

'A bit.'

Dan waits with me in the frozen silence of the stairwell, the occasional door slamming above somewhere, clanging through the hollow air, raised voices echoing through from the corridor. The institutional smell of lunch weaves around us, that particular hospital food smell, all boiled vegetables and overcooked meat.

My stomach lurches, and suddenly I need Jake and my home so bad I gasp.

When we get back to the ward I flop down on my bed, beaten. When will I ever have the strength to get out of here?

'Never mind,' Dan says. 'Next time. You did really well, getting that far, you'll be fine.'

'Sorry I fainted on you.'

'Will you stop apologising, woman?'

I lie back on my pillows and glance around the bay. Amina is propped up reading a book, all serious eyes and rigid back. Kat is asleep. Barbara is on her chair, staring at nowhere in particular, feet shod in her maroon slippers. Jodie isn't here. Violet's curtains are closed and low voices emanate from her cubicle. 'Violet, flower, let's get you sat up for a bit of lunch, shall we? You're all clean and sorted now. It's okay, lovely. It's okay.'

I think Violet is sobbing.

JAKE SCRAPES THE chair noisily on the polished floor. 'Oops, mum, sorry, didn't mean to wake you.'

'Hi, Jake.'

'Nan asked me to tell you to get well soon,' he says, clearly uncomfortable, shifting in his seat.

'Did she?'

'Yeah. She seemed to mean it.'

'Right.'

'And Grandad too. I mean, he didn't say it or anything, but I can see it in his eyes, like, when I'm telling them how you are and all that.'

'Mmm.'

'Honestly, Mum. They do love you.'

'Okay.'

I know they do, in their own way. We are our own little family, Jake and me, us against the world, but although my parents haven't been easy, they've been there for me, taking care of Jake when I am in hospital, sending him presents for Christmas and birthdays, keeping up some semblance of happy families.

Jodie is back on her bed, scrolling through her phone. No sign of Kane this afternoon, thankfully. 'You seen Violet?' she says.

I look over at Violet's bed. Except there's no bed, just a gaping space where her bed should be.

I look at Jodie.

'Don't ask me. I was out for a fag and when I got back she'd gone.'

I swallow. 'You don't think…?'

'Nah. Made of stern stuff, that one. She'd bite Death on the arse if he came visiting, tell him he was common as muck and to shove orf.'

Kat wanders over. 'She's just gone for an x-ray. She's too poorly to sit up so they took her down in her bed.'

I exhale.

It's funny. I don't like Violet. Or at least I didn't like Violet. But I want her to be okay. I need her to be okay.

'I've been asking that nurse all afternoon for some morphine,' Jodie says, flinching. 'It's like pulling teeth today, trying to get anyone to take any notice. I could be dying here, for all they know.'

'Moan moan, whinge whinge,' Jake says.

Jodie gives him a look.

Violet's husband Brian walks into the ward, all rigid and stiff and drowning in his frown. 'Where is she?' he says to no one in particular.

Kat goes to him, whispers softly. He nods, his brow furrowing further, and sits on the edge of the chair in Violet's bedspace, all abandoned and lost. His body is tense, wired as if he is going to snap any moment, his hands clasped together in his lap so tightly the whites of his knuckles are showing. Kat drags a bucket chair up and sits with him, but they don't talk. She just sits, and he sits, and they wait together.

'I hope she's okay,' I say to Jodie.

'She will be. She has to be, because she's got to come on this little trip.'

'What trip?' I say without thinking, then watch as Jodie's face falls. 'Oh. That trip.'

'What trip?' Jake says.

I shake my head at Jodie. 'Nothing.'

Jake plugs his earphones in. I can hear the tinny music from here, and wonder how it doesn't blast his skull apart.

'You're as bad as Kat.' Jodie's voice has a whiny tinge to it.

'Kat?'

Jodie bends forward towards me, keeping an eye on Kat. 'I told her about our plan.'

Our plan?

'And she said it wasn't a good idea.'

Well, it's not, really.

'But then I said, what if it's Barbara's only chance? What if we are the only ones who can help a lonely old lady see the sea one last time? And then she goes, well, maybe, but only if it's all planned. And I go yeah, it will be, and she says we should clear it with Sister Harris, and I go we're not at school or in prison, we can do what we like.'

I try to avoid her gaze.

'You promised,' Jodie says, all young and petulant.

Jake pokes his head between us. 'What you two on about?'

'Nothing,' Jodie and I both say together.

Jake shrugs and goes back to his game.

I flop back on my pillow. I did promise, kind of. I made a promise to collude with a madcap plan, to liven up our drab lives in this drab place, to make-believe a tale of a world where elderly ladies get their dying wishes and sick patients get to go on trips to the seaside. I said yes because I am Penny who says yes. Penny who said yes to an abusive husband. Penny who is going to say yes to a ridiculous scheme dreamed up by an unstable girl with a speciality in wishful thinking.

Sister Joy breezes into the ward, her smile all sunshine and warmth. 'You asked for some morphine?' she says to Jodie, holding out a small vial of oramorph.

''Bout time,' Jodie says, and Joy's face falls. 'Only kidding. I know you're busy.'

'We do our best.'

'I know. Listen, Sister, would it be okay if we take Barbara for a little bit of fresh air, say in the Peace Garden? She's always stuck in here with no visitors, and she's a lot stronger than she was a few days ago, isn't she?'

Sister Joy folds her arms, regarding Jodie and then glancing over at Barbara, nestled in her armchair, all angles and tissue-paper thin skin, support stockings all crinkled around her ankles, blue veins running down her bare legs like someone has drawn on her with a biro.

'I think it would do her the world of good,' she says.

Jodie smiles at me and her smile is a blaze of triumph.

BRIAN DOESN'T LEAVE Violet's side for the rest of the day. When she is wheeled back in from wherever they took her she is flopped down in her pillows, her face pasty and puffy, cheeks shrunken into themselves, fluttering eyelids purple and heavy with veins. Somehow, though, her expression is as growly as ever, stamped with the general air of disdain and disapproval that never quite leaves her. I had a teacher like that once, always viewing the world through a lens of displeasure. I was often on the edges of his antipathy, desperate to find ways to placate him but never quite succeeding. His lips lived in a constant snarl and his nose in a perpetual crinkle at the world in general and me in particular.

I'VE BEEN OUT of school for a month. I'm behind in my studies and my stomach is a pit of dread as I enter my tutor group. I stare at the scuffed floor, hitching my bag further up my shoulder, my hair falling over my eyes in straggly clumps. Mum said my new perm would make me look chic, but I know that in reality I look like I am walking round with a large shower puff stuck to each side of my face. I've barely recovered, but Mum says I mustn't dilly dally any longer. Pull your socks up, Penny.

When I get to school I slouch my socks down and try to make my hair straight and invisible.

As I go into the classroom it falls silent. Hot fear snakes through my bones, turning them to molten lava. I feel heavy as a ton of bricks and sink down onto my chair, resting my head in my hands.

'The wanderer returns!' Mr Lewis stands at the front of the class, a piece of chalk in his hand, staring straight at me. No sign of anything amusing at all plays around his deadpan face, his dead-fish eyes, his sardonic line of a mouth. He claps his hands together. Once, twice, three times, slowly, slowly, an invitation a pile of thirteen-year-olds are only too happy to take him up on. The whole class joins in, slow hand-clapping me for making it back to school. My cheeks flame with heat and the room shifts around me, spinning into strange swirling shapes and colours. I feel sick. A black mist creeps in on the edges of my vision.

'Penelope.'

Darkness. I can't hear. It's as though the air has turned to gloop around me, slowing everything down.

'Penelope.' The word comes in slow-motion, low and insistent, dragging me by the hair back through the tunnel.

'Penelope. Stop playing up.'

It's a shout now, a screech through my roaring ears, a wake-up call that snaps me out of my faint. Mr Lewis is in my face, eyes bulging as he shouts at me, so close I can smell something that reminds me too uncomfortably of my dad and what he likes to drink in the evening. I lower my head again, my hair a waterfall of lacquered curls scratching my desk. Maybe tonight I will cut them all off.

A bang on my head, sudden and sharp, exploding through my brain until stars race through my vision. The board rubber. He has the board rubber there in his hand and he has whacked me with it. There's a gasp and then a shocked silence.

'Get yourself together,' he says. 'It's bad enough that you've missed so much school, without coming in and messing around and not speaking when you're spoken to. Insolent girl.'

I steal a glance round at the class, at my few friends, all sitting with wide eyes and closed mouths. No one will say anything. No one ever does.

School might be the best days of their lives for those who fit in and thrive in the knowledge that they are liked, but it's the worst days of our lives for those of us who don't. It can be a place of great mental and physical cruelty, a place where adults allow unspeakable things to happen to children because that girl isn't really a bully, she's just mucking around and besides her dad is the chair of governors. It's a place where memories are made that echo through the hollow corridors of your mind years later and conjure up the sheer heart pounding panic you felt back then when Claire Jacobs and Nicola Smith cornered you in the far reaches of the playing field and then rained their rage upon your head and shrieked that you were an ugly little wimp and please stop trying to get into their crowd because it's never going to happen. You want to shrink into the slimy green walls in the girls' toilets and get subsumed within their depths because they can't be any deeper than the hatred and bile spat out at you every day. It's a place where you stand shivering in the playground and get picked last because everyone knows you are hopeless at P.E and most other things.

Mr Lewis and all those others are consigned to history, but he is part of my history. He is part of what makes me Penny who never quite manages to be enough. I am tired of nice Penny, of yes Penny, but I don't seem to be able to stop her saying yes. I collude just as much as that class of kids did back in the eighties, to keep things quiet and simple, to allow the tough stuff to go unchallenged.

Because that's who I am.

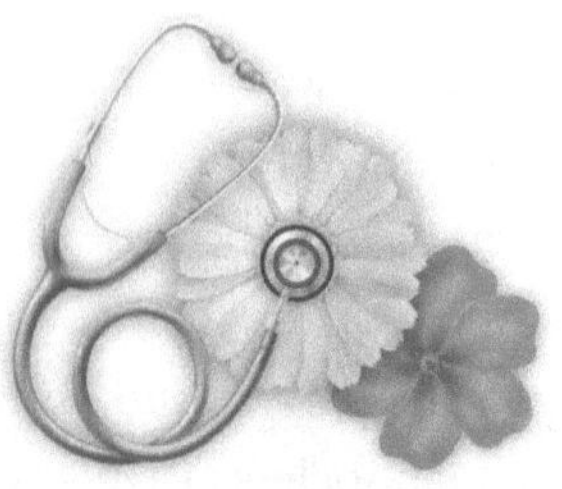

Chapter 13

Dr Chowdhury has arranged a CT scan for me. 'I'm a little worried about the damage to your lungs from all these recent infections,' he says. His medical students are with him today, all big, scared eyes and tensed up brows, watching his every move. 'And with this latest pneumonia, and all your little friends down there.' He chuckles, and his students stare at him as if they haven't got any idea what he is talking about.

'I had one a couple of years ago,' I say.

'I know. I have it here. I want to compare it, to see how we're doing with treating you.'

'Oh. Okay. Thank you.'

'They should be here for you shortly.'

I know what 'shortly' means in hospital. It means hours, or perhaps days. But today the porter is here within half an hour, whistling and grinning and greeting Ernesto with a wink. It's my rainbow hipster friend.

'You still here?' he says to me, whizzing a chair over to my bed and helping me into it. I wrap myself in my dressing gown and he drapes a blanket over my knees. 'Bit cold out there in the halls today.'

In the radiography department it is busy, cluttered with patients in wheelchairs and on beds, and outpatients dressed in great big coats with the cold of the day imprinted on their cheeks. 'Won't be long,' a nurse says to me, and I prepare for the long wait, pleased I remembered to grab my phone.

Messenger is clogged with a hundred messages all clamouring for my attention. Jen is there, asking me if I feel like another visit. I say yes, please, and wonder if she will come. Karen asks me if I feel better and when am I coming home. My online book group are discussing *The Midnight Library* and they all have long opinions that scroll for miles. Jake's class parents' WhatsApp group are discussing the upcoming mock GCSEs, asking how long each other's kids revise each night, how to balance their screen time, how to keep them active.

My own parenting is shipped out, left to my parents who didn't like parenting me very much. They don't care much about Jake's screen time and certainly don't police his revision. Another parenting fail, then. I shut down WhatsApp and scroll through a subreddit about parenting teenagers. Not a great idea.

An hour later I'm in the scanning room with my hospital gown on, loosely tied at the back. 'I'm just going to inject a little bit of dye,' the radiographer says. 'It's to help the doctor read the contrast in your lungs. You may feel like you need to go to the toilet, but don't worry.'

I'm not worried about that, but I am worried about the scanner, the oversized polo mint they send me hurtling into. It wraps itself around my body and seals over my head, as though I am enclosed in a coffin and I can't get out, even though the practical part of my brain knows it's not that bad. The scanner powers up around me and lights whizz through their rotations, slowly at first. 'Breathe in,' the automated voice commands me, 'hold your breath.' I can't, not for long, not for long enough, come on please let me breathe out. Don't worry, the radiographer says, her disembodied voice echoing through the tube, just hold it as long as you can.

That's not long at all.

Whizz, whizz, revolutions of blazing brightness, over and over like rainbows pelting by at the speed of light, the low buzz of the scanner snaking through my bones. I am shaking, cold with fear and weariness. 'Nearly done,' the voice says after too long. I can't hold out. My hands are rigid beside me on the trolley, quivering with the effort to avoid smashing out at the walls entombing me. My skin prickles with sweat.

'Okay. All done.'

My journey out of the scanner feels as though it takes a thousand times longer than the one in.

'We'll send the scan to your doctor,' the radiographer says kindly. 'You look like you could do with a bit of sleep. Well done, I know it's not always easy.'

'Thank you. Sorry,' I say.

'What for?'

'Just, um… being a bit useless in there.'

'You're not useless.' Her eyes are lit in a weary smile. 'You're just ill.'

AFTER LUNCH JODIE announces that she is going to take Barbara to the Peace Garden for a practice run, and that we are all coming with her. That's me, Amina and Kat, at least. Violet is deathly pale, though less still than she was yesterday, propped up slightly on her bed. Her greying, brassy hair lies in damp stringy ribbons on her sweat-soaked brow. 'I want to come,' she says. 'I need a cigarette.'

Jodie shakes her head. 'No, you don't.'

Sister Joy strolls into the bay, scanning one of the charts. 'You all here still?' Her smile is as warm as her name. 'Can't get rid of you lot, can we?'

Jodie is standing by Barbara's bed. 'I thought we'd take Barbara in the garden, like we talked about yesterday? The sun's out for a change. And she's all chipper today, aren't you Barbara?'

Barbara is sitting in her chair, fiddling with her dressing gown belt. She does have a little more colour in her cheeks, and her eyes are bright. 'I want to go in the garden,' she says.

I'm glad it's Sister Joy here today, not Sister Harris. I'm not sure she'd stand for any garden trip shenanigans.

'I think that's a wonderful idea,' Joy says. 'Give me a minute, and I'll fetch a chair for her. Are you going too, Penny? Do you want a chair?'

'Yes. I mean, yes, I'm going, but I can manage with a walker. Dan wants me to walk more, so…'

Joy bustles out of the ward, leaving the chart stranded on Amina's bed.

'I'm coming too,' Kat says. 'Could do with some air.'

'Amina?' Jodie says.

Amina looks up from her phone. She looks a little grey round the edges today, as if she has a black and white Instagram filter applied to her face. She shakes her head. 'No. Not today. But thank you very much for asking me. Another day, though, please.'

Amina is always so polite.

Sister Joy trundles back into the bay pushing a blue hospital wheelchair with one hand and pulling a walking frame with the other. 'There we go. She'll love this. We'll get her all wrapped up warm, she'll love a little sunshine on her face, she's been stuck in that corner for so long, God bless her. Don't keep her out long, though, will you? It's chilly out there.' She sees Kat sliding her slippers and dressing gown on. 'Oh, you're going too?' Her face crinkles in consternation. 'Just keep warm and don't stay out long. It'll build you up a bit, ready for home in a few days, won't it?' She turns and looks at me. 'When is it for you, Penny?'

'Should be next Monday or Tuesday, all being well.'

'Me too,' Kat says. 'The doctor said I'm doing well.'

'Well, good. Now, don't go getting yourselves cold. I don't have to tell you that—' she gestures at Jodie with disapproving eyes, '—you're always out there anyway, all weathers, with your smoking. Her, too.' She casts her eyes over at Violet, a shadow crossing her face. 'She's a little better today, but she's staying right here. Now. Do you want one of the healthcare assistants to help you?'

'Just to get Barbara in her chair, and get her oxygen all sorted,' Jodie says, wheeling the chair over to Barbara who sits up like a Year One child in assembly, all ramrod straight and eager. Pick me! Pick me!

'I'll just fetch some oxygen,' Joy says, going out of the ward.

Jodie beckons to Kat. 'Come on. We can get her in between us.'

'I can get in myself, young lady,' Barbara says with unexpected clarity.

'Oh! Well, okay then, let me just take your arm, though.'

Barbara shrugs Jodie's arm off and eases herself out of her bedside chair and into the waiting wheelchair with a face set in grim determination, a series of grunts and a spattering of somewhat ripe language. Jodie takes her arm again as she stumbles, and this time she allows it.

'Bit cold, this chair,' she says. 'Could do with some nice padding.'

Kat laughs. 'It could that.'

Her oxygen tube is still attached to the vial on the wall, stretched out taut over the gap. Joy bustles in with a cylinder and an oh of surprise. 'That was quick! You're a sprightly one, young lady, aren't you?'

Barbara giggles.

Joy hooks her drip over the drip stand on the back of the wheelchair and connects up her oxygen.

We get her all tucked in with her warm fleecy dressing-gown, slippers and two blankets tucked round her from her neck down to her feet. 'I feel like one of them mummies,' she says.

'Right,' Sister Joy says, stepping on the brake and whirling round with the chair to face the doors. 'You've all had your lunchtime meds and IVs, haven't you?'

We all have.

'Have a nice little trip out, then, ladies.'

Jodie's eyes are merry as she whispers in my ear, 'Little does she know.'

Joy pauses. 'It's nice, how you all look out for each other. Don't see that very often.'

I cling hard to the walker as we make our slow way out of the bay and out of the ward, a ponderous procession, all dressing-gowned up. If we do go along with Jodie's preposterous plan, we'll need coats and proper shoes, not dressing gowns and slippers. I'll have to ask Jake to bring some clothes in for me. Socks. I'll definitely need socks, now I'm free of the stockings of doom.

'You okay?' Kat says, turning to me as I loiter at the back, behind her and Jodie who is pushing Barbara's chair.

'Mmm. Just a bit slow, sorry.'

'You're always apologising, you know.'

'Oh. Sorry.'

Kat laughs.

Heat rushes to my face and I fumble for words. 'Oh, sorry… um, I mean, yeah, that's true.'

'You don't have to be so sorry all the time.' Her blue eyes are intense with meaning and something like power. 'You can be more at ease with yourself.'

I shrug. I don't know what to say to this confident, tattooed vicar who seems to carry the wisdom of the world and a whole load of compassion besides. Whenever she talks to me I get a lump in my throat, as if the tears I haven't shed for many years might be pushing somewhere close to my eyes, as if her presence unlocks something secret in my wildest places, something I'm not sure I want to visit.

We push through the doors into the coolness of the corridor, soothing after the artificial heat of the ward. It stretches out before us, long and rambling, reaching far and away into more departments and wards and theatres and the intensive care unit. It's a hub of activity, medical staff rushing to and fro, admin staff striding down the hallway with clipboards and buff files laden with endless pages, patients shuffling along with drip stands, and early visitors waiting outside wards to be allowed in. The Peace Garden is quiet, though, no one else braving the cold, despite the weak sunshine pushing through the November sky. I lean on my walker and turn my face to the sun, closing my eyes and allowing its fragile rays to stroke my face.

Jodie parks Barbara by the bench and lights up. She sees me watching her and throws her palms up, cigarette clamped in the corner of her mouth. 'Don't worry, don't worry, I'm not coming near you.' She wanders over to the other side of the garden where a path snakes through the fallow flowerbeds and stands staring into space, puffing away. Kat and I sit down on the tatty old bench and it creaks in dismay.

'You okay, Barbara?' Kat says, turning to Barbara and tucking an edge of blanket underneath her shoulder. She reminds me of Jake as a baby, all swaddled in his pram, cocooned from the nasty world out there.

She smiles and the glow of it lights her faded eyes. For seconds I get a glimpse of who she once was, the Barbara who married Bill and loved him for sixty years. The glint of light in her eyes has an edge of mischief but an edge of something else, as well, a darker edge, an edge that tells of sadness and weariness. I wonder what her life has been like. I wonder if she's always been ill, like me and Jodie. I wonder who she really is.

'I know my mouse is somewhere near,' she says.

Kat and I exchange a look.

'Are you warm enough?' Kat says.

'Ooh, girl, I'm toasty. Don't worry about me!'

We sit in companionable silence, watching the clouds race across the sun and the bare branches of the fruit trees waving in the chill breeze. I shiver and wrap my dressing-gown tighter.

Jodie finishes her cigarette and wanders over. 'She's loving this, isn't she,' she says, nodding to Barbara, who has her face upturned to the afternoon sky, a smile playing round her cracked lips.

'She is,' Kat says. 'But we shouldn't keep her out too long.'

Barbara shakes her head. 'I'm fine. Stop fussing, woman. I like it out here.'

Kat smiles. 'I'm glad.'

'Used to sit out in the garden with my Bill. He liked to grow vegetables, he did. Didn't always turn out so well, mind. You should've seen some of his carrots. They were all bendy, they were, and I says to him, expect me to peel those things? And he says yes, I expect you will, because you can do anything with food. And he was right, too.' Her face clouds over and she picks at a corner of her blanket. 'He was my rock.'

No one says anything, but Kat tucks the blanket back around Barbara's arm, and keeps her own hand on top of it.

'Listen,' Barbara says, after a few moments have passed. 'You hear that bird?'

I strain to hear. I can't hear much, but there is a muted shrill of birdsong, a ghost of summer mornings, reminding us of nature's glory even in winter. 'I hear it,' I say.

Barbara leans her head back on the chair, smiling.

Jodie is grinning away. 'What's tickling you?' Kat says.

Jodie gesticulates at Barbara. 'It's just, she's doing well, isn't she? If she's like this we can do it, can't we?'

'Do what?' Barbara says.

Kat shakes her head at Jodie.

'Y'know, Barbara. I mean, we can keep bringing you for some fresh air.'

'You will take me to the sea, though, won't you?' Barbara says, unaware of the hope whispering through the air and through our weary minds.

Maybe Jodie is right. Maybe we *could* do this thing.

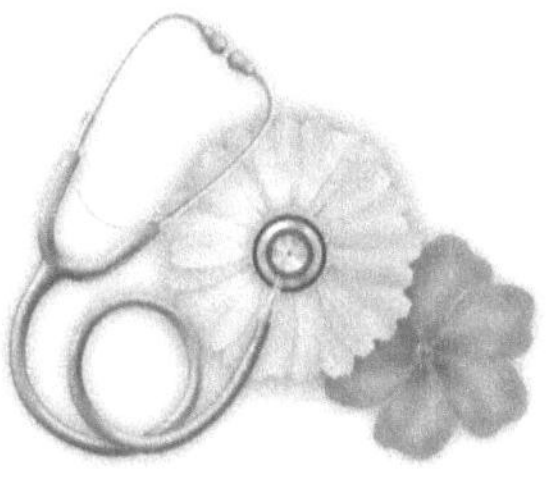

Chapter 14

'SOMEBODY GET THIS man off my bed!'

I try to wake up, open my eyes, but they are pinned shut, as if I am being held down, my limbs immobilised. Wake me up, wake me up somebody, I try to say, try to scream, but no sound comes out of my mouth.

'Nurse!'

I wake up with my chest in a vice, confused and disorientated. Where am I? There's a clamour in the bay, a whoosh of air, patters of feet, outraged shouts.

Over the bay Violet is on her feet, quivering from head to toe, her face screwed up with rage and something like fear. A nurse I don't recognise is standing next to her, telling her to breathe. Nicki dashes into the bay and over to her bed and pulls at something. Someone. A man, lying on Violet's bed.

Harold.

'I got back from my smoke and found him there!' Violet waves her arms around. 'In my bed, cheeky as you like! Get him out of there, nurse!'

'Harold!' Nicki says.

No response.

She shouts in his ear. 'Harold! You're in the ladies' bay!'

Harold stirs and groans. I wonder how long he's been there. He opens his eyes and closes them again, then opens them wide. 'What...?'

Nicki slows her voice down. 'You've got in the wrong bed, flower. In the wrong bay.' She looks around at Violet and me and Jodie. 'He's in this bed space in Bay D. Must've used your loo and then forgot where he was. Now, Harold, let's get you back to bed, shall we? Poor Violet, stood there shivering when she's been so poorly. Kelly!' She hails a healthcare assistant lingering at the door. 'Get some new sheets for Violet's bed, quick now.'

Kelly scuttles off. There's clearly a pecking order of healthcare assistants in here, and Nicki is most definitely at the top.

Violet wraps her arms around her chest. 'It's a jolly good thing I wasn't in that bed when he got into it.' Her mouth is a thin slash of disapproval.

'It's a bit funny, though, isn't it,' Jodie says, a smile curling the edges of her mouth.

Violet purses her lips and her nostrils flare. 'No. Not in the least. Get this man out of here, nurse. This is why I asked for a room of my own! This always happens.'

Jodie smirks. 'What, when you're in with the commoners, you mean?'

Violet sticks out her chin and sniffs.

Jodie doesn't leave it be. 'An' what, so you're saying random dudes climb into your bed every time you come into hospital? Lucky you.' She catches my eye and grins.

Violet huffs. 'Stop being so—'

'What? So chavvy? So gobby? You don't seem to care so much when you ask me to light your fag for you.'

'Come on, Harold.' Nicki has Harold on his feet at last, taking firm hold of his arm. He looks older than he did last time I saw him, his face criss-crossed with jagged lines, sparse hair all askew, eyes wild. His dirty pyjama top is inside out.

'Where am I?'

Nicki leads him out of the bay. 'Let's get you back, flower. It's okay. You're okay.'

He shuffles along with her like a small child with his mother, clinging to her arm, head hung low, compliant and silent. I think he has tears in his eyes.

'Come on, petal. Everything is going to be okay.'

Nicki, somehow, always makes everyone okay in the end.

When the doctors' rounds begin, I am sitting up out of bed. I want them to see that I am doing well, that I have more strength, that I will be able to go home next week. This morning, for the first time in ten days, I managed my own shower. I sat on the fold-down chair, water pummelling my face and my body until I folded myself into it and wished it would never stop. I scrubbed the built-up filth out of my bird's nest hair and then brushed out the tangles.

I sit here in my clean pyjamas and fleecy dressing gown, scrolling through my Facebook feed, my stomach squirming as I wait to see if he has the CT results and what they will show.

He strolls in with his entourage packed closely round him. They take an age looking over the patient charts, whispering to the nurse who is still dispensing our morning meds. I hear snatches of conversation, of my name and Jodie's and Violet's names. Another doctor stands at the end of Barbara's bed, trying to get her attention. Barbara's mouth is slack, open in a soft snore. A junior doctor who looks a whole lot like a very young Himesh Patel is talking to Kat, her curtains closing off the sight but not the sounds. 'We're pleased with your progress,' he is saying.

Jodie leans over to me. 'Wish he was my doctor. Hot or what?'

Kat says, 'Can I go home then?'

'Not yet,' he says, in a voice barely broken. 'The consultant wants you in a few more days, to make sure you're all clear.'

Dr Chowdhury keeps giving me sidelong glances, talking in low tones to his students and juniors at the same time, hunched over an iPad. His face is lined with a strained frown. He catches me watching and nods at me, coming over and pulling the curtains around us. Just me and him, today. My heart beats faster, my palms spiky with sweat.

'It's not the best news.'

A shiver explodes in my stomach.

'But not the worst, either. It's as I thought, though. It's spread – see here.' He shows me the CT image on his tablet. Even I can see the blotches that look like a child has splashed a bubble print on the surface of my lungs. 'Unfortunately, there's further scarring.' He scrolls back to another image, my CT scan from a couple of years back. 'Look, here – and here. You had hardly any in this lobe, but now, well, you can see.'

I can see. It's spreading, degenerating, progressing, whatever word you want to use. Maybe one day my lungs will simply collapse in on themselves, one great big bubble about to pop when the damage is too crushing.

'I know it's upsetting, Penny. But you're strong. Look how quickly you've thrown this one off. You were in quite a state when you arrived less than two weeks ago. I have to admit I was worried. You were nearly sent to the high dependency unit, that first night, you know, but you rallied on the oxygen. You'll be fine. Just keep on with the physio and the meds routine, and, well, it could slow down.'

None of what he is saying helps, but I smile up at him anyway.

'It's probable that eventually you'll be looking at a transplant,' he says softly. 'Not for a long time, I hope.'

I swallow and look down.

'There's every reason to be optimistic. Try to keep positive, Penny. You have that son of yours to keep you going, don't you?'

I do.

There is an ocean of tears swimming inside me, trying to spill out, but it stays there all confined, threatening to burst its bank and break me into pieces. I wish the tears would flow, and I wish a little bit that I could drown in them.

'You okay?' Kat says to me as Dr Chowdhury pulls back my curtains and moves on to Jodie.

I shrug.

'Sorry, I don't mean to pry,' she says. 'It's just, I can see you're upset.'

I fiddle with a loose thread on my dressing gown.

'You know, if you ever need to talk…'

Go away. Go away and leave me alone.

'Yeah. Thanks.'

I don't trust anyone. Don't want to trust anyone.

Kat gives me a soft smile and the dry tears push harder and I curse my frailty.

'It's okay. You don't have to say anything.'

'Just leave me alone.'

Kat shrinks back. 'I'm sorry—'

'You always have to be Mrs Perfect, don't you?' I bite down on my lip, trying to suck the words back from the shocked silent air. Why did you say that, Penny?

Kat falters. 'I…'

I shake my head, trying to clear away the noise. 'I'm sorry. I'm sorry.'

'Please don't do that. You're right, I should butt out.'

She hasn't done anything wrong. It's Karen who is always the perfect one, always the one I can't compare to, the one who so highlights my shortcomings. Why am I throwing all my rubbish out at Kat, at this sick patient next to me who seems to care?

I am beside myself, this dried-out broken husk, wishing I could put myself back together and inhabit a space where light got in and shadows didn't lurk.

Kat leans back into her pillow and closes her eyes.

I pick at the bleeding skin around my nails. 'I just, I mean, the doctor just told me that things are getting worse with my disease.'

Kat doesn't reply. She sits up, moves her body round to face me and sits on the edge of her bed, hands on her knees, those intense blue eyes ablaze with great unsettling compassion.

I tear off a flap of skin and flinch. 'It's just that… I don't know. That I just wanted to be a good mum.'

Where did that come from?

Kat gazes at me. Like she actually cares enough to climb into this moment with me.

I can't stop the words. 'I could never be a normal mum, you know? Like the others in the playground, all taking their kids everywhere for this and that, for sports and scouts and whatever else. Jake's been like a prisoner in my home with me, sometimes, when I'm too sick to do anything, and now I'm just getting sicker. It's just not fair, you know? Why do some people get an easy time of it in life and not others?'

Kat nods. 'I know.'

A heat blooms in my throat. 'Do you? You have it all, don't you? I mean, I know you're ill now and everything, but, like, you're not usually are you? And you have this man who adores you and so many friends and…'

Stop, Penny. Stop being a joy killer. Stop being here.

Kat stares down at her hands. Her fingernails are spattered with the remains of pearlescent purple polish, and nearly all of her fingers are laden with rings, silver and gold and white gold. Her engagement ring is a large sapphire set in a star of diamonds.

Marcus never bought me an engagement ring at all.

'No one's life is perfect, Penny,' she says softly.

'All very well for you to say. Probably why you have faith and all that. 'Cause you haven't lived like someone like me.'

Shut up Penny shutupshutup.

Kat droops, but she doesn't turn away, she doesn't tell me where to go. A dark shadow cuts through her eyes, dulling their power.

I gather myself together. 'Sorry. Sorry.'

She breathes out slowly. 'People's lives are mostly messy. You might think I have it all, but what if I look at you and think you have everything I want?'

Her voice is raspy, broken up, shards of meaning slicing through her words.

I stare at her.

'What if you have the one thing I can't have?'

A lump clogs up my throat. *Jake.* 'Oh. I'm so sorry. You mean…?'

She blinks and looks down.

I lean in towards her, grab her hands. 'I'm sorry. I always say the wrong thing.'

'I don't want you to apologise, Penny. I just wanted to share with you that we're not always what we seem on the outside, and pain can go deep.'

'I'm so sorry.'

Kat puffs out her cheeks. 'Will you stop apologising, woman?'

I try to smile. 'I'll try.'

'I'm sorry about your disease,' she says, squeezing my hands. 'That's rubbish.'

'Yeah.'

'But you'll be out of here soon? Back home with Jake?'

I lift my shoulders.

'And before that,' Kat says, suddenly grinning, 'we have a special trip to go on, don't we?'

Sister Harris wanders into the ward, rubbing sanitiser into her hands and surveying the patients, bushy eyebrows raised. 'Well, well, well. Not you lot again!'

Jodie laughs. 'Can't get rid of us that easy, Sister.'

'Hmm. Very rare, actually, to have the same patients in a bay for so long. It's usually like Piccadilly, all comings and goings all hours of the day and night.' She looks at Kat. 'You cast a spell, or said a prayer, or whatever you do?'

Kat smiles enigmatically.

'Still, you'll all be off home before we know it, won't you? We don't want you lot clogging up these beds longer than you need to.' She grins round at us, warm brown eyes sparkling, and then plucks Barbara's chart from the end of her bed.

'What?' Barbara says, straining forward to hear. Her hair is standing straight up, a thin white shock of it, as if she's stuck a finger in an electric socket. 'Did you say I can go home?'

'Not quite yet, Barbara my love,' Sister Harris says, scouring the notes. 'Few days, though. You're doing all right, aren't you?'

I'm not sure she is, really. I heard her doctor discussing her with one of the nurses yesterday, talking about discharging her back to her care home. It wouldn't be long, the doctor said, that would be the best place for her to go more comfortably and quietly, among her familiar things with familiar people. Jodie heard her, too, and said that we should get planning, because this was going to be the only chance Barbara got. What if we missed the opportunity, and they came to take Barbara away, and she never saw the outside world again?

Nicki comes back into the bay with Kelly in her wake. 'Heard you took her for a little fresh air yesterday,' she says to Jodie, nodding her head at Barbara. 'Did her the world of good, that did. Such a kind thing to do. You going to take her again today? She's kept on about it ever since, she has.'

Jodie grins. 'That's the plan. And tomorrow. Every day.'

Sister Harris doesn't look convinced.

'You make it sound like you're all here to stay for good.' Nicki winks at Sister Harris. 'You only want to stay for the five-star service, I know.'

Kat laughs. 'You're right there. And the gourmet cuisine.'

'Of course.'

'Well, not me,' Violet says, screwing up her nose. 'The food in here is disgusting. And they let men wander in here in the dead of night and get into our beds. And even after all that they still won't give me my own room. What's the world coming to?'

Jodie hisses something under her breath. I think it's probably something Jake would say.

Amina clears her throat. 'Will you stop moaning, woman. You are lucky to have this health care, in this country. You should be grateful, not all this whinging all the time.'

We stare at her.

And then Jodie laughs. 'Too right, Amina. Too right.'

Violet crosses her arms, rolls her eyes and sniffs loudly.

But she doesn't say anything.

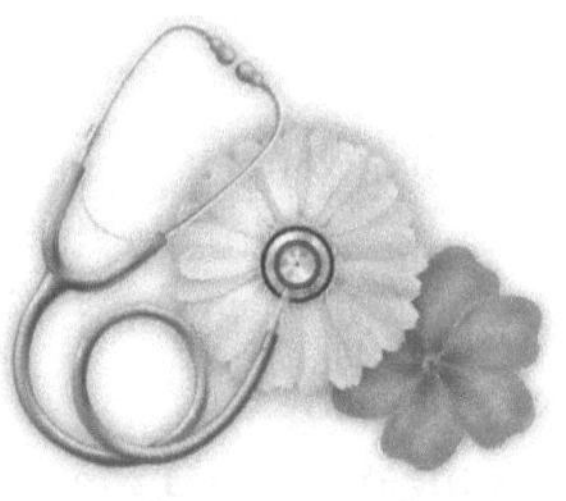

Chapter 15

IT'S MORNING AND the early shift is doing the changeover. They stop at the foot of each bed in the bay, catching up the new shift on each patient. They talk about us but not to us, as if we are not really there. 'Penny Fielding, in with pneumonia. She's on day eleven of fourteen days tobramycin and ceftazidime and responding well. Just needing three hourly obs now, keep an eye on her blood pressure please as it's been a bit low. She's off the oxygen now and looking to go home early next week. Oh, and she needs a new cannula in, can you do that one Laura?'

I'm glad I'm doing so well, but I wish they would look at me, acknowledge that I am a person, I am here and I can hear. They move on to Jodie en masse and talk in low tones I cannot quite catch. They'll be saying she can go home in the next few days, too. All of us on the ward, in fact, are like different people; if not sprightly, at least a little more colour in our cheeks, a little more wind in our sails. A few days back I was washed up on some distant shore after a great storm, battered and bruised and half-drowned, but I've crawled slowly up the beach and now I'm on my feet, a little wobbly but on my way to recovery. I look over at Violet; she looks different to how she looked the other day, less dishevelled, less hollowed out. She is drinking a cup of tea and eyeing the crowd of nurses with great suspicion.

She catches me looking at her. 'The doctor is going to let me go home today. He said so yesterday.'

'Oh, that's good, then,' I say. I don't think he did say that, actually, but I don't tell her that. I think he might have said something about her going home sooner rather than later, but not as soon as this. She's pale round the edges, dark shadows under her eyes telling the tale of where she has been over the past days.

Amina says, 'You cannot go yet.'

Violet scowls at her. 'The doctor said—'

'No, what I mean is, you must stay, so that you can be with us on our outing to the seaside.'

Violet frowns harder. 'Don't be silly, woman. That's not actually going to happen, is it? It's some ludicrous scheme of Jodie's. We played along, is all.' Then she mutters something else under her breath. Something possibly about not being interested in the opinion of certain people.

Amina just shrugs.

Funny, that's what I thought at first, that it was all some kind of game. But now my stomach drops at Violet's words and I realise that I do, after all, want to go along with this bonkers plan. I want to make Barbara glow, and there's something more than that. I look around the ward, look at each of these ladies in turn, women I had never met in my life two weeks ago, women I'd never have dreamed of being friends with. I would care, I suddenly realise, if one of us was moved out of the bay tonight. As I look at them something washes over me; a feeling of solidarity, strength, and something like hope, too.

I will be disappointed if we don't, somehow, make this thing happen.

Amina clasps both hands over her mug and gazes over at me, then back at Violet. 'I think we can do this. I think that Barbara needs us to. All of us.'

'Well, you can do it if you like. I will be home and warm and catching up on *Eastenders,* thank you.' Violet scowls up at the defunct TV system, the wretched thing Brian couldn't get to work even after pouring thirty quid into it. Even Jake couldn't work his usual techy magic on it. It's ancient tech, he'd said, shrugging his shoulders and conceding defeat. The youth of today, Violet had said, and Brian had muttered something about how disgraceful they all are, and how he would complain to the hospital and get his money back.

'Well, we'll be on the beach, watching the sea and the sky,' Amina says, her eyes far away.

'And flaming freezing,' Violet says smugly.

After the doctors' rounds, Violet is silent, shrivelled up like a daffodil that bloomed for a day then wilted, staring into space. Nobody asks her if she is going home.

Jodie is chipper today, blazing with energy and excitement. 'I think tomorrow is the day,' she says, her eyes flicking left to right, standing by my bed and wielding her phone at me. 'Saturday is always quieter in hospital, anyway. No one on to us a hundred times an hour for bloods and physio and whatnot. I've checked the weather forecast, too, see here, and it's basically the best weather in weeks. A sign, I reckon.' She glances at Kat, who lifts her shoulders gently. 'Says it's gonna be dry all day, well, most of the day, anyway. Bit nippy, but it is November. If we go, like, straight after lunch, that's always dead time isn't it? Hardly anyone around. Besides, we'll just say we're going to the Peace Garden as usual.' She waves her arms around, gabbling at a hundred miles an hour, barely pausing for breath. It's like the air itself is breathless, grasping hold of her every word, all of us leaning forward apart from Barbara, who is sleeping, and Violet, who slumps back in her chair. She's listening, though, the lines on her face vivid in motion, twitching up and down in disapproval then softening a little, and then hardening once again.

Jodie takes a deep breath in, and I can hear the hiss of her wheeze. 'Yeah, so it says there might even be a bit of sun in the afternoon. Might warm it up a bit. And we only have to be out the van for a bit, like.'

'Okay.' Kat holds her palm up. 'Look. If we're seriously thinking about this, we should think about each aspect of it. So, you say, Kane could drive us in his van – does it have enough seats, and does it have seatbelts?'

Violet mutters something about health and safety gone mad.

Jodie nods furiously. 'Yeah. It's a minibus, all kitted out and everything. Space for the wheelchair too. And he's a safe driver.' She pouts at my doubtful look. 'He is, 'cause he's been a lorry driver before. So you don't have to stress.'

'Right,' says Kat, scratching her head, possibly wondering, like me, why Kane is no longer a lorry driver. 'And where is this beach you are thinking of? Does it have a car park?'

'Well there's this little bit of beach, not far. Not many people know about it 'cause it's not got shops or nothing like that. But you can literally park right on the sand. Honestly, you'll love it. It'll be perfect. I only know about it 'cause my mum used to take us there as kids, used to say it was her hidden gem.'

'Hmm. So you can drive onto the beach. Are you sure?'

'Yeah, for definite. We honestly won't have to do any walking unless we want to just walk down to the water from the van and everything.'

'You've thought it all out.'

'Yeah.'

'What about getting to the van, then?' Amina says. 'We are not very strong.'

'Kane will help. He can take us down one at a time if we need. But most of us could probably make it out there now, couldn't we? Kat? Penny?'

We both nod.

'Violet can, she's fast on her feet when she wants to be, like when she wants a fag. 'Specially with that frame thing. She's like a little kid charging along behind a baby walker, aren't you, Vi?'

Violet turns her back to us, the rigid line of her shoulders a palpable statement of non-intent.

Jodie shrugs. 'Ah, she'll come round.'

'I suppose I could manage,' Amina says. Then her shoulders drop. 'I mean, if it is okay, that I come with you?'

'Don't be so daft. Course you're coming.'

Amina smiles, and her eyes light the whole room.

Violet sniffs.

Kat taps her finger against her lips. 'Okay, so, say we can all get to the entrance and Kane brings Barbara in one of the hospital chairs. Where will he park? And how will he get Barbara in? Those chairs don't collapse down, you know, and they're heavy beasts.'

'It'll be fine,' Jodie says. 'He'll find a space. And even if he doesn't, he'll get us down there then go and get the van and bring it right to us. And he's got a ramp thing. Stop stressing.'

'I suppose that could work,' Kat says, though her voice drips with misgiving. She sounds like she knows she should be the grown-up here, she's the one in a position of authority, the sensible, clear-headed one. I can almost see the thoughts whizzing round her head, eyes flicking here and there as she computes the likelihood of this working. 'It's only a little trip. Hardly different to going to the Peace Garden, really. And they don't actually mind if you go out of the hospital sometimes, you know.'

'True,' Jodie says, 'I've been out for meals and stuff, when I couldn't stand the grub here any longer.'

'So it's just like that, isn't it?'

'Exactly.'

But it's not really just like that. When patients go off ward and off premises, they're generally up to it, and they're generally not confused eighty-seven-year-old ladies who might die any day. Perhaps if they're with safe family members, but even then I can't see Sister Harris complying.

'Tomorrow, then?' Jodie says, and gazes round the bay at each of us.

Nods. All nods, apart from Violet, who remains stiff and implacable, and Barbara who is fast asleep, dreaming of crashing waves and sand between her toes.

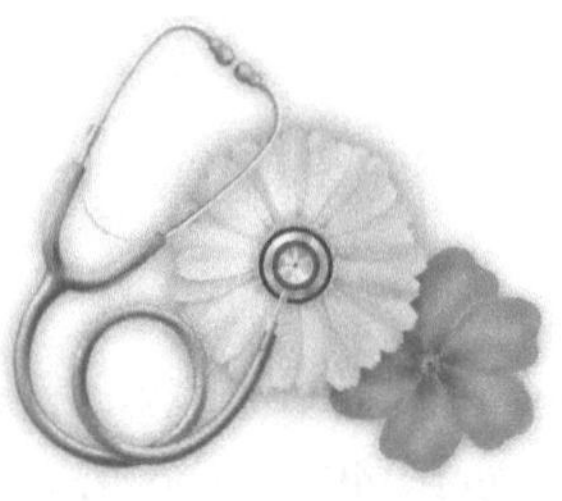

Chapter 16

LATER IN THE day the bay is full of visitors. The hospital is buzzing with that Friday afternoon feel, patients being discharged before the weekend, doctors rushing round with their tablets and their bulging files. Everything has to get wrapped up on a Friday, because things shut down over the weekend, some things anyway. Patients still get admitted and diagnosed and treated. But everything else gets pared down, especially for patients like us who are almost ready for home. There's less stress in the ward, less rushing from here to there with obs machines and drips and oxygen canisters. Perhaps that's all going on in the other bays, but here we are ready for the relative calm of the weekend. Outside my window the sky is heavy, clouds like sheets all draped across the heavens in a hundred layers of white and grey.

Kat has five people around her bed, an older couple and two younger women, all leaning in and laughing uproariously, with Nate on the chair right next to her bed, holding her hand. 'Oh, by the way, did you remember my coat?' she says. 'For tomorrow, I mean, for that little outing I told you about.'

Nate drags something out of a Tesco bag.

'Nate!' she says, rolling out the name and her eyes at the same time. 'Seriously?'

'What?'

'It's hardly my big winter coat, is it? Don't think this is going to protect me from the November wind, do you? What are you like, bringing me a great boiling onesie for a hospital ward and a festival raincoat for a cold winter day?'

Nate scratches his head and casts his gaze over at the wall.

Kat grabs his hand. 'You daft sod.'

He smiles like he knows a secret, and then picks up a corner of her dressing gown. 'Can't you go in this?'

'I suppose.'

Jake has brought me some clothes in, but they're not very suitable. He's managed to unearth my baggiest pair of leggings, the ones with the waist that's almost gone, prone to falling down whenever I walk more than two steps, and an old grey jumper that doesn't look like it's been washed in a while. They look like all my other clothes, tired and worn and greyed. 'I didn't know what to bring, Mum. I knew you'd want something warm, if you're going outside.'

I haven't told Jake anything much about our plans. I've just told him we're planning a little wander out of the hospital grounds and so would prefer some outdoor clothes.

'I brought this as well.' He reaches into his rucksack and pulls out my black parka, and I sag with relief. 'And these, for your feet.'

Ballet flats. Tiny, thin ballet flats. 'Jake, I said my ankle boots.'

'Couldn't find them.'

I sigh. 'Socks?'

'Here.' He plucks out a pair of big red fluffy slipper socks. I'm not sure they'll jam into the ballet flats, but they'll keep my feet warm, I suppose.

'What about my hat and gloves I asked you for?'

He brandishes a bulging Aldi bag at me.

'What's that?'

'Well how was I supposed to know which hat and scarf or whatever you want?'

'Jake, did you just tip the entire contents of our hat and gloves basket into this bag?'

He shoots his eyes off to the side and twists his mouth in a wry little grin.

'Jake!'

'Doesn't matter, does it? You can get what you want and I'll take the rest home.' He shoves the bag on the floor under my chair, then gazes at me. 'Listen, Mum, I... I made you something.'

'What?'

He rolls his eyes. 'There's no need to look so surprised. I do occasionally do nice things, don't I?'

'Umm, yes...'

'Wow.' He scowls. 'Well, this time I have, anyway.'

I grin at him. 'What do you want? Money for a takeaway? New trainers?'

'Muuum!' He stares at me, more exasperated than amused.

'Sorry. Just trying to be... I mean, just a little joke.'

He grunts.

'So, show me then,' I say. 'What've you made?'

His cheeks flush with colour and he stands there, his backpack on the floor, twisting his hands together.

'I just made you this.' He bends and digs into the bag, then drops a large envelope onto my bed. I stare. Jake doesn't make things. Jake doesn't do things that are not on the computer or the phone or the football pitch. Jake doesn't do things for me.

'Well open it, then.' He gazes at his bitten down fingernails. I pull a card out of the envelope, a piece of computer photo card folded in two. Turn it over and stare.

'I know sunflowers are your favourite flower. And I know you can't have flowers in hospital. And I know you think real cards are a bit boring and all that.'

I swallow, overcome.

'I did it in GIMP.'

'Um—'

'Oh Mum, don't look at me with those what are you into now eyes, like you think I'm into something creepy. It's an open-source graphics program.'

'Oh. Okay.'

'And so here, I like free drew the petals using the paintbrush tool and then I gave them an alpha mask and kind of used this gradient to fill them, like orange to yellow, see here?'

'I, um—'

'It was actually this method I found on YouTube. And you see this centre bit, right, I just wanted it to be like unique or something, not like any old photo you can get off the internet, so I made the pattern myself then imported it as a bucket fill and, oh, you don't need me to witter on about all this.'

'I do.' And I know I do. I need to hear all this stuff I don't understand the slightest edges of, and he needs to tell me. 'I do, actually.'

He reddens. 'Okay, so, I did that and then I did kind of this thing for the background, I know your favourite colour is purple so I got all these different purple textures, see here, I did them all as layers and then blended them together, and then I thought, well I thought it sort of looked okay, actually.'

'It looks more than okay. It's brilliant, Jake. I love it.'

His flush deepens. 'Well, it's not Banksy or anything like that. But it was kind of fun. Nan lets me go on the computer more than you do so... so this.'

Mum probably does that to spite me. She's done it at every turn, at every parenting decision, taking the opposite tack deliberately and sneakily, undermining me in the most insidious of ways so I couldn't challenge her, not with Jake so precious and me so alone. I shove the thought away. That doesn't matter right now.

'I love you, Jake.'

'I miss you.'

'I miss you too.'

He leans towards me and circles me in his arms, carefully, like I'm made of china. I draw him in and hug him close, his cheek against mine like when he was small and he would press his face against mine and tell me he loved me mummy. I inhale the scent of him, chewing gum and stale curry and Lynx, and think about how I did this all alone. Okay, he's not perfect. He's annoying and rude and sometimes arrogant. He thinks the world exists for him alone at times and his room is like an antechamber to the underworld with plates and glasses culturing unusual species and clothes thrown in great piles together on the floor, dirty and clean all mixed up. He is messy and insensitive and ungrateful.

But he made me a card with an amazing piece of computer artwork on it.

I wish his dad could see him now, the baby he abandoned because he wanted to live his life and I had spoiled that for him. I wish he could have been the kind of dad who cuddled him as a tiny newborn smelling of baby oil, could have swung him in the air as a toddler and kicked a ball in the garden with him as a small boy with legs that never stayed still. I wish he could see him now as the young man on the cusp of adulthood, changing every day, his voice deepening and his legs lengthening, my skinny gentle giant who made me a card with a sunflower on it that looks like all the colours of day and night together. But his dad didn't want to know. He's the one who missed out.

He's the one who left bruises that blossomed on the inside of my mind and my soul, as well as the other ones, the ones he hid so well. But I don't want to think about those.

'I thought it kind of looked like sunrise. Like the flowers are kind of the sun. Actually, that sounds lame.' He shakes his head.

'It doesn't sound lame at all. I love it. It's like the sunset with all the colours exploding in the sky and the sunflower is the dawn breaking through the night. I love it. You could do more of this stuff, you know. People would pay good money.'

Jake scowls. 'Whatever.' He fishes in his pocket and pulls out his phone, and in seconds he is lost to me, caught up in his online world. His eyelashes lie on his cheeks like they did when he was a baby, all full and fanned out and dark and heartbreaking. I remember holding him close through unsettled nights and days that seemed to last forever, no partner to come in and relieve the burden at the end of the day. I held him tight through the years, through tantrums and bleeding knees and bad behaviour and school reports that weren't always complimentary. I held him tight when his first girlfriend dumped him because he wasn't as cute as Alex James. He was a cuddly baby, a huggy child, a boy who always needed touch to sustain him, even through those difficult pre-teen years. He still needs me now, I realise, perhaps more than ever, in his uncouth, grunting, gentle and sweet way, he needs my love and my patience.

He needs me to be here and to not get even more sick.

I want to sink into the colours he created for me, to pretend that they are my colours after all, that I deserve them, or maybe even that I could be them.

I reach out my hand and stroke his face. He glances up at me for a second and rolls his eyes; I'm surprised they are not worn out from the copious rolling he puts them through every hour of every day. 'Muuum,' he says again, but he doesn't ask me to stop. Instead he leans into my touch, his acne-puckered cheek rough against my hand, dark hair flopping forward.

I did this. I did this all alone. I recovered from abuse and I brought up this young man who made me a sunflower card.

'I do love you, Mum.'

'I love you too.'

'Nan and Grandad love you too, you know, in their way. Grandad's been on about coming in to see you.'

'Has he?'

Jake nods, but his eyes reflect the doubt that burns in my own, and he looks down at his hands. He knows Dad could have come in to see me, any day, but he hasn't. He never does.

I lean back into my pillows and watch Jake as he stabs at his phone, his thumbs working furiously as he battles some unknown monster.

Over in the opposite corner, Barbara is sitting up in her chair, wide awake. She's watching Jake with a gaze full of longing. 'Let's go and chat to Barbara,' I say to him. Surprisingly, he doesn't complain, doesn't make a murmur, just flings his phone down on the bed, drags two bucket chairs to her space and helps me over, holding onto my arm.

'Hello, Barbara.'

She nods her head. 'Yes. Hello, love. And you, lad.'

Jake nods. ''S'up.'

Barbara regards him with questioning eyebrows.

'How are you?' Jake says.

'Oh, I'm very well, dear.'

I take in her face, ravaged like a map full of contour lines, watery, weary eyes blinking against the light of the ward. Not well, not really.

Now I'm here I don't know what to say to her. I swallow. 'You feeling better, then, Barbara?'

'Pardon? Speak up, dear.' She fiddles with her hearing aid and it shrieks in squeaky rebuke.

'I just said, are you feeling a little better?'

'Oh, yes, darling. Yes. But…' She leans closer and beckons me in with a wizened, arthritic finger. 'But that rat was here again. I saw it.'

This again.

'The rat's gone, Barbara.'

Jake smiles at her. 'There's no rats in here, no need to worry.'

'The rat is after my mouse.'

'It's okay, Barbara.' I try to channel Kat, to take her hand, but she snatches it away and hisses at me.

'You don't know. You can't see it. But I can.'

It's Jake that steps in for me. 'I promise it's gone,' he says, looking into her eyes. She gazes back at him with a kind of wonder.

'You promise?'

'I promise.'

'The rat was in our house. Me and Bill's. It got in the loft and we could hear it scrabbling at night, patter patter patter on the ceiling. I thought it was the ghost.'

'The ghost?' Jake says.

'Oh, pay no mind of me. Just a silly old woman. But Bill, he says to me, that's no ghost, that's rats that is. And he was right. But now they won't leave me alone, see. They chase my mouse all the time.'

'I'm sorry,' Jake says.

Barbara flaps her hand at him. 'Ooh, no doubt you'll be thinking I'm just some daft old bag, saying a load of stupid things. But I'm still all here. Most of me.' She chuckles, and Jake smiles, and I do, too. 'Bill always said I'd forget my head if it weren't screwed on, he did. Said I was scatty as anything but that he still loved me to the stars. That's what he always said.' She gazes off to the side, eyes fixed on the wall but on something more inside her memories. I think about what her life must have been like, with a man who loved her for sixty years. I think about Kat with Nate and Amina with Bilal, men who are faithful and kind and loving, men who are nothing like Marcus or my own father who failed me a thousand times over in his disappointment and disapproval. Maybe I don't have to worry so much about Jake, if there are men like Bill and Nate and Bilal in the world; maybe Jake can be good and kind as well. I gaze at him as he sits quietly with Barbara, his hand on her arm so gentle, and I can see him for who he is, finally, through the haze of stroppy teenager and grumbling adolescence, through the haze of what I always dreaded he might become because of who his father is. He is nothing like Marcus, I see in a moment of raw clarity, joy jumping through my bones. He is Jake, he is my boy who cares about me and about a lonely old woman who is worried about rats.

'I'm going home tomorrow, they told me,' Barbara says suddenly.

My stomach sinks like a stone. 'Oh, did they? That's… I mean, that's nice, to be going to a nice place.' I scramble desperately through my mind for words to say that will console somebody who is going to a place to die, and through my own raging disappointment. 'What time… did they say when you'll be going?'

'Oh, in the morning, I expect,' Barbara says.

Our plans crash to the ground in a pile of dust. Barbara won't get to see the sea after all, she won't get to feel the sun on her face or the wind in her hair.

I take her hand. 'I'm sorry,' I whisper.

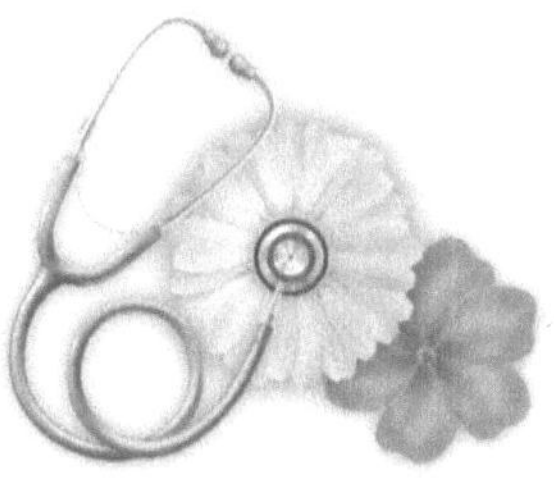

Chapter 17

'IT'S NOT GOING to happen.'

Jodie, Amina and Kat stare at me.

'What?' Jodie says. She blinks and then gawps at me as I share Barbara's news.

It might not be such a bad thing, I'm thinking. It really was a daft idea all along, after all. I mean, what were we thinking? Playing with the idea of taking a sick old woman to the beach in the middle of winter? We've been like schoolchildren gleefully planning to wag off lessons, but possibly never really intending to go through with it. I am bathed in a strange mixture of disappointment and relief. But mostly disappointment.

'Well, we just have to delay her transport,' Jodie says. 'And anyway, everyone knows that when hospital transport is arranged for the morning it doesn't come until late afternoon.'

True.

'But that's no good,' I say. 'What if they come when we're out? We'll be wasting their time and that's unfair.'

Jodie's shoulders sag.

Amina takes a deep breath in. 'I know this might seem an out-there idea, but what about if we actually ask the nurses? Tell them of our plan?'

Jodie shakes her head. 'Sister Harris'll never have it. You know that.'

'But I do not see another way. Maybe they will say it is a good idea, if we tell them we have it all planned out.'

'They're not going to say yes,' I say.

Amina rubs her chin, staring at the ceiling, and we stare up at it too, gazing at the discoloured tiles, patches of damp crawling over the edges, one of the recessed tile lights flickering and sputtering. We sag together in defeated silence.

'But what about if we just tell one?' Amina says.

Jodie perks up. 'What about Nicki?'

I shake my head. 'She could lose her job. She'd want to help, wouldn't she? She'd see this is what Barbara wants, but then she'd get in trouble for allowing it to happen and not letting any of the other staff know.'

Jodie puffs out her cheeks. 'But we're not doing anything wrong! We're only going for a bit of fresh air.'

'But it's where we are going that's the issue,' I say. 'You know that. Taking a vulnerable person off site. It's not on, really.'

Kat has been sitting silently, her hands busy with a crochet hook and a half-finished blanket, wave after wave in all the colours of the sea and sky. Blues and greens, turquoise and purple. I gaze at it and wish I could swallow myself up in its liquid depths. She looks up at us, her hands stilled for seconds, crochet hook paused in mid-air. 'We could at least ask Nicki or someone else what time the transport's coming for her.'

'They won't know,' I say.

'They'll know vaguely, won't they?'

'And then maybe we could say to them, could we just take her to the Peace Garden one more time?' Jodie says.

'It feels wrong,' I say.

Kane struts into the bay wearing a white Adidas tracksuit, working away at some chewing gum. 'All right?' he says to us, slumping down on Jodie's bed and digging out his phone.

Jodie simpers apologetically at us and turns towards him, sitting down on her bed next to him. He shoves her over. 'Can't you go on the chair? You're always hogging the bed.'

Kat raises her eyebrows at me.

Jodie does as she is commanded, obediently settling herself on her chair. 'Sorry. Just a bit knackered. Wanted to put my feet up.'

'Well, what else do you do all day in here? I've been out working, unlike some. Putting food on the table.'

Seriously, why does she take this?

Why did I take it?

Jodie looks down at her bunny slipper-clad feet. 'Well, I am in hospital, to be fair.' Her voice is small, the words hushed, almost like she doesn't want him to hear but still can't help saying them. She's a faded version of herself around him, like someone's been in and turned down her dimmer switch until her usual glow is so dulled it can barely be seen. But the glow hasn't gone out altogether.

Kat can't be doing with it, it turns out. 'Who do you think you are?' she says to Kane. 'Your girlfriend is ill. She's in hospital, you absolute loser. Get off the bed and let her lie down.'

Kane is speechless for seconds, then his face contorts into an ugly leer. 'Who the hell do you think you are, Mrs Vicar, telling me what to do? Oh so holier-than-thou, you are, just like all your types, think they are better than the rest of us, think they can tell us what to do. Well, you sour-faced bitch, I will do what I like, and at the moment I like sitting here.'

Jodie shakes her head at Kat, eyes big and wild and pleading. Kat flushes deep purple and grips her crochet hook so tightly the bones of her knuckles strain through her skin as she raises it slightly as if to position it to stab hard into Kane's leg.

Jodie takes hold of Kane's hand. 'Listen, babe, we was just sorting out the trip tomorrow. There's a bit of a set-back but I'm sure it'll be sorted.'

'It better bloody had, I'm taking time off work to ferry you lot round the countryside.'

Jodie nods furiously. 'It will, don't worry. We're just sorting it out, aren't we ladies?' She gazes round at each of us in turn, imploring us with her pale, beseeching eyes, posing a question that doesn't need to be asked.

Kat recovers herself first. 'It's fine. We'll be ready.'

I nod, too, smiling away as if Kane is my best friend and I can't wait to make him happy.

Amina flattens her lips, but doesn't say anything.

Brian shuffles in grasping a bulging Waitrose bag and sits down by Violet's bed. He is wearing brown cord trousers that barely graze his ankles and a dirty checked shirt missing some of its buttons. 'Look at the state of you,' she says, sitting up and brushing him down. 'Look like the cat dragged you in. Honestly, you men, you fall apart without a woman to sort you out.' She clicks her tongue loudly, sneaking a glance at me.

'What's eating you?' Brian says, unexpectedly.

Violet scowls at him and her scowl is so loaded with scorn I wonder if he will melt in the heat of it. 'Doctor says I have to wait another few days to go home.'

'Oh dear,' says Brian, but he doesn't sound too disappointed.

'Take that smirk off your face. Just because you can watch what you like on the telly and go and get fish and chips every night. Don't you miss me?'

Brian nods hastily. 'Yes, of course, dear.'

Violet huffs. 'Yes dear this, yes dear that.' She looks at his bag. 'That my coat?'

He nods.

Her face sags. 'You needn't've bothered. I'll not be needing it.'

Brian shrugs. 'Might as well leave it here for when you come home.'

She shrugs.

'You're grumpier than usual tonight,' he mutters.

Jodie speaks up, ignoring Kane who is immersed in his phone, spreading himself out until he takes up every last inch of her bed, like Henry VIII on his throne. 'It's 'cause she says she's not coming with us tomorrow, but she wants to really.'

'I don't want to go, not with them lot. They laugh at me.'

Brian looks bemused.

'Oh get a grip, Violet,' Jodie says. 'We're all just joshing, got to get through the day somehow. Stop sulking like a stroppy toddler just 'cause you can't go home today and watch *Eastenders*.'

Kane looks up with a sly little smile, and then looks down at his phone again. It seems he's fine with Jodie dishing out home truths to other people, then.

Violet puckers up her mouth. 'Well, I never.'

Brian exhales slowly. 'She's right, though, dear. I mean, I mean…' he stops, stumbling over his words, as Violet stares daggers at him.

'What, *dear?*'

'I just mean, it's just, you cut off your nose to spite your face, sometimes. I just want you to be happy.'

'Happy?' she says, wrapping splashes of great derision around the word as if it is foreign to her, as if she cannot imagine what it even means.

'Yes. Happy. And there's been times this last two weeks, in here, with these women… there's been times I've seen you smiling, like your old self, like the Violet I once knew.'

'Oh, what, so you want your young model Violet back? The one before COPD? The one before Covid?'

He strokes her arm. 'That's not what I mean, and you know it. I've just seen some kind of, I don't know, spark or something, in you, like you've been recharged somehow. I reckon this little outing would do you the world of good.'

Violet looks away, pouting.

'You should go,' he says softly.

'You tell her, Brian,' Kat says.

I sit amazed at this Brian I haven't seen or guessed at, out of the old shell of seriously henpecked husband, out of the old cliché of husband who is useless without wife. This Brian has something about him, something Violet may have tried to clobber out of him over the years.

Maybe the Violet he is talking about is in there somewhere, too.

I think again about Marcus and how he used to talk me down instead of up. Brian is patently not perfect, but he is on her side, he is for her, he wants her good. Of course, Marcus always told me he wanted my good, but it turned out my good was not good enough.

❧

I'M IN A bar on our honeymoon in Tenerife. I'm tired and hungry; we've been out on a boat trip around the south of the island, feeling the warm breeze on our faces. It's been a little taste of heaven, a time out of time when my body behaved as I wished it to, and I feel hopeful about the world and my future with my new husband. I know I've made the right choice, marrying Marcus, because he always wants nothing but the best for me, and no one has ever wanted that before. He picks out the outfits I should wear because he has a good eye, he knows what suits me and what doesn't, he only wants me to wear things that flatter me. I still can't believe that someone cares this much about me. I have a stunning figure, he tells me, I should show it off more, show a little more leg and wear lower cut tops to enhance what I have. I'm a little on the skinny side, he says, a little loose in places, but some more sessions at the gym will sort me out, will make me a better version of myself, a version he is even more proud to be seen with. Perhaps a little cosmetic surgery at some point. It's not that he's not proud to be seen with me now, of course, I know he is because he says so, he says that other men envy him when they see him with me; it's just that I could be even better.

'Are you wearing that?' he says, wandering into the bar in a loose evening suit, crisp white shirt with unbuttoned collar flashing an enticing hint of deep tan. He'd been in the shower when I got myself ready and shouted through the door that I'd meet him down here. I wanted to be sitting here on a stool, sipping at a cocktail and looking alluring in my short summery dress and sandals. I'd pinned a purple flower clip in my hair and thought I looked exotic and mysterious, all flushed with happiness and sunshine, a brand-new bride head-over-heels in love.

'What do you mean?' I say, wilting under his gaze like fresh spinach chucked in a pan of boiling water. I flinch at the slightly sardonic upturn of his mouth.

'Well, it's hardly flattering. It's a bit loose, to be honest.' He takes hold of my arm and grabs my cocktail, downing it in one gulp. 'Let's go and get you into something else, shall we? I was thinking that red dress I bought you, the one with the zip, you know.'

I go with him, of course, because I always go with him. He's right, you see. He knows what suits me better than I do, and he knows the dress I am wearing is too loose, too flowing, too floral; it skims my curves instead of clinging to them. The red dress squeezes the very bones of me and makes me breathless, but I know it looks good because he stands back, tapping his finger against his mouth with a satisfied – and somewhat lascivious – look creeping through his eyes. 'Hmm. Much better. Now, the shoes. Those sandals don't really go, do they?'

They don't, of course. He's right, as ever. It's lucky that he bought me some red stilettos to go with the red dress, isn't it? I push my feet into them and ignore the nip at my toes, trying to stand tall and stately and model-like. He stands there and inspects me, dissecting every part of me, still finding me wanting. I can see it in his eyes, hooded with disappointment. I've not tried hard enough. I should have been more careful with my make-up. I should have styled my hair differently. I should have been a different woman.

'You should take that flower thing out. It doesn't go with the look.' He grabs hold of the clip and yanks it out of my hair, throwing it on the floor. I wince. 'Now, how about you put it up in a knot? More classy, with that dress. Yes, that would work.'

He stands and stares while I brush out my loose brown waves, flecked with new blonde lights in the sun, and twist my hair into a tight knot, securing it with a gold barrette. I glance in the mirror. It looks severe, dragged off my face like that, tightening my skin and giving my eyebrows a slightly quizzical look. I tease out a few tendrils at the front and twirl them around my fingers.

'Now some lipstick. That new scarlet one I bought you, not the light pink one you wear. You need something dazzling.' I dig out the lipstick, an expensive brand I'd never normally buy, and slick it on to my lips. I look like a vampire, I think, with my slightly harsh looking hairdo and the scarlet slash across my mouth. I look like one of those slutty women with guitars in that Robert Palmer video.

I like the flowery dress more.

He stands back, assessing me with inscrutable eyes. 'You'll do,' he says, taking my arm and swinging me round, then pushing me towards the door. I totter on my heels, almost banging my head on the wall, and he laughs. 'Clumsy kitten. You could do with some deportment exercises. Stand up straight, like you've got a book on your head. That's it! You've got it. Now just see if you can keep it up, you look so much better!'

He keeps his hand on my back as we travel down in the lift, rigid against me, digging in whenever I slouch.

'This is my new wife,' he says to the bartender, who smiles politely and pretends that he didn't just half an hour ago serve a cocktail to a smiling girl in a pretty dress with a flower in her hair who looked a whole lot like me.

'WHAT ARE YOU wearing, anyway?' Kane's harsh voice cuts through my memory and jolts me anew with my stupidity. I can see it all too clearly, now, when I listen to Kane, when I see how he looks at Jodie, when I take apart the meaning in his words. I can justify myself a million ways: I didn't have a father I looked up to, or who showed me how men should respect women. I didn't have an upbringing bursting at the seams with love and fun and joy. I didn't know how to be in a relationship, how to assert my own needs when they seemed so very unimportant next to my need to please this man who showed so much interest in me, how to be my own person when that person seemed so lacking. I look at Jodie, now, shrinking under Kane's gaze, and dig my nails into my palm, furious at myself and Marcus and Kane and a little bit at Jodie for being so sparkly and joyous yet so ebbed away by this man who doesn't love her at all, at least in any healthy way.

'I… I know I need some new pyjamas,' Jodie says, twisting her hands together. She is sitting on the edge of her chair, shivering a little, Kane sprawled out on her bed like a great big St Bernard flopping over every corner, stabbing furiously at his phone.

'You look like a chav,' Jake says to him.

I look at his tracksuit and almost laugh out loud.

'You look like a twat,' Kat says, and this time I do.

'Do you want me to take you tomorrow, or what?' Kane says, his voice all loaded with threat. He's hard to take seriously, though, all manspread out in white nylon.

'Well, not really,' Kat says, 'but it's not like we have a choice of chauffeurs, is it?'

Jodie strokes his arm. 'We do, babe. I promise. They're just joking around. Right?' She gazes at us with imploring wide eyes.

I remember doing that, too, and so I say, 'Yes. We do. Thank you, Kane.'

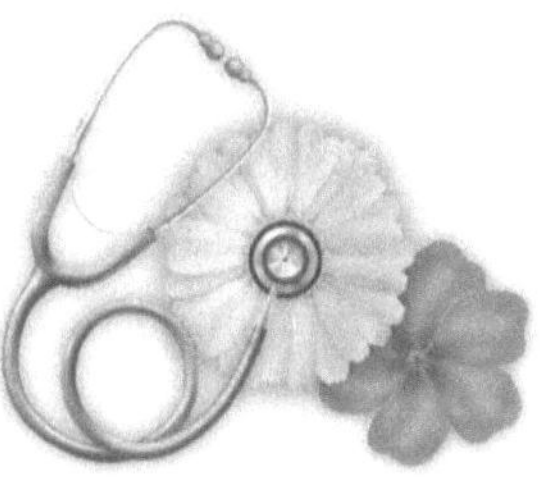

Chapter 18

EVERYTHING IS GOING wrong. It's like this place knows we are trying to bend the rules and it's pressing back at us, conspiring against us in every way. Our evening IV round is so late I've given up on trying to stay awake, and when the nurse comes at one o'clock in the morning I wake with a jump and can't get my heartbeat to slow. 'Shhh, now,' she says, deftly inserting the syringe into my IV port. 'Go back to sleep.'

The lights are still on in the ward, blazing out in time with the beeps of various IV drips, a turbulence of sound across our bay and through the doors to the other respiratory bays. I give up on sleep and binge watch *Casualty*, catching up on three episodes I've missed. Nothing like watching hospital dramas in hospital. All the patients always seem so well, somehow, so alive with colour and spark, wandering around the hospital without stopping for breath or stumbling because their legs have turned to liquid. The medical staff go straight to the patients when they're called and give them their medication when they need it. It's a sanitised version of the real thing.

I fall asleep at some point in the middle of my third *Casualty*.

I almost sleep through my early morning observations, only slightly waking when Ernesto wraps my arm in the blood pressure cuff and it squeezes hard, expanding the loose flesh on each side of it until I feel like my skin will burst into lots of tiny wrinkly pieces. I sleep completely through my early IV, waking up to find the tube still attached, the empty bag dangling from the TV unit above my head. I unscrew the IV from the port and clip off my line, suddenly needing a wee.

That's when I notice there's something different about the ward.

Someone different.

A nurse and two healthcare assistants are buzzing round Amina's bed. Only it's not Amina's bed, not anymore. Amina isn't there. Instead there's an elderly, very sickly looking woman, face smothered by a large CPAP mask, sparse white hair hanging in ratty tendrils round her face. Her chest moves up and down too quickly, her hands opening and closing like a newborn baby's. Her face, almost lost beneath the mask, is translucent, like a thin layer of cellophane over shrivelled flesh, eyelids fluttering and mouth agape as if trying to force air to be there when it is not.

Jodie is sitting on the end of her bed, eyes wide, watching the staff sorting out the woman's oxygen line and drip and catheter.

'Where's Amina?' I whisper to her. My heart is a stone in my stomach. Amina was doing well yesterday, she was all ready to go home tomorrow, she was fine.

Jodie shakes her head. 'Dunno. I just woke up and she was gone.'

Sister Joy comes into the ward with a pen in one hand and a clipboard of notes in the other, scanning through the top page. My first thought is that it's a good thing she is on shift today, rather than Sister Harris, but then I remember. Barbara is going to the home and Amina has gone.

'Where's Amina?' Jodie shouts over to Sister Joy, who hangs the file on the end of the new patient's bed and turns to face us.

'She's been moved.'

'Is she okay?'

Sister Joy nods. 'She's fine. But we're full, you see. We needed the space for a sicker patient. Amina is in another ward to finish her treatment before she goes home.'

'But we didn't get to say goodbye,' Jodie says.

Joy gazes at her. 'I'm sure you'll be able to see Amina before she goes.'

'But where is she?'

Sister Joy shrugs. 'Not sure. The night staff sorted her out. Listen, I need to sort this lady out, so I'll have a look for you later. Okay?'

Jodie nods mutely. We both know she won't have time to do something like that, even though she's one of the kindest.

Sister Joy turns away and Jodie clasps her hands together. 'Oh, wait, before you go, um… do you know when Barbara is going today?'

Sister Joy puts her hands on her hips. 'I am not psychic. They will come when they come. The doctor will see her first, could be any time after that. You know how it is. But I think it's planned for this morning, before lunch at least.' She turns back to the new patient and picks up her chart again, skimming along the lines with her pen.

Jodie casts her glance down to her hands and picks at her fingernails, a slight quiver rolling round her mouth.

Kat is still asleep next to me, and Violet must be outside. I stare out of the window. It's a clear day, watery winter sun breaking through the clouds, patches of blue sky and great tall sails of white cloud splashed across the canvas, fighting each other for space. I can almost breathe in the crispness of the air, the mellow taste of autumn conceding to winter; smoke and mulchy leaves, a woody kind of taste in my mouth. I suddenly want to be outside, to do what we said we would do, to taste the air and the salt and the sea breeze.

But how can we, with Barbara going and Amina gone?

Jodie nibbles at her nails, staring at the wall as if it might open and reveal a Grand Plan for us, but it is as blank as my mind, as pale as Jodie's saddened eyes.

After breakfast, we brood in silence. Even Violet is quiet this morning, having huffed and puffed at the inconvenience of having a new neighbour without even being consulted about it. You moaned about your last neighbour, Sister Joy said, and Violet said that at least she knew where she was with her, and where was she anyway, and why didn't she even say goodbye? No one is in the mood for our usual morning chatter, where we set the world to rights over watery porridge and cold floppy toast.

Jodie gets out of bed and teeters over to Barbara's bed in a hospital gown tied loosely at the back, showing most of her rear to the world. Thankfully she does have some baggy greyed knickers on, all too evident now as she bends over the end of Barbara's bed. They look like they once had a unicorn pattern. What is she doing, I wonder disinterestedly, what is she up to now? I dig my phone out and scroll through Facebook. It's about time I replied to some of these messages, people who really seem to care, who want to know if I'm okay, when I'm coming home, how I am feeling.

I look up as Jodie climbs back on her bed, a tiny smile frisking around her lips. I narrow my eyes at her. 'What's so amusing?'

She shakes her head and puts her finger on her lips.

'What were you doing?'

'Nothing.'

I shrug, turning back to my phone. There's a message here from Karen:

So sorry hun that I haven't got to come and see you. It's been crazy this end, you know what it's like, with the girls and everything, I've not had a min. But I'll come and see you when you get out, I promise. Love you sis. Xxx

A couple of doctors are arriving with their teams, smaller teams today, only a skeleton staff on a weekend day for the sickest patients, walking briskly into the bay, a group of them immediately breaking off and shutting themselves in with the new patient. Alice, I hear them calling her, and think about my friend Jen whose daughter is named Alice. How Jake and her were fast friends as toddlers and small children, but grew apart as the years morphed them into awkwardness around each other and Alice wanted to hang out with the cooler kids.

Jodie is grinning full on now, glancing over at Barbara and then at the staff congregating in the middle of the bay, consulting together.

'What's with you?' I say.

Kat has her eye on her, too. 'Did you do something?'

Jodie raises her eyebrows. 'What d'you mean?'

One of the doctors makes her way towards Barbara, greeting her and plucking her chart from the end of her bed.

'Did you do something to her chart?' I say, following Jodie's line of sight.

Jodie giggles. 'Maybe.'

'Jodie!' Kat and I both say together, appalled.

Jodie is unabashed.

'You could get into big trouble for that!' Kat says. 'And so could the staff. You have to tell them. Now, look!'

Jodie sits in smug silence.

'Jodie!' I say again. 'Just tell the doctor now. You can't do that!'

But Jodie sits there like a queen in state, chin high in the air, her face all wreathed in self-satisfaction. She brings her hands together in a prayer pose and says 'Yes, Sensei,' in a ridiculous growly voice. 'I'll tell 'em later, boss. I promise. When we're back.'

I glance at Kat, whose face is all rumpled up. Probably thinking, like me, that she should say something if Jodie won't.

None of the doctors are here to see me, or Kat, or Violet, or Jodie today. Only the new lady and Barbara, I assume to quickly sign her off. But the doctor with Barbara is speaking to a nurse in low concerned tones, snatches of her words floating over to us as we strain forward to hear. We can't hear enough, though, not with the machine screeching through the bay. It's only when the doctor moves away we see Barbara, sitting up in bed looking strangely peaceful, tiny frail hands gathered together in her lap. Jodie's over there quickly, bending down to her level. 'All well with you?' she says, an edge of anticipation to her voice. I sit on the end of my bed, leaning forward to hear more clearly.

'Well, I was, you know, darling? Thought I was for it today, into that home, they said. Said it'd be nice in there, all quiet and such, back with my things. But I know why they're sending me back there, I'm not stupid.'

'So are you not going?' Jodie says. 'To the home, today, I mean?'

Barbara shakes her head. 'Said I was a bit high, my temperature, earlier. That nurse was on about those night staff forgetting to mention it in handover, said who could she trust to do their job round here? Said it's fine now, but they want to just keep an eye for another few hours. Was funny, doctor said it'd been steady for days and then this sudden rise early this morning. Might be going later, they said, but not 'til tonight, or tomorrow. Probably Monday, though, love, you know how it is on weekend time.'

Jodie grins round at me and Kat, a big grin loaded with triumph and I-told-you-so. Kat heaves a great big sigh, and it reminds me of the sighs I would give when Jake was little and got away with something he shouldn't have done in the first place. Slightly irritated yet a little bit amused, a little bit okay with what he had done. Perhaps that's what it is with Jodie; she doesn't do rules, she doesn't follow orders, unless it's Kane giving them. She does what she thinks she needs to do to help someone out. And she gets away with it, because she is Jodie.

'I didn't want to go anyway,' Barbara says, smiling up at Jodie. 'Prefer you lot in here to those near-dead lot in there.'

I catch Kat's eye.

'You lot make me laugh, you do.'

'You make us laugh, too, Barbara,' Jodie says gently. 'We're gonna take you for a little walk later, okay? Little bit of fresh air for you.'

Barbara's eyes light up. 'You taking me to the sea at last?'

Jodie winks over at me. 'Don't be daft. You know we can't do that. We're taking you for a little wander somewhere nice.'

Barbara clasps her hands together. 'Ooh, lovely.'

Sister Joy is listening in. 'We'll just have to keep an eye on her temperature to check you can do that.'

Jodie smiles. 'I've got a feeling her temperature is gonna be fine.'

IT'S QUIET WHEN the doctors have left, like it usually is on a weekend, though there is an unending stream of different healthcare professionals attending to Alice. A pharmacist, phlebotomist, physiotherapist and radiologist are all here at different points through the morning with their various bits of equipment. 'Poor thing,' Kat says, eyeing Alice's curtained-off cubicle.

Jodie says, 'I wonder if she needs a trip to the seaside?'

We all laugh, even Violet. 'Are you coming then, Vi?' Jodie says to her with a sly wink over at Kat.

Violet bristles. 'My name is not Vi, and you know that, young lady.'

'So? You coming with us?'

'Coming where?' Nicki breezes in with the tea trolley rattling like a sack of old bones in front of her. 'You all going for a little outing, are you?'

I look at Jodie. Has Nicki rumbled us?

Jodie plays it cool. 'Just to the garden, like usual. Just trying to get Violet here to join in, she was a bit of a grumpy cow yesterday, weren't you Vi?'

Violet narrows her eyes.

'Well, she was out there for her smoke earlier, weren't you flower?' Nicki says, heaping sugar into Kat's tea. 'She's fine out there, aren't you?'

Violet shrugs. 'I suppose.'

'So?' Jodie says.

Violet sniffs.

Nicki laughs. 'You lot and your little walks. Still can't get rid of you, though, can we? You'll all be gone next week and then what'll we do round here?'

'You'll have more time to do your job,' Kat says.

'Too right, flower. Too right.'

BY LUNCHTIME I am sick with nerves. Everyone seems prepared, ready to do this thing. Barbara's temperature has stayed steady and

Sister Joy has pronounced her 'fit for a little walk'. Jodie has been on the phone to Kane, speaking in low hisses then assuring us that all is well and he will be here at two-thirty sharp with a chair for Barbara. We'll be back for three-thirty, or at the latest three-forty-five, she says. Twenty minutes there, twenty minutes on the beach, twenty minutes back. Back for visiting at four. Easy as that. Does everyone have warm clothes? Kane is bringing her coat in, she says, but she's just wearing her pyjamas under that. She's dressed in them now, all ready, out of her undignified hospital gown. She's wearing a tatty Justin Bieber T-shirt and her pink leopard print fleece pyjama bottoms. I say yes, Jake brought me some clothes in, and Kat says Nate was rubbish and forgot her proper coat so she'll have to wear her dressing gown.

Violet stares at Jodie. 'You'll be too cold with just those and a coat.'

'Nah. Hot-blooded, me.'

Violet shakes her head and turns around, rummaging in her bedside cupboard. 'Here.' She holds something dark and fluffy up to Jodie. 'You can borrow this, put it on over that tiny little T-shirt.'

'What are you, my mother?'

'You want it or not?'

Jodie grabs it from her. 'Let's have a look.' She shakes it out and then cackles loudly. 'Oh my actual days, Violet, where do you wear this?' She holds it against her, a big fleece jumper with a badly rendered laminate picture of a wolf howling at the moon. 'This wolf looks like a crazed psycho.'

Violet humphs. 'Well, actually, I got it on holiday. Brian has a matching one, too.'

Jodie snorts. 'Where'd you go on holiday to get that?'

Violet sniffs. 'Skegness.'

'Lol,' Jodie says.

'You want it or not?'

Jodie slips it over her head. The sleeves are too long and it almost reaches her knees, but it looks warm. 'I wouldn't mind.'

'Thank you, Violet,' Violet says.

'Thank you, Vi,' Jodie replies.

'What about Barbara?' I say, taking her in with her thin cotton nightdress and maroon fluffy slippers.

'We'll wrap her in that huge great dressing gown and then a load of blankets, like we do in the Peace Garden,' Jodie says. 'Stop stressing, Penny. She'll be fine.'

Lunch arrives and I am so churned up I can't eat it, but I'm not really sure I'd want to eat it much anyway. It's a vegetarian lasagne, Nicki says, but the lasagne sheets are like sloppy gloop and the vegetables overboiled pulp glued together with the pasta. It's like someone in the industrial kitchen at wherever it is this hospital gets its meals these days has thought to themselves, ahh, I know what to do with all those bits of broccoli we boiled to death and never used, let's stick them between a few lasagne sheets and put it in the microwave and call it vegetarian lasagne. That'll do those fussy veggies.

I push it away and drum my fingers on my lap.

'Will you stop that?' Kat says, shovelling up her meat-of-doubtful-origin stew. 'You're getting me all riled up now.'

'It's only a bit of fresh air, Penny,' Jodie says.

'You got your coat and everything, Violet?' I say.

Violet sits with arms folded, mouth a thin slash. 'If Amina isn't going, nor am I. I… I never got to say goodbye to her. We should find her first.'

I stare at her and I want to rail at her, to pour out a rant about how she treated Amina and didn't deserve to say goodbye. But I wonder if, deep down, she knows that.

'I don't know how we can,' I say. 'Unless Nicki can look, or Sister Joy, but they're rushing round everywhere with that new lady today so I don't want to disturb them.'

'Well, I won't go, then,' Violet says.

'Whatever,' Jodie mutters under her breath.

'An hour and a half to go,' Kat says.

I feel sick.

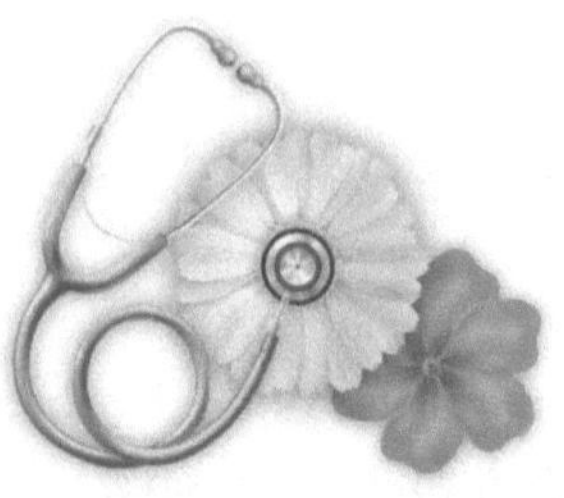

Chapter 19

I SHOULDN'T BE doing this. I know I shouldn't be doing this. I thought about asking on Mumsnet: Am I Being Unreasonable to join five other sick women from my hospital ward on a jaunt to the seaside to give an elderly lady her dying wish? YABU, they would say, You Are Being Unreasonable, 98% would say I was unreasonable and 2% would vote You Are Not Being Unreasonable just to be obtuse. I'd get told to give my head a wobble and get a grip, to stop being so stupid and think about the practicalities of such madness, that I sound like hard work and do I want to kill an old lady? So then I thought about asking on Reddit, but quickly gave up that one at the thought of Jake's face whenever I mention Reddit, as if he is amazed I am aware of its exIstence, as if it is his domain only.

I know in my head though what I don't need randoms on the internet to tell me. This is crazy, foolish, bonkers. Even if it's only an hour's trip we shouldn't be going. We're breaking the rules. We might get sicker. It's the middle of winter, cold and grey and damp, and we all have lung conditions.

But my heart is larger than my mind. I get dressed quickly, taking care around the cannula site, a sense of something like excitement bubbling in me, like the waters of a lake rippling at the coming of a storm. I don't do things like this. I keep the rules and keep the peace. But Jodie is a life-force, a wind rushing through the ward and through all of our minds, spinning our thoughts until we cannot do anything but follow her lead. For the fiftieth time, I ask myself what she is doing with that awful man.

She has tucked her pyjama bottoms into a pair of Ugg boots and balances on the edge of my chair, picking at her nails. 'Come on, Violet,' she says. 'You've got to come.'

Violet sticks her chin out. 'I don't want to go without Amina. Did you not hear me the first time?'

'We don't know where she is. You know that.'

'It's not fair to leave her, though, is it? Not when she was part of it all. I just don't think we should.'

Jodie runs her hand through her hair. 'Since when were you so bothered about Amina? You've always been vile to her, if I'm being honest with you.'

Violet turns her face away.

'Okay, look, you don't have to come. Listen, I'm sorry about Amina and everything, but Barbara's the one who counts here.'

Violet says nothing and keeps her arms tightly folded, staring back at Jodie with rebellion in her eyes.

Jodie shrugs. 'Whatever. Where's Kat?'

'She's in the loo,' I say. 'Says she was just getting ready.'

Jodie nods, and then gapes, and then laughs out loud, her gaze locked on the doors behind me. I turn round. Kat is walking into the bay dressed in a Chewbacca onesie and Doc Martens, the purple shawl her friends made for her around her shoulders, a lightweight purple raincoat draped over her furry arm.

'Awesome,' Jodie says. 'You have style, lady.'

Kat does a spin and laughs. 'I have warmth, at least. Might as well make use of this thing.'

'Love it,' Jodie says, then rubs her hands together. 'This is going to be so much fun!'

'Bit too hot in here though. Got my fleece pjs on under this baby.' Kat wipes sweat from her brow.

I look at Jodie, in her strange get-up, and Kat in her onesie, wondering how she still manages to look so effortlessly cool, and wish I had something more exciting than a baggy old jumper and saggy leggings. At least I have a coat, though, at least Jake remembered that. I can feel the nip of cold through the gap in my window. I cram my unsuitable ballet flats over the ridiculous red slipper socks, far too puffy for the shoes.

Kane turns up, whistling and slaloming one of the blue hospital wheelchairs in front of him. 'Everyone ready?' He seems buoyant today, full of energy and excitement, his blue eyes sparkling. He does a double take at Jodie, and stands back, nose crimped in disdain. 'What the hell is that?'

She wilts under his gaze.

'You're not wearing that, are you? It makes you look like a fat old lady.'

I can almost see Kat's hackles rising, standing proud from her skin, emanating waves of antipathy. I shake my head at her. *Not now.*

Jodie says, 'I'll take it off.' She peels the jumper off, and the Justin Bieber T-shirt looks even flimsier, even more insubstantial than before.

'Hmm,' Kane says. He crushes her tightly to him then just as quickly pushes her away. 'I'm all ready for you ladies.'

Jodie simpers, looking round at us as if to say, here's my wonderful man, look how amazing he is, look how helpful he is.

'Here's your coat,' Kane says, shoving a jacket at Jodie.

'That's not my winter coat,' Jodie says, holding it out in front of her; a lightweight denim jacket with a thin fabric hood.

'I don't like that one,' Kane says. 'Makes you look a bit chunky, babe. This one's hot.'

Jodie nods. 'Okay. Yeah. Yeah, you're right.'

'You should take the fleece,' Kat says, her face all puckered up. 'You'll be too cold.'

'We won't be outside long.'

'Still, you should take it. Wouldn't harm, would it? You could just leave it in the van if you're okay without it.'

Jodie shrugs. 'I guess.'

Kane says, 'Don't expect to be seen with me in that thing.'

Nicki wanders into the bay. 'What you lot up to now then? All in your gladrags like that? Bit dressed up for your little garden jaunt, aren't you?'

'Just going for a little walk. Maybe a little bit longer than usual,' Jodie says, gazing back at Nicki without guile. 'Bit chilly out there, is all.'

Nicki looks Kat up and down. 'Nice onesie.'

'I know, right?' Kat says, smiling. 'My daft other half decided I needed it in here, bless him. Thought I'd pop it on for a little bit of air.'

'Hmm,' Nicki says, giving her a sidelong look so dripping with suspicion it's almost written on her face in sharpie pen. 'Right. See you have the chair for Barbara. She's doing well, isn't she? Much better than in the night. Be careful with her, though, won't you? Don't keep her outside too long.'

'We won't,' Jodie says.

'I'll just hook up her oxygen, then,' Nicki says, fiddling with Barbara's tube and connecting it to the cylinder by her bed. 'Right. Let's get you into your chair, flower.'

Barbara claps her hands together. 'We're going to the sea!'

Nicki looks at Jodie, eyebrows pinched together in a point.

'Ah, you know how she is,' Jodie says, rolling her eyes around. 'She'll be on about her mouse next.'

'Is my mouse there?' Barbara says, right on cue.

'See?' Jodie says, weaving her arms into the jacket, which is a little too small and far too thin. Her T-shirt is a little short, revealing an expanse of belly and a tattoo I'd never noticed before. *Kane4eva,* it says, in matching style and slightly dodgy quality to Kane's larger more visible one on his bicep. It looks sore.

Nicki helps Barbara into the chair and wraps her up, in her dressing-gown and socks and slippers and two blankets tucked in under her legs and a third around her shoulders. She looks snug and warm and happy.

Violet stares at her, a dark shadow crossing her eyes, but she doesn't shift from her bed.

Nicki smiles tentatively. 'Hmm. Well, off you go then, ladies, I wouldn't want to keep you from your fresh air.' She forms her fingers into quotation marks around the last two words, and I glance at Kat. Does Nicki know? And does Barbara know, really, after all our attempts to keep it from her, or is it her usual wishful thinking?

It doesn't really matter now, I suppose. I look at Barbara, installed in her blue hospital wheelchair, all wrapped in blankets, drip stand inserted into the slot on the chair, oxygen cylinder stowed in the holder attached to the back. I see the great anticipation written on her, her eyes alive with hope like a child on Christmas morning.

'Did you bring a scarf or anything?' Kat says to me.

'Oh, nearly forgot!' Did Jake take that bag away last night? I peer under the bed and find it there, abandoned on the floor with a scarf spilling out. I rifle through the bag but can't see my favourite black bobble hat.

'Get a move on,' Kane growls.

What the heck. I'll look later. I hitch my handbag further up my shoulder, hook the Aldi bag over my arm and catch up with Kat, waiting behind Barbara's chair at the entrance. We wave to Violet, who turns away and doesn't wave back, and Kane leads us out of the bay, pushing Barbara through the double doors and then weaving through the ward to the main doors into the corridor.

'Slow down, babe,' Jodie says, grabbing hold of Kane's arm. 'We can't keep up. Penny can't walk very fast.'

Kane powers ahead, like he's in some kind of race, and I don't have a chance. Kat and Jodie might have a little more fitness than me, but they're huffing and puffing, faces paler than ever in the harsh overhead lights of the long hallway. I stop for a moment and bend over, gasping.

Kane skids the chair to a stop and scowls around at us. 'Look. Van's on yellow lines,' he says in tones stuffed with anger and tension. 'Had to park somewhere close and those disabled bays were all full up.'

He sounds outraged at those disabled bays all being full up, as if those annoying disabled people have no right to fill them up when someone important like him needs the space.

Jodie's shoulders stiffen and Kat lays a hand on her arm. 'Look, Kane, okay. You go at your pace and we'll catch you up, okay? You take Barbara to the van and get her in, you can do that, right?'

Kane looks at Barbara, tiny and bony and lost in her blankets, and flexes his muscles. 'What d'you think?'

He takes off towards the main entrance. Barbara squeals and then shouts, 'Faster!'

Kat takes my arm and Jodie comes round the other side of me and takes the other. 'Slowly does it, Penny. Slow and steady.'

We're near the entrance when I feel a cautious tap on my shoulder. I whirl around, catching a blurry glimpse of a woman in a turquoise hijab and a big blue puffy coat, standing behind me with her hands clasped together.

Jodie glances at her, narrowing her eyes, and I worry that she must think us rude. But then Jodie steps back over to her and enfolds her in a huge hug.

She beams so brightly I can see it all in her eyes. 'You were not going to go without me, were you?'

She is wearing a green *salwar kameez* under the coat, and patent black stilettos.

'Amina,' I say. 'You look nice.'

Nice? Seriously, Penny.

But Amina thanks me. 'I hope it is okay that I wear this. It is important for me.'

Kat touches Amina's hand. 'We're delighted you found us. And of course. You don't have to ask. And awesome shoes, by the way.'

Amina touches her head. 'It is just, when I am outside, like this, outside of the hospital, I wish to wear this.'

Jodie gazes at her, biting down on her lip, a myriad of emotions crossing through her eyes. I can see the fight in her mind, and the moment the better part of herself wins. She punches Amina on the arm. 'We're just so damn glad you made it. Where were you?'

'They put me on the day surgery ward. But I knew you were going now, so I came now too.'

Kat's brow crinkles. 'Day surgery?'

'It is because, they say, because I am most well out of all of you, and they needed the bed space where I was for somebody very sick. And the space I am now is the only bed space they have in all the hospital. It is very busy in there, but I go home tomorrow, so I do not mind. But I was sad when I could not say goodbye.'

'We were sad too,' Kat says, taking Amina's arm and leading her towards the entrance. 'Kane's waiting outside with Barbara, so we'd better—'

'Wait! Where is Violet?' Amina stares around at me, then Kat, then Jodie, then at the doors. 'She is with Kane, yes? With Barbara?'

Jodie shakes her head. 'She wouldn't come. Without you, I mean.'

Amina's eyes widen. 'Without me?'

'Yeah,' Jodie says. 'But we have to go—'

'You are sure? She would not go without me?'

I nod. 'She thought we were wrong to go without you, when you'd been a part of the plans, and when you're such a part of us.'

'But I must go to her. Get her and bring her.' Amina pulls her arm away from Kat's and whirls around, swishing away, calling over her shoulder. 'Wait for us, please, outside. Please wait.'

'Don't worry,' Kat says. 'We'll be at the entrance. In the van. Make sure she is warm enough, that she brings a coat, okay?'

Amina has disappeared into the gloomy distance of the endless corridor.

'She's so much better,' Kat says.

Jodie takes a deep breath in and exhales slowly.

'Okay?' I say to her.

'It's just, Kane, you know, he's waiting. He doesn't like waiting.'

I bet he doesn't.

'It's okay,' says Kat. 'We'll go and find him now, and we'll talk to him. I'm sure he'll be fine.'

Jodie doesn't look so sure, but follows Kat as she walks slowly towards the main entrance, allowing me time to walk with them at my snail's pace. Each step is still painful, and I wish I'd done more with Dan, wish I'd built up my muscles further, that I was just that slight bit better.

I take a breath in and grit my teeth as I push through the doors to the outside world.

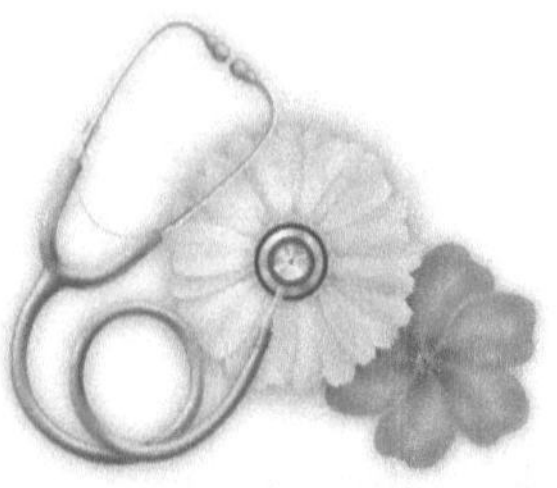

Chapter 20

THE COLD AFTERNOON hits me in the face, stealing my breath, the late November sun peeking through the low-lying layers of cloud. It's captivating, the wide grey sweep of the sky, drawing my gaze up away from the mass of cars and the ambulances and all the people. I stand there for a moment, allowing the few feeble rays of sunshine to caress my face.

Jodie pulls at my arm. 'There,' she says, pointing over at a confusion of cars and vans and a hospital minibus all jostling for position near the entrance. Kane is there in the centre, leaning on a beat-up old minibus with the words 'Oak Green Primary School' in faded green Comic Sans, and an equally faded image of an oak tree in full bloom across the battered, filthy panelling. I wonder how he got hold of it, and then decide not to wonder too much. He's parked it across two of the disabled parking bays and stands there with his arms folded and a cigarette hanging out of the corner of his mouth, with Barbara next to him in her chair, her eyes sparkling in their pale reflections of the patchy blue of the sky peeping through the grey. He spots the three of us as we make our way over, threading between two taxis. He grunts and slides the door open.

'How are we getting her in?' Jodie says, staring at the gap between the ground and the step. 'Thought you had a ramp?'

Kane shakes his head. 'I can lift her. I told you that. Just need a bit of a hand.' He grasps the bar at the front of the chair, underneath Barbara's maroon-slippered feet. 'Come on. Get the back.'

'Me?' Jodie says.

'Who else? Them lot don't have the strength, right?' He peers over at me and Kat, then shades his face with his hand, staring at us and the entrance behind us. 'Where's that other one? That grumpy old bint?'

'She's coming,' Kat says. 'And Amina, too. We'll just have to wait.'

Kane shakes his head. 'Nah. See, I'm not waiting round here anymore. That jobsworth over there already gave me a load of lip, an' I says to him I'll just be five mins, an' that was ages ago. Said he'd fine me, and I says I'm picking up a handicapped lady, an' he swore at me, I'm not even joking. Those people taking up these here spaces'll be out any sec.' He sweeps his arm round at the disabled bays, a look of disdain creasing his face. 'So help me up with her, babe.'

Jodie breathes in.

'Now.' He says the word quietly, softly, but it's loaded with menace, and it reminds me too much of Marcus.

Jodie grips hold of the handles on Barbara's chair. 'I'll help,' Kat says, shoving Jodie aside and taking hold herself.

'We'll do it together.' Jodie grabs one handle and the bar at the side, and they lift together, Jodie's breathing rapid and sputtering.

'Let me,' I say. I'm going home on Monday, after all. I'm much better than I was. I grab the bar at the back, and we all heave Barbara and chair into the van together. I'm not sure if it's my imagination, but it doesn't feel as though Kane does much of the work at all. Sweat prickles at my brow and I breathe hard at the exertion. Kane looks down at me from his position in the van, eyebrows slightly raised, mouth all sardonic and contorted.

'Get in then.' He grabs Jodie's hand and yanks her into the minibus, so hard she's almost flying, tripping up over the plate as she lands on the floor next to him. He laughs. 'Stupid cow.'

'Don't talk to her like that,' Kat says.

'You want me to take you, or what?'

Kat shrugs.

'You okay, Barbara?' I say, climbing into the minibus and sitting down. 'You warm enough?'

It's chilled in here, the air sagging in a sense of worn-out hopelessness around us, as if the vehicle has given up on life, yearning for the days when squealing children bounced on its seats and threw up on its floor. A musty aroma coils through the dusty air and makes me cough.

Barbara stares around her suspiciously. 'There's rats in here.'

She's probably right.

'We should get her in one of the seats,' Kat says. 'Belted up.'

Kane shakes his head. 'We gotta go. No time for that faffing around. She's fine as she is.'

Kat stares up at him, tilting her head to the side. 'No she's not. We get her in the seat. Do you not care about safety? What if there was an accident? It'd be your fault if she got hurt.'

'As if there'd be an accident,' he says, his mouth all twisted up with a great big scoff. 'I'm an experienced HCV driver, actually.'

'Well, then, actually, you should know all about safety protocols,' Kat says, head tilted even further over.

He doesn't reply to this.

'Come on,' Kat says to Jodie. 'Let's get her in the seat.' She leans in closer to me and whispers, 'Go slow.'

We lift Barbara, gently and so exaggeratedly slowly Kane begins to turn purple. He jumps out of the minibus, kicking at the wheels and then slamming the sliding door closed so hard the whole thing judders. He flips his cigarette on the ground and then clambers in through the driver's door. 'Take your time, why don't you.'

'We will,' Kat whispers.

'What's so funny?'

'Nothing,' Jodie says. 'Just helping Barbara.'

'Well, will you hurry up? You asked me to do this, so show some gratitude and get on with it.'

We settle Barbara onto her seat and cross the tattered belt over her body gently, then tuck the blankets around her. She looks as lost in her seat as she does in her wheelchair and her hospital bed, a tiny white-haired bird, all of her pale and white against a sea of 1980s bus-seat cover, all violent geometric reds and blues and oranges fighting with one another for space.

Jodie clicks the belt into the buckle and draws back. 'Right.'

'You ready, then?' Kane's voice is all irritation barely smothered, like a pressure cooker about to burst its lid open.

'Just need to get us belted in, now,' Kat says. 'Give us a minute.'

He drums his fingers on the steering wheel, blowing out his cheeks.

We draw our seatbelts across with meticulous languidness. Kat's seatbelt seems to stick repeatedly. 'Oh dear,' she says, winking at me as she pulls the belt across her over and over again and then yanks it hard. 'I think this one's broken. Give me a minute while I try that one.'

I laugh under my breath as Kane slams his fist on the window.

In the end we can't procrastinate any longer.

'Finally,' Kane hisses, turning over the engine. It sounds like a tractor and I wonder if it moves like one. He pulls out towards the entrance, and curses again as a taxi pulls in front of him. He leans on the horn and lifts his hands as the taxi driver leans out of his window and scowls at him. 'Will you get out my way?' Kane shouts, but the taxi driver doesn't get out of his way. He sits there with engine idling, ignoring Kane's increasingly frenzied yells.

Jodie looks at Kat, who is grinning away to herself in the corner. 'What? You been praying or something? To slow us down?'

Kat smiles wider.

'They're taking ages,' I say.

Kane slams the wheel.

'Look!' Jodie says, pointing to the entrance, where Amina is rushing through the doors, her bright clothing glinting in the daylight. Behind her is Violet, stumbling along with her walking frame, dressed in a huge puffy silver jacket zipped up over the Dressing Gown of Doom. Jodie's face lights with glee. 'Wonder if Brian has one of those, an' all.'

Kat gives me a sideways glance and I laugh out loud at the hideous incongruousness of Violet's get-up. Her full-length dressing gown, poking out of the silver coat like a bad onesie that forgot its legs, garish lace details at the cuffs and a zip from top to bottom. A toilet tent, that's what Jodie had called it.

Jodie drags the door open and screeches over at them. 'Over here! Violet! Amina!'

Kane slams the dashboard.

They bring a violent wind in with them, with Amina's rippling hijab and the hideous gown, and they bring more laughter too. Violet is bright and glowing and has a face full of garish make-up, all smudged bright blue eyeshadow and a slash of scarlet lipstick, blusher that looks like a clown got a bit wasted; one hand grasping her walking frame, one arm threaded through Amina's, the mouth that is usually turned down drawn back in a wide grin, showing wonky, yellowing teeth.

Jodie says, 'You look like the love-child of an astronaut and a pair of seventies curtains.'

Violet doesn't stop grinning.

Jodie helps Violet up and lifts the walker in, stowing it next to the wheelchair.

'She came back for me.' Violet hacks and pants, her chest rising and falling rapidly as she sinks down into one of the seats. 'There she was, in that funny headscarf thing, running into the bay. Thought I was hallucinating, but it was her.'

Amina squeezes in next to her and I wonder if she is offended by Violet's careless use of language. But she leans into Violet's shoulder and grins. 'Sorry we took a while. Madam here had to prepare herself to be the belle of the ball.'

I think that Violet has tears in her eyes. 'She came back for me.'

'Well, I was not going to leave you, was I?'

Violet swallows. 'She said I had to come. So I did.'

'You belong with us,' Kat says.

Violet stares at her and then around at all of us, doubt clouding her eyes and creasing her face up, not into its old familiar pattern of distaste at the world, but into something more like uncertainty.

I look at her and can only imagine her thoughts. She's been the outsider in our ward and probably the outsider in her life, always looking on with great disapproval, a disdain that so obviously masks the pain she is in. She's put a shell around herself, I think, erected a boundary of haughtiness and superiority, but underneath it all she's just got the same longings as the rest of us. She just wants to belong.

'I think you've changed me,' she says.

I am seeing a butterfly emerging out of its chrysalis, in flashes of glorious colour, beating its wings and flying free into a new world. Violet, in her polyester dressing gown and smeared blue eyeshadow, her silver coat and pink slippers, is a wave of colour and light.

I want to take hold of some of that wave and wrap it around myself.

'This bus is a bit of a dump, though, isn't it?' she says, her mouth flattening back into its usual shape.

We all laugh.

I look around at all of us here in this very possibly stolen minibus, a motley crew of six sick women, one wheelchair, one oxygen cylinder, one drip stand, one walking frame, a hideous dressing gown, a Justin Bieber T-shirt and a Chewbacca onesie. The flowers, Nicki always calls us. We're the flowers of Bay C. A tide of something warm steals over me; something more than fondness, like a wild longing somewhere inside me being slowly soothed, like something in the depths of me is opening as much as it is in Violet.

The taxi finally moves out of the way, its charge safely installed, and Kane guides the bus haphazardly around the entrance and out of the car park. For the first time in two weeks I am out in the world, away from my safe place, from the routine of meds rounds and obs checks and healthcare assistants with tea trolleys. I'm out in the world where normal people go to work and have energy, where people laugh and cry and make their way through life, where people drive a thousand cars all over the roads to a thousand different places. I stare out of the window, shaken by the rawness of reality, by how easily I have become, once again, institutionalised in a world where I am taken care of and ruled over by hospital routine. It's almost too free out here on the road, where anything could happen, too scary, the skies too open and the horizon so wide it might swallow me up.

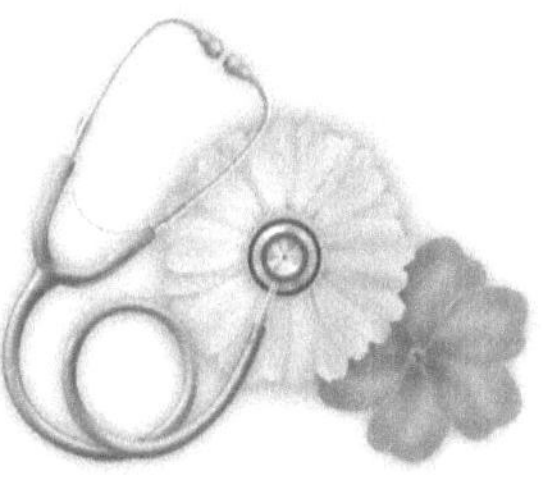

Chapter 21

KANE DRIVES TOO quickly. The old minibus weaves and undulates worryingly as he slews round corners as though he thinks he is Lewis Hamilton, the chassis screeching and the suspension groaning as we bounce up and down over speed bumps that Kane doesn't appear to notice. It does indeed move like a tractor, but like a souped-up tractor on speed.

'Easy, babe,' Jodie says. She's sitting up at the front next to him, her hand on his knee.

He shoves her hand away. 'You wanna get there quick, don't you?'

'Well, yeah, but—'

'Well then.' He changes down a gear as he moves out to overtake a pootling red Micra, the gearbox crunching and the bus hopping forward as he releases the clutch too quickly. 'Stupid pile of garbage,' he mutters, sticking his middle finger up at the window as he passes the Micra, then growling when the Micra driver gives him the same back.

'I've got a quicker route,' he says, turning around to face us and grinning. 'Better than that piece of crap.' He motions to an ancient SatNav, stuck to the windscreen with its mount peeling away at the edges, worn wire trailing down to the cigarette lighter. 'I'll get you gals there in no time.'

'Thanks, babe,' Jodie says.

'Thanks, babe,' Kat mouths at me, rolling her eyes.

He stamps on the brake as we swing sharply into a bend and see an actual tractor dead ahead of us, trundling along at a snail's pace. We jerk forwards into our seatbelts.

'Wheee!' Barbara says, patting her hands up and down on her lap. 'Faster!'

'She's like a kid on a fairground ride,' Kat says.

She's all wide-eyed with wonder and smiling with glee. 'We're going to the seaside.'

'We are,' Kat says.

'We're going to see the sea!'

'We are.'

Barbara starts humming *Oh I Do Like To Be Beside The Seaside* in a quavering croon, and one by one we join in. Amina's voice, it turns out, is both rich and powerful, like liquid gold, like an ocean I want to plunge into.

'You should go on *X Factor*,' Jodie says.

'You sound nice,' Violet says.

Amina glances shyly up at her, eyes sparkling, then looks quickly away out of the window, twisting her hands together in her lap. I gape at Kat, raising my eyebrows in Violet's direction. Did she actually just compliment Amina?

'You lot are bloody noisy,' Kane says.

We sing louder.

'Will the lot of you shut up?'

Jodie turns to us, shaking her head slightly. I, too, have caught the edge in his voice, and gaze around at the others, motioning at Kane and pressing my lips together. But Barbara is away with the fairies, warbling away in a strangled soprano, hands waving round in the air.

Kane tightens his hands on the wheel.

Jodie strokes his thigh. 'She's okay, babe, isn't she? I haven't seen her so happy before. Let her be?' Her voice is a wheedling whine as she leans into him and whispers something else into his ear. The edges of his thin lips turn up in the ghost of a smile, and he shrugs.

The tractor plods on ahead of us, spewing black smoke from its exhaust. 'Stupid great tank,' Kane shouts, winding his window down. 'Get out of my way!'

The tractor driver does not take any notice and does not get out of Kane's way. At the next slight widening of the road Kane manhandles the bus around the tractor, missing its huge tires by an inch and drawing a cloud of colourful language from the irate driver. He floors the accelerator and a few seconds later slews off down yet another unsigned country lane, boxed in by hedges flying by in blurs of evergreen and winter-starved trees bowing in the sharp November wind.

Jodie shivers.

'Please put your jumper on,' Kat says, plucking the discarded wolf fleece from one of the empty seats and passing it to her. 'You'll catch your death.'

Jodie turns her head slightly, studying Kane's disapproving profile. 'I'll be okay.'

Kat touches her arm. 'Put it on.'

Jodie shakes her head.

Barbara gets more excited by the minute, bouncing up and down in her seat, cackling away with a loud wheeze. 'Step on it, boy!'

'Yes, ma'am,' Kane says, veering round another bend in the road too quickly.

'Are we nearly there yet?' Barbara says.

'Have some patience, woman! I'm doing my best.'

'Are you sure this is a quicker way?' Jodie's face is creased with doubt as she peers out of the dusty windscreen at the narrow road ahead. It constricts into little more than a farm track in the distance, heading towards a copse of trees and what looks like a gate and a cattlegrid.

Kane turns to her and gives her a look that reminds me uncomfortably of how Marcus used to look at me when I said the wrong thing, which was most of the time. It was a look that would freeze my insides, that would stop up my mouth and keep the words from spilling over further. I would swallow them back down and then say I'm so useless, sorry. And he would say yes, you are, aren't you, and I should think more before I speak. And I would nod firmly, up and down, and then stroke his arm and tell him that I loved him and loved that he wanted the best for me and I would keep on trying, and please forgive me Marcus and give me another chance.

Jodie looks down and shakes her head slightly, saying no more as Kane pulls up to the track, stops, scratches his chin and fiddles with the crap SatNav that wasn't as good as him. Says nothing as he reverses too quickly all the way back up the unsigned country lane to the junction where he passed the stupid great tank and joins the country lane we were on originally. Still says nothing as we catch up with the stupid great tank and sit right up its rear end for the next few minutes, until it chugs off down another track, the driver waving out of the window and then flipping the bird in a final farewell.

It seems to be taking too long to get there, but I don't seem to be able to worry about it, because time is different out here, it's languid and silent, without the stress and strain of the ward. I gaze at the sky rushing by and long for more of its great open wildness.

We're on a narrow road running parallel to the sea. There's hardly any traffic on the road, just the odd car approaching behind us, hovering at our rear in juddering impatience and then overtaking as soon as they get the chance, Kane muttering obscenities at each driver who dares to pass. The grey sea peeps out from beyond scrubby grassland and scraggy bushes and broken-down drystone walls to our right. There's just the hint of a sparkle off the water, a pale reminder of long summer days in the warmth of the sunshine, where the sea shines turquoise under a cloudless sky. I close my eyes for a moment, imagining the heat, the enticing invitation of the water.

'There!' Jodie shouts, a moment too late as we pass the entrance to a barely visible track, a crooked sign at its mouth flashing by. 'You've gone past it.'

Kane jerks the bus to a halt. 'You weren't looking hard enough. I'm the driver, you're supposed to tell me when we're there.'

'Sorry.'

Kane grunts and throws the minibus into reverse. There's a car coming up behind, a silver Yaris, but he ignores it and starts backtracking quickly towards the entrance to the track, the tyres squealing in protest. The car behind toots its horn but Kane takes no notice, backtracking until he's almost touching its bumper. I turn in my seat to see the driver sitting there with her brow crinkled up, her palms raised in a question, an older woman refusing to be intimidated by this idiot. She sits there and she does not move, and Kane sits there and he does not move.

'Just keep going and turn round somewhere else, for heaven's sake,' Kat says, shattering the taut heaviness. 'It won't take a minute.'

'No,' Kane says.

'Why does she put up with that great big bully?' Violet whispers to Amina, except her whisper is more of a loud hiss, and Kane hears it too.

He turns around and narrows his eyes at Violet, a vein pulsing in his neck. 'You wanna drive? Is that it? You want me to go and leave you to it?'

Violet rolls her eyes.

'No, she don't mean that,' Jodie says. 'She just means, just… we should turn around.'

'Why don't you stand up for yourself?' Violet says.

Kat gives her a sideways glance, an imperceptible shake of her head, a softly whispered 'Not now.'

Kane sits with arms folded tightly, staring straight at the driver in his rear-view mirror. I can just see his eyes reflected; pale, cold as ice, holding in place with stubborn arrogance. We hang there in tense silence for what seems like minutes until the woman buckles and then breaks, shifting her gaze away and her car into reverse. She limps back down the road, past the track, all without so much as a last glance at Kane. He laughs out loud and revs the bus noisily as he reverses the rest of the way, grinding the gears then fishtailing into the track, slamming the horn as a final flourish. 'Ha,' he says.

The writing on the wonky sign to the beach is almost obliterated by weather and time. All I can see is the word 'bay'. The beach is only a little way down the track, and Jodie was right, you can drive right onto it. The sand is dark and packed-in, that gritty kind of sand, not the light golden sand you can dig into and stream between your fingers. More like a mud-flat, really. But it's still sand. It's still a beach. It stretches off both ways into a wilderness of nothingness, sky meeting ocean in shimmering grey desolation.

'Godforsaken place, this, isn't it?' Violet says.

'What did you want, the bloody Seychelles?' Kane brings the bus to a juddering halt, halfway between the entrance and the creeping tide.

'No, it's great,' Kat says. 'It's the sea and it's a beautiful crisp November day, and we're here. What d'you think, Barbara?'

Barbara sits stock still, staring out at the ocean, her eyes reflecting the blue-grey in their faded glow. She lays her hands on the window, her blankets slipping down, revealing the whiteness of her stringy arms. Her veins are like bulging estuaries in full flood, pushing starkly through her skin like the map of her life cannot be contained any more. 'I think… I think my mouse is here.'

'Then let's get you outside, shall we?'

'Oh, yes. Oh, yes, please.'

'What is this beach, anyway?' I say as Kane lopes round to the sliding door, dragging it open through a lingering rusty growl as it resists his pull. 'I've never been here. Didn't even know it was here.'

Jodie points to another tiny, battered sign on the edge of the beach near the track. *Sea Bay.*

'Imaginative name,' Violet says.

I'm all of a sudden infused with energy. I snap my belt open, grabbing my bag, and pile out of the van after Amina and Violet, helping Violet out with the walker. The cold air hits me in the face and steals my breath. Kat and Jodie help Barbara into her chair and they can hardly contain her, bubbling away and bouncing like a toddler being restrained in her buggy. They take hold of one arm of the chair each. 'Help us out, Kane,' Kat says, and Jodie looks at him with scared eyes. He is leaning on the side of the van, lighting a cigarette.

He sighs, then grunts, then grabs hold of the bar across the front of the chair, dragging it forward and pulling it down with little care for its angle, Barbara tipping dangerously towards the sand. She grips the arms and giggles. 'You are a one, young man.'

Kat sighs.

'Thought you weren't coming out of the van,' I say to Violet, who is leaning on her walker, gazing out at the sea. 'Thought you hated sand.'

Violet screws up her nose. 'Might as well, now I'm here, I suppose.'

'Did you bring that hot chocolate?' Jodie says to Kane, when Barbara is safely down on the sand, the wheels of her hospital chair sinking just slightly into its marshy surface.

Kane nods. 'Anything for my princess, right?' He chucks her under the chin and then kisses her full on the mouth, holding his cigarette too close to her blonde hair. 'I said I would, so I did.' He climbs back into the bus and scrabbles around under the passenger seat. 'Here.' He brings out two large tartan flasks and a nest of disposable cups. 'Even remembered the cups. What d'you think of that, then?' He winks at her.

Jodie wraps her arms around herself. 'I think you're brilliant.'

He hands the flasks to me and Kat. 'I'm gonna stop in here, let you ladies go and look at the sea or whatever.' He climbs back into the minibus, flops down on one of the double seats and splays his long legs out over the aisle to another seat. He digs out his phone. 'Rubbish reception here. Don't be long, will you?'

'We won't,' Jodie says.

Barbara is animated, as if the wind has caught hold of her and swept through her fading body. 'I want to feel the sand.'

Kat starts to shake her head, but Jodie smiles and looks back at Kane. 'Kane's got a beach chair or two in here, haven't you babe? An' a picnic rug too. Keeps it just in case.'

Kane shrugs. 'Mmm. Under those seats at the back, I think.' He makes no move to go towards the seats at the back, so Jodie clambers up, panting, scrambles over Kane's legs and crouches down herself.

'One's broken.' She pulls out the remains of a rusty old camping chair, the poles of one leg snapped in two, and shoves it away. 'This one's okay though.' She tugs out another chair, opening it out; a smaller one, lime green, the back shaped like the face of a frog, cartoon eyes bulging from the top corners.

'That's a kid's chair,' Kat says, taking it from her.

'And this.' Jodie drags out a faded old blanket, the plastic shredding away on its back, pink and white candy-striped fleece covered in what looks like a hundred crusted picnic remains and drink spills. 'Here!' she says triumphantly, holding it aloft. 'We can all sit on it.'

Barbara claps her hands together. 'I want to sit on the frog chair.'

Jodie shoves the blanket at me. It smells like mildew. I shove my handbag back in the bus, my arms too full of flask and rug, weighed down with the Aldi bag full of hats and gloves still hooked over my arm, and start slowly down the beach with Kat, who is pushing Barbara, the chair responding sluggishly, the wheels catching on the grit and groaning in protest. Kat has the wolf fleece draped over her arm.

It's not far to the water's edge. We inch down towards it and I stare up at the open, clouded sky, breathing in the salty crisp freshness of the air and listening to the plaintive cry of gulls. I dump the flask and bag on the sand and lay out the blanket, and for the first time in weeks I feel like I can breathe again and it's wonderful and wild and invigorating.

Jodie tugs off her Ugg boots and long stripy socks, curling and uncurling her bare toes in the damp sand. 'Hey,' she shouts, flinging her arms to the sky, 'I just thought. We've come from C Bay to Sea Bay! How about that!'

Kat says, 'I know which one I prefer.'

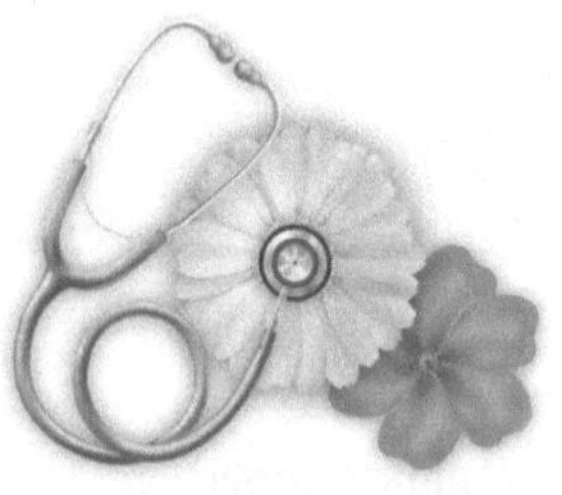

Chapter 22

THE PICNIC RUG is a square of smallness, made for a couple cosying up with a bottle of wine. The frog chair is tiny, but Barbara is tinier, and she giggles and claps her hands as Kat and Jodie help her off the wheelchair and lower her in. The poles screech and I worry it will collapse under her, but it stays put, one side listing slightly. They wrap her tightly in the blanket, gathering in her cannula and oxygen line. Her drip bag is empty, the line stretching taut and tugging at her arm, so I detach the connector lock from her port, clipping off her tube and tucking the end into the bandage around her arm. Her knees poke out from under her dressing gown, her support stockings all crinkled at her ankles, legs extending in front of her like sticks, criss-crossed with blue and purple veins vivid against the near translucency of her skin, her slippered feet resting on the sand. Kat lays the other blankets out over her legs and tucks them in all around her until she is cocooned in a blue waffle shell.

Violet stands back, leaning heavily on her walking frame next to Barbara's chair, her face a picture of disgust as she looks down at the picnic rug. 'You're not getting me onto *that*.' She struggles with her walker, shoving it through the sand and placing it next to the rug, on the other side to Barbara's frog chair.

Jodie laughs. 'You're no fun, Violet.'

Violet's face tenses and then just as quickly softens, the deep-set lines around her eyes smoothing out just a little, her mouth curving into the edges of a smile. 'Could do with a cig,' she says. 'Got any?'

Jodie plucks a cigarette packet out of the pocket of her jacket. 'Of course. I'll join you.'

Kat and Amina and I squeeze as much of ourselves as we can onto the rug. It slips and slides and buries itself in the gritty sand, leaving our legs splayed out over the naked ground. The sand is cool against my thin leggings and I shiver, pulling my parka tightly around me and my hood up. Kat hunches next to me in her onesie with the hood pulled right up, Chewie's face smiling kookily out at us. Amina shivers. Somewhere in the far distance a dog barks.

'Wait a sec.' I remember the bag, discarded on the sand nearby, and tug it towards me, opening it up and rummaging through. 'There's a few things in here. Hats, scarves, gloves. You're all welcome to them if you want.'

'Good thinking,' Kat says.

'More by luck than design. Jake couldn't be bothered to look for my hat, so…' I begin to pluck out some of the contents. 'Oh my days. Sorry about this.' I still can't find my lovely black bobble hat, but I do find a Bristol Rovers hat and scarf set, a West Ham hat, some red children's fingerless gloves and a fleecy Santa hat amongst other sundry items. My favourite black wool scarf is here, though, and I wrap it around my neck, slipping on some football gloves and a tatty old beanie hat of Jake's, pulling my parka hood up over it.

Jake never even supported Bristol Rovers.

'We should put that hat on Barbara,' Kat says. 'It's biting out here.'

Barbara submits to Kat sliding the hat on her head and the child's gloves onto her hands. She smiles out at the sea, diminutive and lost in a mountain of blankets and a Bristol Rovers bobble hat. Amina and Kat both find some non-matching gloves, and we sit in silence and enjoy the quiet of the beach and the rolling of the sea, watching Violet and Jodie, standing slightly away from us, puffing away.

'It's nice to be out in the fresh air, I must say,' Violet says.

Kat raises her eyebrows at me, and I almost laugh out loud at the irony of it.

Marcus used to smoke, even though he was a fitness nut and knew that it messed my lungs up even further. I was just being picky, he said, he smoked outside, what more did I want? It wasn't like he was smoking right in my face in an enclosed space or anything, he was being as considerate as he could and all I did was complain. Sorry, I would say, sorry, I know you're thinking of me, it's just that it makes me wheeze and it hurts. But then he'd remind me that if I made more effort to get fit my lungs would get stronger and I wouldn't have such an issue with him having the odd cigarette at the end of a really hard day at work. He deserved it, after all, he was the one bringing the money in round here, yet here I was denying him a little bit of comfort. Sorry, sorry for putting myself first, I would say. And then he would go and smoke the cigarette and when he came in he would take me in his arms and hold me tight and I would cough and cough until my chest ached.

'Another one?' Violet says, when they're done, but Jodie shakes her head.

'Nah. We don't really have the time. Just a sec.' Jodie straggles up the beach and says something to Kane, then starts picking her way back towards us. Her toes are blue against the sand. He says something back to her in a shouty voice, then comes out of the van and follows her, muttering.

'Give us it, then,' he says.

Jodie pulls her phone out of her pocket and fiddles with it for a moment, then hands it to him. 'Here. App's open.'

'Go and get down with the rest, then,' he says to her, and Jodie smiles eagerly up at him as she comes back to Violet's side.

Violet allows herself to be guided over to her walker and holds on to Jodie tightly as she lowers her down to the seat. 'Ouch. My poor legs. I'm not stopping down here long.' She sits awkwardly, legs shaking. Jodie squeezes herself down onto the rug with the rest of us, shivering.

I hold the bag out to Jodie. 'Take some,' I say. 'It's so cold.'

'Haven't got all day,' Kane says, lurching down the beach towards us, scrolling through Jodie's phone.

Kat passes the wolf fleece to Jodie. 'You almost forgot this.' Jodie gazes at it, then glances at Kane, chewing on the inside of her cheek. Then she quickly shrugs her jacket off and pulls the fleece over her head. The jacket is even more ill-fitting over the fleece, barely meeting in the middle, the howling wolf displayed in all its tacky glory.

'Thank you,' she says. 'Can I have the Santa hat?'

I pass the West Ham hat up to Violet. Its wool is unravelling, more well-used than the Bristol Rovers one. She screws up her face but slips it over her head, saying nothing. She pulls out a pair of gloves from the pockets of her silver puffer jacket. They are black leather and look expensive.

Kane hovers near Violet, pulling a face at the wolf jumper. 'You quite ready?'

'Kane's just gonna take a photo of us all,' Jodie says. 'Smile, everyone!'

Kane comes around to the front of us and stands with the phone held out in front of him and a sulk screwing up his face. We smile up at the camera and Jodie kneels next to me and throws her hands up in the air, then lowers them at the look of disdain written over Kane's face.

'Done,' he grunts, turning on his heel and setting off back up to his minibus.

'We made it,' Jodie says, relaxing onto a patch of sand next to the blanket, which is too full of the four of us, and dusting the clingy sand from her feet. 'We're here. We're at the seaside, Barbara!'

Barbara is alive with light. She looks around at us all, giggles, then looks around again, flinging her hand over her mouth. 'You brought me.'

'We did.'

'I never thought you really would, you know.'

We edge closer to her and Kat lays her head lightly on her knee.

'I want to feel the sand.'

Kat looks doubtful.

'Let me feel it,' Barbara says.

Jodie and Kat gently remove Barbara's maroon slippers and her off-white support stockings, revealing wrinkled feet with purple blotches and discoloured, yellowing toenails curling around under themselves. Jodie places the shoes and socks up on Barbara's wheelchair, behind us, just in case the tide comes in and catches us off guard.

Kat digs into a small bag she has on her lap. 'Can I do this?' she says to Barbara, holding up a tiny pair of nail scissors and some bright red nail polish.

Barbara stares at her, and then nods. 'Yes. Yes, poppet.'

'It's quick dry stuff. Sixty seconds.' Kat takes Barbara's left foot and starts trimming the nails, slowly and carefully, and we watch in silence as she paints each toenail until they are all glittering with vibrant scarlet.

'They match my gloves,' Barbara says.

'Leave them a minute.' Kat clips her bag closed and sits with her legs drawn up to her, gazing out at the sea.

After a few moments Barbara stretches out her feet, splaying out her toes and pressing them to the sand, burrowing them in. 'Now bury my feet,' she says to Jodie.

'Sand's a bit chilly,' Jodie says.

'I don't care.'

Jodie plucks handfuls of sand and gently pats them over Barbara's feet, digging further in until two mounds of sand take shape, cutting off Barbara at the ankles. Barbara stares at them, her face serious, something dark crossing her eyes. 'Bill used to do that. Only he'd bury me up to my neck, he would, and I'd be lying there pinned under this great mountain of sand, and he'd be there laughing at me. Then he'd say, you still look beautiful even under that lot. That's what he'd say. Then he'd leave me right there, all up to my head in his sand cave, then he'd be back with ice-cream cones, saying oh no, looks like I'll have to eat both of these seeing as you're all tied up. And I'd leap up out of the sand and it'd fly everywhere, and we'd sit and eat ice-creams with bits of sand in them, and they were the best things ever.'

We sit there and feel the wind ruffling at our hair. It blows the fake fur on my hood into my eyes and I blink it away and wonder if the prick of tears is only my imagination.

'He sounded lovely,' Kat says softly.

Barbara stares out to the horizon.

'You take your shoes off,' she says to us. 'You should all feel it, like me.'

'But it's cold,' Violet says, shivering.

'It's wonderful,' Barbara says.

So we do. I slip off my ballet flats and my fluffy socks, Amina kicks her stilettos off. I wonder fleetingly what on earth moved her to wear them when she knew where we were going. Kat unlaces her Docs and throws them aside.

'Go on, Vi,' Jodie says.

For once, Violet doesn't correct her. She shrugs, then meticulously removes her own slippers and socks, placing them carefully in the basket underneath her seat, away from the harmful reach of the damp sand. She draws her frame closer still to the rug, and places her bare feet on it, toes just poking out of the Dressing Gown of Doom and edging off the rug, distaste twisting her mouth as fine grains of sand skitter up towards her.

I curl my own toes into the cold sand and breathe out slowly, remembering the sandy ground in the village I was born in, how I would run barefoot and free, catching my feet on scrubby bushes and falling flat on my face and getting up again grinning as Haki stood laughing his head off at me.

We sit together on this rugged November beach, gazing out at the grey Bristol Channel, the horizon heavy with hazy grey mist under a watery sun. I turn my face up, closing my eyes and feeling the weak rays stroking my eyelids.

'My mouse is here, I think,' Barbara says.

No one replies.

'But I want to feel the sea, as well. I want to feel the water.'

Kat shakes her head. 'It's too cold, sweetheart. It wouldn't do you any good.'

Barbara's face falls. 'But I want to feel the sea. Bill and me, we liked to take off our shoes and socks and paddle together, only sometimes he'd jump right in, clothes and all, and pull me in with him.'

'Maybe just a little bit?' Jodie says.

Kat frowns at her.

'How about if we bring the sea to you, Barbara?' Amina says. 'Here, give me one of those cups you have, Jodie. I will put the sea into here for you.'

Barbara's brow crinkles, but then smooths. 'Yes. Yes. You bring me the sea.'

Amina glides down to the water's edge, her *salwar kameez* glittering in the pale sunlight. She scoops seawater into the polystyrene cup and brings it back to us. 'Here is the sea.' She takes one of Barbara's feet in her hands, brushing away the sand, and dips her finger into the cup and then caresses it over Barbara's foot, tracing the line of a vein so tenderly Barbara must barely feel it. Then she dips again and strokes more water over Barbara's foot. Barbara sits transfixed, clasping her hands together.

'Do the other one.'

Amina's eyes crinkle up in a smile as she gently lays Barbara's foot back down and takes the other one in her hand, repeating the process. The sea seems to lap in time with her strokes, the creeping tide weaving in and out, in and out, the sound of it like the sounds I listened to in shells I picked off beaches like this when I was small, when we had come to the UK and I was lost and alone and longed for the great open skies and all the colours again. Listen to the shells, my father said to me, hear the sound of the skies and the water and the great trees waving in the wind. And the sounds were always there.

'What about some hot chocolate, then?' Jodie says, unscrewing the lid from the first flask.

'Good idea,' I say. 'How about we just have a little cup, then we go back?'

'I don't want to go back yet,' Barbara says.

'Nor do I,' says Jodie. 'Let's have this, at least. Let's sit a while longer.'

'Okay,' I say.

Jodie has the flask open. She wrinkles her nose and sniffs at its contents. 'What the hell, Kane? What's he gone and put in here?'

But Kane is back in the minibus, warm and oblivious.

'What is it?' I say.

'It's bloody brandy,' Jodie says, then splutters out in laughter.

Kat rubs her nose. 'We can't give Barbara that. We can't have that, really. Not sure IVs and alcohol mix so well.'

Jodie shrugs. 'I reckon it'd be okay.'

Barbara says, 'Brandy? Give me a little nip of that stuff!'

'Is it the same in the other one?' Kat says.

I open the flask next to me and give it a sniff. 'Phew. Hot chocolate.'

Jodie relaxes. 'He must've had a moment. Like, I mean, he must've meant to put it in both, then got distracted or something.'

'Yeah right,' Kat says.

'Why do you hate him?' Jodie screws the lid too tightly back on her flask and slams it on the ground, turning to Kat with pleading eyes. 'What's he done to you?'

Kat shakes her head. 'Let's just have the hot chocolate.'

I pour it into six cups, just half a cup each until the flask is empty of every last drop. I hand them out and we sip at it. Amina helps Barbara, whose hands are too shaky to hold the cup. It's lukewarm and a bit watery but it tastes like all the goodness of the world rolled up into each tiny, sweet drop.

'Put us a nip of that there brandy in here, will you?' Barbara says to Jodie.

Jodie looks at Kat, who shakes her head.

Barbara narrows her eyes at Kat like a schoolgirl caught in a misdemeanour. 'Spoilsport.'

'The tide's creeping in,' Violet says, shifting backwards as if the frigid water is going to crawl over her bare feet and consume her at any moment. 'Look. It's closer to us than it was.'

It is closer, but not that much closer. There are a good few feet between us and the lapping waves, which gurgle and drag at the surf.

'Tell you what,' Kat says. 'Let's wait till it's nearly up at where we are, and then we'll know it's time to go. Okay with everyone?'

Jodie nods with enthusiasm and Amina and I say yes, good plan. Violet and Barbara both sulk, for different reasons.

We sit in silence, finishing our drinks and gazing out to the misty sea. I shiver as another cloud bank blots out the sun, smothering its paltry warmth. I keep my gloved hands round my cup, drawing out the little heat left in it. The water is increasingly choppy, the waves further out more turbulent, white froth dancing on their tips as the ocean bows and leaps to the sky.

'My little mouse was born near the sea,' Barbara says suddenly. I'd thought Barbara was extra lucid today, with little mention of the mouse or the rat. We should be getting back. She's getting tired and confused.

But Kat moves closer to her. 'Tell us.'

Barbara's mouth is downturned in a thin, mottled-blue line. She picks at the edges of the polystyrene on her empty cup and gazes up at the darkening sky. 'I called her my little mouse because she was so tiny. She was born too soon, you see. She looked like a baby mouse, all shrivelled and tiny with little bright eyes that went dull too quickly. She had downy dark hair all over her body.'

We sit frozen.

'We were going to call her Margaret, you see. Maggie, she'd have been. Our little Maggie Mouse. She was only tiny, smaller than my hand. There was lots of blood. But I knew she was a she, deep in my heart.'

I can't find any words.

'We were on the beach when it happened. Felt the pains, like I'd never felt before, they were sharp and wrong, I just knew they were wrong. I says to Bill, this isn't right, this isn't. I says, this one's on her way, she's coming too soon.'

Silence sags between us.

'Never had no more after Maggie Mouse. They never came, see. And then Bill went, and I was alone.'

Kat takes her hand, and I crawl around to the other side of Barbara and wrap both of mine around her other hand. It feels like a handful of broken flower stems, encased in that crepe paper you get wrapped round delicate items from Etsy. My heart aches.

Jodie shifts until she is kneeling in front of her. 'I'm so sorry, Barbara.'

The dog barks again, only this time it's even further away, a ghost of a bark, a thin cry through the windswept silence.

Barbara stares out to the sea. 'We went to the hospital, but it was too late. She'd come, see, my little Maggie Mouse, she'd not waited long enough.'

No one says anything.

'We never even got to bury her. Wasn't much of her, they said. But I saw enough of her. I saw her little mouth and her eyes. She was still my baby girl. I wanted a service, like, in the church and everything, but it was only a miscarriage, they said. Doctor told me I shouldn't think of her as a baby, I should just move on. But I knew she was. I imagined her every day, how she'd grow, what she'd look like, what she'd wear, who she'd be now. My baby died and I wanted to say goodbye proper and I never did.'

Kat pats her hand so softly, gazing directly into her eyes with such love I can almost taste it.

'And now I've got no one left, have I? Not even Bill. No family left in this world.'

Jodie leans in closer and strokes Barbara's thin white hair, pulling the hat further down over her ears. 'We are your family now. We are the Bay C Family.'

I want to squeeze her hand but don't dare. I might crush her frail bones.

Kat says, 'Would you like me to say a little prayer for Maggie Mouse?'

Barbara stares out at the rolling grey ocean for a while. Then, in the tiniest gasp, she says, 'Yes.'

Kat whispers words into her ear and I watch tears track her sunken cheeks like the blue veins that lace her skin. The wind blows Kat's words away and we sit in the silence of their breath.

'My feet are cold,' Barbara says. I look down at them. They are blue and white all at once, and the red of her nails is like blood on snow.

'Get her socks and slippers,' Kat says, and Jodie heaves herself up. She coughs, a little too pale herself, but she shrugs me off when I offer to get them.

'They're only just here,' she says. She gives the stockings and slippers to Kat, and I help Kat clean and dry Barbara's feet with the corner of the picnic rug, and slip them back onto Barbara's feet.

'They're like ice,' Kat says, shooting me a concerned look.

'We should think about going.'

'I don't want to go,' Barbara says.

Kane shouts down from the minibus, but his shout is snatched away by the gathering wind, which is churning up the sand. 'What?' Jodie shouts back. He shouts again, but we can't hear him. 'I'll just go and see what he wants,' she says. 'Listen, get your stuff together, we should probably go. Anyone know what the time is?'

Kat digs out her phone from her little bag, and glances at me, wide-eyed. 'It's already after half three.'

Jodie scowls. 'It's 'cause he went and took his own stupid route here. Look, give us a sec and start sorting your shoes out.'

She digs her own dampened, sandy feet into her socks and Ugg boots and stomps back off up the beach towards the minibus and

Kane, who stands there with arms crossed and a cigarette hanging from the corner of his mouth. He says something to Jodie and she glowers and says something back to him. He starts shouting, waving his hands around, then he grabs hold of her arms. Even from here I can see he's squeezing too hard. He is hurting her.

Kat pulls her Docs on, grimacing as they resist her, sticking on the dampness of her skin. 'What's he doing?'

'I don't know,' I say.

'I said, didn't I,' Violet says, 'I said he's a bully. Just look at him now!'

Kane has his arms clamped tightly around Jodie, squeezing her firmly against him. I can hear her coughing, but he does not ease off. He draws her in harder, whispering into her ear.

She shoves back at him and shouts something at him, then stops and pats his arm, trying to inch back closer to him. But he pushes her away, his massive hands pressed into her chest as he jabs at her. She stumbles.

'We need to get back up there and help her,' Kat says, struggling with one of her boots.

Amina is up off the rug, shoving her feet into her stilettos, floundering up the sand towards Jodie but making little progress. Violet struggles to get herself up from her walker seat, moaning about her stiff old bones. I pull on my socks and shoes and drag myself to my feet, then tuck my arm into Violet's, helping her up. The afternoon chill catches at my chest and I gasp. It must be below freezing out here.

'Leave me alone!' I hear Jodie yell in a high, strangled voice, as she shrugs Kane's hands away from her and turns away, looking back at us, her face ravaged with something like pain.

'Fine,' he shouts.

Jodie lurches back towards us, her hair flowing loose and wild and whipping her face as the wind rips the Santa hat from her head.

'Are you okay?' Amina says, reaching her and laying her hand on her arm.

Jodie shrugs her arm off.

'Sorry,' Amina says. 'I was just a bit worried for you.'

'Oh, take no notice of him. He's just messing around. He's just being a bit of an idiot.'

'He doesn't deserve you,' Kat says, picking up the hat and giving it back.

Jodie looks at her feet.

Kat helps me lift Barbara back into her wheelchair and we wrap her up again, tucking the blankets in around her slight body and her hat over her head, covering her ears from the bitterness of the mounting wind. I don't mention the racking pain that roars through my body as I straighten up.

It's then we hear an engine, cutting through the wind and shattering the quiet of the bay. Jodie whirls round quickly, her face an oh of horror. 'He's going. He's going without us.'

We watch in disbelief as he reverses the minibus, knocking over the tattered *Sea Bay* sign and skidding into an untidy turn, then swerving up the entry track towards the main road and out of sight.

He's gone, and left us all alone.

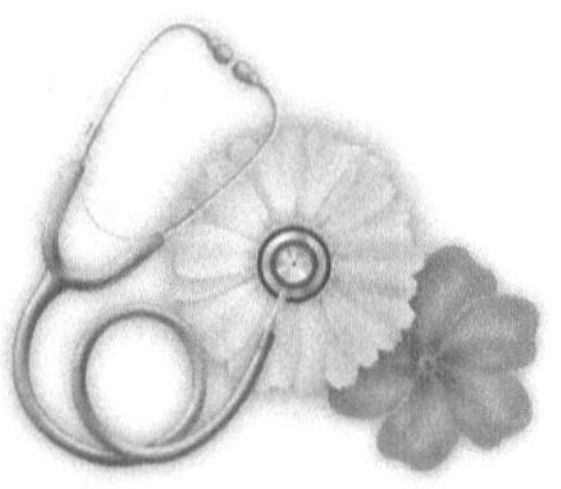

Chapter 23

'I'M SO SORRY. I'm so sorry.' Jodie stands there, her entire body shaking, wringing her hands, tears streaming down her cheeks. 'I'm so sorry. We had an argument. He told me I looked fat, that suddenly he could see how fat I was, sat there in the sand in this stupid jumper. He told me I looked ugly and I kind of just told him he was no oil painting and then he grabbed me and said all this stuff to me, and then he was pushing me and it hurt, and… and I'm so sorry, he's just gone.'

Kat lays a hand on her shoulder. 'Jodie. You've done nothing wrong.'

Jodie's eyes are wild. 'But I have. He's gone. If I'd not argued back, if I'd not said that stupid thing about the oil painting, he'd not've gone.'

Kat's jaw is tight. 'It's him that's the issue. Not you. It's never been you, Jodie.'

I know that Jodie thinks it is her and that it's going to take her a while to believe that it's him, after all. Sometimes even now I still think everything that happened with Marcus is my fault. Even fifteen years later I sometimes wonder what would have happened if I hadn't led him to the edge of it all. Maybe he wouldn't have hit me. Maybe he would have stayed, and Jake would have had a father. But it's as if this beach, these women, this whole surreal afternoon, have all sparked a new clarity in the recesses of my mind. It's as if I can suddenly see clearly. Half-truths I have told myself for years become downright lies, shame I have carried is starting to melt away, like so much slush after the snow melts. I hope it will pour down the drain and be gone forever.

Jodie drags her hands over her face, batting the tears away. 'It's my fault.'

Kat sighs. 'No. It's not. He's a loser, lovely. But we've got other things to worry about now.'

'What are we going to do?' I say.

Violet shakes her head. 'Never trusted him. Never should've come.' She is clinging so tightly to her walker her knuckles strain against her skin.

Kat turns and snaps at her. 'Look, will you stop being such a grumpy mare? We're here, and Barbara's felt the sand and the sea.'

Violet huffs. 'Charming, I'm sure.'

Kat has no patience left for her grumblings. 'Just stop it. Just stop being so up yourself you keep the rest of us down. It's fine. I'll call one of those wheelchair accessible taxis for us, the ones with enough seats. It's fine.' She digs her phone out of her pocket and stabs at it. 'You have to be kidding.'

I go colder than the very cold I was already.

'No damn reception,' she says. 'Not one bar. Nothing.'

'I'll check mine,' Jodie says. 'Might be a different network.' She fishes in her jacket pockets, frowning. 'Oh no, wait… Kane. The photo. He never gave me my phone back, did he?'

I stare at her.

She presses both hands to her forehead. 'You couldn't make this up. What about yours, Penny?'

I shake my head slowly. 'My bag… it's in the minibus. I didn't think I'd need it and the sand was too wet and I had too much stuff. Has no one got a phone? Amina?'

I try not to worry too much about getting my handbag back.

'I forgot it. It is in the hospital, on charge,' Amina says slowly.

'I don't believe this,' Kat says.

Violet doesn't even have a phone. Those new-fangled things, she calls them, a look of distrust stamped on her face. You'll never get her using one of those things. Except when she wants one of us to call Brian for her and tell him to bring her a clean nightie and decent food, that is.

'Can't you get the internet?' Amina says to Kat. 'I mean, have you any data at all?'

'Nothing.'

'What on earth are we supposed to do now?' Violet says.

I look around me wildly, as if I might find an answer somewhere in the wilds of the ocean or the grit of the sand or the multitude of greys in the sky.

But the sand is silent and the sky is hostile. No one has a phone and there is no one else on this frozen lonely beach that stretches for miles. And the tide is creeping in.

'I heard a dog, earlier,' Kat says, shielding her eyes and searching the horizon in every direction. 'Someone was out here somewhere.'

But there is nothing. No dog owner materialising out of the mist, ready to rescue us with a working phone.

Nobody.

'Are there any houses, shops nearby?' I ask Jodie, but she shakes her head.

'There's a caravan park over there, see? And there's a café and shop up there too.' She points into the distance where a few tired-looking static caravans sit behind a boundary of scraggly naked trees. 'But it's all closed down for the winter. Besides, none of us are going to be able to get there, are we? Let's face it.'

None of us can walk more than a few metres, let alone miles to some battened down caravans in the vain hope the owner might be around out of season.

Barbara stares dreamily at the sky. 'Look. The sun is starting to go down.'

I gaze out at the sea. The sun is low behind the gathering layers of cloud, but there is a break in the grey as rays play and reflect on the water, muted corals and pastel peaches draping the horizon, as if through a gauze curtain of mist. The colours gather and race through the heavens, twisting and whirling like ribbons, a dance of glory as the sky begins its fade into darkness. The clocks went back a couple of weeks ago and the nights draw in early. I shiver and pull my scarf tight around my face.

'Can we watch it? The sunset?' Barbara wheedles like a small child, seemingly unaware of our plight. 'One more sunset. Bill used to take me to the beach at sunset. We'd take this tartan flask, like these ones today, full of hot cocoa, and watch the sun go down beyond the sea. He'd bring these deckchairs, he would, remember them ones with the blue stripes? He'd have them under his arm then he'd set them up and say here, my queen, take your throne, and then he'd pour out the cocoa and we'd just sit and gaze at it, the beauty of it all. We did it when we were young and when we were old too, we did, and those deckchairs, well, they never even got broken. Still got them in the shed, but I don't go in there now. I don't want to use them chairs now.'

We stand there and stare at her. What are we supposed to do now?

Jodie sinks down onto the sand and puts her head into her hands.

'Are you sure there are no houses nearby?' Kat says. 'I think I could walk a little distance.'

'I, too,' Amina says.

Jodie shakes her head. 'Don't think so. There's a village, further down that main road, but it's miles away, like literally about three miles I think. We used to go in the little shop there and buy drinks and crisps to bring here. An' I don't know about houses, but I don't think so. Not that I've noticed before, anyway. An' I've been coming here since I was small. It's nice in the summer, honest.' Her words pour out in a rush and suddenly she wilts, rubs at her forehead, squeezing her eyes shut against tears that spill out regardless and crawl down her cheeks. She looks too pale to me, too worn out. Maybe this was too much for her, after all. Maybe it was too much for all of us. Maybe we've done a really, really stupid thing. I look at Barbara and my stomach cramps with anxiety. She looks warm enough, all cocooned in her blankets, but what if it rains? What if no one comes by? What if we can't find anyone? We could die of exposure out here, all of us, stranded on a freezing beach in the middle of winter. Why did I go along with this stupidity? Why am I Penny who always says yes?

Kat crouches down next to Jodie. 'Look. It's no good getting all upset. We're just going to have to get ourselves up to that road, and flag someone down. There'll be someone.'

Violet narrows her eyes. 'Can we all get up there?'

'It's not so far,' I say. 'Look, we can see the top of the track from here. We can. We have to.'

I know it's going to just about finish me off, but I also know I will manage it. Whether Violet will I'm not sure, or Amina, who looks grey and shattered, her head bent low as she shivers, arms clasped tightly around herself, or Jodie, who all of a sudden looks as though she should be tucked back in her hospital bed with a warm drink and hot water bottle. I've never really understood that saying about all the colour draining out of your face, but as I watch Jodie now it happens to her before my eyes. She looks like a ghost, almost translucent with paleness and fragility. She was the strongest of us all, I thought. She has to be the strongest of us all, but now it seems like Kat might be.

Or even, maybe, me.

'Come on,' I say. 'Let's start walking, before it gets too dark.' I fold up the frog chair and the picnic blanket and stow them under my arm.

'But I want to watch the sun go down,' Barbara says, her mouth quivering into a pout as Kat gets hold of her chair and begins to push it slowly back up the beach. 'I want to see the sun setting again. Just once more.'

Kat stops and looks at me as if I must suddenly have the answer. Her eyes are wide and scared. My heart is beating too quickly as I kneel down in front of Barbara and place my hand on her knee. She feels skeletal, even under the tightly tucked-in blankets. 'Barbara, darling. I know you do. But look. Jodie's a bit poorly, and you're getting cold. We need to get back.'

Barbara's mouth is set in a stubborn line. 'I want to see the sunset.'

Violet tuts and opens her mouth to speak, but Amina turns to her, placing a finger against her mouth and shaking her head, and Violet shrugs and looks away.

I pat Barbara's knee. 'I know. But look, we've all seen the sea, haven't we? We've all felt the sun on our faces. We've all felt the sand between our toes. And now we can see the sun starting to go down, can't we? See it now, Barbara, look. It's low in the sky, it's blazing its last rays of the afternoon just for you.'

Barbara gazes up at the sky and her eyes widen. The sun is fighting one last battle against the fiercely gathering clouds, battling to show off its final fuzzy glory of the day, reaching out weary fingers to touch our faces one more time.

'It's about to plunge into the sea,' I say. 'But it's just shining on you for a while longer.'

Barbara closes her eyes and keeps her face upturned to the setting sun. Her face seems alight from within, the muted winter colours dashing over her luminescent skin and morphing into the hope of spring. On a cluster of rocks out to sea a flock of cormorants stand proudly and shriek at the fading skies.

'It's beautiful, isn't it?' My knees hurt from kneeling on the rough sand, but I don't care too much. I gaze up with her, to the arch of the heavens, the subdued colours of misted sunset. I'd forgotten how big the world is, cooped up in hospital and in my small life. I'd forgotten the heights and depths, the widths and lengths, but here they are all laid out before me, and they make me want to cast off my pain and dance on the sand. I am a tiny dot in a huge great universe, but I can see there is a vastness inside me, too, a wide expanse I've barely explored the edges of. And somehow, today, it's like I'm pushing open a new door, gazing at a new scene, and it's wild and raw and beautiful.

I turn back to Barbara. 'It's time to go, now. You ready?'

She nods, a tiny smile quivering at her mouth.

I nod at Kat as I drag myself up, steadying myself on the arm of the wheelchair. As we trudge up the beach, Jodie links arms with me. 'Didn't know you was so poetic. All that about the sunset and whatnot.'

I used to write little poems, once upon a time, to go with the pictures I painted. But Marcus said that they sounded ridiculous and that I should concentrate on building my body up so I could go out and get a normal job in an office. I gave him a poem I wrote about him, when I first met him and I was starry eyed with passion. I was proud of it, I was certain that my verbs sang and my adjectives danced, that my words bounced with colour. I thought that, at last, someone was giving me inspiration to give the best part of myself, this new man who loved me, who wanted to help me so much that he chose me out of a gym full of gorgeous, toned, fit women who had normal jobs in offices. I put oil to canvas and created a portrait of him where I brought out the mischievous sparkle in his eyes and the lustre of his hair, and then I scratched out my little poem on the canvas and wrapped it up for his birthday, my stomach tense with nervous excitement. He opened it and he laughed. What the hell is this, he said, and then, when he read the poem, he laughed even more. You really wrote this? Have you any idea how crazy you sound, Penny? Then he stowed the canvas at the back of our wardrobe and we never spoke of it again, and I never wrote another poem and I never painted another picture.

'I'm not really,' I say.

'You are,' Jodie says. 'You put yourself down too much, you do. You can't see who you really are.'

That's because I don't think I know who I really am. But I think I might know a little bit more than I did two weeks ago, and I think that little bit more is something I like, and I think I might want to keep exploring and start throwing off all the bad things I thought I was before. That might take me a long time, though.

At the entrance to the track the *Sea Bay* sign lies battered and broken, already covered over by a layer of sand. 'Goodbye, Sea Bay,' Jodie says.

The track itself isn't all that long. Maybe thirty yards. But those thirty yards seem like a thousand right now and we drag our feet, taking it in turns to push the wheelchair so that we can lean on it. Violet leans heavily on the walker, almost bent double as she plods along, the small plastic wheels catching and sticking in the sandy gravel. Nobody has breath to say a word as we slog our way up to the road, the bitter wind buffeting our faces. I keep my eyes to the ground and concentrate on my feet. One foot in front of the other, Dan would say. Keep going, Penny, you can do it, a little at a time, one, two, one, two. Amina's stilettos clack in time with my thoughts and I zero in my focus to the sound they make. Clack clack clack clack one two one two. They are scuffed now, their patent shine dulled by sand and salt and gravelly path.

'Why on earth did you wear those things?' Violet says suddenly. Perhaps she's seen me focussing on Amina's feet. Perhaps the sound of her heels are the only thing we can all concentrate on right now, our only rally call to keep on going. 'They seem completely unsuitable!'

Amina exhales slowly, turning to face Violet. Her brown eyes are sunken, the darkened rings around them a messy circle of pain and suffering. 'Because they are what I like.'

'Good for you,' Kat says.

Violet's lip curls. 'Silly girl.'

Don't spoil it, Violet, I want to say. Don't spoil it all now, not after all of this, not after what Amina did for you back at the hospital, not when we've come this far.

Amina just laughs. 'I am a silly girl. And I do not care.'

'Right on,' Kat says, and fist punches Amina.

Jodie is unusually quiet, and says nothing at all.

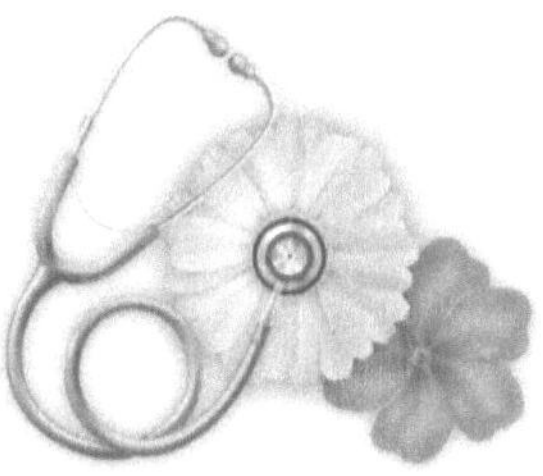

Chapter 24

THE NOT-SO-main-road stretches off into a desolated, silent, carless distance. The sea crashes behind us, rolling waves lurching higher as the wind picks up and the sun goes down. It's an uninhabited wasteland, scrubby tired grassland waving listlessly in the wind, a few sad splashes of colour breaking up its winter captivity. As we drag up to the road we stand there and we gaze in both directions, as if by looking we will conjure something – someone – up.

But nothing. No one is in sight.

'What do we do now?' Violet says, wrapping her arms tightly around herself and looking at me. Why is she looking at me?

'I don't know,' I say.

Kat pulls her onesie hood further over her head. 'All we can do is wait. We wait for a car and we flag it down. Surely someone'll stop for us, when they see Barbara and everything.'

Barbara sits there in her wheelchair, backed onto the grass verge next to a crumbling drystone wall, bundled up in blankets and face pale with cold, yet smiling like she knows a secret, her faded eyes sparkling with merriment. She is the only one who seems completely unmoved and unworried by our plight.

'Yeah,' I say. 'I'm sure someone will be along in a minute or two.'

We stand there and scan the horizon. To our left the road stretches off into the mist-clogged horizon, and to our right it curves into a bend not far from where we are. But we cannot see anything and we cannot hear anything.

'My legs hurt,' Violet says, leaning over her walker and breathing heavily.

Mine do too. They feel wobbly as well, fragile and insubstantial, as if any moment they might shatter underneath me and slam me to the ground.

'I am sure a car will come soon,' Amina says, sliding her arm through Violet's and placing the walker next to the wheelchair, by the wall. 'But let's get this set up for you, to have a little sit. A little bit of shelter here for you, from the wind.'

A car does come soon. It is coming now, hurtling around the bend at far too high a speed for this kind of road.

Kat waves at it.

Then it screeches past us without slowing, its taillights disappearing too quickly into the distance.

'Damn it,' Kat says.

We wait five more agonising minutes for another one. It comes and it goes again, slowing slightly to look at us. I realise we must look an odd sight, with our manic waving, with our strange attire and selection of walking aids. We must look like a tableau in the London Dungeon, or a diverse hen party who have drunk too much and got lost somewhere in the wilds of the countryside.

Jodie stumbles back against a low section of the wall. 'I can't stand no longer.' She hunkers down and lowers her head to her knees.

I sit down with her, my legs wobbling so much that I almost sprawl right over her. I hold out the frog chair to Amina, who takes it and sits down so gracefully she might as well be in a period drama, all crossed ankles and folded hands. Kat stays standing, shading her eyes as she stares up and down the road. There's nothing much to shade her eyes from, because the sun is low behind us, almost swallowed up by the sea. It must be almost four by now. Nearly dark. The sky draws closer over us, layers of clouds like great shrouds suspended across the heavens in rows and rows of whites and greys, so many shades I can't take them all in, silver-grey and blue-grey and purple-grey and a grey so dark it is nearly black, so low the sky itself might break and fall on us any minute.

Violet groans loudly as her bones squeak and click. 'I need a fag.'

'Kane took them,' Jodie says.

I look at Jodie and worry. Her skin seems even paler than before and she is breathing too shallowly, tiny gasps escaping from her mouth and forming puffs of cloud in the frozen air. She needs oxygen, I think. We should have brought oxygen for her.

We should have done so many things.

She is shivering in her wolf fleece and thin denim jacket with its useless cloth hood. I drape the picnic rug over her shoulders and she pulls it around herself, tugging the Santa hat further over her ears. I must thank Jake for not bothering to search for my favourite hat.

We sit there like drooping flowers as the darkness draws in around us and the road remains empty. Another car comes, and goes, and then a white van, which slows to a crawl, the driver opening the window and hollering at us then leaving us with an obscene gesture to remember him by, the woman in his passenger seat screeching with laughter.

'Seeing the best of humanity out here,' Kat says dully. We huddle further into our coats and dressing gowns and blankets and the sun drops below sea level behind us back at the shore.

Jodie sniffs and I realise she is crying again, only this time it's more silent, the tears scurrying down her cheeks, leaving great tracks of misery. I sit closer to her and put my arms around her, and she leans into my shoulder. Her body is rigid and shivering all at the same time so I pull her closer and unzip my parka, then I wrap it around as much of her as I can and try and infuse warmth into her. 'Don't cry,' I say, helplessly.

'But it's my fault.'

'It's not,' Kat says. 'You have to see that.'

'I did this, though. It was my idea. I dragged you lot out here, you kept telling me no, don't be so stupid Jodie, and I wouldn't listen, would I?'

'Please don't blame yourself,' I say. 'We all went along with it, didn't we? We're free agents.'

'If anyone is to blame, it's that great oaf of an ex-boyfriend of yours,' Kat says.

Jodie peeks out of the top of her blanket at her, eyes widened. 'Ex?'

'Well, I bloody hope so,' Kat says. 'Left us all high and dry out here, knowing we're all vulnerable, including an eighty-seven-year-old. What kind of person is he? Is he someone you really want to be with?'

Jodie gazes up at the murky sky. 'I don't know. He loves me, really, though. He's just a bit, I don't know, a bit impulsive sometimes. He'll probably be back any minute, saying he's sorry, he never meant to, he just got a bit cross, that he loves me really.'

'He loves himself, sweetheart,' I find myself saying. 'And I know that, because I've been there.'

'You have?'

I search under the picnic rug for Jodie's gloved hand and take it in mine, squeezing it softly. 'I was with someone like that.'

'Jake's dad?'

'Jake's father, yes. He's never been any kind of dad to him, though. Never even laid eyes on him. Ran off with my so-called best friend and decided he didn't want to be burdened with a kid.'

'Bastard.'

'Right?' I lean my head on hers. 'But you see, it was the same. He said the same things to me, about loving me I mean, about doing anything for me. Always made me believe it was me in the wrong. Made me think I could never be enough, or do enough, to deserve him.'

Jodie picks her fingernails.

'But it's him who didn't deserve you,' Kat says.

'I never thought that,' I say. 'I always thought he was right. Thought it for years, that somehow it was some, I don't know, kind of like a deficiency in me, that I hadn't managed to keep hold of him, this man who seemed to want the best for me.'

'But he wanted the best for himself.'

'Yeah, I guess. And that's just what I see, in Kane. He's only all about Kane.'

'But, he always says he loves me.' Jodie's voice is devoid of its usual colour. 'He calls me his princess, see.'

Kat snorts. 'That's 'cause he sees himself as some kind of prince, like some kind of saviour dude. He wants any glory for himself.'

'That was Marcus, too,' I say softly. 'Kept making it about him, and then it was too late, before I saw him for who he was. I thought I was lucky, see, thought any woman would want someone like him, so charming, so handsome, so thought it was my fault when he… when he did stuff. Took me a long time to realise it wasn't, to be honest with you, even now I still think like that, sometimes.'

It's Christmas when it happens. I am newly pregnant, and bursting with excitement about telling Marcus. We haven't planned this, it just happened, probably because I wasn't careful enough. Maybe I forgot my pill or something. But I know how excited he will be, how he will whirl me in his arms and tell me that I am beautiful and that he can't wait to be a daddy. When I pee on the stick and see the blue cross stark against the white plastic my pulse speeds up, and just for a moment I panic, but then joy sweeps through me like a wave of warmth.

He comes in from work late. He's been busy with clients toning up for Christmas parties, working until late into the evening, bringing in the money that means I can be kept in style, living in his sumptuous flat with its view over the town and out to the hills.

He's gruff with me tonight. I've prepared his favourite meal, medium-rare steak with hand-cut chips. I used to be vegetarian before I met Marcus, but he told me it was making me unhealthy and that it was important we ate together and developed the same tastes, so I started eating meat again. I don't ever tell him that I don't much like it, because it would hurt him and I don't want to do that. So I keep quiet and force the meat down. It's good for me. Lately, though, I've been wondering, I've been thinking about asserting myself. Maybe he will be proud of me, just another step along the way to the new me he has created.

'What's up with you?'

I'm twitchy, perching on the edge of my seat, wringing my hands under the table. For some reason I'm nervous to tell him this news that will change our world. I can't seem to find the right words for it.

I shrug. 'Nothing. Just… I just—'

'Spit it out.'

I gulp in a breath and exhale slowly. 'I just have something to tell you.'

He stabs his fork into a great hunk of steak and shoves it into his mouth. 'What?' he says, around his loud chewing, one eye on his phone on the table. I flinch for a second as a wave of nausea pummels through my body.

I bite down on my lip.

'Out with it,' he says. 'What excitement do you have for me today? Did the kettle break down? Did you finally hoover my office? Did you manage more than half-an-hour of your Davina fitness DVD without collapsing on the floor like a great beached whale?'

My mouth is dry.

He looks at me, scowling so loudly it is almost audible. 'Are you going to tell me, or what?'

'I'm pregnant.'

He doesn't respond for a few moments. He stares into my eyes, then back at his dinner, then into my eyes again and his eyes are fading into pinpricks of ice. My stomach lurches as cold reality hits me in the face. How long will I keep lying to myself about him? About our relationship?

'What?'

'I'm pregnant. Look. Here.' I dig out the test stick I'm sitting on, wrapped up in a ribbon earlier in my eager excitement.

'What is that?'

'I—'

He whips it from my hand and looks at it, and then back at me, and then back at his dinner.

Everything turns to slow-motion as he scrapes his chair back, picks up his plate and hurls it at the wall behind me, rivulets of gravy cascading down the Farrow and Ball eggshell paint that he picked out. He's out from the table and round to me before I can take in what is happening.

My heart is beating too quickly and sweat prickles at my armpits. 'I thought you'd be pleased.'

He doesn't speak any more words to me. He sets his mouth in a grim line and his eyes are narrowed and pinched together as he gets right into my face, like he does when he kisses me except this is not like that. This time he yanks at me, pulling me out of my chair, and I stumble and trip against the wall behind me, falling to the ground. He stands over me, crunched up on the floor, and then his hand is flying to my face before I can move out of the way, and then all I can feel is an explosion of pain and all I can see is a burst of dizzy light.

Later on he says that he knows he shouldn't have done that, but it is my fault because I shouldn't have got pregnant. A part of me wants to say that it takes two to tango but I don't dare. He doesn't say sorry, exactly, but he goes out and he buys me some flowers and says that it's because he loves me so very much, and because he has got me so far, and now pregnancy will undo all his good work and make me sick again. It's only because he cares so much that he got so angry. So I turn to him and snuggle into his neck and say it's okay, I understand why and I'm sorry I was careless. I say please don't stop loving me. He shushes me and says it's fine, it's okay, we can get rid of it, and Penny please don't tell anyone about this because you know I didn't mean it.

'He hit me because I got pregnant. With Jake. And other times, too. I always thought it was my fault.'

Kat gazes at me and her eyes are pools of pain.

'I got away a few months later, but those few months I couldn't see him for what he was. He wanted me to terminate the pregnancy, but I didn't want to, and he hit me then, as well. And then he left.'

No one says anything for a few moments. We listen to the whisper of the wind in the trees, and I think it sounds like the cry of a girl who is lost.

'Kane never hits me, though,' Jodie says. 'He'd never lay a finger on me.'

Kat shakes her head. 'Stop minimising his behaviour. We've seen how he manhandles you, Jodie, how he grabs you that bit too tightly.'

Jodie's shoulders tense under the blanket.

'We've all seen it. He pushes you around, darling.'

'No he doesn't.'

'Yes,' I say. 'Yes, he does.'

Jodie's mouth quivers. 'But he's there for me.'

'Not here for you now, is he?' Kat says, and Jodie says nothing to that.

'But we are,' I say.

Jodie stares up at me through brimming eyes. 'Aren't you mad at me?'

'No,' I say.

'A little,' Kat says, and then laughs, and then Jodie smiles just a little bit.

'Look at you now,' I say. 'You're free and you're magnificent without him. He dampens you down, Jodie. He makes you into a paler you, and none of us like that, do we ladies?'

'It is true,' Amina says. 'He makes you into someone you are not. And you always are saying to me, I am controlled, I am forced to be with Bilal and I should set myself free, but you know that it is you who are controlled and me that is free. But it can be like that no longer. He has let you go free and you can take your wings up and fly away now.'

Jodie gazes at the sky.

'You are glorious without him,' I say.

'And so are you, Penny,' Kat says. 'You are glorious and you don't realise quite how glorious.'

'We're all glorious,' Jodie says, smiling through her tears. 'We're the flowers who are blooming even on this gloomy day.'

'We might be flowers, but we'll be the dying flowers if we don't get back to that hospital,' Violet says. 'There hasn't been a car for ages. I hope one of you has a bright idea, because this just isn't working, is it?'

She's right. We have been sitting on this verge for over twenty minutes now, and nobody has come to our rescue. Kane hasn't had a change of heart and returned, probably because he doesn't have much of a heart. And if no one comes, we will wilt away and die.

'I don't know what to do,' I say, and everyone seems to wither before me, as if they were blossoming for a moment but then the summer died. I turn to Kat. She's the sensible one. She'll have something up her sleeve. 'Do you?'

She just shakes her head, and then she lowers herself onto her knees on a patch of grass and closes her eyes.

'What are you doing?' Jodie says.

Kat is silent.

Amina puts her finger on her lips, and whispers, 'What do you think she is doing?'

Violet wrinkles her nose. 'Whatever floats her boat, I guess. Lot of use it's done so far this afternoon.'

'Shut up, Violet,' I say, and she looks up in surprise, and I am surprised too.

The darkness draws in further, bringing the cold with it and the damp we can feel under our bottoms and through our bones. Jodie wheezes too loudly and I worry.

Barbara puts out her red-gloved hand, palm upwards, a look of wonder in her eyes. 'Snow!' she says, and she sounds like a small child gazing out of her window on Christmas Eve, voice high with excitement and the promise of what is to come.

'You said it would be dry all day today,' Violet says to Jodie with baleful eyes, shivering and zipping her silver coat up to the top, burying her mouth and nose.

Jodie sticks out her chin. 'It said that! Well, I mean, it said it might snow tonight, through the night like, but it said there would be sun through the day, then might get chilly towards late afternoon. Not that it would snow this early or nothing.'

'But there it is,' I say.

It only comes in slow floaty flakes, at first, but it is as if time slows down as I gaze at them. I can almost make out the complex intricacy of each one, as if an artist has taken time to craft them from nothing into an explosion of great and mysterious beauty.

'I don't like snow,' Violet says.

Why doesn't that surprise me? She doesn't like sand, either, or the sea, or very much at all. Yet it seems she might like us a little more than she did. She liked us enough to come on this doomed outing.

'It's too cold,' she says, 'snow, I mean. And wet.'

'Look,' Jodie croaks. 'There.'

Something is coming over the horizon to the west of us. It takes shape as a battered rust-coloured people-carrier trundling slowly down the road pulling a huge old caravan. The car is a Zafira, I think. When Marcus and I got married I used to plan out our life, how we would have three or four children and buy a Zafira with seven seats and travel the country with our happy brood. Marcus would be a good father, I thought. He'd bring them up to be the best that they could be, to be useful and wholesome people.

The car draws closer. Through the murky dusk I can just about make out seventies-style floral curtains waving slightly in the windows of the battered, ancient caravan, which looks like something Jeremy Clarkson would like to play racing games involving fiery finales with.

Kat scrambles to her feet and is out on the road in seconds, ready to flag the driver down. The rest of us remain sitting, steeped in lethargy and apathy. Why should this one be any different?

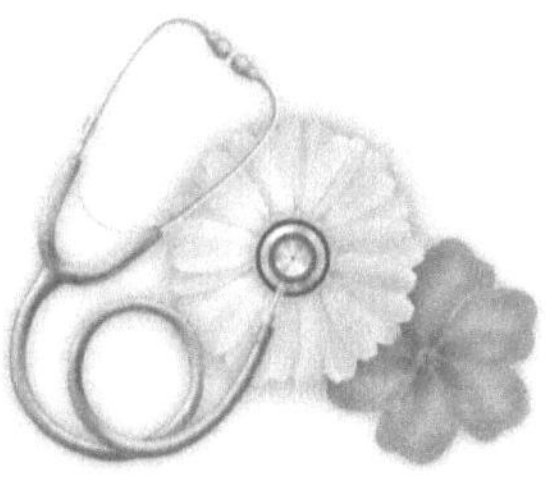

Chapter 25

KAT IS NOT taking no for an answer.

'It's too dark,' I say. 'He might not see you.'

She shakes her head. 'He's going that slowly.'

Something is making a very unhealthy sound and I'm not sure whether it's the car or the caravan, a kind of clanking, shrieking sound, amplified with each second as the getup limps closer. It seems to take an age to get here, and Kat shifts from foot to foot in impatience, waiting until the driver is in sight to start waving her arms around. She doesn't just wave, though. She shouts, too, and her shout is a high-pitched screech: 'STOP! STOP!'

The car squeals to a halt and the driver opens the window.

'What the hell is this?'

Nobody knows what to say to that, so we stay silent. None of us can form many words anymore, anyway. Even Kat is quiet, spent in her heroic efforts to bring this thing to a stop and get us out of this intolerable situation. I heave myself off the wall and join Kat next to his open window.

'What do you all think you look like? Granny's night out gone wrong, is it? Little too much of the sherry and now you've got lost? What do you want?' His shadowed face cuts in a frown so spiky his skin is sliced in ribbons. 'I don't have time for this. I have to go.'

'You can't,' I say.

'Yes, I can. Get out of my way.'

'No,' Kat says.

He stares her down and she stares back until his eyes drift off to the side, widening and then creasing up into even deeper crevices. 'Wait, is she okay?'

He's looking at Barbara, whose face is almost buried between her Bristol Rovers bobble hat and her blanket shroud. She has her hands stuffed inside her dressing gown and she is slumped down as if all of a sudden everything has become too much for her.

'No,' Jodie says, 'she is not okay. We have to get her to the hospital. *You* have to get her – all of us – to the hospital.'

He has long, ratty, mousy-brown hair tied back in a messy ponytail, thinning on top, and bulbous eyes like a dead fish. He grimaces at us, revealing protruding teeth and a gold incisor.

'I bleedin' don't,' he says, and starts sliding his window up. It sticks and shudders and he curses.

'It's the rat,' Barbara says, her quivering finger pointing straight at him.

'I'm out of here,' he says.

Jodie drags herself out in front of his car and bangs on the windscreen. 'You. Have. To. Help. Us.' It's like she is dredging up some pocket of energy she didn't know she had and spilling it all out in one great big splurge.

'No. I. Do. Not.'

Kat steps nearer to him and lowers her face so she's on a level with him. She flinches a little and I wonder if he has bad breath. 'Could you at least phone the police for us? Or at least a taxi, or something – anything? Our phones aren't working.'

He shakes his head. 'I'm not calling the pigs, or no one else. Get out of my way, you freak.'

'Can you not take us into town at least, or even the nearest village, if you can't get us to the hospital? Then we can get help, and you can get on with your important business.' Kat spits the last two words out and his eyes narrow into slits at her. If slits could still bulge out, that's his eyes right now.

'No,' he shouts. 'If you don't get out my way I'm gonna run you over.' He's looking at Jodie now, who is still leaning on the centre of his bonnet.

Kat puffs her cheeks out. 'Listen. Do you want a sick old lady dying on your conscience? Do you? Because that is what is going to happen if you don't help us.'

His eyes shift sideways.

'You can fit us all in this thing,' Kat says. 'Just drop us somewhere, anywhere that's not out in the wild like here. By a house or something.'

He chews on his lip and his incisor glints.

He looks at Barbara again. 'Where am I supposed to put that great big chair thing?' And then he turns his gaze to Violet, with a slight sneer twisting his mouth, probably at the Dressing Gown of Doom/Spaceman combo. He points to her walking frame. 'And that piece of crap there?'

'Well,' Violet says, her hand skittering to her throat, 'I never heard such rudeness.'

Kat points to the caravan he's trailing. 'Well, you've got that great big piece of crap there, haven't you? I think we can probably get a chair and walker in that thing between us.'

He shakes his head, his lips pulled back from his teeth in a pouty kind of snarl. 'I'll do that. Don't need you lot interfering in my caravan.' He crashes his door open and wrenches his bulk out of his beat-up seat, the old fabric torn and faded. 'I am only doing this for her,' he says, nodding at Barbara. 'But I can only take you to the next village. No further. I'm on holiday, and I'm late.'

'*Holiday?*' Kat mouths at me. I can't imagine anything much worse than a holiday in a bashed-up old caravan in late November.

'I'll have to put the seats down in the back,' he grumbles, slamming his door closed against the snow and stomping round to the boot. He yanks the seats into place, all the time letting out a stream of obscenities even Kane would pale at.

'An' you expect me to just lift that thing into my van?' He nods at Barbara's chair again, his eyes popping even further out. Maybe they will fall out altogether and lie on his mottled red cheeks, continuing to give out their glares of incredulity and creep around me with that slight lascivious look I'm picking up.

'We said we'd help,' Kat says, hopping from one foot to the other. 'But can we get a move on, please? You need to go on holiday, after all, don't you?'

I don't know where she is getting the energy to argue with his level of obnoxious, but inside I'm applauding her and wishing a little bit that I was her.

He huffs like a great whale expelling air through its blowhole. 'Well, you lot get her sat in the car, then, and I'll sort this thing out. And give us that.' He whips the walker away from Violet who wobbles and teeters and falls against Amina, and drags it over to his caravan, shoving a key into the door and slamming it open.

Kat and I help Barbara into the front seat. She is less sparkly than she was just moments ago, fading by the second. A wave of heat hits us as we open the door, and it feels good. 'Ah,' she says. 'Now we just need a cuppa and everything'll be right as rain.'

'Or snow,' Amina says.

I stash the oxygen cylinder in the footwell next to Barbara and then wheel the chair over to the driver, the wheels that were never meant for anything more than hospital corridors and outdoor concrete walkways faltering on the rough-surfaced road. 'Here you go.'

He spins round and glares at me. 'Get out of my way. Get into the car. I'll do this.'

'I can lift it up to you,' I say.

He bares his teeth at me and suddenly his eyes are more than a watery bulge of unpleasantness; now they are terrifying great orbs of menace.

'Okay. Okay.' I show him my palms and back away slowly. I try and see what's behind him in there, what he's being so precious about, but it's in heavy shadow and I can only make out vague shapes. He steps out of the van and grabs the chair, then tries to shove it in, but it doesn't want to fit. With a great deal of drama and huffing and puffing, he pushes it through the door, a little at a time, shouting curses at it and back at us. I hold out the frog chair, and he snarls so much I feel like his mouth will crack in two.

In the car it is so warm the windows have steamed up. I clamber into one of the back two seats, with Jodie in the other, and Amina, Violet and Kat in the middle row of three. We let out a big collective sigh of relief as we sink into the ancient seats, where, despite rusted springs poking up through the tatty fabric, it's like we've suddenly landed in great luxury. The bulge-eyed man slams the boot down over me and Jodie and we look at each other and giggle. 'It's like I'm a kid again,' Jodie says, 'sat in my dad's boot when he had too many of us kids in the car to fit. That's before he naffed off and left us all alone with Mum, though.'

He climbs into the driving seat and thumps his hands down on the wheel. He mutters to himself and does a whole lot of sighing and tutting. 'Why I agreed to this madness I'll never know.'

'Because you have some heart underneath all that lot,' Kat says.

'Shut up. Shut the hell up. You're not making noise in my car, if you want me to take you any further at all.'

Jodie whispers, 'Your prayers suck, Kat. You pray for rescue and we get Dodgy Caravan Dude after like about half-an-hour waiting.'

'Yeah,' Kat says, 'but he has a seven-seater car.'

Jodie laughs. 'Touché.'

'What's your name, young man?' Barbara says to Dodgy Caravan Dude. Kat turns to Jodie and me and we splutter.

'Do you not understand shut up?'

'Well,' Barbara says, 'how rude.'

DCD starts driving painfully slowly up the road.

'Go faster, man,' Barbara says, seemingly oblivious to the livid air of rancour pervading the car.

'Will someone shut her up, or I'll do it for you.'

'Barbara, dear,' Amina says, putting her hands on Barbara's shoulders, 'just close your eyes. Have a little sleep while we drive. Let the nice gentleman drive in peace.'

'Pah,' Barbara says, but buttons her lips together and closes her eyes, leaning back into the seat.

The warmth of the car begins to lull me back into hope and tiny sparks of energy ping through my body, creeping slowly into my bones and weaving through my mind. I feel sleepy, all of a sudden, but sleepy in a good way, like when I have managed a walk and I feel good for being able to exercise.

I wonder to myself why this car and caravan will not go any faster, but I don't dare say a thing. I am desperate to get back – Jake might be there by now, turning up for visiting hours at four o'clock, and the staff on the ward will be getting increasingly concerned. If only we could call them.

I tap Kat on the shoulder and lean forward to whisper into her ear. 'Is it worth checking your phone, see if it's got any reception yet?'

She nods and pulls it out, then her face falls. 'Not one bar. This thing is useless. Kept saying to Nate I need a new one but never got round to it.'

'Did you tell Nate, where we were going?'

She shakes her head. 'Not specifically, no. He knows we're out for a walk though. But he'll be worried we're not back. I wish I'd told him more, but I kind of thought he'd say I shouldn't go, and then I'd feel bad about going.'

I swallow and grab hold of my nerve. 'Umm, hi,' I say loudly, to get the attention of our reluctant driver. 'Could we possibly borrow your phone? I mean, we won't call the police or anything, if you don't want that, but can I just call my son, so he can let the nurses know we're okay and everything?'

DCD brings the car to a screeching halt, slewing it into the verge and half into a bush. The caravan lurches from side to side, and now he's really angry. He turns round and gives me that glare again. 'No phones. No one is calling anyone. Do you want me to let you out here?'

I gaze out of the window, hoping for a lit-up house, for any signs at all of civilisation. There is nothing, just wild rural countryside, fast turning ghostly white, crystals dancing in the beam of the headlights.

'No,' I say, shaking my head from side to side. 'No. Sorry, please, just take us to the next village.'

'No more words from any of you?'

I zip my thumb and finger across my mouth.

He yanks the steering wheel to his right and floors the accelerator, the whole thing squealing as it wrenches itself out of the mangled bush. 'Damn it.'

He manages to wrestle the thing into compliance and drives on. Snow falls harder, drifting over the car and settling on the windows. He turns the windscreen wipers to full and curses again.

The sound of them swishing across the glass is strangely soothing, their rhythmic scrapes and groaning squeals mingling with the warm fug in the car, settling my ragged pulse and dragging me into a fitful doze.

I jolt awake as the car comes to a rolling stop. I'm confused for a few seconds, looking around me and trying to work out where I am.

'Damn thing's broken down.' DCD turns, scowling, spitting out his words. 'Stay here while I try and get this sorted out.'

Kat digs her phone out again, but her resigned exhale tells me all I need to know.

'Are we near the village?' Jodie says sleepily.

'I don't think so,' I say, peering out of the window at the whitewashed landscape. All I can see are fields of snow, stretching on for ever, falling away on both sides, and skeletal trees with their winter-bared branches bending and twisting to the grey skies. Way up ahead I think I can see something that might be a light, but it's too far to tell.

DCD pops his bonnet and slams his door closed after him, leaving us sitting in silence, the car cooling far too quickly. There's a slight acrid stench in the air, the engine overheated by dragging a great ancient caravan in these conditions.

'It's one thing after another, isn't it,' Kat says.

No one replies.

Jodie huddles deeper into her blanket and stares out of the window, her eyes paler than ever as they reflect the barren snowscape.

'At least we're indoors. At least we're not still out there on the road,' I say.

'Shouldn't've come in the first place,' Violet mutters.

'Not helpful,' says Kat.

We wait as he clatters and clanks around out there, the car shaking back and forth, the chassis squawking in misery. We wait and we watch as our breath begins to form small clouds in the air.

'Bit chilly in 'ere,' Barbara says.

For some reason this tickles me, and I laugh out loud. The others look at me as though I've lost the plot, and I stare down at my hands.

After too many minutes I hear him shout, 'Finally!' and then he slams the bonnet down and wrenches his door open. 'Right. Out, you lot.'

'What?' Kat says.

'Get out. I'm late and I can't dilly dally no longer for you lot.'

It's not our fault your useless car broke down, I want to say.

None of us move. I watch as his face changes before us, his eyes narrowing, the door light revealing a pulsing vein in his neck as he leans in.

'The village isn't far,' Kat says, though I'm not sure there is a village up ahead at all.

'I don't care. I've got to go the other way.' He points to a road up ahead, a tiny country lane that looks like it might lead to some desolate farmhouse in the middle of nowhere. 'I've brought you this far. Besides, there's a bus stop right there.' He points over to the other side of the road where there is, indeed, a bus shelter, one of those old-fashioned wooden ones with three sides enclosed. 'You can get a bus somewhere, I'm sure one'll be along soon. Now, piss off.'

I'm not at all sure about the bus. I'm not even sure any buses come along this lonely road anymore. With its snow covering it looks like something from an alien planet, so far from civilisation nothing and no one ever comes here. We haven't met another car since we started out, back at the beach.

'I'm not gonna ask you again. *Get out of my car.*'

'I don't want to get out of the car,' Barbara says.

'I don't care.' His face is turning a strange, ghostly shade of purple in the reflection of the snow in his side mirror. He bends further in and scrabbles in the glove box, plucking something out and then holding it up. It glints in the light over the rear-view mirror.

Kat draws back and shakes her head at me. 'He's got a knife,' she hisses. 'Come on.'

He stands there brandishing the knife at us as we crawl out, leaving Barbara on the passenger seat. It's one of those multi-tool penknives; my dad had one of those back when I was a child, but I wasn't allowed to touch it, because I was clumsy.

His hand is shaking. 'Hurry up.'

'What about Barbara's chair?' Kat says.

DCD makes a sound like a dog's growl and pulls the caravan keys from his pocket. 'Wait here. I'll sort it.'

'Don't forget my frame,' Violet says.

'Shut up, you silly old cow.'

Violet shrinks against the car and doesn't say anything else.

A few minutes later he's still not out of there. The caravan is shaking and the air is blue with his cussing. 'We should give him a hand,' I say, and march back to the caravan door before any of the others can stop me.

He's stumbling round in the caravan, shoving at the wheelchair which is wedged in the doorway. 'Why the hell didn't you bring a proper folding wheelchair on this little jaunt of yours?'

None of us answer. He slams his shoulder at it and then stumbles backwards over the walking frame, sprawling out on the floor behind him and hitting his head on one of the cupboards. 'Ouch! Bleedin' thing.'

Violet peers over the chair and into the caravan. 'Are you all right?'

'Get out of the way. Leave me alone.'

'We should try and inch it out, little by little.' I grab hold of the bar across the front and pull it and then push it back. It's stuck fast but as I wobble it back and forth I feel a little bit of give. 'Okay. Look, it just needs to go back in and then come out at another angle, tipped over a bit, yeah, then bring it round the door, that's it.' Kat and me edge it forwards and then back until it's loose, then gently ease it out and lift it down onto the snow.

Violet is half in the caravan before we can stop her, bending over DCD and reaching out to shift her walker away from him. 'I can't get up this step,' she says. 'I think he's hurt.'

He drags to his knees and shoves at the walker, almost knocking Violet flying back from the door. She falls back against Kat. 'Steady,' I say. 'We should go. He'll be fine.'

Violet shakes her head, peeks back in and stares around at the interior, eyes widened. Her hand flies to her throat. 'Oh, my word.'

'What?' Jodie pushes through, trying to see around Violet.

'He has a van full of those pad things,' Violet hisses at us, one eye on him, still on his knees behind the upturned walker.

'Pad things?' I say.

'You know. The telephones.'

I'm mystified, but Jodie jumps in. 'You mean iPads, right?'

Violet nods furiously. 'Yes. The pads. Stacked end to side.'

Jodie has her head in the van now, squashing herself up against Violet in the doorway. She whistles. 'Woah.'

'What?' says Kat.

'Ain't just iPads in there. He has like a million tons of weed or something.'

We stare at Jodie for a second and then he's up on his feet and hurling the walker at Violet, who stumbles back into Jodie, who stumbles back into me. We back away, gaping up at him.

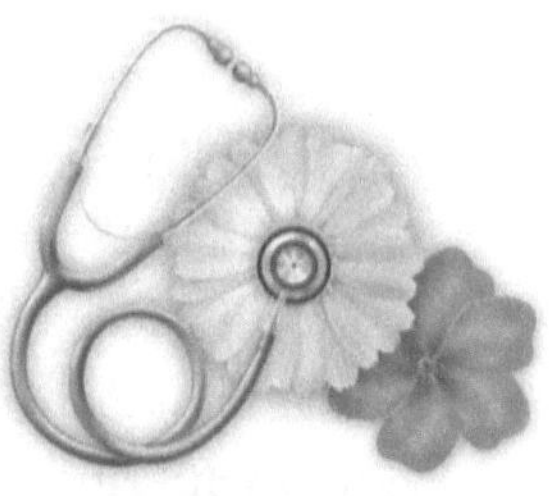

Chapter 26

HE STANDS IN the doorway of the caravan, baring his teeth at us like a caged zoo animal. He has the knife in his hand again and wields it at us, a vein in his temple bulging almost as much as his eyes. 'I told you not to interfere in my caravan.'

Violet takes hold of the walker then starts backing towards the car.

'Stop.'

My pulse pounds at my throat.

'Get over here. You, give me that phone.'

Kat has her phone out, her brow all crinkled up as she searches for a signal. She holds it to her chest and glares at him. I nudge her. 'Give it to him.'

'He won't do anything,' she says, loudly enough for him to hear. He jumps down to our level, almost tripping over the step, and holds the knife out towards her, his hand quivering. She flinches but doesn't avert her stare. 'He wouldn't hurt a bunch of sick women.'

'Give me your phone. I'm not having you calling the pigs soon as I'm out of here.'

Jodie grabs Kat's phone and places it in his upturned hand. He looks at it and sneers. 'Can't get much for this piece of shit.'

Kat shrugs. 'Needed a new one anyway. You're doing me a favour.'

His face darkens further, mottled patches of purple livid against unhealthy grey. 'Any other phones? Turn out your pockets.'

Jodie says, 'None of us have any.'

'Expect me to believe that? Think I was born yesterday?'

We shake our heads and show him our turned-out pockets. He grabs Amina's hijab and yanks it up. 'Got one under this thing, have you? Hiding it from me?'

She blanches and cringes away from his touch. Violet grabs his arm and shoves him away. 'Leave her alone. She doesn't have one.'

'What about the old bat in the car?'

'She don't even know how to use one of them things. And neither do I,' Violet says. She is almost spitting with rage.

He shoves Kat's phone in his back pocket and stands there staring at us, scratching his head like he doesn't know what to do next. He looks slightly lost and out of his league, like a little kid caught stealing from the corner shop because his mates dared him to.

I swallow. 'Look. You can go. It's not like we can tell anyone, is it, not right now, out here.'

'But you'll tell the pigs when you get home.'

'Yes,' Kat says, 'we will.'

He rakes his hand through his hair. I notice that the knife is lowered now in his other hand, and feel sure that this man will not hurt us further than leaving us stranded at a bus stop at dusk, out in the sticks of nowhere in a snowstorm in sub-zero temperatures. Perhaps he hopes we will merely perish out here and take his secret with us, perhaps he thinks he can wash his hands of us now because he's done his bit.

Something bright behind him in the caravan catches my eye, and I edge towards the door, ignoring Kat's hand on my arm and the vehement shake of her head. I square up to him. 'Now we know all about what you're up to with this whole get-up here you've got, I think you owe us something else, seeing as you're leaving us out in the cold.'

He squints through the shadows at me. 'What are you talking about, woman?'

I push past him and he grabs hold of my sleeve, but I shake him off and scramble into the caravan. It reeks of mould and damp and something more; something living, or maybe dead. Its loud floral curtains clash with yet another floral design in orange and brown on its seats, frayed and torn with foam spilling out at every corner. Stacks of iPads teeter haphazardly under the table between the two long seats, and great clear bags full of smaller bags packed with marijuana lie scattered on the seats and the floor. This is no professional crook. On the seat to my right is a bright orange sleeping bag and a fleecy green blanket. 'I think we'll take these.'

It's like all his spirit has drained out of him. 'Whatever. But hurry the hell up.' He glances from side to side as if suddenly a whole convoy of police cars will come screaming out of the frozen silence and bear him away.

I smile to myself as I gather up the sleeping bag then drape the blanket around my shoulders. It's even bigger than I thought and trails down onto the floor, so I scrunch it up and double it over.

As I move towards the doorway a sound stops me still and I whirl around. It's high pitched, like a squeak, and my first thought is that Barbara's plaintive prophecies about rats are at last coming true in this battered-up old van that clenches me so tightly in its mildewed, time-slipped grip. But then the squeak turns into something longer and more pitiful.

'What on earth—'

'Get out of my caravan.'

I ignore him and move closer to the sound, which has turned into a full-on yowling. It's coming from a cardboard box on one of the seats at the rear of the caravan. 'What have you got in there?'

DCD scowls at me and shrugs. 'Nothing.'

The Nothing is making a sound so piteous my heart sinks into my stomach. As I edge closer to the box I see little air holes punched into it. I pull the flaps open, and inside the most exquisite white cat I have ever seen cowers away in one corner, its entire body quivering.

'Oh,' I say.

'Leave that alone. It's mine,' he yells, and at his voice the cat arches its back and hisses, its fur standing on end, then cringes further into the corner, shaking violently.

A commotion sounds outside. It sounds like a car, crawling up the hill towards us. DCD turns his back and ushers the others away, hissing at them. 'Get back behind the van. Don't let him see you.' I see the glint of the knife again as he holds it out, and I also see that his arm is even more unsteady than before.

I look at the door, and then I look at the cat, and I make a snap decision. I've suffered for too many years under the hands of a bully, and while it's in my power I won't let another creature suffer the same fate. I slide my arms around the cat's belly and gingerly lift it to my chest, waiting for it to spit and hiss at me just as it did at its master's voice. But it's strangely compliant, curling into my parka as I zip it up to the neck. I pull the blanket tighter around us both, hiding its little head from sight, feeling it quivering against me and then, just slightly, relaxing. It's a ball of warmth in the midst of a great chill as I step into the doorway of the caravan with the sleeping bag over my arm. Outside the other car is approaching slowly and I step back as it comes to a stop, a filthy

Landrover that looks at home on these roads. 'Can I help out?' the driver shouts out. 'Are you broken down?'

DCD has obviously managed to get the others out of sight around the other side of the caravan. 'You're all right,' he shouts back. 'Just fixing something on the van. I'm all good to go now.'

'Well, if you're sure,' the other driver says, and then he's off before one of us can shout out, roaring away up the road and cutting a deep tread through the snow.

I should have called to him. I should have made him see us. But all I could think about was DCD and his knife, far too close to the others for comfort. I don't think he'd hurt us, but I can't be completely sure.

He finds me standing in the doorway holding the sleeping bag tightly to me. I made sure to close the flaps on the cardboard box and I'm glad, because he pokes his head in and glances over at it. 'Are you quite done?'

The cat stiffens against my chest and I try to breathe slowly, to calm it.

'Yes,' I say. 'Thanks. I mean, for the ride. And the blanket.'

He slams the van door and skits back round to his car. 'Get this old bint out of my car and then get out of my way.'

By the time we have Barbara arranged back in her chair, oxygen cylinder safely stowed in its holder, and into the bus shelter, all we can see is the caravan's one working taillight, flickering and fading into the foggy distance. I crash my palm against my forehead. I didn't even look at the licence plate.

'Well, he were a right barrel of laughs, weren't he,' Barbara says.

Kat snorts. 'Oh, Barbara.'

Barbara screws up her nose. 'Well, it's true.' She shivers suddenly and I gaze around us, taking in this predicament in which we find ourselves, this tiny frozen shelter in a wasteland of oblivion. It's three sided, so at least the snow doesn't drive in over us through the sides, and the storm is blowing north so doesn't drift too much into the shelter. Small mercies, I suppose.

'You'd best get praying again,' Jodie says to Kat. 'Only ask for someone a bit more human.'

'Look here.' Amina is clearing a small transparent box attached to the side of the shelter. It's a timetable, but it looks old and grubby and I wonder if it is in use at all or if we are going to find some relic from the eighties. She leans in and squints at the tiny font enclosed in the smeared laminate. 'Oh.'

My stomach clenches.

'What?' Kat asks.

'There are buses on weekdays on this route, two times a day, but not weekends.'

The shelter presses in on me, its shadowy corners suddenly a whole new depth of darkness trailing out into a limbo of hopelessness.

I unzip the sleeping bag and signal to Kat to help me lift Barbara slightly and slide it underneath her frail body. She has no weight to her, she feels like an insubstantial puff of breath in my arms. I pull the bag around her, blankets, oxygen line, and all, and zip it all the way round so she is completely enclosed. I pull the tog at the top so that her head is covered and her little white face with its nasal cannula pokes out of the puckered elastic, her Rovers hat askew, her skin stark against the violent orange of the bag, almost as white as the snow gathering in great drifts outside on the road. She gives me a wan little smile.

There's a bench running right across the shelter at the back and somehow, in a great providence I can't quite take in, it has room for us all, with Barbara to one side in her chair. I drape the blanket over Violet and Jodie, and find that it's big enough to go round Amina as well as they huddle together into its fleecy warmth. 'Could do with a nice hot water bottle,' Violet says.

Jodie says, 'We left the frog chair in the caravan. Kane won't be happy.'

'Wait, what is that?' Kat says, peering closely at my neck. 'That flash of white? Did you get snow in your coat?'

I unzip it slightly and the cat peeks its head out at them, blinking in the snow-glare and giving a tiny mewl.

'What, what did you… you took his cat?'

I scratch the back of my neck and throw my gaze out to the driving snow.

Jodie whistles. 'Woah.'

'What if he sees and comes back?' Amina says, her brow all puckered up. 'He will be so angry. He scared me, with all those drugs.'

'Drugs?' Barbara murmurs.

'He had a load of cannabis in there, all packaged up,' Kat says.

'He won't come back,' I say, maybe too confidently. 'He was itching to be away to whatever he was doing. He won't know, anyway, as long as he's driving. Besides, he just wants to get as far away as he can, doesn't he, I mean before we manage to get hold of the police.'

'Let's hope so,' Kat says, rubbing her hands together. She's wearing a mismatched pair of Jake's goalie gloves.

Barbara stares at the cat with a wide-eyed gaze. 'Bring him to me! Here, puss! Come to Barbara.'

I look around at the others, uncertain. Jodie nods at me. I slowly bring the cat out and the others gasp. It is strikingly beautiful, its coat fluffy and magnificent, even whiter than the snow outside. Its eyes are a piercing blue, slicing through the shadowy gloom in the shelter. I take it over to Barbara and she reaches for it, folding it into the top of her sleeping bag, where it curls into her shoulder and closes its eyes as if it has come home. A few seconds later I hear a low purring sound.

'It likes you,' Kat says.

Barbara beams. 'I am going to call him Snowy.'

'I like that you took him,' Kat says, turning to me. 'I think you're stupid, but I like that you took him.'

'He was afraid,' I say. 'He was so scared. I could hardly leave him there.'

Barbara has her face almost buried in the sleeping bag, kissing Snowy and crooning loving words into his fur.

Kat and I squeeze onto the bench with the other three and we wrap the picnic rug around our shoulders. All we can do now is wait. I try not to think about how cold my feet are, my slipper socks and thin flats no match for the gathering snow.

'Anyone want some brandy?' Jodie says, reaching over to Violet's walker where the flasks are stowed in the basket underneath. 'It'll give us a little warmth.'

Kat looks dubious.

'I want some,' Violet says. 'An' I want a fag too.'

'Sorry,' Jodie says.

Violet looks down at the floor. 'Just wish I had better shoes.' She kicks out her feet, shod in their pink slippers which look less fluffy and more bedraggled now. 'My feet are like ice. That husband of mine, never thought to bring me proper shoes in, oh no.'

Jodie bends down and tugs off her Ugg boots. 'Here. Mine are still kind of dry. And my feet aren't ice like yours. See, I've got these great big socks on under here.'

Violet looks at her with wide eyes and a faltering mouth.

Jodie pushes the boots at her. 'Go on. I'm fine.'

'You're sure?'

'Here. Get those silly things off.' Jodie bends down and pulls them off Violet's feet. 'Flaming Nora. No wonder you was cold! These are wet through.' Then she grins up at Violet. 'No loss, really, is it, these horrible old things?' She shoves them under the seat of the shelter. 'RIP, hideous slippers.'

Violet's eyebrows begin to knit together and then, after a moment, they relax as a tiny smile flutters at her mouth. 'Why are you so kind to me?' she asks, slipping her feet into the Ugg boots and sighing. 'Why d'you put up with me after how I was?'

'You're an okay old stick,' Jodie says.

Violet blinks and gazes out at the snow.

'There will be someone along soon,' Amina says. 'We will get back. I know we will.'

'Let's just hope it's not another Dodgy Caravan Dude,' Jodie says.

'Give us a nip of that brandy, then,' Violet says, and Jodie takes a little swig herself and passes it on. We all sit there in a row passing the flask between us.

'It's a bit like communion,' Kat says.

THE SKY HANGS low in foggy ribbons of all the colours of grey and the snow tumbles outside the shelter in great cascades of whiteness. We sit, bundled up and huddled together for warmth, and we wait. The brandy sits warm in my belly and releases a tiny ball of something like happiness in me.

'We're like a nativity scene,' Jodie says. Kat raises her eyebrows in a question. 'Well, I mean, this could be like the stable, and then you're in an animal costume, right, so you're like the ox or the donkey or whatever, and Violet could be like the shepherd in her dressing gown, and Barbara's a Wise Man 'cause of that bright orange thing, like a cloak or something, and Amina's Mary with her blue headscarf and all that. And Snowy is the little lamb.'

'So who's Joseph?' I say.

'That's you because of that stripy blanket.'

'You must be the angel, then,' Kat says. 'With that halo of blonde hair poking out of your Santa hat.'

And with the magic she has somehow wrought among us today.

'I wish I had some wings to fly away and bring us back home,' Jodie says.

Violet says, 'I don't think a Star Wars bear and Santa Claus were present at the first Christmas.'

No cars come by. The road stretches out in infinite snow-numbed silence, the winter trees silhouettes of writhing bone stark against the sky. I wonder what the time is, but DCD took Kat's phone and nobody has a watch. I wonder what they are thinking, back at the hospital, and if they have called the police. I think about how stupid we were, to not tell them what we were up to, and it makes me think about how Marcus always told me I was a loser who could never do anything right. Yet through the dark haze of my thoughts a new light is poking through, like the ethereal luminosity of the falling snow, shining on my insecurities and highlighting them for what they are. I think about Kane and how Jodie shines without him, and I know that I want to shine, too.

'Are you okay?' Kat says to me.

I realise that tears are crawling down my cheeks and I blink at the strangeness of them. 'I never cry.'

'It's okay to.'

'It'll be the brandy,' Violet says.

'I just… I was thinking about my ex. How he didn't really love me at all.'

Kat finds my hand under the blanket and squeezes it.

'I think Kane was the same,' Jodie says. 'It's like, he told me he loved me, and all that, but he didn't really act like it, did he?'

'No, he didn't,' Kat says.

Jodie rubs her face. 'No man's really loved me. My dad ran away when I was young, just like your Jake, Penny. He beat my mum around and I was glad to see the back of him. My mum was different when he left, but she always said he loved her, really, that he just got a bit angry sometimes. Kane said I was his princess, but it was on his terms, I suppose.'

'You'd hardly had a good role-model for a loving partner,' Kat says.

I nod. 'It was the same with Marcus. It was always on his terms, as long as I did what he asked of me and became the person he wanted me to be, it was fine. But as soon as I said no, it wasn't fine anymore.'

'He hurt you,' Kat says softly.

'He hurt me more in here.' I point to my heart.

'You should never have to become somebody you are not to please another,' Kat says. 'Especially when they are subjecting you to emotional abuse.'

It feels right to me, somehow, that the first time I am confiding all of this in its raw candour to others is here, in a frozen wasteland, with five people I have come to love. I taste the unfamiliar saltiness of tears on my tongue and think it tastes a bit like all the colours in the world. 'But how do I move on? It's like... like he still has a hold on me. Like I look at myself and still see that person he wanted to change, and I keep trying to please people to cover it all over. I don't have any strength in me, not like you, Kat, or you, Jodie.'

Jodie shakes her head. 'I don't have a lot myself. I didn't have the strength to bin him off.'

'I have less than you think,' Kat says, staring out at the snow.

'You will, though, Jodie. You will find the strength,' Amina says.

Jodie lifts her chin and I notice the blue tinge around her lips and the translucency of her skin and the dark shadows around her eyes. 'I won't have him back. Not after this.'

I pick at a loose thread on one of my gloves and think about what Kat said, about not having to become someone different, and wonder where I went wrong, and how I can find a better path. 'So how do we? I mean, how do we get out of this... I don't know, almost this like ticker-tape thing that keeps going round and round in my head. It's like I can never escape from the words, like they just keep on squeezing me tighter and tighter. I don't know how to get out.'

'But you are getting out,' Kat says.

I gaze at her, and wonder if she might be right.

'I've heard it described as graffiti on the heart,' she says. 'When words get written on us for many years, and it's really hard to scrub them off. I've often found it's about forgiveness. Setting yourself free from bitterness.'

'But I can't ever forgive him,' I say.

Violet leans forward. 'I can never forgive my dad, neither. There's some people you just can't forgive.'

I think about my parents, too, and to a lesser extent, my sister. I think about what it might feel like to let go.

'What happened with your dad?' Kat says gently to Violet.

'He thought all that mattered was appearances, see. So when I got pregnant, when I was just sixteen, he threw me out and said he never wanted to see me again.' She looks at the floor, her mouth quivering. 'My mother, she was always kind, and it broke her. She wanted me to stay, but in the end she did as she was told. They did, in those days, you know.'

Amina leans her head into Violet's shoulder. 'I am so sorry.'

'He's fifty now, my son, and my father never even met him. And it's not even like I'm close to my son, either.' She gazes at

Amina. 'I was so awful to you, but you know what? It's because I was jealous. I was jealous of your family, how they love you. There. I said it.'

Silence hangs low in the shelter, and we mould ourselves into it.

'Forgiving isn't saying that it's okay, what the other person did,' Kat says. 'It's about letting yourself off the hook. About kind of climbing out of those bars and saying no, I'm not letting this person have any power over me anymore. I'm not going to live chained up to him just because I hold so much hate in my heart for him.' She pauses, gazing up at the driving snow. 'It's sort of like saying, I matter too much to allow him to have any influence at all over me now, so I'm going to let that go.'

I look at her. The fine lines around her eyes are creased up and her mouth sits in a grim line. She knows of what she speaks.

Jodie stares at her, frowning, pulling at her gloves.

'You let yourself off from the bonds of misery,' she says.

'I don't know if I can,' I say.

'Sometimes it's the words that are powerful. Sometimes just saying them breaks the chains. You might have to say them over and over, but after a while you realise that you are getting slowly free. When I had to do it, it took a long time. But it works. It works.'

Jodie shakes her head.

'You have this kind of peace,' I say to Kat. 'How do you, all the time?'

'Not all the time. Sometimes I'm crippled with anxiety, but I've found in my faith a stillness, like in the depths of the ocean in a storm if you swim down far enough there's a warmth there, a stillness underneath the waves. It's kind of like that, but it's not this magical thing I can just snap my fingers and get. It has to be a choice, sometimes, for me it's a choice to go on with it but then peace is there and it's beautiful and it makes sense of stuff even when everything sucks. And it's like that with forgiving, too.'

Even though the world is frozen around us, the silence is warm.

'I think I know what it's like. To be forgiven,' Violet says softly, her eyes on the lip of the roof where snow settles and drips down, captured into tiny icicles, framing the shelter in a riot of frozen fairy lights that sparkle against the backdrop of slow-falling snowflakes. I think about how each one is a work of craftmanship, yet such an insubstantial puff of nothing on its own, how it's only when the snowflakes come together that they build something: great dazzling mountains of beauty and power.

Amina says, 'I also had to forgive a bad person. It was not my family, but somebody else who did something to me.'

Jodie moves closer to her.

'It is okay. It is well. I agree with Kat. Maybe it is the time for all of you to move away from this sadness that is deep in you.'

Maybe it is. I think about Marcus and how he didn't really love me at all, and wonder if I loved him or loved the idea of him, loved him out of duty and because he saved me, and somehow that sense of allegiance masqueraded as love in my messed-up mind. Maybe I really did love him, but never understood love in its fullness. Not in the essence of it I catch the edges of when I listen to Barbara talk about Bill or Nate whispering to Kat, or even as I watched Brian wait for Violet when she was taken away for a scan with an imprint of great anxiety on his face, and watch them together in their somewhat dysfunctional, disdainful us-against-the-whole-world kind of way. Maybe it's because I never really knew what love was as a child, or if I did it was a clumsy kind of love, a love couched in terms and conditions. 'I don't think I've understood love,' I say.

Kat says, 'Look at Jake.'

I gaze out over the mist-clogged horizon as if I can conjure up his face out there, his grumpy teenage face, headphones clamped over his ears, eyes rolling so much they might disappear into the back of his head.

'You know love because you try to love your son unconditionally,' she says. 'And that's what love is, at its purest and best. It's patient and kind, it's not proud, it doesn't dishonour others. It's not self-seeking and it keeps no record of wrongs. It always protects and always trusts. It always hopes and it always perseveres.'

I catch my breath as something like a wave of heat pounds through my body.

'Very poetic,' Violet says.

'It's from my favourite book.'

I think about all those attributes of love and think about how I feel about Jake and realise that's what I've been missing all along, there in front of me as I strived and persevered and loved him through a life that hurt too much, as I protected him and tried not to fail him, though I often did. And now, no more of this. Time to let go of the things that have caged me in for too long, of the words from my parents, from Marcus, from kids at school that wounded me in deep places. It's time for me to be free.

'Listen,' Amina says, leaning forward slightly and tilting her head to the side.

I can't hear anything through the heavy, muted silence of this kingdom of snow.

'I hear something too,' Jodie says.

And then I hear it. An engine. It shatters the dampened quietness, its throaty roar sounding pained and weary, a little bit like us. I suck a breath in, flinching as a stab of pain flashes through my chest, and drag myself off the seat. 'It's a car. We have to stop it.'

But it's not a car.

'I thought there were no buses on Saturdays,' Jodie says, her eyes wide as she gazes at the stuttering vehicle limping over the foggy horizon and cutting slowly through the unrelenting snowstorm towards us.

'It's out of service,' Kat says, peering out of the shelter and shaking her head. 'It's all dark.'

'I don't care,' I say. 'That bus has to stop. That bus is going to stop.' I grab the picnic blanket and I drag myself out of the shelter and into the middle of the road, the snow soaking through my thin shoes and socks and sending icy shivers through my feet and up through my legs. Nobody follows me. They sit pinned to the seat, steeped in pain or weariness or apathy or all three.

'He won't see you, Penny,' Kat shouts dully. 'You'll get run down.'

But I don't care. I take up the rug and I start waving it madly. I feel like Bobby from *The Railway Children*, standing in the middle of the track waving massive red bloomers in the air, hoping against hope the train will stop before it hurtles into me. Only I'm waving a dirty old candy-striped picnic rug and snow is driving down all around me, shrouding my body and my mind and icing up my bones.

As I wave it over my head, back and forth, my arms strain and pain rips through my body, and it's almost like time stands still as the bus grows in size and its grumbling engine fills up the silence. Suddenly I think about Jake, and what he will think if I die here now. I think about how his life has been too full of sacrifice, how because of me he has missed out on a normal carefree childhood, how he has been catapulted into the role of carer a thousand times too many. Will he miss me, I wonder, or will he finally be free to live his life without the great big burden that is me?

I catch a glimpse of the others in the edges of my vision, their weary huddled shapes blurring against the shadows of the shelter, and I grit my teeth as I wave the blanket. Back and forth. Back and forth.

The bus has to stop.

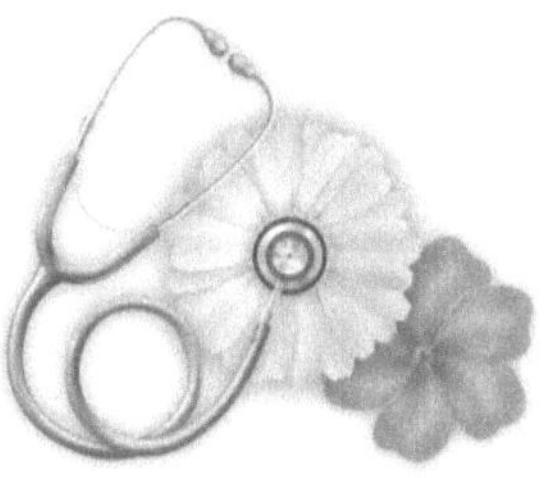

Chapter 27

THE BUS SHOWS no signs of slowing as it draws closer, its engine a spluttering growl, a cloud of black smoke spitting from its exhaust and painting the air in sooty darkness.

I marshal my strength and stand as tall as I can, waving the rug over my head then flapping it up and down, my arms shaking with exhaustion. I can't do this. I am going to faint. I need to lie down.

I shout as the bus comes nearer and the driver looms into view through the murk. I scream at the top of my lungs and I jump up and down and I don't know where my body finds the energy.

It screeches to a halt inches from me, its headlights picking out a great flurry of dancing footprints where I have jumped and leaped and poured myself out. The driver throws his window open and leans out. 'What in the name of all that is holy?' he shrieks in a broad Irish brogue. 'What in heaven's name are you doing, woman? Do you have a death wish?'

I can't find any words left in me. They are swallowed up by a rising tide coursing through my body and dragging my feet from underneath me. I am wet cardboard, floppy and bendy with nothing to hold me up. I fall to my knees in the snow and lower my dizzied head as my breath comes thick and fast. The edges of the world turn to black around me as I fall harder, and then I am diving through the snow and plunging deep into the frozen ground.

I CAN HEAR Jake knocking on my bedroom door. Mummy, Mummy! There are no words in my mouth, my throat is closed up as my breath is whipped away by a surge of pain. Mummy! I will help you Mummy. He is in the room with me, he is pulling my duvet over me and then he is stroking my hair. Are you okay, Mummy? Are you okay? I try to nod, to say yes, Jake, please don't worry about me, but my words are stifled into a grunt. I'll help you Mummy, just wait there. Then my world falls into mist until he comes back, gently rocking my shoulder. I've made you some dinner, Mummy, to help you feel better. He has a tray with a cup of lukewarm tea because I told him never to use the kettle and a jam sandwich and there is jam all over the tray and his sticky fingers. He puts it on the bed with me and then he climbs in with me and he won't let me go and he says please get better, Mummy, please.

'PENNY. Penny.' Someone is shaking my shoulder. Is it Jake? I open my eyes and the freezing world presses in on me. Where am I? 'Penny! Are you okay?' Kat is gaping at me, eyes wide with worry, and Jodie is with her too, and all I can think about is Jodie in her socks in the snow. 'Come on. We'll help you.' They each tuck an arm into mine and help me up, and even though I am still sagging like damp cardboard now I have something to cling to. 'It's okay,' Kat says, as I begin to hyperventilate and the world tilts on its side. 'Shh. It's okay. You did it, Penny. You stopped him. We're going to be okay.'

I sense a soft whisper of breath on my neck. I find Violet behind me, her arm on my back, steadying herself with the walking frame. She whispers to me, 'You're a brave girl.'

'What is all this?' the driver shouts out of his window.

'Let us in,' Kat says.

He stares at us. 'I can't do that. I'm not allowed to do that. I'm not in service, pet.'

'Please.'

He stabs at something on his panel, and the doors hiss open, complaining in a slow high-pitched screech. He comes out into the snow, his curly greying brown hair like a halo in the light spilling out from his cab. He folds his arms and takes us all in, stopping and staring as he catches sight of Barbara, lost in her sleeping bag, a huddle of orange peeking through the shadows in the shelter.

'Holy Mary, Mother of God.'

Kat says, 'Oh, you're religious, then? Catholic, I take it? Good. So, what would Mary say? What about your mother? What would your mam say to you now, when faced with six women who need to get back to the hospital and need your help? What would she say?'

He crosses himself and steps back, stumbling against the lip of the door. 'I'm out of service.'

Kat points to something hanging from the rear-view mirror in his cab. 'Nice rosary.'

He pushes out his cheeks. 'I'm not supposed to.'

'We know that. You told us. But you can take us, can't you? You're not going to leave a bunch of sick women out here in the cold and the snow?'

'I've got to take this old bus back to the depot. Last time, like. Can't take passengers in her, she's not fit for it. Health and safety and all that.'

'D'you think we care about how fit this thing is?' Violet says. 'You can fit us in there. You've got seats in there.'

'They're not very nice.'

Kat laughs.

'Would you like us to sit out here and die?'

He runs his hand through his hair and gazes around at each one of us. His hair is almost white at the roots, his eyes a piercing green. He'd have been a bit of a looker in his youth, I reckon. Still is, really.

'It's up to you,' Kat says, her eyes hard on the rosary beads.

He shifts and then gives a short nod. 'I can get you into town, at least, I suppose.'

We don't need to be told twice. Kat turns back to fetch Barbara and the rest of us crunch our way through the thickening snow over to the open doors. It's one of those old-fashioned buses, no low floor for easy access, just a high step with a grab bar up the middle. Violet puffs and pants as she grips hold of the bar and drags herself up. Amina lifts her walker in after her, her hijab shimmering against the falling snow as she spins around to help Jodie up.

Jodie says, 'She's like that song from the olden days.'

'What song?' I say.

'That stilettos in the snow one.'

A sharp pang through me, memories I don't want to remember, school buses and playgrounds and reports that spoke of my uselessness. '*Kayleigh*,' I say softly. 'And less of the olden days, thank you.'

'Can't get that thing in here.' The driver gestures at Barbara, sitting in her chair by the door. 'Won't fit. I haven't got a ramp in this baby, you know.'

Kat stares at him.

'Gonna have to leave it here.'

She shakes her head. 'But… but it belongs to the hospital.'

'I don't care if it belongs to the King. It's not coming in my bus.'

'Haven't you got like a luggage thing on the side?'

'It's not a bleddy luxury coach, you know.'

'We'll have to leave it,' I say, standing in the doorway and clinging to the pole as if at any moment my legs might give up and send me sprawling down onto the floor, which looks like it's probably not been cleaned for a good while.

'Do you know how much those things cost?' Kat says.

'We've no choice, have we? We'll send someone back for it. No one'll nick a hospital wheelchair from a bus shelter in the wild ends of the countryside.'

Kat raises her eyebrows. 'Don't you believe it.' She shrugs. 'But yes. Could you help me get Barbara on to the bus, then?'

The driver takes one look at me and shakes his head. 'Sit down, pet. You're fit to collapse. Here.' He guides me to the single seat nearest the driver's cab, up at the front. My limbs are shaking so much that I am jerking in every direction. 'You look like you need a bit of the good stuff,' he says.

'Already had some,' I say.

'What have you lot been up to?'

No one replies so he shrugs and then slings himself out through the doors and lifts Barbara in her sleeping bag into his arms. 'She's nothing to her, has she? Ugly sleeping bag, that.'

Kat slides the oxygen cylinder from the holder on the chair and gathers up the trailing tubing.

The driver screws his brow up, his eyebrows so thick they tangle up together like a thicket full of brambles. 'Wait a sec. What's she have in there? Is that a cat? No pets allowed on these buses.'

Kat levels him with a look. 'Really?'

He stands and stares at her, hands planted on his hips, and then he casts his eyes down. 'Not like I'm not already breaking the rules, is it.'

'You're doing a good thing,' Kat says.

'And you're a wee gobshite.'

Kat laughs.

'Come on, get yourself settled, all of you.' He lowers Barbara tenderly onto one of the double seats. 'One of you'll need to sit with her. Keep her steady. Not like I have any seatbelts or anything like that. But it's your funeral.'

I really hope not.

Kat sits down with Barbara and straightens her up a little so she's not sliding down the plastic covered seat in the nylon sleeping bag. She places the oxygen carefully under the seat and then puts her arm around Barbara and nods at the driver.

'Ye lot sound like a whole load of steam trains,' he says. 'You all got asthma or what?'

'Pretty much,' I say. 'All in the hospital. In the chest ward.'

'Most of us got screwed lungs,' Jodie says, peeling off her soaked-through socks.

'What in the world are you all doing out here, then? Are you mad?'

'Probably,' Kat says.

Amina and Violet are sitting together on one of the double seats, and Jodie sags down on another, curling up and laying her head on her arm. She closes her eyes and I think about the dark rings around them and how they look even darker than they did.

The driver goes back outside and moves the wheelchair back into the bus shelter. He didn't have to do that. There's something good about this man, some inner integrity I am only catching the edges of, something diametrically opposed to DCD and Kane and Marcus.

'Are we all quite ready, then?'

We murmur assent and he gets himself settled back in his cab. He starts the engine and it coughs and splutters and he bangs the steering wheel and yells at it to come on me auld girl. It would just about finish me off, I think, if we're now broken down out here.

'She's almost done for,' he says, trying the engine again. 'Come on, pet, one last time?'

This time it responds to his coaxing and turns over, the bus shivering and rattling as it crackles and then roars into life.

As he drives away I look out of the window behind me at the bus shelter where a blue hospital wheelchair sits abandoned, drip stand still in place with empty IV bag attached, stark and desolate against its backdrop of weathered cedar wood and drifted snow. Maybe by the morning it'll be so deeply buried it will be lost to the world, like we might have been if this out-of-time bus that looks like the set of a ghost story hadn't loomed out of the mist and whipped us on board.

Amina and Violet huddle together into the big fleece blanket and Kat lays the picnic rug over Jodie, who is tumbling quickly into sleep, tucking her bare feet into its faded folds. I wrap my arms around my chest and shiver. There's no heating on in this thing and the cold saws through my bones. I sit here in the murky darkness, watching the bleak landscape rolling by, darkening shades of grey chasing the remains of day through an angry sky.

I have a thought, and I don't know why I didn't think of it already. My mind must be slowing, numbing along with my frozen limbs. I lean over so I'm closer to the driver. 'Do you have a phone? Can I just call my son to let him know we're all safe, and then he can tell the ward?'

The driver shakes his head. 'Sorry, darlin'. It's me being all thumbs, see. Mine got all smashed up the other day, silly eejit dropped it on the pavement and that was that. So it's in with the repair bloke.'

'Oh.'

'Sorry.'

'Don't worry. Do you have, I don't know, like a radio, like a walkie talkie thing?'

He smiles wryly, shakes his head. 'Not in this old girl.'

'Maybe we should stop as soon as we get to the next village,' Kat says. 'Then we can at least let them know.'

'I'm not stopping in a village in this. Trouble enough getting her started just now. Only another quarter of an hour or so into town. You can phone someone from the depot.'

'Can't you take us to the hospital?'

He massages his temple. 'Can't get this old thing through that mare of a car park. Not in these conditions.'

'I bet you can.' I cross my fingers under my knees.

He shakes his head and makes a face like Jake makes when I ask him to tidy his room or bring his extensive collection of crockery down to wash up.

Silence drapes us in its soporific potency as we relax into the rhythmic chugging of the bus and swishing of the windscreen wiper, watching the white world stagger by. The bus struggles up hills and through the village we'd hoped DCD might drop us in. I gaze out of my window at the empty stillness of its snow-shrouded streets, and think about how I'm glad he didn't, after all. Nobody would want to come out of their warm houses to help a bunch of women who look like they've had a few too many out on a jolly.

I look round at the others. They all have their eyes closed. Snowy pokes his little head out of the zip of Barbara's sleeping bag and nestles back into her neck. I think Jodie is snoring slightly, though that might just be the rumbling growl of the engine.

Violet's head is tucked into Amina's shoulder, and I think about how far they have come.

How far we've all come.

I fold my arms more tightly around myself and stare out of the window. The world out there is an alien planet lit in unearthly luminosity, the snow dancing on the windows and colonising the fields. I feel my bones melting like the snow that trickles down the glass, dragging me down into something a little bit like relaxation, and close my eyes.

'I'm taking her on her final journey.'

I blink and look up at the driver, who is peering ahead into the storm, both hands clenched tight around the wheel as if the bus might skid out of control any moment.

'What?'

He glances at me and then chuckles. 'Oh, no, I don't mean…' He thumbs back towards Barbara. 'I don't mean it's her final journey.'

It might well be, though. And that might be our fault.

'No, I mean this old beast here. She's been out of service a good while now. She's obsolete. Useless.'

A bit like me, I start to think and then catch myself. *No.* Not anymore.

I gaze around the shadowy interior of the bus, taking in its torn red plastic seats, splodged with years of spilled drinks and other nameless things, its mould-rimmed windows streaming with condensation, one of them flapping open at the top and conceding the creep of the frozen outside. Tired, tattered adverts line the sides. No electronic display or information screen for this old dinosaur. It's a relic of times past, of buses I would get to school when we moved to England, when I sat at the very back and hoped Jamie Harrison or Nicola Smith didn't notice me so they could steal my bag and laugh at my charity shop coat and the haircut that my mother thought was so chic. It echoes with the ghosts of years, with sadness and poverty and daily travail.

'It's 'cause of all them yummy mummies, see,' he says.

'Sorry?'

He scratches his chin and then grabs the wheel as the bus swerves slightly towards the verge. A car is coming the other way, too quickly for this weather, dazzling full-beam headlights shattering the gloom. 'Idiot!' He stamps on the brake and it squeals back at him, and for a moment I'm afraid we're going into a skid, the bus suddenly weightless, the other car too close. Our driver sits on his horn and the other car swerves round us, honking back. 'Tosser.'

'The yummy mummies?' I say after a few moments' silence.

'Oh, yeah. Well, see, firstly it was for the handicapped people. The ones in wheelchairs, so's they had a ramp and everything. And only too right, I say.' He nods his head firmly. 'Took too long coming, if you ask me.'

What is he on about?

'But then those parents had to go and stick their oars in, you get me?'

'Those parents?'

'Yeah, those entitled mummies, those snowflakes with their tanks.'

Snowflakes with their tanks? Jake would like that. I file it away in my mind.

'Why they can't just have one of those little buggies like we did when mine were wee, I just can't imagine. No, has to be those supersized prams these days. They're like Audis. Those mummies are like Audi drivers, cutting up and pushing in and getting in the way so they can have their seat that they are so entitled to. The Lord forbid you suggest they fold up for some poor sod in a wheelchair. It's all, first come first serve, I know my rights, I'll sue the bus company. I tell you, it was simpler in the days we drove these old things around all the time. A load less hassle.'

'Oh,' I say.

Inside I'm thinking, can we just get back now? Can I just have some peace, a chance to close my eyes and screen out the weary day before I have to face the inevitable music?

He seems to be waiting for more of a response, so I force my eyes to resist the heavy pull upon them. 'How come these ones are still around, then?'

'They're not, really. Great big diesel engines that screw the environment. Only one or two left, rotting in some yard somewhere. This one's going for scrap, eventually. Only used on a quiet route it was, up 'til a year or two ago, this one here. Got complaints about it, we did, too dirty and outdated. Can't say as I blame them. All going towards electric, all that carbon neutral, nowadays. An' then of course there's the fact it's no good for wheelchairs, and you have to go with the times, don't you? You have to make sure you've done all you can to include them folk. An' too right as well. This here bus, she's done her last. It's kind of fitting she goes out like this, doing her bit for others like she always did.'

He pats the steering wheel, and I want to cry a little bit.

'What's your name?' I say.

He pauses for a moment, then clears his throat. 'It's Cal. Callum O'Mahoney at your service, madam.'

'And will you keep on driving? The new buses, I mean?'

'I'm doing that now, but I reckon it's time I was put to seed an' all, for sure.'

'You're not that past it,' I say, grinning at him.

He smiles back, a great toothy grin that lights his eyes. 'Got some life to live yet. Got the grandkids, the littluns to keep me going. But I'm about done with all this.'

'Are your family local?'

'Some of them, but some of them back in Dublin. I miss them. They'd have me back like a shot, they say, but my wife was from here, see, and I can't bring myself to go home, not while she's here. I mean, not here. She's passed, like, but she's still here, you know?'

I nod. 'What was her name?'

'Nancy.'

He goes quiet, after that, and I watch the world go by. The bus stutters through another village and up to the outskirts of town. The lights draw us in with their promise of hope and warmth, blurring through the falling snow.

'Nearly there,' he says.

I wonder about him and this bus. I wonder why it's been all the battered and broken-down vehicles for us this afternoon. First the old school minibus, then the caravan, now this.

Maybe it's because we're all a little bit battered and broken-down.

Maybe it's because they all brought us glimpses of hope, and even joy, in their own weary ways.

He guides the bus through the town boundaries and onto the ring road, where snow is mulched into slush and cars throw up splashes of icy sludge as they hurtle by. Jodie coughs in her sleep and it rattles her entire body. I twist my hands together and take a deep breath in. 'Listen,' I say, leaning forward. 'I know you could get us there. To the hospital. See her?' I point to Barbara. 'She needs her medication. We all do. And I just don't think we could actually cope with another wait. We've been through a lot, you see.'

'But I'll get in trouble, see, pet, if it breaks down, or there's a problem in the car park...'

I look at him, and look at the others, and then I swallow. 'Please.'

He doesn't reply.

I give him the briefest outline of our unlikely tale, about the beach and how we were stranded, and Dodgy Caravan Dude. He stares round at me, aghast, when I tell him about what was in the caravan. 'Holy Mary, woman.'

'So you see, I think we're done. And you're the only one who can help us now.'

This new audacity tastes foreign and enticing. Just yesterday I'd have said yes, that's fine, please don't put yourself out, sorry to be such a pain. But I'm digging up something new today, and it feels a bit like freedom.

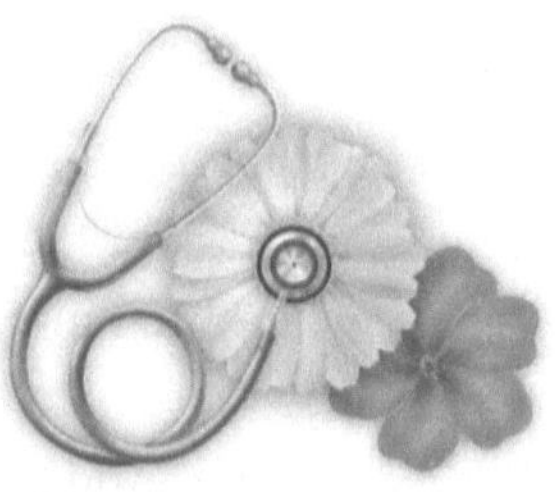

Chapter 28

CAL LIKES TO hum to himself. He's humming as he pulls the bus into the entrance road to the hospital and hums louder as the packed-out car park looms up to meet us. Cars abandoned everywhere, on verges and double-parked, angled steeply up banks and engulfed in snowdrifts. It's chaos out there, with visiting hours plus the weather leading to utter carnage, drivers inching their cars around hunting for spaces, getting into arguments, shouting at the car park attendant. Cal is already stressed after hitting town in rush hour, the streets clogged with snow-pelted traffic, people just wanting to get home into the warm.

'No way I'm getting through that,' he says, shaking his head.

'You don't have to go through it.' I point at the main entrance, to the side of the car park, where taxis linger, where people fight over disabled parking bays and an elderly lady with a walking frame stands alone, shivering. 'Just go round to the main entrance and drop us there.'

'I can't block that.'

'Kane did,' I say.

'I don't care what Kane, whoever the jeff he is, did. I can't block that entrance.'

I exhale. 'I don't think there's much choice.'

He puffs out his cheeks and then shrugs as he slams the bus back into gear, the ancient system squealing back at him. The bus leaps forward, like a car driven by a learner who doesn't quite get the clutch yet, and then crunches through piled up snow and slush as it limps down the entrance road. 'I'm in so much trouble.'

'You're doing a good thing,' Kat says. I look round at her and notice how her face is fading into grey.

'Hmm,' Cal says.

A car beeps its horn as Cal manoeuvres the great beast around it, narrowly avoiding taking out its wing mirror. 'Idiot's going the wrong way,' he mutters. He swings round the entrance curve and pulls to a halt behind an idling taxi, the bus juddering as he slams the brakes hard. We all jerk forward, and Kat holds tightly to Barbara. Jodie lurches awake, almost tumbling from her seat, and sits up, rubbing at her hair. 'What's happening? Where are we?'

'We made it,' Kat says. 'We're back.'

Jodie stares round, wide-eyed, taking in the lights of the entrance, the great glass sliding doors, the huddle of smokers gazing up at us in the bus with weary and curious eyes. 'No way.'

'Yes way,' Cal shouts from his cab. 'Your hospital, my ladies.'

He seems just a little more relaxed, now he's parked up, just on the edge of fidgety, his hands still clamped tight around the wheel.

Jodie starts clapping and then Kat joins in and then the rest of us, even Barbara from under her orange nylon folds. Snowy shifts and mewls then pushes his little pink nose into Barbara's cheek.

Cal rubs his face and smiles shyly round at us. 'No need for that, now.' I'm sure he's blushing beneath that great salt-and-pepper beard. 'Now. Let's get you out of here and up to your beds.' He swings out of his cab as the bus doors hiss open, and gazes around at us, sprawled out with little resource left to get ourselves from here to the ward. He scratches his chin. 'Give us a sec.' He bounds down the step and disappears into the main entrance.

'What do you think they'll say?' I say to Kat.

'Well, they'll all be there, won't they, our visitors I mean. Nate'll be there and who knows else for me, I'm guessing Jake'll be there for you, and Amina's lot, in her ward, I guess. Will Brian be there, Violet?'

Violet nods. 'He'll be there and he'll be worried.'

'He'll say you're a disgrace,' Jodie says, and Violet's mouth tightens for a second, and then relaxes just a tiny bit.

'It's Sister Harris I'm worried about,' I say. 'She'll be livid when she hears.'

'Lucky she's not on today,' Jodie says.

Kat stands gingerly, gripping hold of one of the bars, her legs wobbling. 'We should get off this old thing. Anyone else feel like their legs won't hold them?'

Mmm, we all say.

'Wait. Look.' Jodie points out of the window. It's Cal with a wheelchair, and behind him is a porter with another wheelchair. 'He's a hero, this Cal dude. He's like… I don't know, like that hot guy from *Transporter*.'

Cal leans through the door, grinning, but there's an edge of worry in the lines that crease his eyes. 'Right. Let's get your friend here in first.' He lifts Barbara tenderly, gathering up her oxygen cylinder and tubing, sliding her into the first wheelchair. 'And you.' He points to Violet.

'Oh, I can walk,' she says. 'I have my frame. Let Jodie go in the chair.'

Amina looks at Violet with something like admiration written across her face.

Kat takes my arm and Amina takes Violet's as we clamber down from the bus and follow the two wheelchairs into the building.

Jodie is slouched low, her Santa hat all askew, her face paler still under the stark criss-crossed tile lighting of the hallway, her bare feet sticking out from beneath the picnic rug. We bring the snow in with us, trailing it from our various footwear. I smile at Violet, incongruous in Jodie's Ugg boots under her garish dressing gown and her silver coat, clinging tightly to her walking frame, her make-up smeared all around her face.

The corridor is a confusion of echoing footsteps and polished floors sliding into infinity. The respiratory ward is at the far end, past the lifts, past the stairs, past x-ray and outpatients, past Wards 1-8, past the Peace Garden where through the windows the snow cloaks the battered bench and sparkles through the late afternoon gloom.

The ward is busy with visitors and staff rushing to and fro. There's an electric kind of energy in the air, an urgency of dread as tangible as the institutional aroma of dinner, a catering supervisor standing dead ahead of us with the food trolley as we turn into the ward.

A sharp intake of breath, a muffle of shouts, a scramble of legs. 'They're here. They're safe. It's okay. Tell the police.'

A shiver flutters through my belly. The police?

Then faces. Angry faces, scared faces, relieved faces, confused faces. And in the middle of all the faces is Jake, and his face is the most beautiful thing I have ever seen.

'Jake.'

He stands and stares at me and runs his hand through his hair. 'Where the hell have you been?'

I put my arms around him and fall into him. He's rigid for seconds then he softens and folds me in and it feels like home.

'Just let me sit down.' I stagger through to our bay and slump onto my bed. Cal lifts Barbara onto her bed and the porter helps Jodie to hers, and then Sister Joy is in the bay and her presence is stiff and foreboding, like Sister Harris on a grumpy day, like a headteacher in a room full of miscreants at detention.

Amina hovers in the doorway. 'I will go to find Bilal. He will be worried. I… thank you. I will come and see you all, before I go.'

As she turns and leaves in a stream of tumbling turquoise, Violet gazes after her. I think her eyes are a little bit wet and wonder if she will mind that her tears will smudge her make-up even more.

'Well, I hope there's a good explanation for this,' Sister Joy says.

None of us seem to be able to form the words we need. We collapse into our pillows, in our coats, sleeping bags, gloves, hats, blankets and all. I feel the warmth of the ward begin to sneak its way through to my skin, and hope it will find its way into my bones before they shatter to pieces.

Nicki is here, standing by Sister Joy, with a grim expression on her face and the vital signs trolley by her side. 'I said you'd probably gone to the cinema. They do that, you know, patients, sometimes. Down to that multiplex. But they usually let us know.'

Brian stands next to Violet's bed, wringing his hands and gazing down at her as if she is a priceless piece of art. He takes her all in, his eyes light with relief, his Adam's apple bobbing up and down. 'What are those monstrosities on your feet?' he says.

'Where have you been, Mum?' Jake says, sitting down on my bed and glaring at me. 'We've been here, like, nearly an hour or something.'

My mouth won't form words.

He shakes his head at me, as if suddenly he is the parent and I am the child who needs to go on the naughty step and think about my behaviour. 'They said they expected you back well over an hour ago. They've been looking for you, all round the hospital, like round the grounds and everything, they said you'd said you'd just gone for a walk.'

'You won't believe it,' I rasp out, and then exhale slowly, gazing around the room. The new woman in Amina's bed, Alice, lies cut off from the world, a mask clamped over her face, the machine's roaring vibration cutting through our uneasy silence. Kat is on her bed with Nate on the chair beside her. She is bent right over, her head in her hands. Jodie curls into her sheets, a blanket draped over her cold bare feet.

'What's this thing doing on you?' Sister Joy says, bustling over to Barbara and unzipping the sleeping bag. 'Let's get you out of it, get you settled back into bed, my darling. Are you okay? Are you cold?'

Barbara shakes her head. 'Warm as toast, my lover.'

'Wait… what is this? What on earth… Nicki! Get this animal off my ward!' Sister Joy steps back away from Barbara, who grasps Snowy closely to her, a look of grim determination on her face.

'You're not taking him.'

Sister Joy frowns so deeply the lines merge into one great big fissure. 'No pets on this ward. Hospital policy.' Her voice softens. 'Barbara. Give the cat to Nicki. Where on earth did it come from?'

'The caravan,' Barbara says.

'What?'

Barbara twinkles. 'They took me to the sea.'

'They what?'

One of the other healthcare assistants hovers at Barbara's bed, bending and looking closely at Snowy. 'Wait… isn't that… Nicki, isn't that that cat in the *Herald?* You know, yesterday? Ain't seen many cats look like that.'

Nicki stares. 'It is, you know. Barbara, where did you find this cat?'

Barbara puffs out her cheeks. 'I just told you. The caravan. The caravan full of skunk.'

Jodie looks at me and mouths *skunk* with big wide merry eyes, and I start laughing, and then Kat starts laughing, and then we're all lost in helpless fits of giggles, and the staff and visitors are standing around us, their faces written with great bemusement and a little bit of alarm.

'What cat in the *Herald*?' Sister Joy says.

Nicki says, 'That one that was stolen. That rich toff's cat, Lady something-or-other. Some guy asked for a ransom of 20k or something. But then he never gave her the cat back even though she paid, left the money and everything.'

The other healthcare assistant nods. 'That cat is worth a mint, but that rich old bat, his owner, she said he was priceless to her. She was offering a reward, like 10k or something like that, if anyone finds him.'

'No way,' Jodie says.

'He's got some poet's name or something,' Nicki says.

'Here, look, he has a collar,' Sister Joy says, bending in and lifting the tag. The tag we all missed in the chaos, and the dark, and the snow. 'Here. Byron.'

'He's called Snowy,' Barbara says.

There's a pause.

'What have you lot been up to?' Sister Joy says, her head tilted to the side.

Jodie shifts herself into a semi-sitting position. 'We went to the sea. Barbara wanted… needed to see the sea one more time and didn't have no one to take her there. So we did. Only it went a bit wrong, my boyfriend… I mean my ex, he kind of left us in the lurch. And then there was this caravan dude, and this bus driver here, Cal, who is like my superhero. And we have to tell the police about the caravan guy.' She stifles a yawn over the last words.

Jake raises his eyebrows at her. 'Cool story bro.'

She sniffs at him. 'True story.' She closes her eyes and curls into her pillow.

Cal hovers in the doorway to the bay. 'I should go. The bus…'

Kat drags herself off her bed and hugs him tight. 'Thank you.'

'You're my superhero,' Jodie says sleepily.

Cal's face is flushed, and I don't know if it is because of the heat of the ward or because he is blushing. He shakes his head as Kat lets him go. 'I'll blame you, you know,' he shouts over to me. 'When the bus company have my arse.'

'Do that,' I say.

As he walks out of the ward I stare after him and think about how some men are, after all, good.

Sister Joy stands in the middle of the bay with her legs planted, her arms crossed and her lips flattened, looking around at each one of us. 'So you've all been out on the coldest day of the year, in the snow, for over two-and-a-half hours? There's all levels of stupid, but this has to be at the top.' She turns to Kat. 'What were you thinking?'

She sounds a whole lot like Sister Harris.

Barbara beckons her over and pulls at her arm. 'They were thinking about me and my Maggie Mouse. And I'm glad they did.' Her cheeks are mottled with sheets of colour, a little bit like she has subsumed the sunset she so wanted to see. She leans back on her pillow, cradling Snowy close, a beady suspicious eye on Nicki.

'We really do need to talk to the police,' Kat says. 'We've quite a story to tell.'

'What you need is to get these visitors out and have a nice cup of tea.' Nicki walks through the ward, sweeping her arms at Jake and Nate and the others. 'And then a bit of hot dinner'll be here any minute. Then we can sort out the police, and hear what you've been up to.'

Sister Joy looks taken aback, as if shocked by a mere healthcare assistant taking charge when she is in the room. But she says nothing. Jake ignores Nicki and stays slouched on the chair next to me, arms folded and long legs splayed out, glancing around the bay with amused eyes.

Nicki turns back to Barbara. 'We'll need to take Byron,' she says softly.

'Snowy.' Barbara folds him tighter to her chest, her arms as white as his fur, and turns her face away from Nicki's gaze.

'We'll get him back to his owner, flower.'

Barbara sticks her bottom lip out and shakes her head, then nestles her face into Snowy's, crooning words about him being safe with her, how he shouldn't worry because he is her darling boy. Nicki tiptoes closer and tries to pluck Snowy from Barbara's arms, but he bucks and hisses at her and she steps back, hands in the air. 'You get him,' she says to Sister Joy.

Joy keeps her arms folded tightly under her ample bosom. 'Why can't you?' She turns to the other healthcare assistant who hovers at the door of the bay. 'Or you?'

'I don't want to get scratched,' she says.

Sister Joy narrows her eyes.

'Okay. Okay. I'll try.' The healthcare assistant creeps over to Barbara and tentatively places her hand on the cat. He arches his back, spits, and bats a paw at her.

Nicki purses her lips. 'We're going to have to get hold of the owner. Quick.'

Barbara glows with a smug little smile.

'Right, Barbara. Just give me your arm, so we can do your sats, just quickly.' Nicki wraps the blood pressure cuff around Barbara's arm and slides the oximeter onto her finger. 'Flaming heck!' She stands back, staring at the numbers on the monitor.

'What is it?' Sister Joy says, her face a mask of concern and not a little bit of anger.

My stomach writhes. If we've made her more ill…

'She's got higher oxygen levels than I've ever seen with her!' Nicki says, showing Sister Joy the screen. 'And her blood pressure – it's right perfect.'

'And her temperature?' Sister Joy says, casting a look of disdain over at me and Kat.

Nicki slides the thermometer into Barbara's ear and waits for the beep. She checks the display and raises her eyebrows. 'Thirty-seve point five.'

'Well,' Sister Joy says.

'She's in better shape than she was this morning,' Nicki says.

Kat whispers, 'More by luck than good management.'

'We went to the seaside,' Barbara says. 'And there was sand mountains on my feet and I sat by the sea and had a nip of brandy.'

Sister Joy makes an oh with her mouth. 'You what?'

'Hot chocolate,' Jodie says dreamily. 'Hot chocolate.'

'I don't know what you did,' Nicki says, 'but she's fitter than a fiddle right now.'

Barbara is bubbling with life and joy, and I know, all of a sudden, that we did something good today, after all.

Jake is staring at me like I am an alien, but that is not unusual. 'Are you going to fill me in?' He glances over at Jodie. 'She looks knackered.'

'It's like Barbara says,' I say. 'We went to the sea. And it went wrong, but it went right as well. I… I realised a few things.'

He shifts his eyes to the side, like he always does just before he senses I'm going to do a Talk at him.

'Yeah?'

I gaze at him and think about how much he has missed out on in his life because he has a mum like me. All those times he missed parties. When he couldn't do the football training he loved because I wasn't reliable enough to take him three times a week. All those World Book Days when all the other parents made homemade costumes worthy of the local amateur dramatics society and I sent him in his Gryffindor robes for the third year in a row (it's helpful when parents model a good work ethic to young children, the teacher said to me with a face full of disapproval). All those National Trust houses we didn't visit together. Not that I much enjoyed National Trust houses when I was a teenager, dragged round by my parents in the hopes of instilling culture into me, and Jake doesn't much like them now, on the occasional visit we manage, trailing around with a scowl on his face and ironic grunts of 'Oh, it's another fireplace. Oh, it's another vase.' That doesn't make up for the fact that he should have had more National Trust houses in his life, though, that while every other family out there are #makingmemories on Instagram and Facebook I am wishing memories away under my duvet. Facebook is for old people, Jake always says, but even if that's true I have never been enough for it.

'I wish I'd given you more,' I say.

The depths of blue in his eyes look like summer.

'But, today, I realised that I'd been beating myself up most of my life. And that I didn't have to do that.'

Jake arrests his eye-roll and grabs my hand. 'You're all right, you know that, Mum. You never have to think you're not enough, or anything like that, not for me. You had a bad lot in life, and then that loser who fathered me...'

I squeeze his hand. 'He gave me the best thing I could ever have.'

Jake's eye-roll resumes its sardonic rotation as he picks up his phone. 'That's slay,' he mutters, and I have no idea what he is talking about.

LATER ON, THE police turn up. We have had our dinner and all our observations and our medication. I think back to my last lot of pills, at lunchtime, and think about how it feels like a hundred years and another lifetime ago. Sister Joy struts around the bay with her mouth all flat with disapproval, yet not quite able to hide the edges of her smile as she looks at Barbara and then at Violet who, for the first time, has not complained about her dinner or the lateness of her pills. All the staff studiously ignore Snowy, curled up in Barbara's blankets, his purr lost beneath the whine of nebulisers. The woman in Amina's bed has not moved and I wonder how she would feel if she were able to be at the beach with the sand under her toes today.

It turns out that the police have spoken to Amina first and that she not only filled them in on every detail, but also memorised DCD's license plate. 'She's a marvel,' Violet says. They want to hear the story from us, too. They want to hear all about the caravan and what exactly is in it, about the man and what he looks like, about how the cat was being kept. They want to know exactly which road he was taking when he abandoned us. They know who it is, it turns out, and they have pictures on their iPad to check with us, Dodgy Caravan Dude gurning in a mugshot. He's well known, they say, bit of a liability round these parts, and now they finally have a chance to catch him, thanks to us.

'Thanks to Jodie,' Kat says.

'We're going to have to take the cat,' the detective constable says, looking guiltily over at Barbara who shields Snowy with wild eyes and hands that curl like claws. 'He can't stay here.'

'He'll be coming with me.'

We turn to see a woman striding into the bay. She is tall and slim, probably in her late sixties or early seventies, wearing a camel-coloured coat and several strings of pearls. She is all haughty imperiousness, staring down at us as if she expects us to bow at her feet. She looks around at each of us and her eyes alight on Barbara, then soften. 'Ah.'

'Lady Caroline,' Nicki says, swiftly on her heels. 'You got here quick.'

'My Byron,' Lady Caroline says, gliding over to Barbara's corner. Barbara takes her all in, looking her up and down, and shields Snowy even more fiercely.

Lady Caroline smiles. 'It's okay. Are you Barbara? Thank you. Thank you for keeping him safe for me.'

Barbara pins her in a beady-eyed glare.

'I need to get him home. He'll want his dinner.'

Barbara looks down at Snowy and then back at Caroline, and there is a slight loosening in her arms.

'I will always be grateful to you,' Caroline says. She gazes around at the rest of us, at Jodie, sleepy and droopy against her pillows, and the rest of us who are edged forward, waiting. 'Which one of you is Penny?'

I inch my hand up slowly, like a primary school child caught in some transgression. She leaves Snowy for a moment and comes to me, her heels clopping on the polished floor. 'Byron is everything to me,' she says to me. It's like all the autocratic arrogance that so marks her features is suddenly washed away into something softer and fuzzier, like the snow outside washes away all the sharp corners and turns them into a thing of beauty. 'I owe you his life. Thank you. Thank you.'

'I would never have left him.'

She gazes into my eyes. 'I can see that. Tell me, was he… I mean, was he hurting? Was he crying?'

'He was fine,' I say. 'He cried a little bit, but he was content when I picked him up. He's not hurt.'

Lady Caroline swallows and pats her over-lacquered white hair, her shimmering eyes swivelled up to the ceiling.

'They're going to catch the man. That officer just said they know who he is and think they know where to find him.'

She nods. 'I'd never have been able to go on.'

I smile at her.

'Now, young lady. I promised a reward, for the person who brings my Byron back to me.' She digs into her Burberry handbag and comes out waving a chequebook in one hand and an old-fashioned silver fountain pen in the other. 'Your full name?'

Ten thousand pounds. What could I do with ten thousand pounds? I think about Jake and what it could do for him. Then I look around the ward at each of the women, at the staff, and through the walls in my mind to Amina, and think about what it could do for more people like us, instead.

'Make it out to this hospital. To this ward.'

Jake gapes up at me, and I shrug at him.

He shakes his head and goes back to his phone, and there is a tiny smile skipping on the edges of his lips.

Nicki and Sister Joy stand stock still, staring at me and then at Lady Caroline as she hands the cheque over. They look at it and then they look at one another.

And then they smile.

'We have so much need,' Sister Joy says. 'We need new equipment.'

Nicki is crying.

'There's one condition,' I say. 'Could you get a new bench, please, for the Peace Garden?'

Nicki laughs out loud. 'We will, flower.'

'That reminds me,' Kat says. 'There's a hospital wheelchair in a bus stop somewhere out on the coast road.'

The DC, standing in the doorway clasping her iPad, sighs. 'We'll have a look for it.'

Nicki shakes her head at Kat. 'Dare I ask how… why…?'

'I'll fill you in,' Kat says.

'Wait,' I say to the DC. 'Kane – the guy who took us to the beach – took off with my bag in his minibus. It's got my phone, my purse. I don't know if you can—'

'I'll get it,' Jodie says. 'Don't worry. I need my phone too.'

'But you're not going to…'

She shakes her head. 'Never.'

Lady Caroline turns back to Barbara and smiles gently at her. The lines on Barbara's face seem to relax, as if smoothed over with an airbrush on Photoshop. She presses her face into Snowy's and then she nods. 'He's ready.'

'Thank you,' Lady Caroline says. 'I'd like to bring him to visit you, if that would be permitted?'

Nicki looks dubious. 'She'll be in the care home from tomorrow, or Monday, more likely. But they might let you in there, I suppose. They let those dogs in, don't they, to comfort the patients and everything.'

Snowy nudges his nose into Barbara's cheek one last time and then allows himself to be picked up and hugged tight to his mistress' chest. He snuggles into her and his body relaxes, but as Lady Caroline walks away from the bed he is gazing at Barbara, pinning her down with exquisite blue eyes until she fades from his vision.

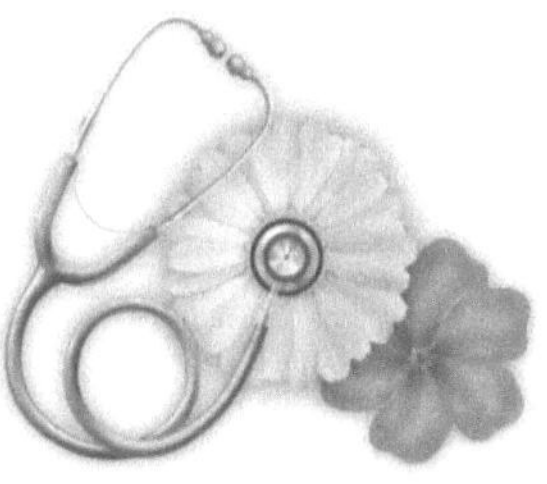

Chapter 29

IN THE NIGHT I am all switched off. My mind is a blank haze of blissful nothingness, carrying me through hours of the best sleep I've had in two weeks, barely waking for my IVs and my observations. In the morning it is quiet in the bay. Alice is propped up against her pillows, and I see her face properly for the first time, free of its CPAP constraint. The indent of the mask still imprints her flesh, leaving angry red streaks that make her look even more vulnerable, even more frail.

Jodie is sleeping, all curled up in a quivering ball, and Violet isn't here. I glance out of the window to the white world outside, the snow still falling, heaped against the walls in great drifts; a good day for a snowball fight, Jake would say. Kat is drinking a cup of tea, pinches of colour in her cheeks I'm sure weren't there before. 'How are you feeling?' she says.

'I'm actually okay,' I say.

'Me, too. I can't quite believe it, to be honest.'

'Pretty sure Sister Joy thought we'd all drop dead of pneumonia last night.'

'What about Barbara?'

I look over to where she is sitting, feet snug in her maroon slippers, dressing gown pulled tight over her hospital gown. Her hair is stark white against the blue of the chair, her face is flushed with marbled pink. I wave at her.

She beckons me over. 'Here. You were snoring, you were.'

'Was I?'

She shakes with mirth. 'Like a great big dog.'

'Umm… thanks?'

'Come and sit down with me.' She pats her bed and I perch on the edge, keeping an eye out for Sister Harris, who might be on shift today. Barbara leans into me and whispers into my ear, 'I found my mouse.'

I draw back and look at her. Is she confused, or is she lucid?

She puts her hand over her mouth and giggles. 'You know I did.'

'I know you did, Barbara.'

'Hey! Off that bed, young lady.' It's not Sister Harris, it's Sister Joy again, bustling in with the meds cart, wagging a finger at me. 'You get back into bed. I've got my eye on you today so you don't go off on another one of your outings. You bad ladies, you.' She says it all with a wide grin curving her mouth and ends it with a tinkling laugh like a mountain stream. 'There's a lady here wants to speak to you all, but I've told her to come back later, when we've got our morning jobs done. She's very insistent.'

'Who is it?'

Sister Joy shrugs. 'She says that she cannot wait until visiting. So I say, I do not care that you cannot wait, this is a hospital. And then she says, she has something good for us, if I let her have half an hour with you.'

The ward settles into the slumber of Sunday morning, with the odd group of doctors consulting together and with their patients. No one seems interested in me or Kat, though Barbara and Violet both get a visit, and Jodie too. I can hear the doctor's booming voice from Barbara's cubicle: 'You are much better, Barbara.' She says it loudly and slowly, as if Barbara is both hard-of-hearing and stupid. 'You can go back to your care home tomorrow.'

'Oh,' Barbara says, and I can hear the wavering in her voice.

'We weren't too happy with what you did,' the doctor says, 'but it seems there's no harm done. You look very sprightly this morning.'

'I went to the sea,' Barbara says.

Sister Joy goes to speak with Jodie's doctor and they hang round in her cubicle for longer than usual, but I can't hear what they're saying, their hushed tones smothered under the beepbeepbeep of Alice's occluded IV drip. Something about morphine, and maybe tramadol, too.

'Are you okay?' I say to her when the doctor has left.

'Never better.'

'Are you going home tomorrow, too?'

'I don't think so.' She seems slurred and dreamy.

A young woman with long, curly red hair and huge black framed glasses wanders into the bay, clutching an iPad and glancing around at each one of us. Her gaze alights on Jodie. 'You're Jodie Hancox?'

Jodie nods and smiles languidly. 'I am she.'

'Good. Good. I'm Sarah Lawley from the *Herald*.'

'Hello, Sarah Lawley from the *Herald*.'

I wonder exactly how much morphine she has had.

'I just wondered if you'd mind answering a few questions for me.' She catches me staring. 'You, too… Katrina?'

'Penny.'

'We probably shouldn't talk to reporters,' Kat says.

Sarah Lawley from the *Herald* smiles and nods. 'I get that. I respect that. Only, we just want to tell a story with a happy ending for a change. See, we've heard about it on the grapevine. About the drug guy and the cat, and about your friend—' she gazes over at Barbara, '—Barbara?'

Jodie nods. 'Beautiful Babs.'

'It's about giving people a little lift, see. We do a lot of bad news, and when something like this comes along – we thought it might be a nice little story, some nice local flavour.'

Jodie's eyes are far away, lost in some land of blue skies and swirling colour. 'Happy ending.'

Sarah furrows her brow at her. 'Yes. Are you okay?'

'I'm grand.'

'She's stoned,' Kat whispers to me. 'We should get that reporter away from her.'

'I heard that,' Jodie says. 'An' I want to talk to her. Tell her the happy story. I like the happy story.'

Kat shakes her head, massaging her temple. 'We like it too, Jodie, but you're a bit out of it.'

Nicki is in the ward with the vitals trolley. 'Everything all right in here?' She raises her eyebrows at Sarah. 'Who are you?'

Sarah shows Nicki her lanyard. 'The other nurse, she said I could come in.'

Nicki shakes her head. 'No reporters. These ladies need rest.'

Sarah says, 'The *Herald* would like to give the respiratory ward a little something. Just in recognition of the good work that you do.'

Nicki pauses.

'What are you raising money for right now?'

'You can't bribe us,' Nicki says.

'I want to talk to the nice lady. Let me talk to the nice lady.' Jodie pouts at Nicki and sits herself up, arranging her pillows behind her.

I say to Kat, 'I think we'd better help Jodie talk to the nice lady, don't you?'

Nicki says, 'Up to you.'

So we do. We talk to Sarah Lawley from the *Herald* and we tell her a story about six foolish but courageous women who went to see the sea. We tell her about how a tatty candy-striped picnic rug and a hideous orange sleeping bag probably saved our lives (and Jodie says that a very disturbing wolf fleece saved hers). I tell her that I'd never dreamed I would have the courage to stand up to a drug dealer or shriek at a bus that was bearing down upon me in the snow.

SISTER JOY BRINGS our lunchtime IVs around. 'You're off home tomorrow, aren't you Penny?' she says, turning to me as she hooks Jodie's clipboard back onto her bed and rubs alcohol gel into her hands. 'You too, Kat, and Violet? Tuesday for you, is it? It'll be all change here. It's a shame really, we've all got used to you lot and your crazy adventures.'

'I think so, yes. The doctor will tell me for sure in the morning. But I feel so much better, despite what we did.' I glance over at Jodie and she gives me a slow, exaggerated wink.

Sister Joy gives Jodie a sidelong look. 'You are a bad girl.'

Jodie bows slightly. 'I know.'

'But look at this woman.' Sister Joy gestures over to Barbara, who is bolt upright in her chair, listening keenly. 'She is like a new woman. She will be running up and down those stairs now and dashing all over the place before we can stop her.'

'They buried my feet in the sand,' Barbara says.

Sister Joy holds the edges of her smile in a sort of half-frown. 'I know.' Tones of disapproval mixed with something like admiration. 'And look at you now! You're like a young lady again, all ready for the dance, with your sparkly eyes and your big grin.'

'I sat in the snow in an orange sleeping bag and had a whole lot of brandy to keep me warm.'

Jodie glances at me and I can't help laughing, and before we know it a great rise of uproar sweeps through the ward, Violet, Kat, Jodie and I carried away over the sea on a wave of mirth. We hack and we gasp and we cough and it's like a great light floods the room. Sister Joy stands in the middle of us, shaking her head and waggling her finger again. 'Like I said, we will all miss you lot.'

I will miss them too.

Amina comes into the bay. She's come to say goodbye, she says, she's been set free and she's off home. Bilal hovers at her side and regards us with a slightly suspicious air of uncertainty, as if he can't make up his mind whether we put his wife in danger or made her dizzy with happiness.

Probably both.

She stands by Violet's bed and twists her hands together. She is wearing her turquoise hijab, and it reminds me of the sea in summer, in its liquid flowing incandescence. She swallows, and then opens her mouth, and then closes it again.

Violet takes her hands. 'I am going to miss you, little Amina.'

Amina gazes up at the ceiling, her eyes brimming with tears. 'I do not know what to say. This is not usual for me, what has happened here.'

Violet says, 'You don't have to say anything.'

Amina gazes around at each one of us. 'I just want to say thank you. Before, I always have felt… invisible, when I am in here. It is like they do not see me, the other patients, because of this—' she touches her head, '—because of the colour of my skin, because of my religion. It is as if they think that they cannot talk with me, laugh with me. I am left alone and I feel alone. But with you… you did not do that to me. You made me feel like I belong, like I exist, maybe like I matter. I had to tell you this before I left.'

Violet picks at her nails, her mouth trembling.

'You, too,' Amina says to her.

Violet scuffs her feet into her slippers – new, equally hideous ones Brian has dropped in for her – and then she heaves herself off her bed and folds Amina into her arms.

Amina's tears spill over.

'You taught me some things,' Violet says.

Jodie, too, drags to her feet, steadying herself on my bed as she makes her way over to Amina and slings her arms around both her and Violet. 'Me too.'

'I would like to stay in touch,' Amina says.

Kat says, 'Here, write down your number, I'll share it with the others when I get my phone back. I think we'd all like that.'

'Yes please,' I say.

AT VISITING TIME, the little Friends man trundles into the bay pushing his newspaper trolley. He stops in the centre and looks around at each of us in turn, an enigmatic little grin spreading over his face. 'I have a surprise for you.'

'What?' Kat says. Nate is with her, leaning in closely and tucking a strand of hair behind her ear.

The Friends man plucks a paper from the rack and brandishes it at us, holding it up high. It's a *Herald*. 'You are celebrities,' he says.

'Oh my word,' Violet says.

Jodie smiles lethargically. 'Go on, then, what's it say?'

Kat says, 'A couple of sentences somewhere towards the back?'

'You're on the front page,' the Friends man says.

What?

'No way,' Jake says.

Friends man spreads the newspaper out on Violet's bed, and Kat and Nate and Jake and I crowd over to see it. Jodie hoists herself up and limps over. 'What's it say, then?'

The first thing I see is a photo of Barbara smiling so widely all the lines on her face are vivid with life and motion. Sarah Lawley from the *Herald* must have snapped it on her phone.

'They've caught him!' Kat says. 'Look!'

I lean over to read the article.

'Read it out to me,' Barbara shouts over.

'"Six hospital patients catch wanted criminal in seaside escapade." That's the headline,' I say.

'Read it all!'

'Okay, okay.' I read the copy out loud and we laugh at the exaggeration and embellishments in the story. Perhaps it was Sarah Lawley's poetic license, or more likely Jodie's morphine-addled imagination. Apparently I defended us against Dodgy Caravan Dude (who, it turns out, is named Gary Cockford), by seizing his knife and holding it against his throat, and Amina high-kicked him with her stiletto heel, '"like this awesome ninja chick,' Jodie Hancox, 31, says." ('She got my age wrong,' Jodie mumbles.) Most of it is true enough to the tale, though, and as I read it I think about how much it sounds like a made-up story, something beyond the bounds of reality. Hospital patients wouldn't go and do something stupid like that, would they?

But there is no judgment in the article. Instead the journalist has written us as heroic, as selfless and self-sacrificial, as kind and courageous women who just wanted to give an elderly lady her dying wish. And there is something true in that, of course, but I know that my motivations, at least, are a little less black-and-white, that there is nuance to this tale that doesn't quite come out in this report. I know that I wanted to be somewhere different, that I wanted to please other people and to say yes, but also know that because I did, I discovered some new things that will help me say yes a whole lot less in the future.

'I did want to help Barbara,' Kat says, her brow all crinkled up as she reads the report again. 'But I'm not this great humble hero they're making out. I kind of like being needed, I guess. I wanted to be part of this thing, to be the person everyone looks to for help. I… I don't always feel like I am enough, I suppose.'

I stare at Kat, beautiful, confident, self-assured Kat, and think about how people might be swimming along so smoothly on the surface when underneath there is a whole maelstrom of emotions and sadness and anger and helplessness threatening to pull them under at any time. I think about how we are so quick to judge people from first impressions, how we have no clue about what is really going on in their lives, how people so often wear a mask, how they say they are fine when they are not. I think about Violet and her behaviour when she first arrived in Bay C, how her words were so soaked in bile, and how they must have sprung from the fear squirming deep inside her and the pain that so gripped every part of her body, from years of rejection that squeezed her into a desert of bitterness and pulled her husband into it with her. How her motivation for this outing was not only born out of the superhuman selflessness Sarah Lawley so hoped to invest us all with; how she wanted to explore this new sense of belonging, something she'd caught glimpses of in the past two weeks in a world she was usually so hostile to and so was hostile back. And Amina wanted to come because she wanted to prove she was a human who existed, to dance into the freedom of being seen, and because she wanted to help Violet, the very person who had so disdained and spurned her. Perhaps Amina's motivation was the best of us all.

I look at Jodie and think about her happy-go-lucky temperament and how it covered over the grim truth of her life with Kane. And then there's me, with my eager-to-please manner and how I so kick myself inside when I do not stand up against injustice or oppression or abuse. I wonder what the world would look like if we were all more honest with one another, if we all admitted our tangled motivations and messed-up emotions, if we helped one another a little more by allowing our own vulnerabilities to stand out and proud.

'I get it,' I say to Kat.

I look down at the article again, reading to the end. There is a quote from Lady Caroline about how immeasurably grateful she is to us for returning her dear cat, Byron, and how delighted she is to donate to the hospital on our behalf. The whole piece reads like a sappy girl-power chick-lit novel, all friendship-in-adversity and women who beat the odds, tenacious, feisty women who are even stronger together. There's a photo of the hospital as well, and one of our bay from the outside I didn't know she had taken. We are all lying in our beds, looking fast asleep and not very strong at all.

'I can't believe it,' Jodie says, and she is grinning from ear to ear.

Jake says, 'I can't even.'

Chapter 30

I LIE AWAKE late into the night, unable to sleep, jittery with agitation about all that has happened and the possibility of going home tomorrow. If I count up my days my last IV wouldn't be officially until tomorrow evening, but I think my consultant will waive that one in the face of my excellent vitals and return to something like health. My cannula is on the edge again, the drug searing through my vein, but I didn't mention it when the nurse came at midnight to push my IV through. Not another one. Please. Not for just one day.

It's quiet on the ward, apart from the screech of Alice's machine which is like background noise now. I wonder how I will sleep at home, in the dead silence of a room without machines. Every so often it squeals and one of the healthcare assistants will come in and gently admonish her for pulling it off. 'I know you don't like it, lovely. It's a horrible great thing, isn't it. But you need to leave it on.' Alice weeps and the healthcare assistant sits with her and holds her hand.

I ask the nurse for one of my prescribed sleeping pills when the hours tick away and sleep doesn't come and I lie stiff with weariness. When she brings it I succumb quickly to its velvet depths, its waters closing over my head and dragging me into sunlight-drenched lands.

In the early hours I jolt awake and wonder if it is morning. The window behind me is a square of dark grey, though, with no signs of dawn breaking up its gloom, and still the snow comes, cascading through the darkness and glittering in the reflection of Alice's overhead light, still on above her bed. I yawn and wonder if I really am awake or if the sleeping pill has sent me into some kind of lucid dream as I become aware of hushed voices from Jodie's cubicle. She has the curtains closed around her, and I wonder if she is on her phone, if she is making up with Kane. I hope not. Not after she has come so far. But then I remember that she doesn't even have her phone, that Kane took it with him.

Another voice floats through the curtain. Kat's calm, soft tones, a low whisper of gentle tenderness. Kat's voice is soothing, floating me away from the weariness of the ward and lulling me back into the arms of my drug-heavy sleep, whispered and gentle and somehow assuring. Is she praying? I think she is praying. I didn't think Jodie was into that stuff.

I am falling, tumbling over and over, tottering on the edge of oblivion, sliding down into Kat's unheard words which tug me deep into waterfalls, drifting into the kind of sleep that you can't easily climb out of, the kind that pins you to the bed and holds you there.

A sudden jolt into consciousness. An impression of something from my dream still weaving through my mind, shouts and crashes and the whirring of machinery. I swallow; my mouth is dry, and reach over for my water, blinking and staring around. My curtains are closed around me, enclosing me in a blue cave with weak light spilling under from Jodie's cubicle. I can hear people moving about, whispering. I think it's coming from Barbara's direction but there's movement next to me too. Jodie is probably getting up to go for her fag, she often does in the early hours, stealing out of the ward like an inept burglar, a look of mischievous rebellion stamped on her face. I hear footsteps leaving her bed and smile. It's all part of the familiarity, the pattern that makes this place my temporary home, the absurdity yet assurance of it all. I close my eyes and begin to slide away.

I don't think Kat is with her anymore. No voices there now, only from the cubicle in the far corner. Muttered voices, worried tones, beepbeepbeep of machines. Beepbeepbeep, calling me into sleep.

Machines in Barbara's cubicle.

Barbara.

They are moving around, stealthy footsteps, squeaking shoes on the polished floor, to and fro and in and out. Whispers and scuffles, a muted commotion of movement.

What are they doing?

Dread settles in my stomach like a jagged stone, cutting through my sluggish languor.

What have we done?

I AM TUGGED awake by the morning light and a sense of doom.

My curtains are still pulled tightly around my cubicle but there is movement outside. The squeal of wheels, the gruff voice of a porter, Ernesto whispering to him. I want to look out of my curtain but don't want to all at the same time.

It's our fault. I know that Barbara had a full, long life, I know that we granted her wish and made her shine, but we tired her out too much, we left her outside in the frozen world too long. I am plunged back into the narrative I so recently began to climb out of:

It's my fault. I am responsible. I should have said no. It's all my fault.

Kat is crying softly from behind the curtain next to me. I swallow over the great lump in my throat and shift myself to the edge of my bed. 'Kat?' I whisper, as if speaking any louder would shatter some kind of sacred aura hovering over the bay. 'Kat?'

She sniffs and then she is up, poking her head through the curtain and then tugging it back so that our cubicles become one, closed against the rest of the bay. Her face is red and tear streaked.

'It's Barbara, isn't it,' I say dully, a pit of dread in my stomach threatening to pull me right inside of it.

She gazes at me and then shakes her head.

'Barbara isn't dead?'

'No.' Her voice is raspy and weary.

I allow the wave of relief to wash over me before I look again at Kat's ravaged face.

'But she is… she's okay?'

'She's fine.'

'Then what…?'

Kat flops back down onto her bed and draws her knees up to her chin.

'What is it?'

She looks at me and her eyes are dark with pain.

'It's Jodie.'

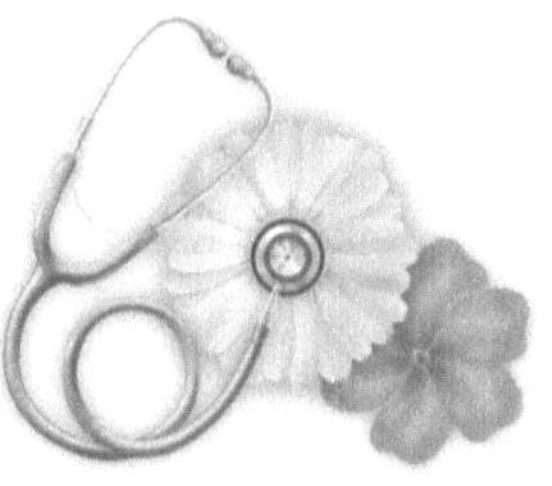

Chapter 31

I AM FALLING off a cliff.

The land is slipping underneath me, relentlessly wrenching at my body. My bones are heavy, dragging me down into the great expanse gaping with malice and darkness.

And then Kat is there, gripping my hands and holding me steady.

Jodie had a heart condition, Kat tells me, a congenital heart disease. She'd known for years that her heart might fail and she was on the transplant list. Her COPD came on top of all that, but it's all she chose to tell us about. Tell me about, at least. She was here on the respiratory ward, being treated for an exacerbation of her COPD, and doing well, but she had a feeling, Kat says, she told Kat that she just knew, and last night her heart began to fail, and later it stopped and would not start again. I think about my dreamlike state through the night: whispers, crashes, beeps, lights. I slept through Jodie dying.

But the doctors never said, I say to Kat, wrapped in her arms after crying out all the tears I keep inside and blinking my eyes at a world that has suddenly tilted. They never said and neither did she. But why would they, Kat says. Why would they say anything to any of us? Patient confidentiality. Patients' conditions are not for sharing with the ward and the world, however friendly they are. I think back over the last two weeks and think about how the doctors would gather round Jodie's bed and speak in muted tones, and how she would smile and laugh and banter at them, how she would say she was ready for home so they'd no need to worry.

'I heard you with her in the night,' I say.

Kat wipes over her face with her sleeve and nods. 'Yes.'

'You were, what, praying?'

'Jodie wanted me to. We do a special little service with the dying. She asked for that.'

'That's kind of nice.'

Nice? Nothing about this is nice.

Kat says nothing.

'So she asked for you. Not Kane.'

Kat nods and smiles softly. 'She said something to me, before she went.'

'Oh?'

'She said that we had set her free.'

The lump in my throat hardens. I remember some words Amina said to her on Saturday, words about how she could now be free from Kane, and so she could take up her wings and fly away.

'She said that?'

'She said she'd never known anyone like us five. That we gave her back her dignity after Kane took it away. She was struggling to speak and I said to her, I said Jodie, please don't talk, please just rest, but she said no, she had to tell me. She said she knew she was dying, she knew she didn't have too long, all the operations she'd had on her heart hadn't done enough, there were structural abnormalities that wouldn't be fixed. Said that she wanted to do one last thing, with Barbara, one last thing for the good of someone. Then she was gasping and the doctor was in there saying no more talking, shush now, and then...'

I take Kat's hands in mine and squeeze.

'Then I did my thing. And sat with her a while. She held onto my hand. They tried, Penny. They tried to revive her but it wouldn't work. I had to leave, to come back here, to listen to it all. How did you not hear?'

'Sleeping pills.'

'Oh.'

There's a bustle in the bay as two of the healthcare assistants start pulling all the curtains back. Sister Harris is there, her face set in a mask of brisk emptiness, yet I can see the cracks at the sides, around her eyes. Violet is sitting up in her bed, blinking back tears, and Barbara is lying back in hers, eyes closed.

Jodie's cubicle is empty.

LATER, DOCTOR CHOWDHURY stands at the end of my bed, his arms hanging awkwardly by his side. 'Now, Penny, I've learned about what you've all been up to.' His eyes flicker over to Jodie's space. 'You were very close. I am sorry.'

I can't find any words, so I nod. The shock in me, at first broiling through me like a wave of heat, has hardened into a rock in the pit of my belly. Later, I will cry more.

'It wasn't your fault, you know.'

I breathe in deeply and exhale. 'But… but if we hadn't been out in the cold… Jodie got cold. She got tired. I could see it on her. She was a bit blue. If we had only stayed—'

Doctor Chowdhury raises his palm. 'You must stop this. This was not the reason. Jodie died because of a long-term issue. Her doctors were surprised she had got to this age, it was thought that she would not survive childhood. You must not think this way.

Instead, you must think about the joy that it brought to her at the end.'

I pick at a loose flap of skin on my thumb and then I wrench it away and hope that the sting of it will burn hotter than the shock and the grief.

And then I think about her face, all lit up with mayhem and mischief, all afire with glowing joy and newly minted liberation. Pale with cold and disease, yet somehow warm with life. She was like the autumn leaves, resplendent in their finery in their final days, blazing with colour as they hurtled to the ground and into their winter of death. She was all the shades of gold, all the splashes of vibrancy.

And then she died.

'Now. Let's look at you.' He takes up the clipboard with my notes and ruffles through the pages. 'Hmm.'

'I'm doing well. I'm so much better.'

'Your vitals are good. It seems your little trip did you good. All that fresh air.' He sweeps his hand around the bay. 'Did you all good.'

'So I can go home today?'

He folds his arms and ponders me, then looks back at my chart and mouths numbers as he counts up days and doses. 'No. No, I think just to be safe I'd prefer you to stay in one more night, for your final IV late tonight. Then we'll get you discharged and home as soon as we can in the morning.'

My gut plummets. I want to go home. I want to go and wrap myself in my blanket and my cushions and Jake's arms.

Jake. Jake will be so sad. Jodie has become important to him, in such a short time; I could see through all their banter, their game of insults, that there was a light between them.

There was a light between us all.

THE FRIENDS MAN is back again, after lunch, when Violet, Kat and I are sitting around Barbara's bed holding hands and saying nothing at all.

'I had to come up here soon as I started my rounds,' the Friends man says, almost gasping with glee. As he takes us in, his face falls and he steps back towards his trolley. 'Are you okay?'

Kat shakes her head.

'Jodie passed away,' Violet says.

'Oh. Oh. I'm ever so sorry.' Lines of concern cut raggedly into his face and I wonder about him, about his background, about what motivates him to give freely of his time to trundle a trolley full of mostly unwanted papers and confectionery around the wards to often ungrateful patients.

'What was it you wanted?' I say, keeping my voice gentle, all of a sudden imbued with the knowledge that this man knows what loss is.

A smile dances quietly around his mouth. 'It's the papers, see.'

'The papers?'

He tugs out a newspaper from the rack and opens it at the second page. It's the *Daily Mail.*

'What the… bring that closer!' Violet says.

'It's all of them,' he says. 'They've all done your story.'

'Oh my word!' Kat says, her hand over her mouth. 'Let's see!'

In the *Mail* there is a photo of us all that I don't recognise. As I look closer, I realise it's the six of us, sprawled out on the beach, on the picnic blanket and an assortment of chairs.

'It must be Kane,' Kat says. 'He took that, remember? With Jodie's phone? He's emailed it in. Probably demanded money for it.'

I don't care if he did, because the picture is there in all its splendour, and it is beautiful. Kat is there smiling up from under the hood of her Chewbacca onesie. I am next to her, huddled in my parka and Jake's old beanie hat with my knees drawn up, a tiny smile on my lips. Barbara, swathed in her waffle blankets on the frog chair, her sparse white hair sticking out from a Bristol Rovers bobble hat, is leaning over towards Amina, whose hijab seems to animate in ripples, even through the stillness of the picture. Violet is sitting stiffly on her walker, the Dressing Gown of Doom pulled over her knees and legs, the space coat zipped up tightly, her mouth twisted with pain or disdain or both. And then there's Jodie, in her skimpy jacket and very disturbing wolf fleece, a Santa hat perched on her head at a jaunty angle, her arms stopped short in mid-air. I remember how she threw them high in abandon and then lowered them at Kane's grimace, and I love that her freedom escaped into this picture.

'Check this out,' Kat says, pointing to the headline and laughing out loud.

ADVENTURING PATIENTS CATCH CARAVAN CRIMINAL. The prose is slightly more exciting and even more hyperbolic than that of the *Herald*. Sarah Lawley probably got a nice little pay-off for this story.

'You ain't seen nothing yet,' the Friends man says. He waves another paper at us and Kat grabs it. It's *The Sun.*

CAT-NAPPING CAMPING CRIME-LORD CANNED IN RUNAWAY PATIENT CAPER.

I look up at Kat and find myself grinning with her.

This one tells the story in colourful pulp. "Five respiratory patients with hearts of gold smuggled an elderly patient with severe dementia out of their hospital ward and took her on a reckless seaside escapade. 'They have given me my smile back,' Barbara Evans, 87, says. Barbara was desperate to see the sea one last time. It's where her husband Bill proposed to her in 1955, Jodie Hancox, 31, who suffers from COPD, says, and where she lost her first and only baby to a miscarriage in 1958. Local tattooed vicar Katrina Omi, 37, who is recovering from pneumonia, says, 'Jodie had this crazy idea and we all went along with it. We thought she was joking and then she wasn't, and before we knew it we were in her boyfriend's minibus heading for Sea Bay. It was surreal but it was about the best day of my life.'" It carries on in the same vein, meandering through our tale with its own brand of overcooked sensationalism, virtue-signalling like mad with its desire to claim its status as a paper that cares for those poor sick people.

Jodie would have loved it.

They've even dug Cal up from somewhere and interviewed him, dragging out his side of the story into melodramatic prose that sounds nothing like him at all. 'I stopped as soon as I saw them. I thought they were out on the tiles, at first. They looked like a hen weekend gone wrong, like a bunch of crazy drunk woman, to be honest with you, but it quickly became obvious they needed my help, so I lifted them all into the bus, one by one, and made sure they were safe. I was just so happy I could help.'

I think about Cal's face when he nearly ran me over, and his overwrought protests about health and safety and buses that needed to be somewhere else.

'I offered to take them straight to the hospital, and there I sourced wheelchairs for each woman and got help to take them up to the ward. It made me late for getting my bus to the depot, but I didn't care. I could only see six sick women who needed my help and I was only too glad to give it.'

I wonder if Cal really did say all that. I doubt it. I think he probably told them a more mundane version, the truth, and they ennobled it in order to make him the saviour of us they wanted him to be. I am miffed that they do not mention that I stopped the bus myself, through sheer stubborn tenacity, in a defining moment that changed my life.

'Does *The Guardian* have it?' I say, hoping that their account will plump for female solidarity more than weak little women with hearts of gold saved by A Man.

The Friends man shakes his head. 'No, but there's a little paragraph in *The Times*. Haven't looked at the others, though. Bet *The Mirror* has it.'

'What does *The Times* say?'

He pulls it out and flips the pages until he finds it, just a short article towards the middle. The headline is less shouty and more bland. 'Patients stumble across drug-dealer.' It outlines the story without fanfare, and includes one of the quotes from the *Herald* from Lady Caroline. It is without spin and without fake heroism and I like it.

Jake is subdued. He sits on my chair and keeps his gaze averted from Jodie's corner, which still remains empty, frozen in waiting for its next patient. He drums his fingers on my bed remote and his dark lashes brush his cheeks and they are damp.

'What do *you* want?' Violet's voice is shrill and harsh across the bay and I look over to her and then to the entrance where a shaven-headed man in a white Adidas hoodie stands in an uncertain, lanky pose, holding a plastic wallet and my handbag.

Kane.

He rubs his hand over his head and stares around at us. He opens his mouth and then closes it again.

Kat says, 'I'm sorry,' and I can't imagine where she digs up the grace for it. I'm not sorry, not for him. I am more sorry than I can say for Jodie and her family and us as those who loved her even though we only knew the edges of her. But for Kane, I cannot find any sorry in myself.

He clears his throat. 'I… brought this bag back.' He holds it up hopelessly, looking around at each one of us, waiting.

'It's mine,' I say, and even I can hear the clipped scorn wrapped around my words.

He shambles over and drops it on my bed.

Jake glares at him.

'I'm sorry. I'm sorry,' Kane says.

No one replies.

'I did love her, you know.'

Silence.

'I'm not a bad person. I didn't mean to leave you all there at the beach. It just happened. I… I did go back, after a while, but you were all gone. Thought you were safe. I wouldn't have left you, you know.'

I have lots of words I could say to this, but I have no energy to waste on saying them out loud.

His face is all crumpled up. 'I'm so sorry.'

Maybe I'm not really sorry that he did leave us there. Maybe I'm grateful for that time spent with Jodie and the others, for the way my life got turned upside down, for the sunset and the snow and the cat and the bus. All because of him.

But I am still angry with him.

'She never told me,' he says, shifting his eyes to the window behind me. 'Why did she never? If she told me I'd of treated her better. I would of.'

Kat presses her lips together.

'She never said nothing about her heart.'

'But you knew she was sick with her lungs,' Kat says.

Kane stares at his feet.

A hot wave rises into my throat and pushes out my words. 'That's not what love is, though, is it. It's not that you treat someone better because they are more sick, or suffering more or whatever. What was it you said before about love, Kat? That it's always patient. Always kind. Not self-serving. Love doesn't come with conditions.'

Kane looks like he doesn't understand what I am talking about.

'You didn't love Jodie,' I say.

He looks smaller all of a sudden, diminished, shrunk back into himself. He shrugs and then he offers me the plastic wallet in his hand. 'Thought you might like this.'

It's the photo he sent to the *Mail*. The photo of us all frozen in time, with Jodie captured in a golden moment, arms in the air, glittering with life.

'Thank you,' I say.

Kane turns and walks out of the bay and out of our lives.

VIOLET HAS BEEN all ready to go for hours. Her discharge forms and medication have finally arrived, and Brian is packing up her things while she discards the hideous dressing gown and dons her silver jacket, with a pink and orange floral scarf that looks like it is desperately trying to escape back into the eighties. Brian is wearing the exact same silver jacket, only in a smaller version. For a moment I can almost taste Jodie's reaction to them, and I feel myself smiling.

A paramedic comes into the bay with a wheelchair and scans the name boards above the beds, settling on Barbara's. 'Hospital transport,' he says to Nicki, who is hovering at the door with some notes. 'Taking Mrs Evans to her care home.'

Him and Brian and Violet and Barbara are a blur of colour as they bend into cupboards and drawers, tugging towels and jumpers off their chairs, clearing their over bed tables of two weeks and more's worth of detritus. They pack up this part of their lives in just a few minutes. Barbara is quavery and weepy, whether about Jodie or going back to the home I am not sure. Maybe it is a mixture of everything. Maybe all her emotions have crowded into one great big river of tears and she can't stop it. I know that because I feel a little bit like that too.

Our goodbyes are too quick and without great drama, even from Violet. I remember the day she came in, when this bay and this bed space was disgusting and so was everything and everyone else, and how as she leaves now her mouth is just a little less twisted up than it was then.

Jake looks at her and Brian, framed in the entrance to the bay, and says, 'Hashtag Briolet, modelling the latest must-have spacewalk jackets in his and hers versions.'

That's something Jodie would have said. I can almost hear the echo of her voice whispering through the bay.

'Keep in touch,' Kat says.

Violet nods, then stops in the doorway, looking back at us, as if she is hovering on the edge of the possibility of saying more. I want to get up, to go over and hug her, but Brian pulls at her arm. As they leave I hear Brian mutter to her, 'It's disgusting, how long they took to get you discharged. Been waiting round all day.'

'It's a disgrace,' Violet says, and then she is gone.

Barbara waves to us as she is pushed out of the door to the bay, wrapped in blankets and wearing her maroon fluffy slippers, a smile toying with her mouth. We wave back, and then she is gone too.

IN EVENING VISITING I am not expecting anyone. Jake left earlier, after hugging me more tightly than usual and telling me that he could not wait for me to come home tomorrow, so we could be together again in our little flat. He would cook for me, he said. Not sloppy macaroni cheese, please, I said.

I lie back on my bed and close my eyes. I am weary and wounded and I just want to sleep and then go home. My cannula stings at my arm and I shift it to try and ease the burning but it doesn't work and I know they will have to change it one last time.

'Penny.'

The voice is familiar. Gentle with tenderness.

Dad.

It is the first time he has come to see me in hospital in years. I look around, searching for Mum, but she isn't there, of course. Just Dad. He looks old and tired, like the years have waged a battle and then won. The lines on his face cut so deeply they look like they have been carved out, as if a sculptor has taken a knife to his flesh. I remember him young and glorious, in Africa on safari with me, lying under great starry skies and pointing out the different constellations. I remember him before the cares of the world got too much and before I became the burden that ruined his life.

'Dad,' I say.

He shifts from foot to foot, his hands jiggling by his side as if he doesn't know what to do with them.

'It's… nice to see you.' All I want is for him to come and sit with me, to throw his arms around me, so that I can cry into his chest like I did as a little girl, so the tears I've locked up for so long can have a safe place to fall on, so he can make everything better.

'I saw you in the *Mail*,' he says.

'You still reading that rag?' I bite my lip and wish I could take the insult back. My politics have never lined up with my parents', and there have been too many arguments that have opened the wound until it is too gaping to mend.

But he smiles softly. 'I wanted to say…'

He stops. Scratches his beard.

'It's just that… I'm proud of you, Penny.'

I stare up at him. His faded grey eyes are troubled.

Proud?

He never told me that he was proud of me. Not in years, at least. Maybe when I was small, when I was doing well at school, when everything about me looked a little bit hopeful and as if I might be something useful in life. But it was Karen they were always proud of, in the end. I was the one who they just had to put up with.

He swallows over his bobbing Adam's apple. 'I… it's just your mum, well, she's very overpowering, isn't she? She hasn't made it easy for me, to be a good father.'

I rub my forehead. 'You can't blame her for that, Dad. You are your own man.'

He purses his lips and then nods.

'I know she wasn't easy, though.'

'She… I don't know, she always manages to make me feel like I'm in the wrong. Like she is the wise one, you know? And I was reading this article and it all just struck me, I suppose, that we – I – have been unfair.'

Unfair? That's an understatement. But I guess I'll take it.

'And then Jake told me about your friend, this girl who died, this girl who brought you all together, this Jodie, and I knew then that I had to come and see you, to come and tell you, to come and say that… that…'

'That what?'

'That I do love you, Penny. I do. And to say that I am so deeply sorry, about Jodie, and… and about all the other things.'

All the other things. I think it would take a hundred years to pick apart all the other things. But he is here, now, and he is my dad, and he is saying sorry. I think back to the words Kat said on Saturday about forgiveness, and about the power that surged through them. I think about what it might mean for me to let go of the restless bitterness that feasts itself on the wounded places inside me.

I thought all the light had spilled out of me long ago and was lost in corners piled up with shadows so deep they vibrated with inky blackness. My colours were twisted up with the light and I was left stranded in grey. But maybe now the corners are releasing their shadows like endless oceans releasing long-buried treasure, and the light is there, and it is catching on kindling and then blazing through my veins and singing through my bones.

I don't think that just because my dad is here today with a sorry and a hug that all is well with the world.

But he is here and that is something and along with all the other somethings it feels a little bit like freedom.

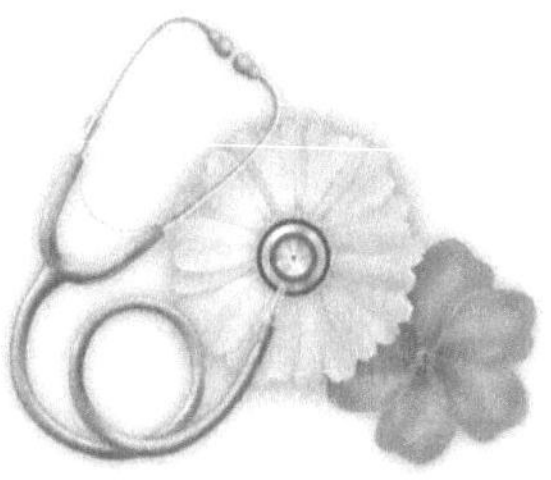

Chapter 32

SISTER JOY IS on the night shift, and I am glad it is her. She does not complain when my cannula will not take one final IV dose, or when Alice cries in her arms, her whole body shaking. She replaces my cannula herself and I barely feel it.

During the night three more patients arrive and by morning the bay is a cold unfamiliar place, like when you move house and go back to the old one and it's not the same anymore. An elderly woman who is confused and distressed is in Jodie's space, and I hold her hand in the early hours when she cries out for her son. He'll come and get her out of here, she says. He will sort all of this out. Tears drip from her eyes and I sit with her, and then Sister Joy tells me to get back into bed and she sits with her, instead.

In the morning Kat and I wait for our discharge forms. We get dressed and sit on our chairs and we watch and wait together.

The doctors come for their rounds and confirm that we are both going home today, and haven't we done well? Doctor Chowdhury says that he doesn't want to see me in here again too soon, do I hear him?

Nicki is here with the tea trolley mid-morning and we are still waiting. 'You two still here? Can't get rid of you, can we?' She makes our drinks without asking us what we want, and they are perfect.

'I'll miss you,' she says. 'Don't get many in as fun as you lot have been. Given us all a bit of distraction, you have.'

'Thank you for all you do,' Kat says.

Nicki flushes. 'Ah, I'm only a humble HCA.'

'Nothing 'only' about you. You've been a rock for us.'

Nicki fiddles with a mug. 'Aw. You're my flowers, you are.'

Kat turns to me as Nicki pushes the trolley over to the new patients. 'What'll you be doing, then, at home, when you get back? What do things look like for you?'

I shrug. 'Not much. Live off the state. Scrounger, and all that.'

'Don't say that.'

I talk to Kat about how I've felt like that for too long. I've been steeped in my own sense of uselessness and had that feeling verified and increased by society's judgment of those in my position. I tell her how I felt in the worst of the pandemic, the whole narrative around it, that people like me were expendable, that we were in the way of the young and healthy getting back to normal, and how I believed it. I believed that I wasn't worth saving, that my life, and me, was useless.

But I don't believe that anymore. Or most of me doesn't. I'm working on it, I tell her.

'Nobody is useless,' she says. 'If you do nothing all day, it doesn't mean you are useless. It means you are sick. But you are valued. You are loved.'

'I'd like to do something more,' I find myself saying. 'I have all this inside me. I want to paint again. To write poetry. I want to help others like me. Always wanted to. But I am scared of letting people down. I start something, and then I get ill, and I can't do it anymore, and then people get disappointed in me, and it just goes on like that.'

Kat levels her deep blue gaze at me. 'You need to stop worrying so about what others think. To live free from that burden.'

If only it were that easy.

'I need some help in the foodbank, if you're interested.'

My heart sinks. She doesn't get it, like everyone else. Maybe she thinks if I start doing something I will get better, that I'm ill because I don't bother. Maybe she thinks that all I need is a job, just like they do at the DWP and the jobcentre.

'I can't be relied on. Flaky as heck,' I say lightly.

'I don't care about that.'

'But that's no good is it, for a foodbank, or anything like that? I might do an hour, and then get so ill I can't do anything for another month.'

'That's fine.'

'It is?'

Kat nods.

'But then I might manage say three weeks in a row, and you'll get to rely on me, and then I'll leave you in the lurch again for maybe three weeks more.'

Kat blows out her cheeks and picks up my hand. 'Penny. It's fine. The whole point of the foodbank is to support the vulnerable. We have many volunteers just like you, and it all runs just fine. People pick up one another's burdens all the time.'

'They do?'

'It's not a workplace where a boss is going to put you on capability for non-attendance. If you can manage an hour sorting out shelves one week and not the next, then great. We'd love your help. We need people like you. People who get what it's like for our clients. And besides, we could do with some artwork, for some publicity we want to do around the town.'

A spark of hope begins to flicker in my wounded soul.

I think about the book I've been reading, the sappy chick-lit about the bakery by the sea, and all those like it. I think about how always in these stories the man sweeps in and saves the wretched broken-hearted girl and her bakery/bookshop/artisan goods store. It's a worldview that suddenly seems so off kilter to me, a world where it has to be a man that saves the girl and saves the world, where all of our problems can be solved by a mysterious, handsome stranger. But I don't need a man to make me better. Once upon a time I fell into that trap, and that man did not make me better, even though he promised every day that he would.

I look at Kat and I think about friendship. I think about how it cannot always be measured only by minutes and hours and days and years of time. It can be measured in the tiniest of things, in the shortest of times, through shared experiences, through profound understanding, through all the little kindnesses, through listening. Through lending Ugg boots in the snow and taking an old lady to the seaside.

'Think about it, will you?' Kat says, and I promise that I will.

LUNCHTIME COMES AND goes. One last hospital meal. It's macaroni cheese. I don't eat a whole lot of it, because it is vile, and because I know Jake is cooking for me tonight. He will make me enchiladas with salsa and halloumi and they will taste like heaven.

Dad is coming to fetch me as soon as I text him that my discharge is sorted. Nate is here already, waiting with Kat and reading *The Guardian*.

Harold wanders into the bay, his shock of white hair standing on end, his pyjama trousers somehow even looser than before, as if they will fall to the floor at any time, leaving him all exposed, all his bones too sharply outlined against the translucence of his blue-tinged skin. He gazes around and knits his eyebrows together.

'I think he's lost,' Kat says. 'I'll get Nicki.'

But Harold shakes his head. 'I'm not lost. I'm looking for her.'

'Her?'

'That one.' He points to Violet's bed space, now taken up by a thin woman who is fast asleep and looks nothing like Violet at all. 'The one who shouts at me. I like her.'

'She's gone home,' Kat says, and Harold's shoulders slump.

'What about her? That gobby one?' He points at Jodie's cubicle.

An icy surge rises through my chest and squeezes my throat. 'She's gone, too.'

Harold droops even more, and then turns and trudges away.

'Jodie enchanted them all, didn't she,' Kat says.

She was a light force, a sweep of nature, a bolt of energy. She swept into my life like a tsunami gathering pace, smashing through my reserve and my pain and my self-doubt. She drew me out of myself and awakened a strength in me I never knew was there. She was irritating, obnoxious and unpredictable. She was a warrior, standing tall even when she had no fight left in her dying body. She taught me about friendship and how to seize hold of the day, about the joy of being alive, about taking crazy chances and lighting up people's lives. Jodie was impossible, rebellious, impetuous, everything I was too afraid to be, she was our anchor point in Bay C, she was our alpha, our chief Flower.

Kat leaks tears like great big rain drops from a ponderous dark cloud. 'I'm going to miss that little imp of a girl.'

Nicki comes over and puts her arms around her. 'It's okay, flower. It's okay.'

WHEN THE DISCHARGE forms come I am packed and ready, my bags on the floor next to my chair, my table cleared of everything but my water-jug and cup, and an old Take a Break that Jodie gave me that I never read. The pharmacist hands me two large carrier bags full of medication and asks me if I have any allergies. Nicki and Sister Harris are in the bay, and Sister Harris tells me to get some good rest and don't even think about any little outings for the next week or two.

When I say goodbye to Kat I cry a little bit more, and wonder if now my tears have started they will ever stop. She folds me tightly into her arms and nestles her face into my hair and tells me she will see me soon. Then she digs into a bag on her bed and holds something out to me. Something that looks like the sky and the sea all rolled into one. It's the blanket she was working on, all finished and glorious. 'This is for you.'

I feel the softness of it in my hands and watch as the colours swirl through my blurry vision. 'But, I...'

'I wanted to give you the sea.'

'I...'

'The colours remind me of you.'

I can't find any words in me, after that.

Dad comes to run me home. He is quiet in the car, brooding, shrunken from who he was yesterday in his uncharacteristic outpouring of emotion. Perhaps Mum has talked him down, told him to stop being a foolish old man, that I'm not really that special at all.

But when he drops me off, he helps me into the lift and into my flat. He carries my bags and he tells me that he loves me. And then he hugs me, and I don't remember the last time he hugged me, and so I hug him back.

Jake is in the kitchen, stirring something in a saucepan. His eyes light up at the sight of me, even though I must be a shocker of a sight, with the bags under my eyes and unwashed hair, my body even skinnier than before, my dark eyes dulled with pain and weariness.

'I'm cooking you your favourite,' he says.

'It smells good.'

'It's macaroni cheese,' he says, and then he is folding me in so closely I can hardly breathe, and he is telling me that he missed me and that he loves me and that everything is going to be okay.

I stare into the pan, full of macaroni cheese, and smile, because I know that he is, after all, right.

Epilogue

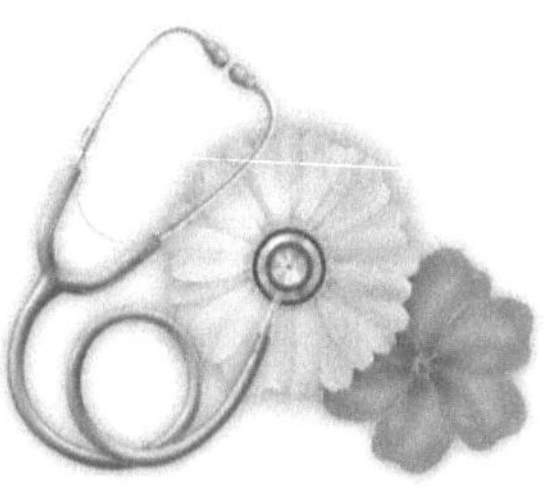

KAT HAS SET up a WhatsApp group for me, her, Amina and Violet. Violet has bought 'one of those telephone things' so she can keep in touch and she loves to watch the YouTube on it but can't get her head around that Facebook thing. Kat has named the group 'The Bay C Flowers'.

The flower that bloomed largest of all wilted too soon, and the flower who opened to the sunshine and the sea air is in a home, waiting to die.

We arrange to meet at the home, the four of us. Amina is in a purple hijab with her black stilettos and kohl-lined eyes. Kat shows us her new tattoo; a cluster of six flowers intertwined, climbing her forearm like ivy up a wall. Violet is dressed in a twinset and pearls under her silver coat.

The home is fragranced with boiled cabbage and a hint of disinfectant, and it takes me back into the hospital bay. Violet says that it smells disgusting in here.

Barbara is sitting up in her bed, face pale and sunken, her eyes holding the edges of a sparkle. She doesn't have long, the harried carer says. Be gentle and calm, please. She's not really allowed so many visitors, but no one else comes, only you and that cat lady a couple of times, so…

Barbara looks at me and smiles a toothless smile. 'Little mouse,' she murmurs. 'Little mouse on the beach.'

I stroke her arm. 'Yes. Yes, with the sun on our faces and the wind in our hair and the sea kissing our toes.'

'And Dodgy Caravan Dude,' Kat says. DCD is serving a suspended sentence now and must rue the day he stopped for a gaggle of women he thought were a bunch of crazies out for a drunken stroll in the wilds of the countryside.

'I don't see the rat no more,' Barbara says. She is puffing like a steam train.

I lay my hand on hers. 'I know you don't. I'm glad you don't.'

Silence falls between us.

'She was a good girl,' Barbara says, and then she coughs, and then sinks into a whole paroxysm of coughing.

We say nothing and we sit with her and watch the sun go down outside her window. It's a clear day in mid-January, a cloudless sky, its pale blue of day chased away by new slashes of coral and indigo that whirl through the heavens like endless ribbons. Barbara gazes out of the window and her eyes are alight with the beauty of it, the colours dancing over the rheumy weariness and transforming her for moments into a young girl by the sea with her new husband burying her in the sand and then bringing her ice-cream.

The sun hangs low and then plunges into the horizon, but the streaks of colour remain there, suspended, written across the sky, as if they will be there for ever more.

By Barbara's bed is a mounted photo of six stupid women in daft outfits on a beach. It catches her eye now and she twinkles playfully up at us, and then she says, 'You saved me.'

Then she is lost to us, her eyes rolling to the side, in another world, muttering about her mouse and Bill and deckchairs. We sit for a while longer, and then the carer comes back and tells us it's time to go.

As we get up to leave, Barbara stops her murmurs and grabs at Kat's arm. 'Come back later. With your oil and things.'

And we all know what she means.

Three months later

I AM BACK in hospital. It's not as bad, this time, and it's not as good, either, but the sun shines outside the window behind my bed and I allow Dan to take me out into the Peace Garden to build up my strength. Spring is blooming out here in all its glory, clouds of daffodils dancing in the borders and the last snowdrops playing on the grass. I take a deep breath in and allow the peace of it to permeate through my battered body. They're missing me at the foodbank, Kat said to me on Facetime, but there's no hurry. No hurry. Just be.

I am sitting on a brand-new bench. It is crafted from the lightest beechwood, shining with new varnish, and it has a silver plaque on the back in the centre. I trace my fingers over it once again and murmur the words aloud, allowing them to spill out into the sun-dappled silence:

In memory of Jodie, who took us out of our sickness and into the sea.

The End

About Resolute Books

We are an independent press representing a consortium of experienced authors, professional editors and talented designers producing engaging and inspiring books of the highest quality for readers everywhere. We produce books in a number of genres including historical fiction, crime suspense, young adult dystopia, memoir, Cold War thrillers, poetry, and even Jane Austen fan fiction!

Find out more at resolutebooks.co.uk

for the joy of reading

About the Author

E.M. Carter is an award-winning author, poet and editor who can't get enough of words. She is the author of *The Flowers of Bay C*, the dystopian Newland Trilogy (*Repression Ground, Rebellion Ground* and *Redemption Ground*), and several non-fiction books.

Liz has been poet in residence for Wellington in Shropshire and a finalist in the Woman Alive Reader's Choice award. For other writers, she offers a freelance service editing and designing book covers and interiors. Liz likes to spend her days clad in fairtrade turquoise dresses trying not to eat chocolate and is proud to be a grammar pedant.

For updates and more, visit emcarter.carterclan.me.uk and sign up to her newsletter.

If you've enjoyed *The Flowers of Bay C*, Liz would very much appreciate it if you could leave a review on Amazon or Goodreads. Thank you so much!

www.ingramcontent.com/pod-product-compliance
Lightning Source LLC
Chambersburg PA
CBHW030532190726
48283CB00006B/1884